China Dolls

BY LISA SEE

China Dolls

Dreams of Joy

Shanghai Girls

Peony in Love

Snow Flower and the Secret Fan

Dragon Bones

The Interior

Flower Net

On Gold Mountain

China Dolls

LISA SEE

BLOOMSBURY
LONDON • NEW DELHI • NEW YORK • SYDNEY

First published in Great Britain 2014

China Dolls is a work of historical fiction. Apart from the well-known actual people, events and locales that figure into the narrative, all names, characters, places and incidents are products of the author's imagination or are used fictitiously

Bloomsbury Publishing Plc
50 Bedford Square
London
WC1B 3DP

www.bloomsbury.com

Bloomsbury Publishing, London, New Delhi, New York and Sydney

A CIP catalogue record for this book is available from the British Library

ISBN 978 1 4088 5325 2

10 9 8 7 6 5 4 3 2 1

Book design by Victoria Wong
Printed and bound in Great Britain by CPI Group (UK) Ltd, Croydon CR0 4YY

For Henry Theodore Kendall

Only three things cannot be long hidden:
the sun,
the moon,
and the truth.

(Attributed to Buddha)

Part One

The Sun

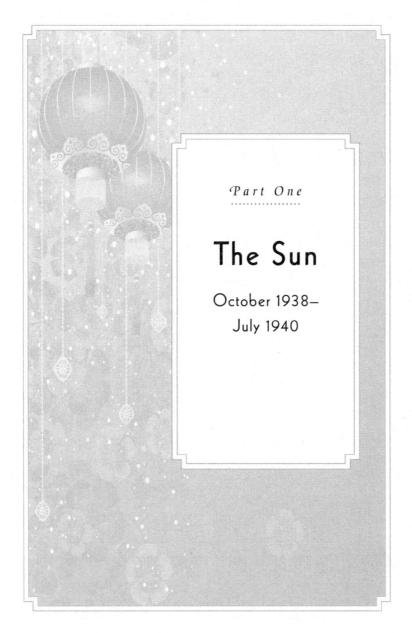

October 1938–
July 1940

GRACE

A Measly Girl

I traveled west—alone—on the cheapest bus routes I could find. Every mile took me farther from Plain City, Ohio, where I'd been a fly-speck on the wallpaper of small-town life. Each new state I passed through loosened another rope around my heart, my legs, my arms, yet my whole body ached and I couldn't shake my vertigo. I lived on aspirin, crackers, and soda pop. I cried and cried and cried. On the eighth day, California. Many hours after crossing the boundary, I got off the bus and pulled my sweater a little more tightly around me. I expected sun and warmth, but on that October afternoon, fog hung over San Francisco, damp, and shockingly cold.

Picking up my suitcase, I left the bus station and started to walk. The receptionists at the cheap hotels I visited told me they were full. "Go to Chinatown," they suggested. "You can get a room there." I had no idea where Chinatown was, so that didn't help me. And I'll say this about San Francisco: lots of hills, water on practically every side, and, it seemed to me, not a single street ran purely in any one direction. Finally, a man at a fleabag took my money—a dollar a day, in advance—and gave me a key to a room.

I washed my hair in the basin and put it up in pin curls, then leaned in to the mirror to examine what remained of my injuries. My forehead had healed completely, but the inside of my skull continued to swim from being banged against the kitchen floor. The skin over my ribs was mottled green, gray, and purple. My shoulder still felt swollen and stiff from being dislocated and then jammed back into place, but the cut on my lip had nearly disappeared. I turned away and sat on the edge of the bed, hungry but too frightened to go out, and listening to the sound of God knows what coming through the walls.

I opened my purse and pulled out the magazine clipping Miss Miller, who'd taught me dance from the age of four, had torn from a magazine and given to me a few months earlier. I smoothed the advertisement with my palm so I could study the artist's sketch of the Golden Gate International Exposition. Even its location on Treasure Island seemed to beckon. "See, Grace, they're looking for six thousand workers," Miss Miller had said. "Dancers, singers, welders, carpenters. The whole works." She'd sighed then. "I wanted to go so many places when I was young, but it takes guts—and talent—to leave everything and everyone you know. You could do it, though." Her few words and that slip of paper had given me the courage to believe I actually could. After all, I'd won first prize at the Plain City Fair for my tap dancing and singing when I was seven and had held the title ever since.

You always planned to leave home, I told myself. *Just because you had to escape sooner than expected doesn't mean you can't still fly to the stars.*

But my pep talk—in a scary hotel room, in a strange city, in the middle of the night—did little to ease my fears. Once in bed, I could practically see the walls closing in around me. To calm myself, I began a routine I'd invented as a small child, running my hands the length of my arms (a broken tibia when I was three; my mom told Doc Haverford I fell down the stairs), slipping along my sides (several broken and fractured ribs over the years), and then lifting each leg and squeezing all the way to my feet (my legs had been a frequent target until I started dancing). The ritual both strengthened and soothed me. I was now alone in the world, with no home to return to and no one to rely on, but if I could survive my father's beatings and the petty prejudices of my hometown, then I could triumph over whatever obstacles the future threw my way. Maybe. Hopefully.

THE NEXT MORNING, I combed out my hair, sweeping up the sides and letting the curls billow below, the way Carole Lombard did in *My Man Godfrey.* I put on the dress my dad bought for me when he took us to Cincinnati to buy supplies for the laundry. I'd chosen a dusty-rose-colored cotton frock, with a geometric print composed of interlocking mustard-yellow and steel-gray squares. Mom said the pattern of the fabric and cut of the dress looked too mature for me—and maybe that was so—but now I considered myself lucky to be wearing something so sophisticated.

Filled with a sense of determination, I went downstairs and onto the street. I asked directions on nearly every corner and managed to find my way to the Ferry Building, where I boarded the boat to Treasure Island, about halfway across the bay and just under the Bay Bridge. I imagined everyone onboard was seeking a job at the Golden Gate International Exposition. As excited as I was, the pulse of the ferry through the choppy water roused my vertigo and my hunger until I felt, once again, dizzy and sick. Once we reached the dock, everyone walked fast, wanting to be first in line for interviews. Me too. I spotted my first palm trees, which was thrilling because they meant I surely was in California. I'd never seen anything like the fair's entrance. Giant towers composed of stacked cubes crowned by stylized elephants bookended the gate. Beyond, I glimpsed spires still clothed in scaffolding. My ears pounded from the sounds of hammers, the buzz of electric saws, the rumble of tractors, bulldozers, and flatbed trucks, and the shouts of men calling out orders and cursing the way they do on construction sites.

"Will they be done on time?" a man's voice asked very close to my ear.

I jumped, spiraling into the terror I experienced around my dad.

I swung around to find a young Occidental man about six feet tall, with broad shoulders and sandy-colored hair. He put up his hands in surrender.

"I'm sorry I scared you." His mouth spread into a contrite smile as I met his deep blue eyes. He looked older than I—maybe around twenty. He extended his hand. "My name's Joe."

"I'm Grace." No last names. I liked that.

"I'm looking for a job as a rolling-chair boy." He didn't bother to explain what that was. "But the real reason I'm here is that I love planes, and I love to fly."

Up ahead, the others from the ferry disappeared through the gate.

"I love planes so much that my parents told me if I got straight *A*s in high school they'd let me take flying lessons," Joe continued, sure of my interest. "I trained in a Piper Cub. I learned how to take off, land, what to do in a stall, and how to pull out of a spin. Now I have my pilot's license."

This told me, among other things, that his family had to be pretty well-off.

"What does that have to do with rolling chairs?"

He laughed and ran a hand through his hair. "Pan Am's Clipper ships are going to be taking off and landing right here at Treasure Island!"

I nodded, pretending interest when I didn't know what in the heck he was talking about.

"I've been chewing your ear off," Joe acknowledged. "Sorry about that. What are you doing here?"

"I'm a dancer."

"Neat." He pointed his chin toward the gate. "We'd better catch up."

When I stumbled a bit in my low-slung heels, he grabbed my arm to steady me, and I instinctively pulled away. His eyes went banjo big. I could tell he was about to apologize again.

"Where are you from?" I blurted, hoping to shift his attention.

"Winnetka, Illinois. I'm going to Cal." Seeing my confusion, he explained, "The University of California. It's over there." He pointed east. "In Berkeley. I live in a fraternity house. How about you?"

"Plain City, Ohio."

"Haven't heard of it, but we're both from the Midwest, and our states are practically neighbors. Friends?"

I nodded. He sure was a nice guy—good-looking, and I liked the way the left side of his mouth tweaked up when he smiled.

"Whew!" He wiped his forehead in mock relief.

He was funny too.

When we had all reached the trailer, a man—wearing gray flannel trousers, a leather jacket zipped halfway up his chest, and a charcoal-colored trilby pulled down to shield his eyes from the sun—jumped on a crate and spoke above the din around us: "A lot of you have come from far away. That's great! We need plenty of folks to get this place up and running. If you're a painter, electrician, or plumber, head over to the Court of the Seven Seas. Harry will lead the way."

Half the folks followed the man pointed out as Harry.

"I figure the rest of you are here to apply for either service or performance jobs," the man in the trilby continued. "If you want to drive one of the elephant trams, work in a concession, become a rolling-chair boy, barker, waitress, fireman, or cop, then go to the Court of Flowers. No flowers there yet, just another trailer like this one."

"That's my cue," Joe whispered. Then, "Good luck!"

He peeled away with a large group. He turned to look back at me, gave me a thumbs-up and another smile, both of which I returned. He strode with such confidence that dust kicked up around his shoes. Through the racket around me, I could just make out him whistling "All of Me." I loved that song.

The man in the hat sized up those who remained. "All right then," he said. "If you're here to be models, dancers, or musicians, you're with me. I'll see you one at a time. After a preliminary look-see, I'll send you on to auditions. If you make the cut . . . Aw, hell," he said with a casual wave of his hand. "You know the drill. Line up here."

One person after another entered the trailer and then exited five or so minutes later with either a grin or a grimace. I tried to prepare myself for the questions I might be asked about my dance experience, and once again my father came into my mind. He may have beat me at home, but he liked to boast to others about how many ribbons and apple-pie prizes I'd won. He'd pushed me to be an "all-American girl," which meant that he let me go to the Rialto to watch musicals to inspire me to practice even harder. I adored Eleanor Powell in *Broadway Melody of 1936,* in which she danced without music. I saw that movie maybe ten times, and then tried to re-create her steps at every opportunity: on the sidewalk outside the theater, at Miss Miller's studio, and in our family's laundry. Of course, the kids in school made fun of me when I said I wanted to be a star. "You? An Oriental girl?" They had a point. It wasn't like there were any famous Chinese movie stars apart from Anna May Wong, and she didn't sing or dance as far as I knew. Then I saw Dorothy Toy and Paul Wing—a *Chinese* dance team—in the whimsically titled *With Best Dishes.* I decided if they could make it, why not me? But would any of that help me now? I suddenly felt very apprehensive and very alone.

When my turn came, I entered the trailer and closed the door behind me as I'd seen others do. The man motioned for me to sit.

"Your name?"

"Grace Lee."

"How old are you?"

"Old enough to sing and dance," I answered pertly. I wanted to be a star, so no matter how desperate I was, I had to act like one. "I'm good."

The man pinched his chin as he considered my response.

"You're Oriental," he observed, "and you're quite the knockout. Problem is, I don't have anything for you."

I opened my purse, pulled out Miss Miller's clipping, and pushed it across the desk. "It says here you need performers for the Cavalcade of the Golden West—"

"That's a big show. Hundreds of performers. But I don't need an Oriental girl."

"What about at the Japanese Pavilion?" I asked, my false confidence instantly eroding. "I came from so far away. I really need a job."

"It's the Depression, kid. Everyone needs a job." He glanced again at my application. "And I hate to break it to you, but you aren't Japanese. Grace Lee, that's Chinese, right?"

"Will anyone know?"

"Kid, I doubt anyone can tell the difference. Can you?"

I shrugged. I'd never seen a Japanese. I'd never seen a Chinese either other than my mother, my father, and my own reflection in the mirror—and Anna May Wong, Toy and Wing, and a couple of Orientals playing maids and butlers on the silver screen, but those weren't in real life—so how could I be certain of the difference between a Japanese and a Chinese? I only knew my mother's thin cheeks and chapped hands and my father's weathered face and wiry arms. Like that, my eyes began to well. What if I failed? What if I had to go home?

"We don't have Orientals where I'm from," I admitted, "but I've always heard that they all look alike."

"Be that as it may, I've been told to be authentic . . ." He snapped his fingers. "I've got it. There's going to be a Chinese Village. Those folks are doing their own hiring. Maybe I can get you set as a dancer from China."

"I'm not *from* China. I was born here."

Unconcerned, he picked up the phone. I listened as he suggested me to the person I assumed was in charge of the Chinese Village. He dropped the receiver back in the cradle. "They aren't hiring dancers in a permanent way. With all the troubles in China, it wouldn't be right."

Troubles in China? I'd read about Germany's aggression in Europe in the *Plain City Advocate,* but the newspaper came out only once a week. It barely covered events in Europe and never in Asia, so I was ignorant about all things Chinese except Chinese rice wine, which my mom made and sold out our back door on Friday and Saturday nights to the men in Plain City—a place as dry as chalk even after Prohibition ended. My mind pondered these things, but they were just a diversion from my panic.

"What about on the Gayway?" I remembered that from Miss Miller's advertisement.

"That's a carnival. I don't see you there at all."

"I've been to a carnival before—"

"Not like this one."

"I can do it," I insisted, but he'd better not try sending me to a hoochie-coochie tent like they had for men at the Plain City Fair. I'd never do that.

He shook his head. "You're a regular China doll. If I put you in the Gayway, the men would eat you up."

My five minutes were done, but the man didn't dismiss me. Instead, he stared at me, taking in my dress, my shoes, the way I'd curled and combed my hair. I lowered my eyes and sat quietly. Perhaps it was proof of how the most innocent can remain safe—or that the man really was of good character—that he didn't try or even suggest any funny business.

"I'll do anything," I said, my voice now shaking, "even if it's boring or menial—"

"That's not the way to sell yourself, kid."

"I could work in a hamburger stand if I had to. Maybe one of the performers in the Cavalcade of the Golden West will get sick. You should have someone like me around, just in case."

"You can try the concessions," he responded dubiously. "But you've got a big problem. Your gams are good, and your contours and promontories are in the right places. You've got a face that could crush a lily. But your accent—"

"My accent?"

"Yeah. You don't have one. You've got to stop talking all perfect. You need to do the ching-chong thing."

Never! My father spoke in heavily accented English, even though he was born here. He always blamed it on the fact that he'd grown up in a lumber camp in the Sierras, where he lived with his father, who conversed only in Chinese. My mother's English was flawless. She was born in China but came to America so early that she'd lost her accent entirely. How she was raised—somehow living far enough from other Chinese that she didn't have an accent—was never discussed. The one time I asked, my father smacked me. In any case, the three of us could understand each other only if we communicated in English. And even if we all had spoken the same dialect, my father would never have allowed us to use it. *Speaking English means you are American, and we must be American at all times.* Reciting sentences like *I hear you cut school again* and *what's the big deal?* showed we were assimilated. But all that didn't mean Dad wouldn't exaggerate his accent for his customers if he calculated it would make them happy.

"I'm sorry," I said. "But I can't do what you ask."

With nothing left to add, I got up to leave. In just these few minutes I'd learned two things about myself: I would never lower myself by faking an accent like my dad did (or Charlie Chan did in the movies), nor would I work naked as a hoochie-coochie dancer. All right, so I had pride. But what price would I have to pay for it? I felt sick with fear and despair.

"Hey, kid, wait a sec." The man reached into a drawer, pulled out a brown paper bag, and then met me at the door. "A ham sandwich and an apple."

Heat crept up my face. I already hadn't gotten the job. Did he have to humiliate me further? Did I appear that down at the heels?

"Take it," he said, pressing the bag into my hands. "From the wife and me."

"Thank you." It would be my first real meal since leaving home.

He gave me a last pitying look. "Have you tried the new nightclubs in Chinatown? I hear they're looking for ponies and canaries." Seeing my confused expression, he explained, "I'm talking about dancers and singers—ponies and canaries. Aw, don't worry about it. You'll learn soon enough. Now head on back to your side of town.

Ask anyone. They'll tell you where to go to find an audition." He gave me a gentle push out the door and called, "Next."

On my way back to the dock, I conjured a nightclub in my mind. *Top Hat, Swing Time,* and *A Star Is Born* all had nightclubs, so I knew just what they looked like: white banquettes, hatcheck and cigarette girls, champagne bubbling in thin-stemmed glasses, men wearing top hats, white ties, and tails, and women swanning about in satin slip gowns cut on the bias that draped over their bodies like whispered kisses. My heart had been set on getting a job at the exposition, but working in a nightclub would be even better. A dollop of confidence: *I will succeed.*

But I still didn't have an inkling about where Chinatown was or where to look once I got there, and that knowledge brought on a horrible wave of anxiety that all but drowned my momentary optimism. For now, I had nowhere to go except back to my hotel room. I already hated that place, with its cockroaches, women with their too-rouged cheeks, and men in their dirty undershirts who came and went, but I wouldn't give up. I *couldn't* give up, because that would mean going home to my father.

THE NEXT DAY, I put on my same rose-colored dress, bought a map, and followed its lines toward Chinatown. The clammy air was depressing. Passing all the soup lines and people—Okies, I guessed—dressed in tattered clothes, gaunt, just standing around, didn't help either. I could end up like them if I wasn't careful. And my body ached from the damp. My ribs and shoulder throbbed when I breathed or raised my arms, but I reminded myself that I'd danced through pain more times than I could count. I swallowed three aspirin dry and silently prayed that I wouldn't have to do a ton of turns if I got an audition, which would be nearly impossible with my lingering vertigo.

At the corner of California Street and Grant Avenue, two peculiar-looking multiple-storied edifices with green-glazed tile roofs sat like guards: Sing Chong Bazaar and Sing Fat Bazaar. What crazy names! Behind the big plate-glass windows were things I'd never seen before:

Chinese furniture, silks, and vases. Then I turned onto Grant and into another world. Coiling dragons painted in bright green, red, and gold decorated the streetlamps. Eaves curled skyward. I passed markets with produce stacked in baskets right on the sidewalk and restaurants advertising chop suey—whatever that was. And the smells! I couldn't tell if they were good or bad—just odd.

But nothing unnerved me more than encountering so many Chinese eyes, mouths, noses, arms, and legs. Here were hundreds—maybe thousands—of Chinese men. They were tall and short, fat and thin, some light-skinned and some very dark. None of them looked like my father. I spotted a couple of older women, moving furtively along the sidewalk, doing their best to be invisible. Farther along, I saw five high school girls, wearing matching uniforms and carrying books. My knowledge of Chinese hair was limited to three examples: my mother's tresses, which she kept in a bun; my father's close-shaved head; and my own manufactured curls. So even the hair was different—long and silky, short bobs, permanent waves, marcels, spiky, wispy, balding, and in so many variations of black. Everything was as foreign and strange as if I'd just disembarked from a boat in Hong Kong, Canton, or Shanghai—not that *I'd* been to any of those places—making me both elated and petrified. Chinatown felt frighteningly enchanted in the way certain fairy tales had once left me unable to sleep. Was that why my parents had insisted on living so far from all this?

I needed help.

"Can you direct me to a nightclub?" I asked a woman wearing what looked like black pajamas and carrying two bags overflowing with onion greens. She refused to acknowledge me. Next I tried to stop a newspaper boy, but he ignored me too. I gazed up the street: so many men here—some dressed as laborers, others as businessmen. Everyone seemed to be in a hurry, moving much faster than folks ever did back home, except for that time the Smith house caught fire and we all rushed to watch the volunteer fire department try to put it out. Now that was a night.

At the corner of Grant and Washington, I found three boys I guessed to be between ten and twelve years old playing in a sandpile dumped in the middle of the intersection. Their pants were rolled up to their knees, their sleeves smashed to their elbows, and their caps askew from roughhousing. Workmen shoveled the perimeter of the pile as cars and trucks honked at the traffic obstacle as though the added noise would cure the problem. I watched it all from the curb for a few minutes. Finally, I stepped into the street. My shoes sank into the sand as I delicately made my way to the little trio, who stopped their horseplay to watch me approach. The oldest boy grabbed two handfuls of sand and let the grains flow through his fingers.

"No one said we couldn't be out here," he said by way of greeting.

"I didn't say they did," I replied.

"Then what do you want, lady?"

My face crinkled. I'd never been called lady before. Measly girl. Hog face. Chink. Chinaman. Little one. Apple-pie winner. Heart dumpling. Kid and China doll just yesterday, but never lady. Act the part!

"I'm hoping you can assist me," I said.

"What's in it for us?" the oldest boy asked impudently.

"A nickel each, if you help me." I pulled out my coin purse, picked through it for three nickels, and held them in my palm. "I'm looking for a nightclub—"

"Oh," he said, his voice rising and falling knowingly. "Won't you get in trouble?"

I dropped one of the nickels back into the coin purse.

"So you're familiar with the clubs," I said. Every boy was curious about the forbidden, and my comment set off all three boys.

"They're barely better than bars—"

"No one wants them in the neighborhood—"

"My dad says they're just a rat's hair above a speakeasy—"

I dropped another nickel into my coin purse.

"You win, lady," the ringleader conceded. "You want to work in a big-thigh show, that's your headache."

"Big-thigh show?"

"Don't you know anything?" he asked. "You really want to let people see your legs?"

As long as it's just my legs . . .

"Please tell me where to go," I said.

I waited while he exchanged looks with his buddies. All I needed was one name to give me a start.

At last, he said, "Wilbert Wong has the Li Po—a cocktail lounge on the next block. He's changing it into more of a club. Andy Wong—not related—runs the Chinese Penthouse. It opened last December with all-Chinese entertainment."

He rattled this off like a town booster. This place was turning out to be a lot more like Plain City than it looked on the surface: a small town, where everyone knew everyone else's business, especially when it came to the taboo.

"I heard Andy Wong is going to change the name to the Sky Room," the smallest boy ventured, which earned him an elbow to the ribs.

"There's Charlie Low's new club. It's not even open yet," the oldest boy continued. "Two years ago, he opened a bar here on Grant Avenue. No Chinese girls or women allowed. What am I saying? No Chinese went, period!"

"How would you know?" I asked, challenging him.

"I *know,*" he responded.

Any boy could spout off about the birds and the bees—and other naughty things—but he often got the details wrong. It would now be up to me to figure out how much of what this little boy said was accurate and how much was gobbledygook picked up from listening to the whispers of older kids.

"Charlie Low's wife is a singer," he continued, "and he's giving her a showplace called the Forbidden City. It's on Sutter Street—"

"Not even in Chinatown," the smallest boy interrupted again.

That appealed to me, because Chinatown was too scary for me.

"Can you point the way?" I asked.

"First, you go . . ."

His voice trailed off, and his eyes widened. The other two boys stared gape-mouthed at something over my shoulder. I turned to see what they were ogling and saw a girl about my age gingerly step off the curb and come toward us. She wore a practical outfit: a gray wool pleated skirt, a long-sleeved black sweater, charcoal-gray wool stockings, and oxfords. She was Chinese, with flawless porcelain skin. She looked *rich,* like out of a movie, except that I'd never seen a Chinese who looked like her in the darkness of the Rialto.

"I know how to get to the Forbidden City," she said in melodious voice. "I'll take you."

Although Joe and the man on Treasure Island had both been perfectly nice to me, I wasn't accustomed to kindness. Now here was a girl, offering to help, as if magically sent. I glanced down at the boys, trying to get a sense of what I should do.

"She's Helen Fong," the ringleader said in awe. "If she wants to help you, let her!"

The other two boys, acting their young ages at last, covered their mouths and giggled. The girl named Helen gave them an unyielding look, and they went quiet but fast.

"Kew, Chuen, Yee, I don't think your mothers will be too happy to hear you aren't in school," she observed coolly. "You'd better hurry along now."

The boys stood and brushed the sand off themselves. When they held out their palms, I paid them their promised nickels. Once they scampered off, I turned to Helen.

"Where to?"

HELEN

Calling to the Heavens

"This way," I answered, but what in the world was I thinking—skipping work, walking through Chinatown unescorted, and talking to a total stranger?

My pace was brisk, and I felt the girl wordlessly tagging along behind me as I wove down Grant. She caught up at a red light.

"My name's Grace," she said.

"Nice to meet you."

"Thanks so much for helping me," she went on, trying to appear composed, I thought, but actually sounding as scared as a fawn panting in fear at the sight of the moon.

"It's nothing," I responded, but it was *everything*. This morning, my brother Monroe had walked me to the door of the Chinese Telephone Exchange, where I worked. After he left me, I'd simply stood there, unable to bring myself to enter the building. I couldn't face another day of listening to the other women talk between calls about what they were going to make for dinner that night for their husbands, how clever their children were, or how hard it was to make ends meet. Those women just weren't pleasant to me. I understood, I suppose. I earned the same five dollars a week they earned and gave every dime to my father for my "upkeep," but everyone knew my family was one of the best and most important in Chinatown.

So there I'd been, outside the telephone exchange, daydreaming about how the thousands of women—wives and concubines—in China's imperial court had once spent their entire lives hidden inside the walls of the palace with no family or friends to love them. To amuse themselves, the women used to catch crickets and keep them in cages near their pillows. The crickets' songs—haunting, calling to the heavens of their loneliness—told not only of their own lives but also of the women who were cared for, but equally helpless, in the cage of the palace. I lived in a traditional Chinese compound right in the heart of Chinatown, with twenty-nine of my closest relatives. A sense of futility had nearly overwhelmed me as I realized my life wasn't all that different from those of the crickets who belonged to the women, who, in turn, belonged to the emperor. Right then, I'd noticed the girl in the street, talking to those silly boys. She looked as lost and lonely as I felt. She wasn't fresh off the boat from China, but she was new to town, of that I was certain—a country bumpkin in her tatty store-bought dress. I'd edged to the intersection. As I'd listened to her conversation with the boys . . . I don't know . . . I felt *compelled* to help her.

Once Grace and I were clearly out of Chinatown, my spirits lifted. No one from the neighborhood was watching me, hoping to curry favor with my father by reporting on my actions. We crossed the street, turned right on Sutter, and continued until we reached a sign that read FORBIDDEN CITY AUDITIONS. NO EXPERIENCE NEEDED. Music wafted down the stairs, enveloping us right on the street.

"Here it is," I said.

"Come with me. Try out with me."

I shook my head. "I can't. I've never had a dance lesson."

"It says no experience needed. We'll stick together. I promise."

Before I could protest further, Grace took my hand. I never would have expected that from a Chinese girl. I shivered. Didn't she know it was rude to touch like that? I guess not, because she gave me an encouraging smile and pulled me up the stairs. I had leapt so far out of my cage—out of *myself*—that I followed Grace like I was the one who was lost and she was now leading the way. Or maybe she was desperate and afraid to go in alone.

In the entry hall, workers—dressed in baggy pants, sleeveless undershirts, and painters' caps—carried lumber and other construction materials. A Chinese woman, sitting at a table made from two-by-fours and a sheet of plywood, handed us forms with spaces for our names, heights, weights, and ages. I wrote down the address of my family's compound. I glanced over Grace's shoulder as she scribbled the name of a hotel in a seedy part of town.

The woman, who I was sure recognized me, took Grace's form and scanned it. "You're seventeen?" she asked, not bothering to look up.

"Is that all right?"

"We've got younger inside. We just don't want you to be *too* young." She pointed down the hall. "You can change in that room on the right. After that, sit with the other girls trying out today. They'll call you when they're ready." She didn't specify who "they" were.

I lingered by the table when Grace walked down the hall.

"If I get the job, how much will you pay?" I inquired.

"Twenty a week," the receptionist answered. I could almost hear additional words pouring out of her mouth. *As though you need it.* Then she bent back to her paperwork.

I could have walked out right then, but I was intrigued. Maybe I could do this. I traced the path Grace had taken and entered the half-finished ladies' room. She had changed into a soft pink one-piece playsuit with short puffed sleeves and little shorts.

"I made this," she boasted, "after I saw Eleanor Powell wear something like it in *Born to Dance.* I couldn't tell the color of the playsuit in the film, but I thought this fabric would look pretty against my skin."

I hadn't been to many movies, so I didn't know what to say.

She glanced in the mirror, squished her curls a couple of times to perk them up, and covered a cut with lipstick. I'd never be so rude as to ask her what had happened, but then she turned in my direction, frowned, and asked me a totally inappropriate question.

"You don't know how to doll up, do you?" she said with a laugh.

She poked around in her bag and fished out a slippery thin pink hair ribbon, which she tucked between her lips. She turned me toward the mirror, ran her fingers through my hair, and then whisked the ribbon from her lips, passed it behind my neck, and pulled the satin strips to the top of my head, where she tied a bow. "That's better!" And it was, because the pink lifted my cheeks' natural color.

We exited the restroom and followed the sound of music and rhythmic tapping. At the end of the hallway, I saw construction framing—for what looked like a bar to the left and a large central room. The stage looked done, though. The place was still a skeleton, but as my mind put flesh on it I began to see a nightclub like the one in Shanghai where I'd once danced the fox-trot . . .

Onstage, as if testing it for the first time, a Chinese man, twenty-six or twenty-seven, or maybe older, wearing cream-colored pants and a blue button-down linen shirt, slid across the floor, spun, and then resumed tapping. His arms appeared simultaneously loose and taut. The slap of his shoes as they hit the parquet—*tat-a-tat*—reverberated through the floorboards and shivered up my spine. His hair was slicked back with pomade, but his athletic steps—rattling now foot over foot across the front of the stage—caused strands to break loose and flop across his forehead. This, in turn, made him flip his head back after every dance phrase to clear his vision. And he was tall—almost six feet—which was extraordinary for a Chinese. He had no musical accompaniment, but his feet tapped out a rhythm that continued to build. *Rah-cha, rah-cha, tat, tat, tat.* Spin. Slide. Now his arms and legs flew—like a windmill. A group of forty or so girls, who sat cross-legged on the floor before the stage, clapped and cheered. Next to me, Grace radiated delight. I couldn't help feeling the same way, because this was a lot better than the Chinese Telephone Exchange.

When the performance ended, the dancer picked up a towel and wiped the sweat from his face. He loped down the stairs, dropped onto a folding chair next to a woman and two men, all of whom had their backs to us. I focused on the girls by the stage. A couple of them were attired in playsuits like Grace, but the rest wore street clothes. I didn't recognize a single girl. Not one of them was from Chinatown. The air I sucked in felt clean and free.

That's when I saw her, one particular girl, who had a spot to herself. Suddenly I wanted out of there, but Grace gripped my hand tightly and pulled me across the floor toward the creature, who was strikingly different from all the rest. Light seemed to glow out of her skin. Her black hair was highlighted by a pair of shockingly white gardenias pinned just above her left ear. Her eyes sparkled, and her lips formed a perfect bow. She wore tap pants and a pale pink blouse with puffed sleeves not all that different from Grace's, only hers had embroidery on the collar and cuffs. Her bare legs ended in ankle socks with delicate lace ruffles and basic black shoes with two-inch heels.

"Sit with me," she trilled when we reached her. "I don't know anyone either. I'm Ruby Tom."

"Helen." Grace pointed to me before putting her hand on her chest. "Grace."

Ruby, excited, continued, "Can you believe Eddie Wu?"

"Eddie Wu?" Grace echoed even as the three of us scrutinized each other to see where we fit in. Ruby and Grace looked poor in their homemade outfits; I was better-dressed than anyone in the room. Ruby's features were willow-delicate, Grace had perfect cheekbones, while my face was a little rounder and softer. Ruby sparkled; Grace could be summed up in four words—skinny legs, big bosom. Otherwise, we looked quite similar: petite, slim, with black curls falling over our shoulders, except that Ruby wore those gardenias in her hair, which made her look like a glamorous crane amidst a flock of chickens. We shifted slightly. We'd finished with our evaluations. *No wind; no waves.*

"The guy who was just dancing," Ruby picked up as though no time had passed. "Isn't Eddie amazing? He's a regular Fred Astaire."

"But he's Chinese," Grace pointed out in a low voice.

"That's why they call him the Chinese Fred Astaire!" Ruby slapped her thigh. Then, "Are you two trying out to be chorus girls? I don't remember either of you from the auditions at Li Po or the Sky Room, though. But you know how it is. New girls are coming every day. Everyone wants a chance—if not here, then at one of the other clubs that are opening."

"Have the other clubs already hired dancers?" Grace asked.

"I didn't say that," Ruby answered. "They just didn't want me. A couple of other new girls are here today too. There might even be more by the end of the day or tomorrow."

"You seem to know a lot about it. Are you from here?" Grace asked.

"Hardly." Ruby tossed her hair. "I was born in Los Angeles. My parents owned a curio shop across from the Orpheum Theater—a hot place for vaudeville when I was a tot. I used to dance and sing outside our store—just for kicks. People would stop, and my brothers would circulate through the crowd with hats, asking for change. We had a wild time!"

Ruby glanced at me. *Well?* But I couldn't fathom what I was supposed to say to someone like her. Among other things, she was what you'd have to call *cheung hay*, a blabbermouth. I elected to keep my thoughts to myself.

"Later we beat it to Terminal Island in Long Beach," Ruby went on, "because my pop wanted to return to fishing. My mom is a teacher. She said she could go wherever children need her, but my parents still weren't happy. They decided we should move to Hawaii."

"Hawaii?" Grace burbled. "So exciting! That's not even the United States. Is that why you talk the way you do?"

"Talk the way I do?"

"Hot? Kicks? Beat it?"

"Sailors! As for Hawaii, it's a protectorate or a territory or something like that." Ruby shrugged. "My family has been there about five years. Now my parents say they want to go all the way home. Beat it while the beating is good. But I told my pop I love glitter. I told him I want to be famous."

"I want to be a star—" Grace began.

"My pop asked why I would want to be in America at all," Ruby continued, once again speaking right over Grace. "He says we'll never be accepted as Americans."

"My dad says that too," I volunteered hesitantly.

But Ruby didn't seem all that interested in what I had to say either. "I went with them to Hawaii," she chattered. "I kept up with my ballet and tap, but I also learned hula. I'll show you how to do it." She took a breath before zeroing in on Grace. "What about you?"

"I've studied ballet, tap, piano, and voice—"

Just then, one of the men sitting next to the male dancer stood and clapped his hands to get everyone's attention. Now that I got a good look at him, I knew who he was: Charlie Low. He'd built the first grand apartment building for Chinese—the Low Apartments—up on Powell. He probably deemed himself the *grandest* man in Chinatown, but if he was, then he would have identified me on sight, and he didn't. He was just a middle-aged lucky so-and-so with a healthy girth that proclaimed to all that he could eat well even in these hard times. But, as they say, *the fish is the last to realize he lives in the water,* meaning Charlie was just another creature in the pond until someone bigger and better—like my baba—pulled him out and showed him what was what.

"I'm Charlie Low," he announced. "This is my wife, a little gal with a big voice, Li Tei Ming." Then he motioned to the two other men still sitting on their chairs. "These two cowboys are Walton Biggerstaff and Eddie Wu. One is your choreographer, and the other is a dancer. You can guess who is who." That earned some giggles, and Charlie threw his shoulders back in response. "This will be the best nightclub San Francisco has ever seen. Okay, so it won't be the first Chinese nightclub, but it will be the first Chinese nightclub *outside* Chinatown. We'll appeal to the most discriminating San Franciscans. I'm talking about *lo fan.*"

Grace frowned. Her ignorance of even the most basic Chinese words amazed me. I whispered, "He's talking about Occidentals—white ghosts."

When Charlie said, "I want girls who can sing and dance," I

started to rise as did a couple of others. Grace and Ruby pulled me back to the floor.

"Wait!" Ruby whispered. "Just listen!"

Charlie chuckled at the reaction he'd gotten. "You kids got me wrong," he went on. "We know most of you don't know how to dance. How could you? You're proper Chinese daughters. Am I right?" The other girls, who'd gotten up, sat down again too. "We want to see if you can move. If you can move *and* you're pretty, then we'll teach you to dance. It won't be hard, I swear. The main thing I want is pretty. Got it?"

"Well, then, we don't have anything to worry about," Ruby whispered again. "We can't miss!"

"I won't have a lot of rules around here, except for one," Charlie continued. "I'm going to hire only Chinese for my floor show. This is *our* chance, and we're going to make this place unique . . . and fun! Now, here's Walton. Consider him your maestro and call him Mr. Biggerstaff."

The tall and lanky *lo fan* got to his feet and spoke in a voice as smooth as caramel. "I want to see you all onstage."

My stomach churned nervously as I followed Ruby and Grace. They *moved* like dancers, which I wasn't. I was clumsy and scared, but a girl a couple of rows over lumbered like an old water buffalo. *Even a crow loses its gait when attempting to roam like a swan.*

"Let's start with each of you walking toward me," Mr. Biggerstaff said.

This part went fast. Either a girl could walk in a straight line or she couldn't. Either she had biggish breasts or she didn't. Either she was short or she wasn't. (Not that any of us was all *that* big—barely five feet or so, and not one over one hundred pounds.) Either she was pretty or she wasn't. Fifteen girls were thanked and dismissed on the spot. They were told to send other Chinese girls who were new to town and wanted work.

"Now give me four lines," Mr. Biggerstaff ordered. Ruby, Grace, and I ended up in the back. "Three steps forward, toe tap, two steps, kick, and turn to the right. We'll do four bars. Start on the right foot. One, two . . ."

Ruby moved well—delicate, like an ibis—but Grace was completely transformed. She was terrific, truly gifted. Charlie, Eddie, and Mr. Biggerstaff could barely take their eyes off her. She shone with each step, kick, and turn. At the other end of the spectrum, I was pathetic, and my dark and heavy clothes made me look even worse. Was I washing my face in a whirl of dust and disappointing myself needlessly?

After several run-throughs, Mr. Biggerstaff asked everyone to get offstage except for the first line. Ruby, Grace, and I went back to the spot on the floor where we'd been earlier, only this time, instead of sitting cross-legged, Ruby slid down into splits and began to stretch. She was unbelievably limber. She was showing off, clearly, doing her best so that Mr. Biggerstaff, Charlie Low, and the others might notice her. I watched as Grace's eyes narrowed, calculating. She held Ruby with her gaze and slowly spread her legs until she, too, was in a complete split, and then she raised her arms over her head and lowered her torso to the floor. Oh, yes, she was better than Ruby. From her impossible position, Grace inclined her head to look up at me. I plopped down next to them.

"I'll never get the steps," I admitted mournfully.

"And you have no natural talent either," Ruby observed. It was the first time she'd spoken directly to me, and it was to say something that sounded pretty mean. But Grace elbowed Ruby, who grinned to show she hadn't actually meant me any harm. "This isn't *real* dancing. You're plenty beautiful, but you need to put some feeling into your walk."

"Quiet over there." Mr. Biggerstaff stared at us sternly. "If you want to talk, go outside. If you go outside, don't come back."

I pulled my lips between my teeth and bit down hard. My fingers twisted in my lap. The longer I was here, the more I wanted this.

"One more time, girls," Mr. Biggerstaff said to the line onstage. "Five, six, seven, eight . . ."

"You can dance if you can count," Grace whispered. "Miss Miller, my dance teacher back home, drilled that into me. One, two, three, four. Five, six, seven, eight. Come. I'll show you." She led me to a corner, where we'd have space to practice. "It's an easy routine—one I could have taught the second and third graders in Miss Miller's school."

Grace explained that we were simply forming a big square. That I could hold in my head, even if my feet were still disobedient.

Ruby came over to watch. She crossed her arms as she studied my movements. "Have you ever seen a woman with bound feet?" She didn't wait for me to answer. "I have. In Hawaii. You need to try walking like *those* women do—like you don't want to put too much weight on your feet."

This time, when I took the first three steps, I pretended that my toes and the bones in my midfoot were broken and wrapped in binding cloth. I imagined myself floating across the floor, avoiding the anguish that any pressure would cause, sending the illusion of fragility, of a cloud drifting over moss. I dreamed I was happy and in love.

Ruby beamed. "Better."

"Much better!" Grace agreed.

Over the next half hour, girls in the first, second, and third lines did their routines twice and then were either chosen for the next round or dismissed. Those who looked sweet and dainty made it through, even if they hadn't mastered all the moves. A feeling hovered over the room: *If you aren't pretty, then it doesn't matter how talented you are.* When our line was called, Grace reminded me to smile, and count in my mind, and not with my lips. (Only problem: I'd been taught never to show my teeth. If I had to smile, then I should cover my mouth with a demure hand.) Ruby told me to relax. (*Aiya!* Like that would be possible.) But as the music played, I saw myself by a pond with weeping willows dripping their tendrils in the water, cranes flying across the sky, and soft fingers on my cheek. Ruby's advice was working. We did the routine twice, and then Mr. Biggerstaff told us to come to the front of the stage. He spoke quietly with Charlie, Li Tei Ming, and Eddie Wu, and then asked me to step forward.

"What kind of legs do you have?"

The question took me aback. I glanced at Ruby and Grace, who gave me encouraging nods. I lifted my wool skirt to just above my knees.

"Higher, please."

I edged the skirt up my thighs. When I'd woken in my bed this morning, I never thought I'd end up here, doing *this*.

"Perfect!" Mr. Biggerstaff proclaimed. "I hoped you might have something useful under there."

Ruby, Grace, and I made it through to the next round. Ruby squealed and hugged Grace and me. (I wasn't raised to be touched so freely, not even by family members, but I was brave about it.) Of the forty or so girls who started out that morning, fifteen made it to the next round for the eight dancers needed.

"Thanks so much for trying out and better luck next time," Charlie addressed those who'd been cut. "The girls who've made it, congratulations. We'll be auditioning again tomorrow and the day after that for additional ponies. On Monday, we'll all meet here again. We're going to see if we can teach you to do a simple tap routine. If you have tap shoes, bring them. If you don't, then I'm afraid you're done here. Oh, and you'll be singing too. That's it for today. Monday then."

"One last thing," Eddie Wu called out. "You, the babe with the gardenias in your hair. I like them. The smell is intoxicating. I'm drunk on you."

Li Tei Ming playfully swatted the back of Eddie's head, Ruby waved him off as though men spoke to her like that all the time, and the other girls in the room covered their mouths to hide their giggles. But I understood what he meant. She had a similar effect on me—as though I'd been sipping *mao tai* from thimble-size porcelain cups at a wedding banquet.

Grace and I clambered downstairs behind the still-glowing Ruby and out onto the street. We were so different from one another, and we could have easily broken apart right then. I could have gone back to the Chinese Telephone Exchange to meet my brother to take me home; Grace could have gone back to her hotel; and Ruby could have gone back to wherever it was she came from. One of us needed to speak. An act of kindness had started me on this road this morning; an act of kindness from Grace now propelled us forward on this new journey.

"I'm guessing you haven't learned how to tap, and you don't own a pair of tap shoes either," she ventured. "What if we take you to buy proper shoes?"

"That would be great—"

"As long as we're shopping," Ruby cut in, "we should get you some dance clothes too. You look more like an old widow than a chorus girl. I want to have an entourage when I'm famous, but you've got to dress the part."

"I accept, but you'll have to let me buy you dinner in return," I offered, figuring neither of them had much money or would know where to eat even if they did.

"Sure!" Ruby answered a little too eagerly. "Shall we go?"

I shook my head. "I can't right now. First I need to go back to where I met Grace this morning. I work near there. My brother always picks me up and takes me home."

Ruby gave me a sideways look, trying to figure me out.

"You need your brother to take you home?" she asked. "How old are you?"

"Twenty," I answered.

"I'm nineteen, and I walk wherever I want to walk," she said.

"But if I walk from one end of Chinatown to the other unescorted," I explained, "the grapevine will have sent out word before I get halfway there. Once someone saw me eating cherries on the street. Why did I get in trouble? Because it wasn't ladylike for me to *eat* on the street. Mama and Baba always say I have to guard my reputation like a piece of jade. Otherwise"—*how did I get going on this path?*—"who will marry me?" I managed to finish.

"Who wants to get married?" Ruby hooted.

Grace dissolved into giggles. I made myself giggle too, but the sound was bitter in my ears. Neither of the other girls noticed.

"My brother picks me up at five," I said. "Will you wait with me?" What was I thinking? Monroe would be taken aback to see me with two outsiders, to say the least. Nothing to do about it now.

We walked into Chinatown. Immediately, I felt eyes on me. At last it occurred to me that someone might have already told my father I hadn't shown up for work today. Nothing to do about that now either. I wanted to push the boundaries. I wanted to see if he'd actually notice me . . . and, if he did, *do* something about it.

The three of us sat on the curb outside the telephone exchange—our knees pressed together, getting to know each other, and discussing what songs to pick for the next round of auditions. This was a new experience for me, at once exhilarating and sickening. A sudden panicked desire to run home and shut the door to my room nearly overwhelmed me. The cage that usually held me came as much from deep inside me as it did from my father. But when I saw Monroe approaching, his strength gave me courage. He wore his usual outfit: dungarees, a T-shirt, and a blue college jacket with CAL written in script on the left breast. I knew the effect he had on girls with his smooth skin, wide eyes, and longish black hair that brushed across his forehead. Ruby would never have a chance, but Grace might do. What would it be like to have someone like Grace live in the compound with us? I let that idea flitter across my mind. I smiled as I rose to my feet. Ruby and Grace got up too.

"Monroe, I want you to meet my new friends. Grace, Ruby." I tugged on my brother's arm. "This is Monroe."

I could read the concern on his face as he stared at the two strangers, especially Ruby.

"Monroe," I went on in a pleading voice, "can you give me another couple of hours? Grace and Ruby are going to take me shopping."

"I'm not sure about this, Helen," he said.

"Please?"

"What'll I tell our ba?" he asked.

"Tell him I had to stay late at work—"

"But you aren't at work—"

"Then I'll take the blame."

He glanced warily from Ruby to Grace. He took his responsibility as my older brother very seriously.

"Please, Monroe, please?" I begged as hard as when I was five and he had a bag of sesame candies I wanted him to share.

It was his duty to watch out for me, but he loved me too. More important, Grace seemed to have caught his eye, just as I'd hoped. He'd want to impress her with his openness.

"You promise she'll be safe?" he asked, his voice demanding truth.

"Absolutely," the two girls replied in unison.

"All right then." He addressed me directly again. "I'll cover for you this one time. I'll see you back here at seven o'clock." He tucked his hands in his pants pockets and nodded at Grace. "Nice to meet you." With that, he pulled his shoulders up under his ears and sauntered back the way he'd come.

We found a telephone booth and looked up the address for a dance shop, then walked several blocks out of Chinatown until we found it. We made it just before closing time, but the clerk volunteered to stay late. Ruby and Grace helped me pick out navy satin shorts and a long-sleeved white blouse to wear for the audition, as well as two pairs of dance shoes—one for regular dancing and the other for tap. Their eyes thinned into slits when I opened my wallet. *Cash!* I ignored them, saying, "I hope this won't be a waste of money."

"Don't worry about it." Ruby seemed sure of *everything*. "We've got two full days to teach you the basics."

. . .

I TOOK THEM to a noodle shop on Grant that I promised was one of the best in Chinatown, but Grace looked as jittery as a wet mouse.

"What should I get?" she asked.

"Pick your favorite. Remember, I'm buying."

Grace blinked. "What I mean is, I don't know what these things are. I've never eaten Chinese food."

"Where did you say you're from?" Ruby pried.

"I didn't say, but I'm from Plain City, Ohio," she answered, guarded.

"Is it one of those places that's too small to have a Chinese restaurant?" I inquired.

"Only about two thousand people live there, so I guess so," she replied.

"Cripes!" Ruby exclaimed.

I shook my head in disbelief. The population of San Francisco's Chinatown was ten times that, and the larger city surrounded it.

"I've never been to a place where you couldn't get Chinese food." After a pause, I asked, "Didn't your mother make it?"

"No."

"That's shocking!"

Grace put her purse on the floor.

"My mother says you must never do that," Ruby chastised.

"Mine too," I agreed. "Do you want all your money to run out of your purse?"

Grace blushed and quickly set the purse back on her lap. "We don't have that custom in Plain City," she said. After an uncomfortable silence, she added, "You haven't told us anything about you yet, Helen."

"I grew up a block from here," I answered. "Baba's in the laundry business—"

Grace brightened. "My family has a laundry too."

"My father doesn't *run* a laundry." That came out haughtier than I intended, and I could see the change in Grace's expression. I tried again, flecking my voice with jasmine petals. "My baba is a merchant.

He sells supplies to laundries: claim tickets, washboards, irons. Things like that. Not just to the mom-and-pops in this city, but to laundries all around the country."

The whole time I spoke, I searched Grace's face. She'd pulled away, but the look in her eyes! Her family's laundry was probably some little hole in the wall in that dinky town of hers.

"My parents are very traditional," I continued. "*Filial piety begins with serving your parents, which leads to serving the emperor* (in our case, the president), *which ends in establishing your character.*" Apparently, Grace wasn't familiar with that aphorism either. "I wasn't allowed to take dance classes, as you know. My brothers and I could speak only Chinese at home. I wasn't permitted to play on the street or in the park. I've never had a girlfriend. I've never even had a girl from school come to my house."

"I'm practically in the same boat friend-wise," Grace admitted.

We glanced at Ruby. She lifted a shoulder. Agreement?

"I have seven brothers, and my dad wished for an eighth son," I told them. "He hoped to get the sound *ba*—for *eight,* which sounds the same as *good luck*. He wanted to walk through Chinatown and have everyone recognize him for his successful business and his eight sons. Instead, I came along and ruined everything."

The waiter set down three bowls of steaming soup noodles. Ruby and I picked up our chopsticks and used them to bring the long noodles to our lips.

"Mama had eight children in ten years," I picked up after the waiter left. "She kept trying for an eighth son, but after me she only had miscarriages and stillborns. It's hard for girls like us. Boys can go to college, but Baba says, '*A woman without education is better than a woman with education.*'" Neither of them seemed to recognize the Confucian saying. "We also aren't allowed to drive. We shouldn't show our arms. We can't show our legs. We're supposed to learn to cook, clean, sew, embroider—"

"Then how can you dance now?" Grace asked, fingering her

chopsticks. "Didn't you say you can't do anything in Chinatown without people finding out about it?"

"And what about your brother?" Ruby chimed in. "Won't he tell?"

I had to think about how to answer them. Today was my first foray into the world of lying. *Tell the truth, but not too much of it.*

"If Baba finds out, I'll be in real hot water," I answered at last. "But Monroe won't tell on me, because he wants to change his life too. He's studying to be an engineer, but he's worried he's going to end up working as a janitor or a houseboy. Something like that happened to another of my older brothers. Jackson was the first in our family to go to college. He graduated two years ago—one of twenty-eight American-born Chinese to graduate from Cal that year—as a dentist. Now the only job he can get is as a chauffeur for a woman who lives in Pacific Heights."

A look passed between Ruby and Grace. *College? An engineer? A dentist?* I bet the chauffeur part sounded pretty good to them too, but I didn't see it that way.

"Baba makes plenty of sweat money in this country, but he says this isn't our real home and that we shouldn't live where we aren't welcome. If one of my brothers gets upset because someone on the street taunted him, calling 'chink, chink, chink,' then Baba says, 'See? I told you so. Go look in the mirror. Your eyes automatically tell you this is not your home.' "

Ruby opened her mouth to speak, but I rolled right over her. "Baba complains that my brothers are too Americanized. He says, 'You might be Americanized, but you'll never be accepted as Americans, even though you were born here.' After that, he criticizes them for not being Chinese enough, because they *were* born here. We all were."

Look who was *cheung hay* now!

"But you can't argue with my baba," I continued, unable to stop myself. "It wouldn't be right. He said he wanted my brothers and me to learn proper Chinese for when we went back to China for good. For months, he went around to the laundries that he supplies. He asked for their old rags, clothes that hadn't been collected, worn-out shoes, hardware, and junk—"

"I had to wear unclaimed laundry too," Grace cut in. "In elementary school, the girls taunted me when they recognized their castoffs. Once the kids caught me wearing Freddie Thompson's old shirt under my jumper—"

"I bet they made fun of you then," Ruby said.

"I'll say. I went in the girls' room, took off the shirt, and tried to give it back to Freddie, but he tossed it in the dirt, saying he didn't want to touch anything that had been on a girl."

"That's what he said. He probably didn't want to touch anything worn by an Oriental," Ruby assessed shrewdly.

Grace nodded. "The boys spent the rest of recess throwing the shirt back and forth, teasing me, but teasing Freddie even worse. Freddie was a tough customer even when he was eight. He fought back."

Grace was trying hard to fit in to the conversation—and Ruby was doing a good job making her feel comfortable—but I had to set them both straight. "I told you, we don't have a laundry. I've never worn people's leftovers, or anyone's hand-me-downs for that matter. My baba packed all that trash in trunks, and we took it to China to give to our relatives."

"Why would you do that?" Grace asked, sounding as unpolished as a servant—one brought in from the rice paddies to work in the landowner's house: dumb, without an ounce of knowledge of how real people lived. But she'd been so nice to me and so open that I liked her despite her country innocence.

"The more trunks we had, the richer we looked," I explained. "The more we gave away, the more important my father appeared. But fortune like that can be won and lost very quickly." I turned and spoke directly to Ruby. "We were only there a year and a half before the Japanese invaded. Baba said it was better for us to come back here and be poor than stay there and be dead. President Roosevelt says times are getting better, but they still aren't that good around here."

"Not where I'm from either," Grace said.

"Or me either," Ruby allowed, the corner of her lip twitching. "That's one of the reasons my parents wanted to move to Hawaii. They could live cheaply, and they'd be closer to getting home—"

"Baba wants all of us to work," I interrupted, and Ruby went back to her noodles. "My other brothers and I are all supposed to chip in for Monroe's tuition, but there aren't a lot of jobs for girls like me. Baba says that no matter how bad off we are, he'll never let me work in a garment factory. Being a maid or working as an elevator operator in one of the department stores on Union Square doesn't appeal to him either."

"But you have a good job already," Grace blurted.

I sighed. "The manager at the Chinese Telephone Exchange is indebted to my father. I've been working there for six months. I hate it, and I'm only making five dollars a week. If I get the job at the Forbidden City, I'll make twenty dollars a week."

Grace croaked, "That much?"

The sum must have seemed fantastical to her. Ruby ran the tip of her tongue over her teeth. Twenty dollars must have sounded like a fortune to her too.

"Didn't either of you ask what the pay was going to be?" When they shook their heads, I said, "But that's the most important piece of information."

Ruby ignored the criticism. "What happens when your father finds out you're dancing?"

I jutted my chin. "Fathers like to give orders and tell you what to do. The next minute? Who are *you*? Get out of my way! Having a worthless daughter isn't just something Chinese say. It's been in our culture for—"

Grace cleared her throat. "My father said I could have anything and do anything I want in America. That's why he forced me to take dance and singing lessons with the other girls in town. He made me do everything they did."

I wanted to ask, *If he's so great, then what are you doing here?* But I didn't, because her talent and her pluck couldn't hide the fact that offstage she seemed barely above a frightened street urchin. But then Ruby saw only her own light and heard her own music, and I was happy to be anywhere but in the compound. Yet as dissimilar as we were, it was as clear to me as chrysanthemum jelly that all three of us were alone in the world—each in our own ways. I saw, *felt,* an invisible string of connection tying us together.

Since the conversation seemed to have reached its end, Grace went back to fingering her chopsticks. Finally, she asked, "Could one of you gals teach me how to use these?"

"You don't use chopsticks?" The idea was astounding.

"I've never seen them before, so how could I know how to use them? Plain City . . ." Grace hunched her shoulders, humbled, embarrassed. "How do you eat soup with sticks?"

"Cripes!" Ruby exclaimed again.

We showed Grace how to pick up the noodles with the chopsticks and dangle them over her porcelain soupspoon before lifting them to her mouth. She was beyond hopeless, but she ate like she hadn't had a meal in a year.

"You'll get better," I promised. "If you can teach me how to tap, then I can certainly teach you how to eat like a proper Chinese."

After dinner, we walked back to the telephone exchange, where we spotted Monroe waiting for us. "If you were going to have noodles here in Chinatown, you should have told me," he said, proving what I'd said about Chinatown's gossip mill to be true. "Next time, we'll all meet there. Okay?"

Grace, excited, grabbed Ruby's and my hands. What was it about these girls and all their touching? Didn't they have *any* manners?

"Thank you," Grace said to Monroe, whose cheeks went crimson. "Thank you so much for letting us see each other again."

I waved goodbye to my new friends and let Monroe escort me home. Most people rented apartments, but not my family. Our home took up nearly a whole block. We occupied an American version of a Chinese compound, with four sides, each with two stories, surrounding an interior courtyard. My six oldest brothers, already married with wives and children, inhabited the side wings. Monroe and I lived with our parents in the back of the compound, where we also had the public rooms. The laundry-supply business faced the street.

Monroe opened the gate, and we walked across the inner courtyard, which was littered with tricycles, balls, and other toys. Suddenly, he stopped and turned to me.

"What are you doing?" he asked gently.

"I'm trying to start my life again—"

"After everything our family has been through, especially you . . . I'm worried you're going to get hurt."

A lot of responses ran through my head, but I wisely didn't speak them.

"You're only just beginning to recover," he went on. "You have a good job. I come and get you every day. Let things return to normal—"

"Nothing will ever be normal again."

"Helen—"

"Don't worry about me. This gets me out of the compound. That's what you all want, isn't it?"

Monroe stared hard at me. I loved him best of all my brothers, but his concern wouldn't help me or change my fate. He sighed. Then he continued to the back of the courtyard and entered a door that led to the dining room. Everyone would just be gathering for dinner, but I didn't want to see all those babies and small children. I also wanted to avoid the kitchen, where my sisters-in-law would ignore me and my mother would struggle for something to say as though anything she could utter could possibly change my status in the household or the world. How could I live in a compound with three generations of my relatives—all so alive with all their breathing, eating, and siring—and still be so lonely?

I ducked through a side entrance, went upstairs, threaded my way along the deserted hallway to my room, and shut the door behind me, but I could still hear the bustle and noise of the family. On a small table next to the window was a plate of oranges—neatly stacked—unlit candles set in pewter dishes, an incense burner, and a photograph. I began to weep.

RUBY

A Real Chinese Girl

On Saturday morning, I left my aunt and uncle's house, took a ferry from Alameda to San Francisco, and walked to the Chinatown playground. Grace and Helen were already there. Sitting on a bench. Talking. Time for work! Grace and I taught Helen steps with one sound—the ball tap, heel tap, brush, and scuff. Every so often, mothers entered the park with their strollers, whispered when they saw us, and then rolled right back out.

"What are they saying?" Grace asked.

"They're calling us no-no girls," Helen answered.

No kidding. But Grace didn't get it. She was a great dancer, better than me by far, which was downright irksome, but she truly acted like she'd just fallen off the turnip truck. I liked her even so. I saw in her what she probably saw in me—that we'd been hit by hard times, that we'd put cardboard in our shoes when the soles had worn out, and that we were on the thin side from too many dinners of watery soup.

On Sunday, same travel time to get to the Chinatown playground. I arrived first. Then Grace. We got to watch Monroe drop off his sister.

"This is the busiest day of the week in Chinatown," he yakked, kicking and complaining, "and you're in the playground!" He gestured to the apartment buildings that surrounded the park. "Lots of eyes up there . . . and everywhere. Ba's going to find out."

He was right, but either Helen wasn't able to think of a better place to go or she was choosing to be deliberately defiant. I couldn't get a read on her. Monroe beat it to the library, reminding Helen with a call over his shoulder that he'd "fetch" her at Fong Fong Chinese Tea Pavilion at five. Then Grace and I spent the morning showing Helen taps with two sounds—the shuffle, scuffle, slap, and flap. She was pretty, which was hard for me to admit, but, man, she was a real cement mixer. By noon, it was clear she simply wasn't catching on.

"It's hard to learn to move well without music," Grace said. "What if I show you something my dance instructor choreographed back home? Every so often, she'd bring out a record of novelty songs. Our favorite was 'Let Me Play with It.'" She started to sing and do the simple routine her teacher had put to the tune. "You let me play with your little yo-yo. I'll let you play with mine."

I grinned at the lyrics, but Helen and Grace seemed to take them at face value. The song was about as easy as could be, though, with those two cracked lines repeated again and again. Helen practiced with steely determination. Aided by the melody, she followed along, pointing her right index finger at an imaginary audience and then at herself at the appropriate spots, putting a little enthusiasm into her footwork, even smiling. And she had a swell voice. In fact, we harmonized quite well together. By four, we'd reached the end of the song—"I'll let you play with mine. I mean it! I'll let you play with mine"—and Helen had learned a passable three-sound tap called the riffle and slurp. And still the mothers who came through the park turned away, muttering under their breath. So what? I was used to that kind of thing.

We sat on a bench and changed out of our taps. Through the open windows around us came the clatter of dinners being prepared, the whines of musical instruments being practiced—badly—and squalls of colicky babies. Men sat on their haunches on fire-escape landings—drinking tea from used jelly jars, smoking cigarettes, and watching us with expressions that combined disdain and desire. I was used to that too.

After Helen fixed my collar—"so you look nicer"—she led the way to Fong Fong. The streets were lively. Laundry workers and waiters, dressed in their Sunday best, took advantage of their one night off, strutting to poolrooms, burlesque shows, and dime-a-dance halls. Helen said some of those men visited the open-air herb shop to buy deer antler, bear gall, and shaved rhinoceros horn to improve and prolong their potency in case good fortune—in the form of a woman—should shine on them in the coming hours. Other men, in business suits, gathered to blab about politics on corners. Women roamed the shops.

Helen pulled us into Fong Fong and bought three Coca-Colas.

"You two have helped me so much," she said. "Thank you—"

Grace and I spoke over each other.

"No thanks are necessary—"

"We were happy to help—"

Helen held up a hand. "Listen." She leaned forward conspiratorially. "I've heard of an apartment close to here. It's not too big or too expensive. If you two become roommates, the rent won't be bad, especially if I negotiate it for you."

"An apartment?" I squinted, doubtful. Hanging around with girls wasn't my idea of a clambake. Especially with either of these two. Grace was a knockout, but so sweet and innocent she hadn't yet kenned onto using what she had. And Helen? She was pretty, like I said, but something was off with her. How could she be so swift on the effect Chinese herbs had on men when she supposedly lived such a sheltered life with her family? Beyond that, I wasn't sure I liked the way she stared at me.

"It's not the cleanest," Helen went on, "but it's not the dirtiest either."

"In Chinatown?" Grace asked nervously.

"Of course it's in Chinatown." Helen sure could be bossy—a regular Miss Know-it-all. "You two need a place to live. The YWCA is full. Cameron House is right around the corner, but that's not right for you. Donaldina Cameron rescues *bad* girls." She lowered her voice. "If you become roommates, you'll be close to where I live, and you'll be even closer to the telephone exchange."

"You won't be working there much longer," I said, confident.

"What if we aren't hired? How will we pay the rent?" People could probably smell Grace's fear all the way in Timbuktu.

"You'll be hired," Helen told her. "You'll be hired before I am!"

Helen didn't mention me, but I had to be a sure thing after the little visit I'd paid to Charlie Low in his office. Nothing happened, and he did a bang-up job of acting like he wasn't thrilled—not with his wife in the building, but she wouldn't always be there. A man is a man is a man. Yeah, I'd wised up after not getting hired at the other auditions. This time I'd get the gig and the dough.

"Do you want to share an apartment?" Grace asked me.

My mother always said it was rude for someone to be so direct, but I answered anyway. "Why not?" Because, really, *why not?* There had to be a first time for everything. "Anyplace would be better than staying with my aunt and uncle in Alameda. It'll be good to get away from my little cousins too."

I watched as they took in those nuggets of information. We'd bumped gums some, talking a bit about this and that. Nothing serious. Nothing too revealing. It was fine by me if we practiced "Oriental silence"—hanging on to information that was no one else's business—but things were bound to leak out.

"You're sure you want to do it?" Grace's voice rose with expectation.

"I'd love to," I answered. "And thank you, Helen. Thank you so much."

"I'm happy to help," she responded. "It will be good to have you nearby."

THE NEXT DAY, Grace and I met Helen at the Forbidden City, where we big-eyed the new girls who'd made it through the weekend auditions. We were back up to forty or so girls for the eight spots, which knocked some of the wind out of my panties. We auditioned in groups of six, and we sang something we'd all learned in elementary school—"Oh My Darling Clementine"—which put us on equal footing and made it instantly clear who could carry a tune. A quarter of the girls were gone by noon. Then Walton—no man was a mister to me—introduced us to the tap routine, which was a lot easier than anything we'd shown Helen over the weekend. He wanted to see how we moved onstage. Did we have presence? Could we hit our marks? Did our simple taps sound crisp or muddled? Did we have nice smiles?

"You, you, and you are in."

Helen, Grace, and I made it through to the next round.

At the end of the day, we found Monroe on the sidewalk. We were physically tired but also exhilarated. We were so close to getting chosen as the Forbidden City's first ponies . . . and now the apartment. Monroe walked with us to a run-down building on Waverly, a block from the playground where Grace and I had taught Helen to tap. Mrs. Hua, the elderly manager, showed us the tiny two-room furnished flat, which had a hot plate and a sink. If we got the place, we'd have to take turns sleeping on the sofa and the bed. Showers would be courtesy of the YWCA. We searched the cupboards and found four plates, three cups, a frying pan, and a wok. It all looked good to me.

I was grateful when Helen took charge. She knew the ins and outs of Chinatown—a place where Grace and I were total strangers. And it turned out she was great at bargaining.

"You want to charge ten dollars a week? For this?" Helen asked Mrs. Hua. "Impossible!"

"Nine dollars," Mrs. Hua countered in heavily accented English.

"It isn't worth five."

"Eight fifty."

"Five. Take it or leave it."

Monroe regarded his sister with embarrassment tinged with grudging admiration. Grace seemed eager for Helen to accept the asking price.

"Eight dollars. No lower," Mrs. Hua came back.

Helen shook her head. "Let's go."

Monroe, Grace, and I started for the door. Mrs. Hua grabbed Helen's sleeve. "Six dollars. Okay?"

Helen pursed her lips as she thought about it. Finally, she said, "All right. Six dollars a week. But I'm not going anywhere until I see the contract. I don't want you changing things after I leave, Mrs. Hua."

As soon as the manager left to get the paperwork, Grace squealed and jumped up and down. "Helen! I can't believe you just did that! My hotel room costs a dollar a day. This is a lot better and for a lot less money."

"Really, Helen, that was pretty neat," I agreed. "Thanks *again.*"

Helen waved us off. "It's the least I can do after everything you've done for me."

Yes, we'd scratched her back, and now she was scratching ours. That's how people get ahead . . . and make "friends." But Helen and Grace were making a mistake if they thought I was "nice" too. I was nice enough, but I was ambitious. I wanted the adoration that comes from being famous and not just a pretty girl from the islands.

Mrs. Hua came back through the door and set the contract on the table. Grace picked up the pen, hesitated, and turned to Helen. "Would you like to live with us? Maybe Mrs. Hua has an even bigger apartment."

Helen nipped the idea in the bud, glancing at her brother. "It's safer for me to be in the compound with my family."

I wasn't sure how she'd be "safer" there, but maybe she could do only so much. She could defy her father by walking through Chinatown with Grace and me, and tempt fate by learning to tap in a very public place, but being on her own—away from her family—might have been the one line she couldn't cross. I might not cross it either if I lived in a "compound"!

The next morning, Helen was sitting on the stairs outside the apartment when I arrived. She had a bag of groceries and some flowers wrapped in butcher paper. Once upstairs, she got straight to work—putting the blooms in a vase she'd brought with her and setting the bouquet on a doily she'd tatted herself. Next, she shelved the groceries. When Grace thumped into the room with her suitcase, the apartment already looked more livable. Grace and I divvied up the space in the closet and dresser. (When Grace thought I wasn't watching, she put five sawbucks in an envelope and tucked it under a sweater in her drawer. Emergency money, no doubt.) Neither of us knew how to cook, so Helen scrambled eggs and toasted bread by holding it over the hot plate. After breakfast, Grace and I brushed our teeth in the sink. Then we went together down the hall and waited in line with tenants from the other five apartments on our floor to use the toilet.

At 10:00, we beat it to the Forbidden City for final auditions. I had this in the bag. Walton asked to see the routine we'd learned the previous week, but this time we had to sing another old-fashioned song—"Let Me Call You Sweetheart"—while we danced. *A cinch.* Helen did well too. What she lacked in dance experience, she more than made up for with her pretty singing voice. When we finished, a few girls were asked to step forward, thanked, and dismissed. The remaining twelve of us rearranged ourselves onstage. I took a place in the front row, wanting to be seen. Walton signaled for the music.

We were making the third turn when Grace came to a dead stop. We were still in the opening part of the routine! I shot an encouraging look in her direction. *Dance!* She struggled to fight back tears. By the time I made my next turn, they were rolling down her cheeks. I liked Grace—my roommate now—but if she were dismissed, then my spot would be sealed for sure.

Eddie Wu bounded onstage, took Grace's hand, and pulled her stage front. "Five, six, seven, eight," he counted loud enough for all of us to hear. "Let me call you sweetheart . . ." They danced the last half of the routine together, adding a flourish or two. They were spectacular, outshining everyone else. When the music ended, Walton and some of the others clapped. Eddie dropped Grace's hand, chucked her chin, and then went back to his folding chair.

Walton, Charlie, and Eddie conferred in low voices, while everyone else tried to cover their apprehensions by adjusting the trim on a sock, going over a move again, or fluffing curls. I stayed perfectly still, with one leg slightly bent and a hand on my hip. Walton asked us to form a single line. Grace stood with her head bowed.

"Irene Liu," Walton said. "Congratulations. You made it."

The second spot went to May Bing. Helen nodded when her name was called. (She'd never be one to show excitement.) Other girls were dropped or accepted until just three of us were left for the last two spots. Grace, another girl, and I held hands.

"Grace Lee, you're in—"

She made it after freezing, then lucking in to Eddie helping her?

"You're our best dancer," Walton added as she walked offstage to where the other new hires clustered together. "Today your nerves showed. Never let anyone see you're scared. Never let anyone guess you've messed up the dance or forgotten the lyrics. You have the potential to be a star, Grace. Act that way, and it will come true."

Only two of us were left standing.

"Ida Wong, step forward please." Walton looked at his clipboard. "Congratulations—"

My stomach lurched, and the room whooshed with shocked exhales. *How could Ida have been chosen over me?* No one could believe it, not even Ida, who was pretty in that cute-as-a-button kind of way. I glanced at Charlie out of the corner of my eye. He lifted a shoulder in halfhearted acknowledgment. My attempt to cozy up to him—a married man—had completely backfired. He must have seen me as trouble. Well, nothing to do about it now. I hopped down off the stage, packed my things, and beat it for the door.

"Abyssinia!" I called to Helen and Grace. Silence. "I'll be seeing ya," I translated.

Grace started to come toward me, but she was stopped by Charlie's call. "You're my glamour girls now. Please gather around . . ."

My eyes swept across the room one last time, and then I left the Forbidden City. I waited for Grace and Helen on the sidewalk, wondering what in the hell I was going to do now. And I'll be honest. I hurt like mad, and I was scared.

Soon enough, Grace and Helen came down the stairs.

"It doesn't make sense," Grace said when she saw me. "You should have gotten hired too."

I looked away. I wasn't about to start busting out the waterworks. I had a little money, but when that ran out and I couldn't pay the rent on my new apartment, then what? Stand in a soup line? Sleep on the street? Beg? Go back to my aunt and uncle's place with all their bawling brats? "It's all right. I'll try at one of the other clubs—"

"Finally," Helen muttered, interrupting me.

It took me a moment to realize she wasn't speaking to me. I followed her gaze and saw a middle-aged Chinese man approaching. He wore a well-tailored suit and carried a copy of *The Chinese Digest* folded and tucked under his arm. He reminded me a bit of Charlie, actually. Black hair, neatly trimmed. Well fed. An air of importance.

"So what the gossips say is true," he said, stopping before Helen. "My daughter has disgraced me."

"I haven't disgraced you, Ba—"

"No? Then what do you call not showing up to work at a job *I* arranged for you? What do you call dancing in the playground? And then there's this!" He pointed at the entrance to the Forbidden City.

"It's a better job. Besides, how can I disgrace you any more than I have already?"

Next to me, Grace looked frightened, like she thought he was going to wallop *her*. I sensed she might bolt, so I grabbed her arm and held her in place. Helen's father stood there—dignified, his hands clasped before him, aware that people—*white* pedestrians—watched us. And the way he stared at me? I understood it right away, because he wasn't the first person to see me for what I was, even if it was rare. The disgust in his eyes made me want to push right back. I struck a pose—a hip thrust forward, my eyes staring defiantly into his face, the fingers of my left hand barely caressing the petals of my gardenias. Grace was a quivering mess, but I wasn't afraid or intimidated at all. And Helen?

"I'll still put my earnings in the family pot," she said matter-of-factly, as if her disobedience and lying would mean nothing to her father. "Now I can give more toward Monroe's tuition."

"If you dance here, you will be one notch above a prostitute," he proclaimed. "Is that how you want people to regard me in Chinatown—as the father of a no-no girl?"

Next to me, a light flipped on in Grace's eyes as she finally put two and two together.

"I won't be hurting the family," Helen insisted calmly. "I'll be helping more than before. And besides, this isn't a reflection on you—"

"Don't be stupid! You have a choice to bring shame or honor on your family. Which is it going to be?"

Helen met her father's disapproval with surprising stubbornness. "You always say you expect me to maintain the proprieties, recognize right from wrong, and not bring embarrassment on our family."

"That's right. Embarrassment!"

"I'm going to make twenty dollars a week," Helen said.

Her father blinked. "Twenty dollars? A week?"

"Are any of my brothers making that much?" she asked.

He grumbled a bit more—"What will our neighbors say?"—but it was clear Helen had won. I guess the money had convinced him. Still, he'd gone down a lot easier than I expected.

"You can do this on one condition," he said, acting like he'd once again gained control over his daughter. "I won't have you walking all over Chinatown . . . at night . . . unescorted. Monroe will drop you off and bring you home."

"Yes, Ba," she answered, sounding both contrite and disappointed, as though he'd failed a test she'd given him.

"All right," he said. "I expect you to be home in time for dinner."

As he gathered himself to leave, he ran his eyes over me again. "And, Helen . . ."

Here it comes, I thought. Now my new friends would know the truth about me. I didn't have a clue about how they would take it.

"One word of warning. Watch out for this one. She's a Jap," he said, nodding in my direction.

Helen acted unimpressed. She gave him a bland look: *As if I didn't know.*

Faced again with his daughter's coolness, he squeezed the newspaper a little more tightly to his ribs and continued down the street. It was a moment of triumph for Helen, utter bewilderment for Grace, and the icing on what had already become a crappy day for me. Grace was the first to speak.

"Why would he say that about Ruby?"

Helen frowned. "You really are a bumpkin," she said. "Ruby is Japanese. Can't you tell?" She pointed to the sign above our heads. "It's the Forbidden City. Like Charlie said, it's for Chinese. The Japs have invaded China, so no Japs allowed. Naturally, Baba wouldn't want me to spend time with someone like her."

My being Japanese wasn't why I didn't get hired, but I said nothing to square the error. Grace stared at Helen—shocked, shocked, shocked. "What are you talking about?"

Helen spelled it out again. "Ruby is Japanese."

Grace looked like someone had bopped her one. "Why would you—he—say that?"

"Because it's true," Helen insisted, her tone superior.

"It's also mean." Grace turned to me. "You're Ruby Tom," she said, positive as could be. "That's a Chinese name. You're a real Chinese girl."

"Ethel Zimmerman changed her name," I said, "because she thought it wouldn't look good on a marquee. Now she's Ethel Merman. My real name is Kimiko Fukutomi. Ruby suits me better, and Fukutomi . . . well . . . I shortened it to Tom."

"That's a Chinese name, right?" Grace repeated weakly. Then she lightly tapped her head with her fingertips—another light going on. "When you said your family wanted to go home, you meant to Japan."

I nodded.

"Oh!" The surprised syllable came out like the first time you put a hand down a boy's pants. "I get it. You're like a Negro pretending to be white." She sighed. "Where I grew up . . . Prejudice, you know—"

"I've always been able to pass," I said, trying to put an end to the commiseration. "I'm good at it. In the Occidental world, no one can tell that I'm different. Even here in Chinatown, most people don't see me as different."

"I did," Helen pointed out. "And my father and brother did too."

Three people out of this entire enclave? I couldn't be too worried about that.

"I'm sorry if you've been hurt," Grace said.

I shrugged. "I'm not hurt."

"We all have secrets," she went on, still trying to comfort me.

I figured that meant I was supposed to ask about *her* secret, but I wasn't fast enough, because she blurted, "I ran away from home. My dad beat me . . ."

Hardly a big surprise, given the bruises her clothes didn't quite cover and the cut she tried unsuccessfully to hide under lipstick, but I nodded sympathetically. "I'm sure you did the right thing."

Neither Helen nor I followed up with additional questions. I can't speak for Helen, but I didn't want Grace to lose any more face than she already had, poor thing. Grace and I now turned to Helen.

"Japanese and Chinese have always been against each other. And it's not just this war," Helen said, her voice as distant yet impassioned as my mother's. "Japan is powerful. It can face any country—"

"Yeah, yeah, yeah." I mean, really. Like this was news? "You want to know what my parents taught *me*? They say all you Chinese think you're great because your culture is so much older than our culture. You accuse us of stealing your language—"

"You did," she responded, not wanting to let it go. "Japan has long held a grudge against China. Japan wants to dominate China politically and militarily. It wants to take control of China's raw materials, food, and labor—"

"I hate all that," I said, repeating what I told my father when he boasted about Japan's imperialistic aspirations. "Those things have nothing to do with me."

"I lived in China, as I've already told you," Helen went on. "When the Jap bombers came, we . . ." She took a breath and held it. "I mean, Monroe and I were walking on the road. We saw the red sun on the sides of the planes. We heard a warning gong from a nearby village, but what could we do? We saw a pilot in one of the cockpits. He shot at us."

"That's terrible," I said. "But those things still have nothing to do with me."

"Really, Helen, you can't blame Ruby for events that happened in another country," Grace threw in, defending me.

"Because it's not *my* country," I added. Again, I'd often said that to my parents, which drove them nearly crazy. "I was born here. I'm an American, just like you and Grace."

Helen stared in the direction her father had gone.

Grace, still anxious, fumbled for something to say. "We're still friends, aren't we?"

Helen gave herself a small shake. Even I—who had known her less than a week—could see that somewhere deep inside a struggle was going on. She shifted her gaze to me, and we locked eyes. Finally, she spoke.

"I will keep your secret."

Was her change of heart a little too quick? My entire life I'd heard about the centuries-long animosity between Japanese and Chinese, but I knew almost nothing about Chinese girls or how one like Helen might think and act.

"What about your father, Helen?" Grace asked. "You'll be disobeying him if you see Ruby."

"How am I disobeying him? He said watch out for her, not don't ever see her. I went to school with Negroes and Mexicans. He didn't like that either, but he had to live with it. Besides," she added, "Ruby won't be working at the Forbidden City, so it's not like I'll be with her every day."

Grace needed to know one more thing. "Are you really going to give all your money to your father?"

"Of course," Helen answered. "My brothers and I all do. He provides for us. We live with him. And he gives us spending money. Anything else you want to know?" The way she asked seemed designed to put an end to the conversation. "Are we set then? Good. Now let's get some noodles."

We began to walk, with Helen in the middle. I peered around her and into Grace's face. She still looked a bit numb from shock and confusion. Between us, Helen wore an expression I couldn't decipher. The three of us were as different as could be, and—despite the sudden revelations—I had a hunch that the two of them were harboring deeper truths, just as I was. In the same way I sensed that Helen and Grace had attached themselves to me like sucking sea creatures, I understood that I had glued myself to them too. The realization shook me something fierce. This was stranger than moving to Hawaii with my parents; defying them with my attitude, smart mouth, and boys; returning to the mainland to live with Aunt Haru and Uncle Junji; or abandoning the identity I was born with for one that might be more practical. Friendship was uncharted territory for me, maybe for all of us. Would the three of us end up as good companions or as vicious enemies?

None of that mattered to me if I didn't get a job.

GRACE

A Few Glorious Minutes

"Smile, damn you. Smile!" Mr. Biggerstaff yelled. It was late November, and we were at his studio, about midway through rehearsals for the Forbidden City's opening. He'd explained that we'd be doing three one-hour shows each night with five acts of dancing, singing, and what he called novelties. In between those acts would be short bridge routines by the ponies, culminating in a big production number for the finale.

"Do it again! One, two, three, four . . . Again! Five, six, seven, eight!" He made us practice at the barre to build our strength: "Keep your knees directly above your feet." He ordered us to do crawling splits across the floor to increase our flexibility: "Wider, wider!" He had us twist into pretzels—all edges erased—to improve our agility: "Stretch. And keep smiling, damn it. Didn't anyone teach you to smile? Show your teeth! Teeth! Teeth! More teeth!"

Mr. Biggerstaff put me in charge of the line. I kept an eye on the other girls—especially Ida Wong, who could be a real nuisance—making sure they hit their marks, didn't get lazy with their turns or kicks, and stayed in time to the music. This caused jealousy among some of the gals, and they stopped talking to me for a few days, but I had to be tough on them, because they were now my responsibility.

"Rehearse, perspire, perfection!" Mr. Biggerstaff encouraged us. "Rehearse, perspire, perfection!" He made us dance and dance and dance. "I want your hop to come on the drummer's downbeat. The kick is on the upbeat. *Listen!* Don't you hear it?"

Everything he asked us to do was easy for me, but most of the other girls had never danced before. They were getting my thirteen years of experience in six weeks. If a girl didn't learn the routine quickly, he went after her, cutting her down, making her cry, but ultimately forcing her to improve. It was hard work and long hours. I forgot the time. I forgot to eat. And for a few glorious minutes each day I forgot to miss my mother or feel bad that I couldn't write to her, knowing that, if I did, my father would find out, track me here, and drag me back to Plain City.

"Take five, girls," Mr. Biggerstaff called.

Helen and I sat on the floor a little apart from the other ponies, who massaged one another's feet, stretched, and gossiped. Every day Helen arrived at rehearsal in a dark wool skirt, long-sleeved black sweater, and charcoal-gray wool stockings, but she quickly changed out of them. To my eyes, it seemed like she was shedding not just layers of clothing but layers of tradition. Now we huddled together—inseparable—watching Eddie warm up for his routine by entertaining us with little combos. He ended with his left leg tipped behind his right, his elbows close to his torso, and his fingers spread wide. He winked flirtatiously, and we clapped. He'd taken a couple of ponies on dates, but he'd never asked Helen or me. When I pointed that out to her, she wrinkled her face like she'd just smelled a glass of sour milk.

After rehearsal, we poured into the street. Fog draped heavy and white over the city, leaving the sidewalks eerily quiet. The melodies of chattering young girls rang through the night like police sirens. As the other ponies melted into the fog, Helen and I headed to Chinatown. For all of Mr. Fong's insistence that Helen always be escorted by her brother, the practice was haphazard at best.

Ruby waited for us in Sam Wo, our favorite café. "I'm starved," she announced.

That first night on the street outside the Forbidden City, something invisible but very strong had clicked between us like cogs catching and holding a tractor wheel. Now, as we ate, we talked about insignificant things.

"The hair on the left side of my head is fine and won't hold a curl," Ruby revealed. "That's why I pin gardenias above that ear."

"My feet are too long," Helen complained, even though they were smaller than Ruby's or mine.

I told them my bosoms were growing too big, to which Ruby agreed, saying, "They're whopping for a Chinese girl."

We ate—I was now adept at using chopsticks—and laughed as Ruby told us about her latest job.

"I don't know anything about housekeeping," she chirped. "The apartment was so nice I was afraid to touch anything. The lady released me. And after only one day! But that wasn't a good position for me, because I'm not neat, and I can barely wash a plate."

We never talked about *deep* things—*why* I'd run away, *how* scared Helen must have been when the Japanese pilot tried to shoot her, or *when* Ruby had made up her mind to pretend she was something she wasn't. Instead, Ruby taught Helen and me how to hula, Helen taught Ruby and me how to make simple soups on our hot plate, and I taught them things I'd learned from the movies, like how use makeup to make our eyes look more dramatic. Ruby and I had to watch our money, so we showed Helen how to make false eyelashes by taking strands of hair from our brushes, winding them around our fingers, snipping them with scissors, and gluing them onto strips, which we then applied to our eyelids. We copied my favorite actresses' hairdos and the way they plucked their eyebrows. We didn't spend a cent, but, along the way, we fell in love with each other. The show kids said we went together like ginger, scallions, and garlic: put us in a pot and you get the perfect dish.

Now, as we lingered at our table, sipping tea and waiting for Monroe to pick up Helen, I got up my nerve to share a little more about myself. I told them about three girls back in Plain City whom I'd named the evil triplets. Velma, who was Finnish by blood, had once been my best friend. When we started kindergarten, we met another girl named Ilsa, also Finnish. The three of us played together all the time, but at the end of first grade, Maude—another Finnish girl—got taken in by Velma and Ilsa, and I was pushed out for good. Soon, their sole pleasure came from teasing and bullying me.

"In fourth grade, the evil triplets told the class not to give me a card on Valentine's Day," I confided, "even though the teacher said that kids needed to give cards to every child in class or not give them at all. The evil triplets argued that I wasn't a proper Christian, even though I was baptized in the same church they were. When I tried to fight back, they chanted, 'Ching chong Chinaman sitting on a fence, trying to make a dollar out of fifty cents.' "

Helen got steamed—"That's awful!"—and Ruby shook her head sympathetically. To have these girls *hear* me and *feel* for me made me like them all the more.

"It must have been easy for you to have friends," Ruby said to Helen, "since you grew up in Chinatown."

"Hardly. When I was little, I was supposed to stay inside with my mother." Helen tucked a strand of hair behind her ear. "When I got to school, the other girls only played with me because their parents said they had to. Those girls are all married now. They have babies." Her voice hitched, and she shrugged. "Plus I now work in a big-thigh show. If I see one of those girls on the street, she looks away. None of them wants to associate with me. Their husbands wouldn't like it. Of the three of us, I'll bet you're the one who's had the most friends."

Ruby nodded slowly, pretending deep thought. Finally, she said, "I've had friends. Lots of friends. Every Tom, Dick, and Harry!"

Helen looked aghast, and then her face cracked as she burst out laughing. Ruby and I joined in. One of the waiters rolled his eyes. *Here we go again.*

"I've never had friends like you," I said after we regained our composure.

"I've never had friends, period!" Helen softly slapped the table for emphasis.

"The three of us are like the Three Musketeers," I said. "We get strength from each other, and we have adventures together. We're all for one and one for all."

"*I* don't plan on being in any duels!" Ruby scoffed good-naturedly.

"Did you ever hear of the Boswell Sisters? Maybe you're like them." This came from a man at a neighboring table, which sent us into a cataclysmic fit of giggles. A man(!) just talked to us. He'd been *eavesdropping* on us! We could flirt with him all we wanted, because we were three girls together. So we broke into song, piecing together the lyrics to "Someone to Watch Over Me" and throwing in some exaggerated arm movements for the benefit of our audience of one, who clapped appreciatively and scooted his stool a little closer to our table.

"Maybe it's better to say we're like the Andrews Sisters," Ruby announced when we came to the end of the song.

"Three friends are better than sisters," I said, even though I'd been dumped by Velma and the other evil triplets. I never wanted a day to come when I'd be excluded by Ruby and Helen in favor of someone like Ida. "Besides, we *aren't* sisters."

"And it's a good thing," Ruby agreed. "Sisters are stuck with each other, whether they like it or not. We *chose* each other. We wouldn't be here now if Helen hadn't found our apartment. So thank you, Helen, *again,* for being right there when we needed someone." She gave a smart two-finger salute to our benefactor. "Anyway, all that makes us better than sisters, like Grace said." Her eyes sparkled. "Hey, what if we put an act together and called ourselves the Swinging Sensations or the Oriental Wonders—"

"How about the Swing Sisters?" Helen suggested.

"We aren't—"

"Sisters," Ruby finished for me. "But so what? We're singers and dancers—"

"You're dancers too?" The man on the stool leaned forward, skeptical.

Ruby stiffened. "Of course! We'll show you."

The customer regarded us in unveiled delight as we jumped up and started pushing tables and stools out of the way. The cooks came out from the kitchen to see what all the hubbub was about, wiping their hands on their aprons, shoving their folded paper hats back on their foreheads. We lined up. I counted, "Five, six, seven . . ." And we broke into "Let Me Play with It."

Halfway through the number, Monroe came in the door, bringing with him a rush of damp air. He scowled as he took in the scene. Our voices trailed off, the man on the stool slid back to his own table, and the cooks slinked into the kitchen.

"Time to go," Ruby said to Helen.

Monroe was clearly upset to see his sister and her friends dancing in a neighborhood restaurant, but he didn't yell or anything like that. Instead, he radiated disapproval. That was fine for Helen; he was her brother. But to me, his attitude was upsetting. He was younger than Eddie Wu and just about the most darling boy I'd ever seen—almost as cute as that boy I'd met on Treasure Island. It probably helped that Monroe was the first *Chinese* boy I'd seen up close.

We waved to the man on his stool as Monroe herded us out the door. When we reached the Fong family compound, he dashed through the main entrance and into the courtyard—his chore done for the night.

"He likes you," Helen said after her brother disappeared from view. "He's always staring at you."

"It's true," Ruby agreed. "Which one do you like more—Monroe or Eddie?"

I shrugged, trying to pretend indifference when I'd never been on a single date. Now, any time I saw Eddie or Monroe, a slightly seasick sensation roiled my stomach and I blushed. (If dreaming about a boy and a man at the same time seems like something only a bad girl would do, then I told myself that I wasn't in Plain City anymore, and

I had some catching up to do.) Eddie appeared to regard my silly comments, hard work in the line, and girlishness with casual indifference, while Monroe . . .

"Sometimes it feels like your brother is taking in every movement, every word, every outfit I wear, and analyzing them—"

"Maybe he's deciding if you're wife material," Helen said.

"Oh, stop!"

Helen's lips formed a gentle smile, and then she slowly backed away from us as though she were a grain of wheat being sucked into a silo. She didn't want to leave us, and we didn't want to let her go, but she never once hinted that she might invite us into the compound to sit on her bed and talk until we all fell asleep. That was something I still missed—and longed for—from when Velma and I were friends.

After the gate swung shut, Ruby and I slowly continued to our apartment. We weren't in a hurry, because nothing and no one waited for us.

"Marry Monroe?" I mused. "He doesn't even know me."

Ruby lifted her shoulders and let them drop. She obviously didn't want to talk about it. Despite her funny stories, being jobless weighed on her. I worried for her too.

With sudden clarity, I understood that Ruby might be more outgoing and Helen might be from a better family, but I linked the three of us together. I was the Velma of the group! Only nicer.

My father screamed, "Measly girl! Worthless girl! You aren't going anywhere!" He bore down on me, trapping me in the corner of our living room. He unbuckled his belt and drew it through his pants loops in a single fast flourish. I had no way to escape . . . The leather lashed through the air before landing on my skin . . . The terrible familiar sting . . .

I jolted awake and lurched into a sitting position. Panting . . . Sweaty . . . I hung my head as I pushed at my fear and feeling of helplessness.

After a few moments, my hands still shaking, I wiped my hair off my face so I could see the clock. It was 9:30 in the morning. I'd gotten to bed from rehearsal only five hours earlier. I lay back down, stared at the ceiling, and let tears run from my eyes to my ears. But I had to pull myself together. In forty-five minutes, I would be going on my first date ever.

I pulled on the silk robe I'd purchased at a curio shop on Grant and padded out to the main room. Ruby had already left to go job hunting, but last night we'd talked about what I should wear, and if Monroe would like me better with or without makeup. I made myself a cup of tea, took it back to the bedroom, and began to get ready. I'd need to spend extra time on my face now to hide the splotches and swelling. By the time I went downstairs, I thought I looked pretty.

Monroe picked me up at 10:15 outside my building and we walked to the corner of Stockton and Clay, joining another two hundred or so people. He told me we were going to a "protest." This was a surprise and hardly the date I'd imagined, but I decided to let the day unfold the way Monroe wanted it to. As soon as we climbed onto the bed of a pickup truck, I knew this was going to be a real adventure. We joined a convoy of cars and stake-back trucks and drove down to Pier 45—singing, yelling, and cheering the whole way—to where a Greek ship, the SS *Spyros,* was docked. Monroe told me the vessel had been charted by Mitsui Company to transport 8,500 tons of scrap iron to Japan. We were there to picket against the shipment. Monroe's decision to bring me here showed him perfectly. He was an ABC—an American-born Chinese, like me. His American birthright gave him the freedom to state his views publicly. He was, as Helen put it, one of those new brooms who wanted to sweep the world clean of all inequities.

"Girls like you need to join the embargo against Japan by no longer wearing silk stockings." Monroe's hair blew in the wind and his eyes shone with fervor. "But everyone can help by keeping scrap metal out of the Japs' mitts so they can't turn it into bombs and bullets to use against China."

Monroe and I grabbed signs, then he boldly took my hand and squeezed it. Together we joined the picket line before the pier. "Victory! Victory! Victory!" Word traveled. More people streamed down the hill from Chinatown to the Embarcadero. Mothers sent drinks, sandwiches, oranges, Chinese buns, and dumplings. One family delivered an entire roast pig! Soon people carried their placards in one hand and roast pork in the other. It was the largest demonstration of Chinese the United States had ever seen. I'd never experienced anything like it, and I guess no one else had either. Monroe had given me this once-in-a-lifetime event. I was glad he'd brought me.

At the climax, the gathering was five thousand people strong. Lieutenant Governor-elect Ellis Patterson, whom Monroe called a liberal and a statesman, addressed the crowd: "Speeches have been made, the press has denounced the shipment of war materials to Japan, all the progressives have expressed themselves for democracy against the aggressor, but you are doing something about it!"

Two hours later, after the demonstration ended, Monroe and I decided to stroll along the Embarcadero rather than get on one of the trucks to go back to Chinatown. He led me onto one of the piers. We silently—nervously—stared into each other's faces until he finally got up the nerve to kiss me. His lips felt thin on mine. For so long I'd dreamed of my first romantic moment with a boy I liked, but this kiss didn't light a fire in me like I had expected it would. Maybe it was unsatisfying for Monroe too, because he didn't try to do it again. He put his hands in his pockets and looked out at the water. I stood there awkwardly, searching for the right thing to say.

"Will you come to opening night?" I asked.

He shook his head and said he wouldn't come—not for Helen, not for me. After a long pause, he added, "I guess I'd better get you home." All the zest he'd exhibited during the demonstration had gone out of him.

So, it was an exciting and adventurous day but a disappointing first date. I felt miserable because I'd failed to please him when I'd let myself hope for so much. I couldn't talk to Ruby about it, because I would have had to tell her that Monroe and I had spent most of our time together at an anti-Japanese rally. I couldn't tell Helen about it either, because he was her brother. All I could hope to do was be a better date next time, if there was a next time, because I wanted to get kissing right.

HELEN

White Snow Blossoms

Mama often liked to recite one of her favorite sayings—*Reshape one's foot to fit a new shoe*—and she expected me to follow her wishes for my life by accepting whatever fate brought me. The peasants in our home village in China lived close to the earth and the cycles of seasons and crops. They believed that *age and time do not wait for people.* And then there was Buddha, who taught *May all that have life be delivered from suffering.* By getting hired at the Forbidden City, I had managed to adhere to all these aphorisms. It was December 22, 1938, and the club would have its grand opening in just a few hours. When I left the compound, Mama and my sisters-in-law were decorating a Christmas tree—an American concession to the little ones in our household. I carried a small bag in which I'd packed a floor-length *cheongsam* that Mama had commissioned for me from one of the finest tailors in Shanghai. I didn't know if I'd have a chance to wear the dress tonight, but you can never be too prepared.

When I arrived at the club, the neon sign that trickled down the face of the building glowed red, gold, and green in lettering that looked like chopsticks: FORBIDDEN CITY. I hurried upstairs. Ornate silk hangings and embroidered tapestries decorated the walls. Chinese urns stuffed shelves and idle corners. Hexagonal lanterns hung from the ceiling. To the left stood the bar, with stools upholstered in red leather and walls covered in bamboo paneling. Just ahead, the main room offered a large open space for our floor show and for customers to dance. Tables—with sparkling place settings lit by little lamps with red glass shades shaped like coolie hats—surrounded the dance floor on three sides.

I pushed through the kitchen's swinging doors into total chaos. The cooks all knew each other, having worked together previously in clubs and cafés in the area, and it showed in their bickering and bantering. Plates and bowls clattered, cleavers clack-clacked against chopping blocks, and cooking utensils slapped the sides of woks. Steam billowed in the air. All this, and not a single meal had been ordered yet.

"Get out! Get out!" one of the cooks shouted. "We don't want you in here." He held up a cleaver. "I'll chop you up if you don't get out!"

I passed through the kitchen to backstage and up a few steps to the dressing rooms. The early birds had secured spots in front of the mirror. I saw Grace, who was extending a leg to slip on opera hose—fishnet stockings so thick they left marks if you sat in them too long. She waved me over, and I waded through other girls patting powder on their cheeks, gluing on false eyelashes, applying lipstick. Irene and May had already changed into their first costumes: long red satin off-the-shoulder Gay Nineties gowns with a slit up the thigh. The necklines and hems were edged with ruffles, which matched the ruffles on the oversize hats.

"I saved you a place next to me," Grace said in greeting. "We can get ready together."

I wished I could change in private, but that wasn't possible, so I began getting into my costume from the bottom up. I slipped on my opera hose under my skirt, then pulled up the corset until it bunched just under my waistband. I unzipped my skirt, let it fall to the floor, and took off my sweater and blouse. I didn't own a brassiere—my mother would have died on the spot if she found one in my bureau, and my sisters-in-law would have gossiped until my brothers condemned me for wearing such an indecent *lo fan* garment—so I wore an undershirt. I turned to the wall and drew it over my head, hoping to avoid prying eyes. Impossible.

"*Waaaa!* What is that?" Ida squealed.

The chatter instantly silenced, and everyone stopped what they were doing to stare. I turned crimson and folded my arms over my breasts.

"Mind your own business," I said.

"But what happened? What *is* that?" Ida repeated.

"It's a scar. You've seen a scar before, haven't you?"

"But on your tittie? It's so red!"

Ida was the coarsest person—man or woman—I'd ever encountered, in addition to being the nosiest. She had piqued everyone else's interest. Even Grace looked at me questioningly.

"I was in a car accident a year ago," I said with a casual shrug.

Fortunately, that seemed to satisfy them, and they went back to getting ready. I kept the scar covered with one hand and used my other to pull my costume up and over my breasts. A second later, somebody called, "Everyone!" followed by a loud knock at the door. Then again, "Everyone"—only this time it must have been addressed to the men's dressing room across the hall. "Charlie wants to see everyone out on the floor."

"Now?" Ida cried out. "I'm not decent yet."

"Now!" came the reply.

We filed out of the dressing room, downstairs to the backstage alley, and then split up—with some of us passing through a velvet curtain on the right side of the stage and others going through a velvet curtain on the left side. Cooks, dishwashers, waiters, and waitresses mingled restlessly on the dance floor. Girls from the front of the house—who worked in the hatcheck room and as hostesses and photographers—lingered near the step to the first raised tier. Van Meisner, our bandleader, and the other members of the Forbidden Knights perched on the edge of the stage, their legs dangling, cigarettes hanging loose from their lips. The Lim Sisters, a new act that had been hired at the last minute, sat at what Charlie had dubbed "the best table in the house." (Bessie, Ella, and Dolores, "the warbling trio," had performed in vaudeville since they were seven, five, and three. None of us had seen their routine, but it was supposed to be a showstopper. We hadn't met them yet either. They were headliners, and we were all curious about them. It was hard not to stare.) Eddie came out in his tuxedo pants, slippers, and a T-shirt with holes at the neck. He leaned against a pillar with his hands in his pockets. Li Tei stood next to her husband.

"This is it," Charlie began. He was dressed for the opening number in a wild double-breasted yellow and blue plaid suit with bright blue velvet lapels and collar. A straw boater balanced on his head, and he kept smoothing the fake mustache pasted to his upper lip with a finger and thumb to make sure it stayed put. "You all made it, and we're all here!"

People applauded, but I was nervous. I not only had to worry about the routines we'd practiced for weeks but also had to remember the last-minute changes Mr. Biggerstaff had made to the production to accommodate the Lim Sisters.

"We're going to show them"—Charlie gestured toward the entrance and all the *lo fan* beyond the door—"that we can accomplish more than just wash dishes, do laundry, sweep floors, or work on the railroad." The men, even the dishwashers, clapped for this. "We're going to show them that you girls have arms and legs." The ponies around me applauded. "Everyone has first-night jitters. Even I have them. Just remember that most of our customers have never seen a Chinese perform. We're going to be great, and we're going to open big." He glanced at his watch. "Finish getting ready. And then have a fabulous night! Let's show the world our stuff!"

"Break a leg, everyone," Eddie called as we dispersed.

We returned to the dressing room to wait for our curtain call. I caught some of the ponies furtively spying on the Lim Sisters as they did their makeup. One of the cigarette girls came back to tell us that customers had started to arrive. The women, she reported, were dropping their furs in the cloakroom to reveal glittering jewels and silk gowns that swept the floor, while the men were shrugging out of overcoats to display perfectly cut evening dress.

"I wish I could see them," Ida said.

"You will," Grace said. "We'll be out there soon enough."

Despite my friend's calm words, anticipation—hers included—made the room feel as though we didn't have enough air to breathe. It was hard to sit still. I tried to focus my mind on the basics of the evening.

At a staff meeting a week ago, Charlie had walked us through what the Forbidden City experience would be like for our customers. The maître d' would escort glamorous couples through the moon gate to floor-side tables. The less well heeled would be seated on the second or third tier, which hugged the main level on three sides. Waiters and waitresses dressed in red silk uniforms would hand out menus—the right side listed Chinese dishes, the left American. Those who didn't have reservations would pay a one-dollar cover charge and line up at the bar. Ruby, if she wasn't there already, would arrive soon. Grace and I had staked her to the evening.

We could hear the Forbidden Knights' tunes all the way in our dressing room. Grace told me the name of each song: "Begin the Beguine," "Heart and Soul," and "Cheek to Cheek." The melodies were beautiful and romantic, and I could practically see couples dancing in my imagination.

"As soon as the set ends," Grace reminded us, "we'll be on."

My stomach lurched. Nerves!

A couple of minutes later, someone rapped his knuckles on the door. "*Fiedee, fiedee, fiedee!*" It was Charlie. "Hurry, hurry, hurry! It's showtime!" Grace grabbed my hand, and together we led the other ponies to the stage-right velvet curtain. Our faces were bone-tight with anxiety. We shifted our feet—some to shake off stage fright, others practicing the moves one last time. We fingered our parasols, praying they'd open on cue. A drum rolled. Charlie stepped through the curtain to greet his guests:

"Welcome, ladies and gentlemen, to the Forbidden City, where we'll give you a new *slant* on entertainment." The *lo fan* laughed at the insulting pun. Charlie knew what he had to say to make them happy. "You won't see any yellow face here. No, siree. We're already yellow! So off we go to yesteryear—when the music was light, times were easy, and the girls were beautiful."

Van Meisner brought down his baton, and the Forbidden Knights began to play "Let Me Call You Sweetheart." Grace went through the velvet curtain first, opened her parasol, glided across the stage, and sashayed down to the dance floor. I followed right behind her with the other ponies behind me. The room oozed rich elegance, reminding me of my favorite club in Shanghai. Everyone was drinking; everyone was happy. We twirled our parasols and tilted our heads just so. We looked exquisite. We looked delicate and breakable—like dolls, like little China dolls. Then we broke into a simple combination—leisurely and rhythmic, in time with the gentle tune. Together, working as a unit where every move and every note were in accord, we supported each other and lifted each other to create a glorious and colorful spectacle. The concentration made me forget the world, made me forget that my father cared so little for me that he let me dance here at all.

We swayed around Charlie, who stood in the middle of the floor, holding his microphone. The dance was slow enough and the lights were such that with each orbit around him I glimpsed people's faces in the audience. They had come as they might go to a curio shop: to encounter the exotic, to glimpse the scandalous, to see a real "curiosity." So far we weren't delivering. But before the audience's mood could coalesce into anything negative, the tempo abruptly changed. The band launched into a rousing "Ta-Ra-Ra Boom-De-Ay." We shouted out the opening syllables, tore off our hats, and tossed them into the audience. We ripped away our gowns to reveal red satin corsets edged with the same fringe that hung from our parasols. Even Charlie got into the act, yanking off his plaid suit to reveal a tuxedo.

This was more like it! Charlie had promised the audience legs and arms, and here they were! Who would have guessed a Chinese girl could move like that? Chinese were supposed to be bowlegged and clumsy. And weren't the women supposed to be submissive? Everyone knew the type. They'd seen her on the street sometimes . . .

"Those women in Chinatown won't even meet my eyes," I heard a man seated next to the dance floor whisper to his friend. (Those would have to be women like my mother, sisters-in-law, or me, who would have preferred to die than look at an ugly *lo fan* like him.)

"I've seen plenty who *will* meet my eyes, if you catch my drift." The other man winked conspiratorially.

The stereotypes about Chinese women were tiresome . . . and predictable. I swirled to the next table and overheard . . .

"They'll give you a disease if you get too close. Have you gotten that close? I've heard that their privates are as different as their eyes."

"You mean slanted, going from side to side instead of front to back?"

It made me sick the way they talked, but I was still glad to be here, happy to have made my choice to be in this world and not caged in the compound.

When the first number ended and we filed offstage, Charlie Low introduced Li Tei. Everyone could feel his pride. "She's a torch singer and good at grand opera too," he promised. I lingered by the curtain to watch as he put a hand to the side of his mouth to confide, "But she'll also sing a Chinese number on request. Ladies and gentlemen, I present my wife, the beautiful and talented Li Tei Ming."

Her *cheongsam* was made of yellow silk with large lipstick-red flowers like giant handprints touching every part of her body. Van Meisner nodded to the band, and the familiar notes of "Loch Lommond" floated through the club. Li Tei sang just one bar—combining a fake Scots accent with her way-down-south Cantonese accent—and once again a feeling of utter disbelief settled over the crowd. When she sang *"Sì, Mi Chiamano Mimi"*—Yes, They Call Me Mimi—from *La Bohème,* it was just too, too much. Unbelievable, really and truly unbelievable.

I hurried back to the dressing room. Irene had changed into her costume for the next number, so she went out to catch Jack Mak's act. After she left, Ida smirked knowingly. "She's so gone on that guy." Once the rest of the ponies were ready, we joined Irene stage left. I guess it hadn't occurred to anyone in the audience that a Chinese man could be a magician either. I could see guests actually scratching their heads, as puzzled by Jack Mak as they were by his illusions. *Did he really just shoot into a box? Now he's opening it! Hey! A dove flew out and over my head!*

We ponies paraded out for a short interlude. This time I dared to look up to the windows into the bar, hoping to spot Ruby, but all I saw were well-dressed men leaning on the sills, watching the show. Charlie passed from table to table with his microphone, joking with customers, teasing them about how many drinks they'd had, asking if the women were wives, fiancées, girlfriends, or something else . . .

As we dipped back behind the curtain, the band broke into "Minnie the Moocher" for the Merry Mahjongs—an acrobatic troupe recently returned from a European tour. When the line "He took her down to Chinatown, he showed her how to kick the gong around" arrived, the acrobats mugged it up for all it was worth. From that night on, they'd be known for literally kicking a gong around, solidifying their reputations as the best Chinese acrobats in America. *Aiya!* As if *that* meant anything!

Another interlude. We wore miniature tuxedos—collars and ties, top hats, gloves, black opera hose, and little sequined corsets. Grace led us through a simple tap number. If a male customer wanted, he could touch a girl's bottom as it twitched by. I managed to stay just out of reach. The spotlight moved to one of the velvet curtains. Expectations rose. Who—*what*—was coming next? The curtain swung open. Eddie stood there in top hat and tails. We kept dancing, hitting such a low and relentless rhythm that I finally understood why we were called ponies. Eddie was smooth and debonair. This wasn't like seeing someone on the big screen. This was real, it was live, and it was happening just a few feet away.

We waited backstage since we didn't have another change. Li Tei

Ming returned for a torch song. My nerves hadn't ebbed much and neither had those of any of the other ponies, but it felt like everything was going well. Then it was time for the main attraction. Our crowd made way for the Lim Sisters, who wore white baptismal gowns and big bonnets. Maybe that had worked for them when they were little girls doing vaudeville, but to my eyes they looked ridiculous now that they were grown women.

"Straight from the Palace in London," Charlie proclaimed, "I give you the Lim Sisters."

The Lims tottered out. I thought their act was strange—who wants to see big babies singing?—but the audience loved them. People here in San Francisco had witnessed so much change the past few years. In the twenties: flappers, alcohol, and money flowing like water. And then the crash: families in breadlines, Okies arriving with all their possessions piled on top of their trucks, and people like those in the audience selling off jewels and property. But as customers watched the sisters perform, you could almost see their hope. It seemed we all wanted to forget.

The big finale: We formed a conga line—with Li Tei at the front—and wove through the club, picking up customers, who hung on to the waists in front of them. *Shake those hips from side to side, and kick! It's the Chinaconga!*

The first show was flawless—like a perfect piece of jade. The audience demonstrated their appreciation by ordering more drinks. Champagne corks popped. Women sipped frothy cocktails from high-stemmed glasses. Men waved to Flo, the cigarette girl, to come to their table to sell her wares. Dinners arrived on big silver trays, with each dish topped by its own silver dome. In the dressing room, the girls jumped up and down, hugged each other, and laughed. How many times had Grace and the others sat in a darkened movie theater and wished and hoped and pined to be up on the screen in that movie, in that scene, in that world? Now they'd brought the illusion off the screen and into this building. The air crackled with adrenaline, excitement, and happiness. Even I felt something . . .

As some of the ponies changed back into their costumes for the first number, I opened the bag I'd brought from home and pulled out my *cheongsam*. The silk was the color of a robin's egg and was printed with white snow blossoms. "You're an unmarried girl," Mama had said when we ordered the dress. "This will make you look fresh and young, while still evoking the frostiness of winter." The dress had marked the beginning of a new phase of my life. Now here I was, starting another chapter. I put it on and buttoned the highest frog to hold the mandarin collar in place. I closed the frogs across my breast, under my armpit, and down my side. It wasn't my best *cheongsam*—not by a long shot—but the girls in the dressing room stared. Until this minute I was the one they distrusted because they could see I had more money than they did. They'd also made it pretty clear they thought that I had won out over dancers better than I was and that I considered myself special because I had Grace—the girl in charge of the line—as my best friend. Resentment threatened to dampen their exuberant moods, but Grace regarded me with eyes of love.

"Look how beautiful you are!"

I waved off the compliment. "I'm going to see if I can find Ruby. I'll be right back."

I left the dressing room before Grace could stop me, then slipped through the velvet curtain and into the club. I sensed Grace behind me, but she didn't follow. As I picked my way through the tables, customers—particularly men—offered their congratulations. I found Ruby in the bar. She wore a bias-cut dress—inexpensive but clinging to every curve. The group of men who clustered around her parted when I approached.

"Wasn't she great, boys?" Ruby asked.

The men all chatted at once, vying for *my* attention.

"Join us."

"Sit with us."

"Let me buy you a drink."

The men tried to one-up each other. Did I want a champagne

cocktail, pink lady, gin fizz, or dry martini? After that, they got down to serious proposals.

"Let me buy you dinner."

"Are you free later tonight?"

"Do you have other girlfriends who'd like to tag along?"

I did my best to be entertaining and polite, but inside I was swooning through the ether of happiness. Then Charlie announced that the second show would start momentarily. I wasn't close to being ready!

I hurried back through the tables but was slowed again and again by admirers. Panic began to well in me. If I didn't get back in time . . . . Once backstage, I ran to the dressing room. *"Fiedee, fiedee, fiedee."* Grace glared at me as a praying mantis would eye a cricket, but she didn't have time to scold me, not when she had to worry about her own performance, her own position, her own life. As Grace and the others filed out of the dressing room, I peeled off my *cheongsam* and threw on my Gay Nineties costume. I went backstage, desperate to join the number. Suddenly, surprisingly, someone yanked my shoulder. It was Eddie—dressed in his tails and top hat. He was furious.

"You stupid bitch!" he hissed. "Are you trying to jam this up for all of us?"

He went on to curse me with words I'd never before heard. When the ponies whisked through the curtain, they ducked their heads and edged around Eddie and me, up the stairs, and into the dressing room. They had to change and be ready for the next routine no matter what happened to me. Only Grace stayed by my side.

"I'm sorry, Eddie." My voice trembled. "This is my first show. I didn't pay attention—"

"Jesus Christ." He drawled out the syllables to emphasize his disgust.

Tears rolled down my cheeks, prompting Eddie to throw up his hands in frustration. Then he gestured to Grace. "Clean her up, for God's sake. We're on in a couple of minutes."

Grace pulled me into the dressing room, where it felt like we were in the middle of a tornado. Girls pitched aside their skimpy undercostumes from the Gay Nineties number and pulled on their black-sequined tuxedo corsets for the routine with Eddie as fast as possible.

"Zip me up, will ya?"

"Is my top hat cocked at a good angle?"

"Do I look fat in this?"

"I've got a run!"

"A seam just split. What am I going to do now?"

Small dramas happened all around us, but not a single pony wasn't aware of my lapse—my irresponsibility—when this job was so precious. But if I got fired, they'd follow the old saying: *Step on her bones to climb the ladder.* And I would just be a lonely girl ignored by the wives and mothers at the Chinese Telephone Exchange.

Grace hastily slipped out of her costume and into her tuxedo outfit. I sat on a bench, weeping. Once Grace was ready, she shooed Ida and the other girls out of the room and kneeled before me.

"You've got to pull yourself together."

That Grace was upset with me was almost more than I could bear. I fought my tears, sucking in my upper lip and biting down hard enough that I tasted blood. Grace grabbed a tissue, and I watched in the mirror as she wiped away the worst of the streaks down my cheeks.

"You need to have a sense of humor about these things," Grace counseled, even as she tried to erase the irritation that chewed at the edges of her voice. "If you don't, you'll never survive in show business. If you miss a step, fall down, or get yelled at, you've got to"—here she began to sing—"pick yourself up, dust yourself off, and start all over again."

I didn't know what in the world she was singing, and it must have showed on my face.

"It's from *Swing Time,*" Grace explained. "The Fred Astaire and Ginger Rogers movie?"

I stared at her blankly.

Grace attempted a new approach, reminding me that she was the head of the line and needed to get me out on the floor or *her* job was in jeopardy.

"Stop crying right now," she ordered. Then she pinched my thigh as hard as she could.

"Oow!" I rubbed my leg. Grace blotted my cheeks with foundation and then used the powder puff so enthusiastically that little clouds of white dust swirled around us. Once my face looked passable, she brought me to my feet to undress and then dress me like I was a small child. Her eyes briefly rested on my scar. Daring for a Chinese girl to stare at another girl's naked breast that way; immodest for a Chinese girl to let another girl so closely examine something so private.

"This isn't just a scar, is it? A whole piece was gouged out." Her eyes met mine. "I feel so bad for you. It must have been a rough time."

"It was, but I don't like to talk about it." I hoped that would put an end to any other questions.

The call came for Eddie's number. I quickly wiggled into my sequined corset, tipped my top hat at a jaunty angle, and started for the door. "You coming?"

This time all eight girls were at one or the other velvet curtain. I spread my mouth into what I'd created to serve as my performance smile and tapped my way through the curtain.

The rest of the second show ran perfectly, as did the third. At close to four in the morning, the last customer disappeared into the night. Charlie met us on the landing between the dressing rooms, where an air of jubilation filled the cramped space.

"Good job, everyone," he said. "But we learned some things tonight. You girls are going to need long gowns or *cheongsams* like the one Helen wore tonight. I want to see all my glamour girls on the floor between shows. Let the customers buy you drinks. Have dinner with them. Dance with them. Make them happy."

The other ponies and I heard this with mixed emotions: I wouldn't be fired (a disappointment to some, a *huge* relief to me); a lot of us, including Grace and me, were not old enough to drink (Charlie told us not to worry about that); and we were all going to join the party that happened in the club every night. I had forgotten myself for a minute, true. But my few moments of enjoyment—for which I could have paid a terrible price—clarified that it wasn't right for me to put happiness first. What had I gotten myself into?

Later, when Grace and I exited onto Sutter, we discovered that the evening wasn't quite over. Ruby waited for us, but there were also men—stage-door Johnnies—making their first appearances to invite ponies out for coffee, breakfast, a hotel room. We weren't about to take them up on any of those propositions.

It was either too late or too early for sleep, so we found a place to get bowls of *jook* and wait for the sun to come up. Ruby bubbled, but I couldn't tell if she was truly excited for us or just wanted to show she hadn't fallen behind. Grace wasn't nearly as thrilled as I'd expected her to be. She'd dreamed of having an opening night . . .

"I need to spend some of my salary to buy a gown," she confessed when prodded.

"Don't worry about that," I said. "I have a closet full of them. I'll give you one of mine."

Grace's shoulders tightened, and she looked away. My offer had made her lose face. *Better to die a beggar than to live as a beggar.* But weren't we supposed to be friends? Didn't friends help each other? Beyond that, we were in the chorus line together. She'd saved me tonight. Lending her a dress was the least I could do.

"Will you give me one too?" Ruby piped up eagerly.

Ruby's reminder that she was in worse shape—without a permanent job—snapped Grace out of her gloom.

RUBY

A Lone Wolf

Two weeks after the Forbidden City's bang-up opening, the three of us were in the apartment, spending Monday, the only day Grace and Helen had off, painting each other's toenails, pinning new hairstyles, and trying on each other's clothes, while I entertained them with my oh-so-humorous Adventures in Unemployment. I was good at getting jobs but not at keeping them.

"So he tells me, 'You move like an angel, but I need an angel who can shine a floor. I said to use elbow grease, not grease!' You can guess the end. Fired!"

I could amuse Grace and Helen for hours with my stories. I was placed as a maid in a tony home in Pacific Heights, only I hadn't been taught that using Ajax wasn't the best way to polish silver. A family on Russian Hill engaged me as a mother's helper, but the children didn't particularly ken to me, and I sure as hell didn't care for them. The father liked me, though, and we had fun until his wife found out. But honestly, why did she have to make such a big stink about a hug and a bump in a laundry room? I signed on as an elevator operator at a department store on Union Square—a highlight in what had been a sorry string of jobs—where I used different accents to entertain the shoppers. "Second floor, gentlemen's suits and other bespoke wear," growled like a Japanese samurai. "Fifth floor, ladies' lingerie," sung as a girl from the islands. "Mezzanine, notions, books, and candy," recited as one of the Mexican girls from my elementary school in Los

Angeles. Customers said I was a hoot; management gave me the bounce. On to cafés in North Beach, Cow Hollow, and the Tenderloin. I knew less about being a waitress than about cleaning a house, unpacking boxes in storage rooms, or selling flowers. It took me a while to catch the brain waves and understand that when someone asked for a bride and groom on a life raft he wanted two eggs and toast, or that a bride and groom on the rocks meant scrambled eggs. Once someone asked for a "rare" waffle. I brought him a plate of batter with a pat of butter on top. Quick as a wink, I was out on my can. "Sorry, slim, but you just aren't working out." Rain off a duck's back, I always say.

"Remember when that customer asked for fried watermelon?" Grace cued me. "He was teasing you, but you went to the kitchen and asked the short-order cook to make it!"

Grace and Helen loved that story for some reason. Fried watermelon. Ha! Ha! Yes, the joke sure was on me. "Fired again!" the three of us sang out in harmony. I laughed as hard as they did. The blues were not in my repertoire.

I didn't want to put the bite on my roommate and ask her for money, but when I couldn't chip in my share of the rent, Grace voluntarily made up the extra amount. "That's what friends do for each other," she said, which was pretty funny given how bent out of shape she'd gotten when Helen offered to give her a dress to wear between shows at the Forbidden City. I didn't see the big deal about taking Grace's money or wearing Helen's castoffs. A girl needs a place to sleep and something snazzy to wear, after all.

On the weekend, I visited Aunt Haru and Uncle Junji in Alameda. They filled me with soba and *natto*—sticky fermented soybeans—slivers of *toro,* and cups of *matcha*. They asked me questions:

"Have you heard from your mother and father?"

"Are you eating enough?"

"Won't you come back and stay with us? We can give you a job in the grocery."

They were the nicest people. They had a small shop not far from the Alameda naval air station. Their customers were lookers, as you might imagine, so working there wouldn't be the worst thing that could happen. But I didn't want to spend my life drinking beer and necking with servicemen—I'd already done a fair amount of that in Hawaii—and even earlier when we lived on Terminal Island not far from the naval reserve, so I turned down Aunt Haru's offer, bowing deeply and repeatedly as my mother would have wanted me to do to show proper respect and humility.

"*Doumo arigatou gozaimasu,* Auntie," I said, using the most polite form of Japanese. "You honor me with your kindness. I'm forever grateful."

My aunt and uncle—as I hoped they would—sent me home with a basket filled with fresh fruits, vegetables, and a five-pound sack of rice, which was a start toward repaying Grace.

And I thought coming here would be a breeze.

I hadn't won any apple-pie prizes or ribbons like Grace had, but even as a little girl I could attract a crowd. That first day at the auditions for the Forbidden City, I told Grace and Helen that I'd always been a dancer, but it was more like I was born to be famous. People *saw* something in me. They were attracted to me. They came to me like bees to a flower or moths to a flame. I'm not exaggerating. I didn't have a lot of talent, but I had plenty of ba-zing.

Way back, when we still lived in Los Angeles, a dancer from the Orpheum Theater came across the street to visit our family's curio shop. She wanted to buy a black lacquer box decorated with flying cranes, but she didn't have enough money, so my mother said, "If you give my girl dance lessons, I'll give you the box." People told my mother that our family had gone to the dogs. Mom, who was about as traditional and strict a woman as you could find on either side of the Pacific, shot them down.

"It's better to be a lone wolf with talent than a monkey dancing for an organ-grinder," she said. "Better to be independent than bow to the Occidental."

But I had to be a proper Japanese girl too. She showed me how to mince when I walked so I'd look delicate and smile behind pressed fingers so I'd look more alluring. She taught me to speak in a high voice, making sure no air—no *life*—came out of my throat. She instructed me to begin each sentence as though everything were my fault: *sumimasenga—I'm sorry but,* or *osoremasuga—I fear offending you but.*

Naturally, I attended my mother's Japanese-language classes. Japanese was of no interest to me, whether at home or in school, and I wished I had a nickel for every time she criticized my use of prepositions. (My pop always said her voice was as beautiful as cherry blossoms floating through the air on a perfect spring morning. On this one thing I couldn't argue. Her voice was beautiful . . . for a nag.) My mother drilled me on honorifics and declensions. I learned the difference between what a woman could say and what a man could say. *Shizukani—quiet*—could politely come from a woman's mouth. But a man could be more forceful: *Damare! Shut up!* I listened when people spoke the common name for a wife—*ka-nai*—which literally meant *house inside.* A husband was called the *shu-jin—person in charge.* But I wanted to be in charge of my own life.

My mother started each class by having her students sing the Japanese national anthem before a portrait of Emperor Hirohito, spiffy in his uniform, sitting astride his white horse, Shirayuki. (This probably wasn't much different than Helen going to Chinese-language school and singing the Republic of China's anthem to a photo of Dr. Sun Yat-sen.) Mom taught class like we were in Japan, stressing single-minded loyalty to our superiors: parents, teachers, anyone older, and, of course, the emperor. The greatest virtues, she told us, were sincerity, loyalty, and obedience. (This couldn't have been all that off the mark from what Helen had learned through her sayings.) My mother educated us about Japan and China's first altercation, back in 663, and taught us that Japan had retaliated with a long chain of invasions that continued to today. (Helen had probably learned the yin-yang version, in which the Japanese were always the villains.) What I'm saying is, we all follow traditions that we believe are right and just, but there are two sides to every story. Still, when I called last year's rape of Nanking a war crime, my mother slapped me and said, "That didn't happen! People made that up!" And then she called me an ungrateful daughter, as though *that* were more evil than raping and killing thousands of innocent women in China.

"I'm not ungrateful or unpatriotic," I fought back. "I love America, and I believe in peace."

"The emperor believes in peace too," Mom said. "He cries for the other countries in Asia that have been crushed beneath the boot of Western imperialism. The Japanese will help our less fortunate brothers and sisters in Manchuria, China, and Korea. This is a time of Friendship, Cooperation, and Co-prosperity."

"Don't you mean the Three Alls policy—burn all, kill all, loot all?"

"*Bakatare!*" My mother spat out the most insulting form of *stupid.*

My parents stopped speaking to me for two weeks after that. Hideo and Yori, my brothers, steered clear of me too. "You were born to be bad," Hideo told me one day, sounding like a gangster he'd seen at the picture show in Honolulu. I wasn't particularly bad, but I did have my own opinions. As a result, I was *komaru ne*—an embarrassment and an annoyance.

Worse, I liked boys and boys liked me, which made my parents crazier than bedbugs. Mom may have encouraged me to dance, but she hadn't properly thought it through. More than three thousand Japanese—*Issei, Nisei,* and *Sansei*—lived on Terminal Island, but the sailors at the naval reserve shared the island with us. By the time I turned fourteen, I knew where I liked to spend my time. So, yes, my pop wanted to fish in Hawaii and my mother wanted to go back to Japan, but they were really getting me out of trouble before I got *in trouble.* But they hadn't thought this through either. The trade winds blew away all orders. White teachers came to school with hibiscus behind their ears and picked them for me to wear. Ocean waves dashed my parents' culture against rocky shoals. Rustling palm fronds whispered freedom and choice. Smooth-skinned local boys spoke with even smoother voices. And more sailors! They couldn't tell if I was Japanese, Chinese, or Hawaiian, and they didn't care.

"Shikata ga nai," my mother moaned. "It cannot be helped."

Mom said I was a *moga*—a modern girl. That was not a compliment. My parents couldn't figure out what to do with me. When my aunt and uncle offered to take me in, my parents gladly let me return to the Land of Rice—mainland America—and I most happily went. And guess what. They lived and worked right next to the naval air station! *Shikata ga nai!* And how!

I'd shattered the mold for a typical Japanese girl. So what? I wasn't like Grace, Helen, or the other girls either, worrying about opinions or dwelling on past disappointments. My desires in life were simple: float above the noise of the world, *live* in my body, and be seen as anything other than just Japanese.

ON A FRIDAY at the very beginning of February, I walked down Market Street, stopping in every shop and café, asking if they needed help. I got the usual brush-off: "We're sorry, but the position has been filled," meaning they wouldn't hire me because I was Oriental. I passed a theater with girls going in and coming out. Curious as a cat, I went inside to find a shapely blond woman of a certain age, interviewing girls for a job at the Golden Gate International Exposition. I filled out an application and took a seat. When my turn came, the woman looked me up and down.

"Are you shy about getting naked?" she asked.

"I've never thought about it before," I answered.

"Think about it now," she said.

Warm days and nights in Hawaii, where I didn't own a sweater, let alone a coat. Humidity so sticky that my parents, brothers, and I would peel down to our underwear and sit in the shallows of the ocean outside our home. Bathing naked in a wooden tub with my mother after my pop and brothers had their turn. The girls in my school, who taught me the hula and told me that their mothers and grandmothers never wore tops when they danced and relied only on their hair and homemade leis for modesty.

"I have nothing against it," I told the woman.

"Nudity is very natural. Consider it art."

If she'd been a man, if the setup had seemed slimy at all, if the job had been for anyplace other than the exposition, I would have skedaddled right on out of there. But when she said, "I could use a Chinese girl," I felt like a big fish caught in one of my father's nets.

"How much you paying?" I asked, trying to sound cheeky.

The woman gave a cunning nod. "Thirty-five berries a week."

That was fifteen dollars more than Grace and Helen made!

"Where do I sign?"

Rehearsals—such as they were—started the next day. I kept what I was doing a secret for now. Grace was a good kid, but she was so wet behind the ears it was flooding back there. And even though I could tell Helen had been around some, she acted much too prim to hear the truth. Besides, with my track record, I still might get fired. I'd have some good stories to tell Grace and Helen then.

GRACE

Pistols and a Cowboy Hat

I went ahead and accepted one of Helen's old prom dresses, which I wore until the gown I bought on layaway at the Emporium was paid off. (I sure as heck wasn't going to sneak into my envelope with my fifty dollars. That money was the barricade between me and going home.) At night, between shows, we looked as pretty as spring flowers in our long dresses as we passed through the velvet curtains and into the dining room. Charlie directed us to particular tables by whispering in our ears. It all seemed innocent enough, so we sat with total strangers. If we still had more shows to do, we'd sip ginger ale or fairy-water tea, which was tea served with a fancy name and a fancier price, but we also ordered the most expensive drink on the menu—a Singapore sling for forty cents—so the customer had to pay.

All we really wanted to do was eat. Most customers ordered for us off the Chinese menu. But me? Given a choice? A steak, of course! As soon as dinner was over, I'd announce I needed to leave for the next show and thank them for their generosity. And that was that . . . at least for Helen and me.

"You girls are so green," Ida ribbed us one night. She was a tiny thing, and she reminded me of a chipmunk—twitchy in her movements and reedy in her speech.

"Look who's calling who green!" Helen shot back. "At least I grew up in a city. *The* city."

"Besides, being green is nothing to be ashamed of," I added, but I wasn't as green as when I'd first started at the Forbidden City. Back then I'd never heard of a no-no girl. Now I knew those were the types of girls Donaldina Cameron rescued. I knew that a free Coca-Cola could turn into something else pretty fast, and I could recognize the particular worried look a girl got when her time of month approached or she was late. I vowed to follow Helen's advice: *Guard your body like a piece of jade.* But I also learned it was easier to spend my salary than to save it. I developed a fondness for lingerie—corsets constructed with Lastex, brassieres made from lace handkerchiefs (which admittedly didn't do much), and cami-knickers in pink or peach crepe for day or black satin or lace for evening. With each passing day, I became less frightened that my father would come searching for me, and my nightmares receded. I no longer had to act like I was carefree because I was sincerely happy, and I didn't have to pretend bravery because I had no one to be afraid of.

After the last show, many ponies met stage-door Johnnies and disappeared into the night; Helen and I met Ruby. Every evening she came to the club, sat at the bar, and let men buy her drinks until Helen and I were free and we could all be together again. Sometimes Helen and I were still so high from performing that we needed to shake things up, so we'd take Ruby to the Pitt Club or the Variety Club, which catered to entertainers after hours, to listen to Harry James blow "All or Nothing at All" when he passed through town, and it was a long jam session with boozing and gambling until six in the morning. Or we might visit the Sky Room for the club's special drink. "What girl doesn't like an angel's tits?" Ruby asked. (And, really, what girl didn't? It was made with white crème de cacao, cherry liqueur, cream chilled in layers, and topped with a maraschino cherry.) Sometimes we just wanted to dance. Jitterbug. Conga. Rumba. And sometimes Ruby bought each of us a gardenia—"So we match"—which we wore over our left ears, showing everyone we were true friends. We found strength in being together, which allowed us to be daring and adventurous. We flirted with men and giggled when they flirted back. We shared clothes—a hair ribbon, a scarf, a sweater, a dress, a gown—and we promised never to let a man come between us like we'd seen happen to girls in high school.

I WENT OUT with Monroe a few more times. He took me to see Chinese opera. (I can't say I enjoyed the caterwauling, but I did like the acrobatics and the way performers seemed to float across the stage like ghosts or butterflies.) Another time he picked me up in one of the family cars and drove me to Mount Tamalpais for a picnic. On our way back, we stopped at the wharf in Tiburon so he could show me Angel Island just offshore—a place he told me was like an Ellis Island for this side of the country.

"People come to America from all over the world," he explained, "but our government is trying to keep *all* Chinese from entering the country." We couldn't see the immigration station from our vantage point, but he told me about it. "They asked us all sorts of questions when we passed through on our way home from China. They treated my brothers, Helen, and me like foreigners, but we were born here."

We hadn't learned about Angel Island at my school in Plain City, and my mom and dad had never mentioned it, but Monroe spoke with such passion that I could envision every detail. He made the place sound like a jail.

"People accept the humiliation because they desperately want to be in America and they want to be American," he said. "You and I are lucky. We don't have a desire to be American. We *are* American."

I stared out at the island and felt sad—for the secrets my parents had apparently kept from me and for the folks on the island right then who, Monroe said, sometimes were held as long as two years before they were deported back to China or were finally allowed to land in San Francisco—if they hadn't already committed suicide. He must have sensed my melancholy, because he pulled me to him.

Things had "progressed." We'd kissed—and we'd both gotten better at it—but never in Chinatown, not even on my apartment building's stoop when we said good night. Monroe said it was because he didn't want to ruin my reputation. Even so, I could tell *he* liked kissing me. I wanted to enjoy it more, but all the time his lips were on mine I was thinking about how I should be acting. He was rich, cute, and my friend's brother, but I felt nervous and insecure around him, like I wasn't good enough.

One day he drove me through Golden Gate Park straight to the ocean. I'd never seen anything so open or so beautiful or so wild. Monroe parked by the side of the road.

"I thought you might like to see this," he said, "being from Ohio and all."

I'd seen enough movies to know I was supposed to wait until he came around to my side and opened my door. He held out his hand, and I took it. The wind cut through my clothes, but I didn't care. We walked down to the water, where the waves crashed, sending up frothy foam and icy mist. He took off his jacket for us to sit on. He started kissing me. The more insistent he got, the more resistant I became. When he started to put a hand up my skirt, I pushed him away. His fumbling was doing nothing to open my heart.

All the way home, he lectured me on rules about Chinese family life that I'd never heard before and concluded were awful. He recited the Three Obediences—*When a girl, obey your father; when a wife, obey your husband; when a widow, obey your son*—and said that he'd expect that from his wife and daughters. Ruby got huffy when I told her about it: "He's trying to get in your pants one minute and bossing you around the next? What a hypocrite!"

I kept going out with him anyway, because I didn't want to hurt Helen's feelings, and, if I'm honest, because he took me places I couldn't afford on my own. The next time I went out with him, he praised me: "You're as American as pink lemonade at a Kansas fair." Then he went on, proving Ruby right. "But, Grace, you'll be better off behaving like a proper Chinese girl."

Helen heard what her brother said very differently than Ruby. "Wear a *cheongsam* the next time you see him, and he'll sing a different tune," Helen counseled. "And it's true. If you want to be a proper Chinese wife, you'll follow the Three Obediences."

Monroe and I went dancing down by the Embarcadero, because at the parties he usually went to all the Chinese girls sat on one side of the room and all the boys sat on the other. "No one would be so brazen as to dance with the opposite sex in public," he said. "If I'm in Chinatown and I see a girl I grew up with," he confided on another occasion, "I have to cross the street so I don't have to tip my hat or say hello. If I went out with her three times, her parents would ask me how much I expect to earn. I have to play for keeps. No fooling around."

What a butt. He was as rigid and disapproving as my father, except he didn't hit me. Helen, again, had a polar opposite interpretation. "A proposal has to be in the air," she proclaimed. "He'll be such a good catch for you. And the best part? If you marry Monroe, you'll be my sister-in-law, and we'll live together in the compound."

But no matter what she said, Monroe and I weren't right for each other. I allowed Helen to indulge in her fantasy, because I was happy she wanted me with her that much. Eventually, though, I'd have to get up the courage to tell her the truth. In the meantime, I was seeing the city on the arm of a respectable young man and getting plenty of free meals. Not true love, but not bad either.

"HAPPY CHINESE NEW Year!" Ruby prodded me awake.

I didn't bother to open my eyes. "Happy New Year to you too," I mumbled. "Now let me sleep." I rolled over and pulled the pillow over my head.

"I have news." She nudged me again. "I finally have a job."

That got me to sit up. "You what?"

"I'm working at the Golden Gate International Exposition." She gave a high, melodious giggle. "The exposition opened last night. I was there!"

"Is that so?" When I'd gotten home at three in the morning, Ruby was still out, but that wasn't unusual. Ruby and her boys . . . Those relationships weren't serious, so Helen and I never had to worry that there might be someone who would try to horn in on our friendship with her. "But how? And what are you doing?" How did she get hired at the fair when I couldn't?

"Being Oriental counted in my favor this time. The fair is all about Pacific harmony—"

"Are you in the Japanese Pavilion?" I remembered that it was supposed to be the biggest and best of the country-sponsored pavilions.

Ruby shook her head. "Not there."

"The Cavalcade of the Golden West?"

"The big pageant? Nah, not that either."

Finally, it hit me. "Are you working in the Gayway?"

Ruby wrinkled her nose. "Don't be upset."

"But, Ruby, the Gayway?"

"It's an amusement park." She let that rattle around in her noggin before changing her mind. "Or maybe a carnival."

"The man who interviewed me when I went there for a job said the Gayway wasn't a place for a girl like me. If it isn't right for a girl like me, then it can't be right for a girl like you—"

She waved that off. "It's Helen I'm worried about," she said. "I know this will be a problem for her."

"For her? *I* don't like it!"

"Grace, be a sport, will ya? I needed a job. You understand that." She stared at me earnestly. "Will you please help me with Helen?"

I put my hands on my head. "Oh, brother!"

"Tomorrow's your day off. Come to Treasure Island and bring Helen. You'll see it's not so bad."

I swallowed hard and agreed.

"Let's go to Chinatown and see the festivities. I've got money now. The day will be on me! Happy New Year!"

"I've never celebrated Chinese New Year," I admitted.

Ruby glowed, triumphant. "Now's your chance. Get dressed."

We spent the morning pushing through crowds, getting a good spot to watch the dragon dance, sampling treats sold from vendor carts, covering our ears when strings of firecrackers crackled and popped on corners. A little before two, Ruby headed to her new job. I continued to explore. At the corner of Grant and Commercial, I saw Helen's family coming toward me on the sidewalk. Mr. Fong strode a yard ahead of the rest of the family, and his demeanor—his importance—sent other pedestrians scurrying out of the way. His seven sons followed behind him. I spotted Monroe and waved. He nodded but didn't wave back. Helen came next, wearing a lavender silk *cheongsam* embroidered with white peonies. A tiny woman, dressed in a navy blue tunic over black pants, with her hair pulled back into a severe bun at the nape of her neck, hung on to Helen's arm for support. She had to be Helen's mother. A group of young women, some carrying babies and others with small children clustered around their legs, brought up the rear. I'd learned a lot in my few months in Chinatown, and I recognized Helen's sisters-in-law as FOBs—fresh off the boat. They were dressed up like Helen, but the way they'd styled their hair and left their skin unembellished by lipstick or rouge made them seem foreign. They kept their eyes modestly downcast and maintained a respectful distance not only behind their husbands but also behind their mother- and sister-in-law.

When the group reached me, I saw why Helen's mother was having such a hard time walking. She had bound feet! I'd heard about bound feet from my dad. He said they were a sign of status. (Whenever he said that, my mom lowered her head.) What I saw looked like deformed stumps. Just then, Helen caught my eyes. The two of us held steady for a fraction of a second, and then she glanced away. Was she embarrassed that I saw the prosperity and status (but also the backwardness) of her family or that she saw me, a common chorus girl? She passed me, didn't say a word, and proceeded on with her kin, with the sisters-in-law and their children trailing behind—squeaking and peeping like chickens with their just-hatched chicks.

THE NEXT DAY, Helen and I met at 3:00, walked down to the Ferry Building, and paid twenty cents each for round-trip tickets on a Key

System ferry to the Golden Gate International Exposition. I figured if I worked up to the Gayway after Helen and I saw a few attractions—the place was huge—she'd be a lot less judgmental. I hoped she'd be able to weave the Gayway and whatever Ruby was doing there into a bigger vision of the world's fair.

When we got to Treasure Island, we investigated the idea of riding on one of the trams, the fronts of which had been decorated to look like elephants, or hiring one of the rolling chairs, which looked like oversize wheelchairs that were pushed by handsome young men, but Helen was too excited to sit. We hurried from attraction to attraction, from pavilion to pavilion, exhibit to exhibit. We ate hot dogs, bags of popcorn, cotton candy, and drank five-cent Coca-Colas. Finally, Helen began to complain about her feet. We collapsed on a bench next to a lagoon, too exhausted to walk another step. It was after 11:00, and the place was lit with beautiful colored lights. I was just about to spill the beans about Ruby when a sandy-haired young man pushing a rolling chair came to a stop before us.

"I recognize you." His smile tweaked up on the left. His eyes were the same bachelor-button blue I remembered, and, of course, he was still tall and fit.

"Joe?"

His lopsided smile spread wider. He nodded at the rolling chair. "I got the job!"

"I didn't."

Joe and I laughed. Helen looked at me questioningly.

"We met four months ago, on my first day in San Francisco," I explained after I introduced them.

"The exhibits are going to close soon." He ran a hand through his hair. "Do you girls want a ride back to the ferry dock?"

I tipped my head slightly to stare at him. "Actually, I was just about to tell Helen about another friend of ours who works in the Gayway."

Helen raised her eyebrows. "What's this all about?" she asked suspiciously.

"Ruby has a job here," I went on. "I thought we could see her together."

"There's only one Oriental girl in the Gayway," Joe interjected helpfully. "I hoped it might be you, Grace, when I first heard about her. It sure wasn't!"

As soon as he said that, I realized I hadn't asked Ruby exactly *where* she worked. This was going to be a surprise for me too. I noticed that Helen's eyes had narrowed. As happy as I was to see Joe again, introducing Helen to the idea of Ruby working on the Gayway wasn't going quite as I'd hoped.

"How much will it cost if you take us to her?" Helen asked.

"Ordinarily fifty cents each for a half hour," he answered, "but it's on the house for you two."

We settled into the chair. I twisted around in my seat to look up and back at Joe. He gave me that crooked grin again. "Gayway, here we come." He took us past the Columbian, Netherlands East Indies, and Argentine pavilions and straight into the Gayway. Here was a man with rubber arms. There was a sword swallower. Just around the bend: a glass eater, a snake charmer, and a fellow who swallowed a neon tube that lit up his innards; a fat lady, a bearded lady, and a lady with no arms, who did everything with her feet, even play instruments! There were arcades, shooting galleries, a flea circus, carnival rides, and a racetrack for monkeys. If the main part of the exposition portrayed the elegant and tasteful, then the Gayway appealed to baser instincts—vulgar, but so much fun.

Joe pulled to a stop in front of what looked like a western saloon with a hitching post. He pointed to a sign that ran across the width of the building: SALLY RAND'S NUDE RANCH.

Oh, God. This was worse than I'd imagined. *Why* hadn't I asked Ruby what she was doing out here?

"Ruby won't be in there," Helen stated with certainty.

"An Oriental girl works inside," Joe said. "You'll see."

"Not Ruby," Helen insisted. "Besides, I doubt *we'd* be allowed in there."

"This is for families, I swear," Joe vowed.

"But it says 'nude.' "

"It's not *that* nude," Joe said. "Sally Rand was one of the most famous performers at the Chicago World's Fair. Now she's here."

"Have you been inside?" I asked.

"You bet!" he answered a bit too enthusiastically.

Helen and I paid twenty-five cents apiece and then waited in a line that moved very slowly. Joe was right. There were people of all ages—even little kids—in the line, but I'd be lying if I didn't say that the majority were men on their own. Joe said he'd made enough money for the day, so he stayed with us. Finally, we entered the building, following the people herded ahead and shoved by those behind. Gene Autry's "Back in the Saddle Again" blared from speakers attached to the ceiling. We peered to our right through plate-glass windows and into a large room. Inside, about twenty girls—wearing cowboy boots, holsters with fake pistols (one in front and one in back, placed at strategic places), bandannas tied around their breasts (or no bandannas at all—just hair taped, glued, or swinging long and loose to meet the decency codes), Stetsons, and nothing else—paraded back and forth in front of the window, posed with a hand behind an ear, whispered to each other. Some of them played badminton, which caused their breasts to jump and wiggle. They may have called this a place for families, but I hadn't seen anything like it in Plain City. I caught sight of a little boy with his eyes bugged out to here. *Boing!*—like in a cartoon. His mother finally noticed and dragged him out.

Helen grabbed my arm. "Look!"

One girl behind the window had set her cowboy hat on the floor so she could swing a lariat above her head. Her black hair swished back and forth across her breasts, concealing her nipples but shimmering like satin against her pale skin. It was Ruby. *Our* Ruby. We gripped the handrail, trying to maintain our position in front of the window as new visitors pushed against us. From where we stood, Helen and I could hear a woman's voice calling orders: "Get off your duff, Betty. Jump a little higher, Sue. Keep that rump up when you bend down to get the ball, Alice."

I rapped on the glass with my knuckles. A girl with curly red hair looked toward the sound. I pointed to Ruby, sending a message that I wanted her attention.

"Hey, Ruby. You have visitors!"

Ruby dropped the lariat—and let's just say she'd never be a whiz at rope tricks—came to the window, and put her hands on the glass. "Helen! Grace! I have a break in ten minutes. When you exit, come around to the side door. I'll meet you there."

Even through my shock, I perceived the energy coming off Joe. I saw the way he stared at Ruby. At first I thought he was embarrassed, but then I realized he couldn't take his eyes off her. His desire jarred open something startling in me. My yearning for him was so deep I could barely breathe. Not once had I felt that way with Monroe. I didn't want to *be* Ruby, but I wanted Joe to want *me* like that.

The crowd surged against us, and we were pushed back outside and into the night. The lights teased my eyes. The cold air nipped my face, but with so many people crowded together it felt as though a thousand hands caressed me.

"I wouldn't call that appropriate for children!" Helen declared. "How could she?"

I shrugged, striving to appear responsive. I stood so close to Joe his clothes brushed against mine and his breath warmed my cheek.

"Will you introduce me to your friend?" he asked.

"Of course," I said.

Helen blinked. Had both her friends gone crazy?

A few minutes later, Ruby—dressed in slacks and a sweater—oozed through a door and onto the Gayway. "You found me!"

Helen started in with a thousand questions: "Do you realize you're practically naked in there? And in front of all those people? What will your parents say if they find out?"

"You looked beautiful," I said. Did I mean it? Not a word, but I was trying to show Joe I could be adult about such things. I took his hand. I'd never behaved so boldly in my life. My fingers lay cold in his palm, but he didn't pull away.

"Ruby, I want you to meet my friend, Joe . . . Joe . . ."

"Joe Mitchell," he said. "I'm a big fan."

"I've only got twenty minutes," Ruby said, not bothering to acknowledge him. I was relieved he hadn't caught her interest. "Forty minutes on, twenty minutes off, from three in the afternoon until two in the morning. Here, let me show you around."

"You three are so tiny," Joe inserted hopefully. "I bet you can all fit on my rolling chair."

Ruby sized him up. "Sure. Take us for a spin."

Joe pushed us hither, thither, and yon, denying Helen and me the chance to grill our friend. The twenty minutes went by quickly. We dropped Ruby back at Sally Rand's and decided to wait for her set to be over. Helen remained quiet, hiding her thoughts, while I gave Joe the third degree. What was his full name? Joseph Eldon Mitchell. How old was he? Twenty. (That's what I'd guessed when I first met him.) His openness encouraged me to ask more questions.

"Are you still going to Cal?"

"Yep! I'm studying political science," he answered. "I want to go to law school eventually and become a lawyer like my dad."

"Do you like California?"

"You bet! I don't miss the seasons in Winnetka one bit." And flying was still his favorite thing in the world. "I'll love it forever." His voice had an endearing way of rising at the end of a sentence as though asking a question. "Not that I've been able to fly since coming to California—"

A little more than forty minutes later, Ruby opened the side door and held it ajar. She wore a kimono. Her nipples pushed against the thin silk. "Sally got mad at me for being late last time. I can't go out with you again. I don't have time to get out of my costume, get dressed, then undressed, and back into my costume again." She laughed at the absurdity of what she'd just said. "It takes time to get those pistols just right! Will you come and get me later? We can go home together on the ferry." Without waiting for an answer, she gave a wave and closed the door.

Joe said, "I've got to leave you too. I need to turn in the rolling chair. But will you come again? We could all meet after Ruby and I get off. I could even come out here one day when I don't have classes or work. Would you like that?"

"I'd love it," I answered, because I really wanted to see him again.

After he pushed off, we found a spot to wait for Ruby near the Headless Woman display. Helen had already spoken her mind, but what was I going to say to Ruby?

I shouldn't have worried, because she started talking as soon as we boarded the ferry to cross the bay back to the city.

"I don't want you girls to zing me from two sides," she began. "I needed a job, and this was the best I could get."

"But how can you be—" I didn't want to say the word *naked*. "You had to have known about this job for a while."

"Ummm." A confirmation of sorts.

"Those nights you were out late the last couple of weeks—"

"Ummm."

"Were you rehearsing?"

"Not a lot to rehearse," Helen quipped.

"We're supposed to be friends," I said, "and you didn't tell us."

"Of course I didn't!" Ruby flared. "Look how you're taking it!"

I peered at her, disbelieving.

"It's not a big deal," she insisted.

"Ruby!" I exclaimed. "You're n-k-d in there!"

"I'm not naked-naked. Sally is very careful about what we show. Besides, we aren't the only nudes on the Gayway. Go to that studio where girls pose without a stitch on, and people can sketch or photograph them for a fee. Go to the movie house that plays reels of nudists playing volleyball. Or go to the Palace of Fine Arts in the main part of the fair, and you'll find a naked woman re-creating a painting by Manet."

"Manet?" Helen burst out, indignant. "Who in the hell is Manet?"

Ruby's and my eyes widened. It was the first time we'd heard Helen curse.

"Well?" she demanded.

"I don't know," Ruby answered with a pixie shrug. "We were told to say that."

She started to giggle, I joined in, and Helen covered her mouth. But what were we thinking? There are consequences to everything.

CONSEQUENCE ONE OF visiting Treasure Island: I now had an honest-to-goodness crush on someone . . . and it absolutely wasn't Monroe. I needed to do the right thing and tell him, even if it disappointed Helen. He picked me up the following Sunday, took me to the Eastern Bakery, and ordered me an ice cream soda I didn't want. I was just getting up my nerve when, surprise! The tables were turned—but definitely!

"I had once hoped my father might approve of you, even though you're a dancer," he began. "But when I saw you on New Year's Day, I realized he never would." Monroe then spent the next half hour telling me why he could never marry me: that I didn't cook Chinese food, that I was an only child so I hadn't learned to care for children, that I didn't embroider, darn, or tat. I wasn't sufficiently political either. I didn't show enough sympathy for what our people in China were enduring at the hands of the Japanese, I didn't appreciate the deprivations of Chinese in this country, and I hadn't been through Angel Island, so I would never understand the terrible things that happened to our people there.

"And you're American-born," he said, as he came to the end of his list. "You'll never act like a proper Chinese wife. You're too *lo fan* for me to marry."

"Have you considered that *you* might be too Chinese for *me* to marry?" I asked, but inside I smarted at being called a white ghost like any tourist who entered Chinatown.

"My father will find a proper girl in China to be my wife. He says he'll take me there to pick her out as soon as the Japanese are vanquished."

"You mean like buying the right apple?" I could barely get out the words.

"If you mean no blemishes, then yes." His eyes narrowed as he appraised me. "You'll never be more than a big-thigh girl."

And that was that. Whether he was dropping me or I was dropping him no longer mattered. I pushed myself away from the table.

"Thank you for the ice cream soda."

"I'll walk you to your apartment. Only prostitutes walk through Chinatown by themselves. I don't want you to be branded a no-no girl. No man in his right senses would want to marry you then."

I thanked him again but turned down his offer. "I'll walk where I want to walk," I said stiffly. "I'll be fine."

As I headed back to my apartment, I felt lucky. I loved Helen, but I could never live in that family, in that compound, and in constant subservience to Monroe with his Three Obediences and all.

"I thought he was American like me," I told my friends later. "But he's much too Chinese. My mom married someone like that—American on the outside but traditional on the inside—and look how it turned out for her."

Ruby agreed, but Helen was very disappointed. She even cried.

Consequences everywhere.

GRACE

Let the Boy Talk

All through the spring, Helen and I went to the exposition whenever possible. We loved the bustle and jumble, the shills and their ballyhoo. Once we got over the shock of seeing Ruby that first time, we saw that, in fact, she wasn't entirely naked. We still didn't "approve" of what she was doing, but she was our friend, and we wanted to show our support, so we always visited her at Sally Rand's. The girls inside the window were constantly doing new things. One time they took turns riding a burro, while the barker called, "Come and see Sally Rand's ass." Joe often came along. Ruby, Helen, and I loved to dance, and he jitterbugged with us to the royalty of the radio "live and in person": Benny Goodman, Count Basie, Kay Kyser, and the Dorseys. You haven't lived until you've been in front of bands like those and danced all out, and Joe and I outshone every couple on the dance floor, cutting loose with our spins, flips, and other tricks. Surprising he could dance so well? Nope. He'd learned his social moves at debutante balls in and around Chicago and the fancier combos at the hotter gatherings that took place late at night after the girls had been presented.

The more I learned about Joe, the more I adored him. He was smart, with all his classes. He pushed a rolling chair from noon to midnight on weekends, and on Mondays, Wednesdays, and Fridays from four until midnight, or later if he picked up a good fare. He'd been raised in Winnetka, which was only about three hundred miles from Plain City. The geographic proximity of our hometowns had to mean something about our values and about who we were as people, didn't it?

"We're a little more open about Orientals in Illinois," he told me one day. "An Oriental and an Occidental can even get married where I live, not like here in California, where it's against the law."

I had no idea laws existed *anywhere* that barred Chinese and Caucasians from marrying. That was rotten news. Seeing my expression, Joe reached over and ruffled the hair on the top of my head.

"Don't worry, squirt," he said. "If you ever decide to hitch your wagon to someone like me, he'll figure it out. Where there's a will there's a way. He might even take you to Mexico to tie the knot . . . Now let's check to see if Ruby's in the window. That Sally Rand sure is something, but it's fun to see your friend too."

I went with Joe, and he still stared at Ruby the way he had that first time, so I also invited him to the Forbidden City to watch *me* dance.

"When that Li Tei Ming started to sing, I couldn't believe it," he said after the first time he came. "She's Oriental, but when she opens her mouth she sounds just like my aunt Myrtle."

How many times had I heard lines like those from customers, who were trying to be polite and complimentary but were really showing their ignorance and prejudice?

"Li Tei was born here," I responded. "Just like I was born here."

"I guess that's what makes you all novelty acts," he said. "Just like Ruby is a novelty—being Oriental and all—over at Sally Rand's."

His comment hurt down to my bones. "We aren't novelties," I said as I bristled. "We're just American girls who like to sing and dance."

"It's true," he agreed. "You're a real hoofer. You're better than the rest of them. You should have your own act. You should be a headliner."

When he said that, I forgave all the other things he'd said and knew that in his eyes, I was special—Oriental or not.

. . .

In May '39, Sally Rand's place got raided, and the headlines splashed across newspapers. That didn't keep people away, however. Everyone wanted to see what the hullabaloo was all about. Ruby gobbled up the attention. But the raid was the last straw for Helen, and she began to stay away. She claimed to be a homebody, and maybe she was, because she never dated, and didn't wear lipstick or makeup except onstage. Ruby attracted men like ants to spilled Coca-Cola. Her attitude: "Men are nothing to get het up about as long as you don't get in trouble." I was saving myself for someone special. That someone was Joe.

My days started to revolve around him. I went to the exposition before I had to be at work, and he joined me before his shift. I dragged him to see special dance performances hosted by countries that didn't have their own pavilions: Cambodia, Siam, and Burma. He took me to see new inventions: electric razors, nylon hosiery, and a television.

"Grace, soon these products will be in our homes. We'll sit on the couch and watch television all night instead of going to a nightclub or the picture show. Entertainment will come to us—all at once, all across the country. Think of the reach that will have. Think of the fame it will bring to the entertainers. And the wealth . . ."

He may have been a college boy, and I loved him, but in some ways, his head was in the clouds. Those DuPont nylon stockings looked neat, though.

I learned the supreme lesson: let the boy talk. Within a few weeks, I knew everything about Joe. He believed in the tooth fairy until he was eight; he hated algebra almost as much as I did; he played football in high school; he couldn't stand lima beans but he loved his mom's rhubarb pie. Blue was his favorite color. He had diphtheria when he was three, and his mom stayed up with him every night until he was out of the woods. His favorite hobby when he was a boy was making model airplanes. He loved his mom and dad, but he wanted to stay in California for the rest of his life. He didn't like taking visitors in his rolling chair to the Japanese Pavilion, because he didn't approve of what that nation was doing in China—which made me glad that we'd decided to keep Ruby's background a secret. She could pass, and I didn't want Joe to hate my best friend. He was moral and concerned about politics—but not a stuffed shirt about it like Monroe.

It wasn't as though I couldn't impress Joe when the opportunity arose. In an effort to attract more business to the Forbidden City, Charlie got the ponies booked to do a dance in a newsreel. On the big day, a bus drove us to the beach. We lined up in the sand, wearing big headdresses that tinkled and glittered with every movement, and embroidered Chinese opera gowns with long water sleeves made of the lightest silk, which draped over our hands a good twelve inches. Our feet dragged in the sand, but our water sleeves floated and blew in the ocean breeze. We sidestepped until we were behind a coromandel screen set up incongruously on the sand to discard our headdresses and gowns, and toss them toward the camera in a manner bound to provoke good-natured chuckles. The music changed to a jitterbug. Now in bathing suits, we swung out from behind the screen. "Well, well, well," the announcer intoned with proper surprise. "What would Confucius say?"

A few weeks later, when Ruby was in bed with cramps, Joe took me to a matinee—the first picture I'd seen in ages—and we saw the newsreel. I sensed what others in the audience felt when we stripped down to our swimsuits. We had moved from foreign Oriental maidens to homespun American gals in a few frames.

"What a great opportunity for you," Joe told me later. "Pretty soon you'll be a genuine motion-picture star."

Now wasn't that better than seeing an electric razor or a television?

JOE GAVE ME a fan from the Chinese Village. A landscape of soaring mountains, pavilions with upturned eaves, and trees bent by the wind spread across the fan's folds. Every night when I got ready for bed, I took it out of my dresser drawer, where I kept the other trinkets he'd given me—a pickle pin from the Heinz exhibit, aluminum coins from the Union Pacific railroad exhibit, and a pair of 3-D glasses. Sure, they were all giveaways—except for the fan and my first precious pair of nylon stockings—but whenever I opened the fan, I thought of Joe. On my days off, I stayed at the exposition all through his shifts, so I could be there during his breaks.

"Grace, you're still a kid," he announced matter-of-factly one afternoon as we walked to the White Star Tuna Resturant to buy a lunch of hot tuna turnovers with frozen peas—the latest in fancy foods. "You're too young for me, and I'm too old for you. Maybe in another ten years . . ."

Even when I surprised him, he always seemed glad to see me. "You again! Great!" Sometimes we sat by the Port of the Trade Winds to watch the China Clipper seaplanes, which offered the first commercial flights between the United States and Asia, taking off and landing in the bay.

"It takes three weeks to travel from here to Hong Kong on an ocean liner," he told me. "The China Clipper has shortened it to a couple of days."

That seemed wondrous, but then I'd never been on a ship, let alone an airplane.

"Maybe one day I'll get to fly a China Clipper," he said. But I didn't see how, especially if he wanted to go to law school.

Joe taught me to drink homemade Cuba libres, which we made by pouring rum into our Coca-Cola bottles. He told me he'd rather have me learn to drink properly with him than from the men in the club, where I might forget how to handle myself.

In August—five months after Joe first approached Helen and me with his rolling chair—he took me to see *The Wizard of Oz*. Sure, it was a kids' movie, but those flying monkeys scared the dickens out of me. Watching Auntie Em and Uncle Henry search for Dorothy made me think about my parents. *Does Mom miss me? What about Dad? Do they wonder where I am and how I'm doing?* But those questions puffed away when Joe whispered in my ear. "The Land of Oz looks just like Treasure Island, doesn't it?"

Just hearing his voice could wash away even the darkest thoughts.

On a Saturday in early September, I sat in the Court of Flowers, watching for him. I could tell as soon as he came into view that he was cross. My stomach tightened: beware. "I had a single fare for the entire day," he complained. "Then the guy stiffed me." Joe burned in a way I recognized from my dad. I got up and followed as he shouldered his way through the throngs, pushing people aside. Of course, trouble finds trouble, and Joe knocked into the wrong person.

"Hey, bub!" the man shouted when Joe didn't stop to apologize. "Are you looking for a beef?"

Joe answered by spinning around and shoving his accuser in the chest. The man lowered his head and heaved himself at Joe, who was thrown into the crowd. People peeled away, making room for the show. Joe regained his balance, planted his feet, and curled his hands into fists.

"Joe! Don't!" I cried.

He shuffled forward. The other man was ready. I had to stop this. I reached out and touched Joe's shoulder.

"Joe—"

He whipped around with his arms raised, ready to lay into me. I closed my eyes and cowered, preparing myself for the blow. It didn't come. I opened my eyes and saw Joe staring at me, horrified.

"I could have hit you." His voice shook, but his hands were still up and clenched.

Behind Joe, passersby pulled the other man away. The space around us quickly filled as the masses resumed their fun, while Joe and I remained frozen. Without breaking his gaze, I slowly straightened my body. The terrible tension melted from Joe as his fists loosened, followed by his arms, and finally his shoulders.

"I don't know what happened," he said. "I'm so sorry, Grace."

I put a hand over my mouth and ran through the crowd until I found a trash can. I threw up. I was still heaving when Joe's fingers began to smooth my hair from my forehead. I flinched; he pulled away. I retched again; he placed a hand on the small of my back. I shook from fright.

"I'm sorry," he crooned. "I'm sorry, I'm sorry . . ."

Usually, at the end of our time together, Joe headed to Berkeley and I returned to the city. But on that night, he escorted me back to San Francisco on the ferry. He was still twitchy, but so was I. I hadn't felt this way since the last time my father beat me to mash almost a year ago. I couldn't stop shivering. Joe wrapped his jacket around my shoulders and took me to Foster's on Jones Street for something to eat. He tried to get me to talk, but what could I say? I was too embarrassed to tell him my father had walloped me for years and that for one terrifying second Joe had reminded me of him. I could never hurt Joe's feelings that way, not when he hadn't *actually* hit me.

"You're a good egg," he said, heartbreakingly apologetic. "My mom and dad would love you."

Just like that, pure joy erased my fear. We still hadn't kissed on the lips, but I could wait.

When we arrived at my building, Joe glanced up and saw that the lights were off in Ruby's and my apartment. He said good night without asking to come up.

A MONTH LATER, the exposition closed. Some said it was for the winter; some said it was because the fair was in such financial trouble that the organizers needed to come up with an improved vision. Now, Joe came to the city on Saturday nights to see me dance. Sometimes he sat with Ruby—who'd gone back to job hopping—and they watched all three shows. Other than that, I rarely saw my roommate, and I didn't see Joe as much as I would have liked either. No kisses. No proposal. Nothing. I told myself Joe was taking his time, because I was young, and he was still a student.

With fewer tourists in town for the fair, the Forbidden City's prospects began to dim. People gossiped that Charlie was bankrupt and that the club was in receivership. Once a week, everyone lined up outside his office to get paid. He hated to part with his cash—whether at the racetrack, in a kitchen poker game, or to compensate his employees. It's true what they said about him: he wept when he paid you. One night he bawled so hard that Ida griped, "He cried so much, I wanted to give him back his money."

I'd seen Charlie weep and had him plead with me too: "You don't really need this, do you? Let me keep it for you." But I always pocketed my pay without an ounce of guilt or sympathy. I had things to buy and things to do. I couldn't contemplate the idea that the club might close.

FEBRUARY ARRIVED. I'D been in San Francisco for sixteen months. It had been five months since that night on Treasure Island when Joe almost hit me, but we'd both gotten over that, and my feelings for him had only grown. Today was the first anniversary of the day we met again at the exposition. One year! That was a lot of jitterbugging and talking. I was ready for something more, and I'd decided that tonight would be *the* night with Joe. I was going to kiss him and tell him exactly how I felt.

I arrived at work and was ready when Charlie called, "*Fiedee, fiedee, fiedee!* Hurry, hurry, hurry! It's showtime!"

I was a bit distracted by my decision, so I had to force myself to concentrate as we lined up behind the velvet curtain. Charlie opened the evening: "I want to introduce you to some lovely southern belles . . . from South China! Grace, Helen, Ida, May . . ."

We began the promenade, our umbrellas twirling just as they had on opening night, only now Charlie put up a hand to stop me, as he did during every show.

"Now hold on a second, little lady," he drawled. "How y'all doin' t'nite?"

"Ah, hawney," I purred back, "I'm all riled up with no place to go." I glanced at the audience. "Will you kindly gentlemen—and ladies too," I added with a tiny curtsy, "allow this gal to show y'all a good time?"

Our customers chortled. They just couldn't make sense of what they were hearing and seeing, but they absolutely loved it. (I earned an extra five dollars a week for speaking my few lines and for bringing tea to the Lim Sisters at the start of the evening. It seemed like a fortune, and yet I spent every dime.)

That night—as every night—we danced close to the patrons, who drank, smoked, and ate by the red-tinged light of their coolie-hat table lamps. They ogled us in our satin peep-toe sandals, skimpy outfits, and amusing headdresses perched at improbable angles. We swished, wiggled, and writhed. We pranced with a single forefinger raised in the air—jazz style—as we gazed heavenward like naughty angels. I scanned the room and found Joe at a table on the second tier.

When the number ended, the ponies and I went backstage, elbowing past the Juggling Jins, who'd replaced the Merry Mahjongs when they'd gone on tour to "kick the gong around" other cities. These weren't the only changes we'd had in the fourteen months since the club opened. When Jack Mak decided he needed an assistant, he'd chosen Irene, one of the chorines, to help him. They'd gotten married two months later. ("I told him no funny business until I have a ring on my finger," Irene said at the wedding. "I couldn't risk getting knocked up.") A new girl, Ruthie, had replaced Irene in the line, and she was nice enough. Tonight, after the last show, she would leave real fast, trying to escape before she had to deal with persistent stage-door Johnnies. Other girls—like Ida—would change slowly, guaranteeing that someone would be outside to take them out.

In the top-hat number, I made a turn, zeroing in on Joe to use as my focal point, and spotted Ruby next to him. The way they stared at each other . . . The way their heads were tilted toward each other so intimately . . . I finally saw it: Ruby and Joe were *a couple*! My breath caught. I missed a step, stumbled slightly, and stopped dead in the middle of the number. Helen sashayed in front of me to cover my mistake. I began to count in my head—*one, two, three, four*—and my body, trained as it was, obeyed, but my heart was frozen.

As soon as the routine ended, I ran offstage. A hand clamped down on my shoulder.

"What's wrong with you?" Charlie demanded.

I bowed my head, praying that this wasn't happening, that perhaps I'd fallen asleep and was having a guilty dream after what I'd hoped to say to Joe tonight.

"It was my fault," I heard Helen answer. "I'm so clumsy and careless. Grace tripped over my feet."

"Is this true?" Charlie asked.

I refused to look up. I saw Charlie's alligator loafers—the ones he always wore on Saturday nights—and my black satin shoes. In my peripheral vision, I glimpsed several pairs of shoes that matched my own, belonging to Helen and the other ponies.

"I count on you, Grace," Charlie chastised. "If you can't do the job, then—"

Helen pulled me away before he could finish. When we got to the dressing room, she said to the other girls, "We've got to help her. Hazel, be a doll, will you, and grab her corset? May, make sure those buckles are tight. Ida, what am I forgetting?"

I was numb as they wrestled me out of one costume and pushed me into another.

"Did you know?" I asked.

"About what?" Helen may not have been the best dancer, but she sure could act innocent.

"Ruby and Joe."

"Don't imagine things," Helen said, but her voice gave her away.

The ponies were uncustomarily silent, soaking in the drama.

Helen sighed. "I figured something might be going on with those two."

"Fiedee, fiedee, fiedee."

It was time for our next number. Helen balanced my hat on my head.

"Why didn't you say something?" I asked.

"I hoped you'd never find out. I hoped even more I was wrong." She led me through the door to the backstage area. "The truth is, I could be wrong. *You* could be wrong. They've met at the club before. You've seen them sit together before."

"But did you see how they *looked* at each other?"

How long had I been making a fool of myself? From that night a year ago, when I introduced them outside Sally Rand's?

At the curtain, I closed my eyes, preparing myself to go onstage. The music for the finale started. I wanted so bad to bolt out of there.

"Grace, you can't lose your job," Helen whispered behind me. "He's just a boy. I take it back. He's not a boy. If what we suspect is true, he's a two-timer who led you on. Mama says a man like that is worse than a horse trying to pull two carts, meaning . . ."

When we went out for the number, Ruby and Joe were gone.

You know the expression "the show must go on"? Forget that! But I did my best to follow the music. When we came offstage, Charlie was right there, his face flushed with irritation.

"Grace is sick," Ida said before he could speak. "She needs to go home."

"Not possible," Charlie said. "We have two more shows—"

"You don't want all of us to get sick, do you?" Ida asked.

Helen put a hand on her stomach. "I'm queasy already."

Charlie sized up the situation, weighing the loss of two girls for the last two shows against the possibility that we all might get sick and he'd lose his entire line for a night or two, or that we were lying. Then he pursed his lips and waved us off with the back of his hand.

The ponies brought me to the dressing room. As they changed into the gowns they wore between shows, Helen and I threw on our street clothes. *Ruby has stolen Joe* pounded in my head. Joe had hurt me, but that Ruby had deceived me was even worse. Anger began to replace my anguish.

"Where do you want to go?" Helen asked when we reached the street. "Do you want to come to my house?"

The invitation was a first. I smiled ruefully. I'd wanted to see the inside of Helen's compound since forever.

"Thanks for the offer, but let's go to my apartment."

"What if Ruby and Joe are there?"

"Good! I'll tear her eyes out," I said, repeating something I'd seen in a movie years ago.

My building was quiet as we went upstairs. I put the key in the lock and opened the door. The lights were off, but I could hear something. I fortified myself, walked to the bedroom, and flipped on the light. Joe and Ruby were naked on top of the covers. He was pushing himself into her. All notions of tearing out eyeballs disappeared as my blood drained out of my head in a sickening *whoosh*. I averted my gaze and saw Helen. Her face was as pale as cream, and her lips were whiter still. I had to look worse. I mean, there we were—two virgins faced with something we'd only imagined. And what I'd imagined was not what was on the bed. I was stunned, destroyed, heartbroken. Joe reached for his shorts. Ruby slipped her arms into her kimono. I covered my eyes and began to weep.

"I'm sorry," Ruby's pretty voice sang to me. "I'm so, so sorry. We never wanted you to find out this way."

Joe kept his eyes down and his mouth shut. He pulled on his pants and grabbed his shirt and socks from the clothes scattered on the floor. As soon as he had his belongings, he rushed past Helen and me and out the door. He'd played me for a sap, and he didn't even have the courage to apologize. He didn't have the conviction to stand by Ruby either. He'd made suckers of both of us. My humiliation was beyond anything I could have imagined. For the first time, I fully understood what it meant to lose face.

"Well," I said at last, "this stinks."

"Grace—"

Hearing Ruby say my name hit me like an electric shock.

"I'm sorry you had to see that," she went on. "We realize you don't know much about sex. Joe and I have always tried to be careful. You usually don't come home until much later."

"You mean this isn't the first time?"

"We waited a long time before I let anything happen, so we've only been *together* for a few months. We were just celebrating the first-year anniversary of when we met. I'll always be grateful to you for introducing us."

Helen grabbed my arm to hold me steady.

"But *I* love him," I mumbled.

"We knew you were sweet on him. That's why we waited," Ruby said sympathetically. "But you kept following him around all the time."

I needed to get out of there.

"Joe was worried about you," Ruby confided in a gentle but straightforward voice. "We both were. You're so nice, but you didn't even graduate from high school. You're not in the same world as we are. You can't play at the same level." She paused. "Oh, honey, you're out of your league. It's time you learned that."

Here's how I heard what she said: I was some dumb rube from the sticks, while she was gorgeous and half-naked all the time.

"Do you love him?" I asked.

"Don't be such a kid," she answered like she was trying to be helpful and teach me what was what. "You work in a nightclub. I work in a nudie show. You need to grow up."

When I recoiled, Ruby finally had the decency to glance away.

"We're like the Three Musketeers, remember?" For the first time, I heard a hint of anxiety in her voice. "We promised we'd never let a man come between us, and I meant it."

"How could I have ever liked you?" I asked.

"We thought, what you don't know won't hurt you," she continued, going back to sounding like a know-it-all big sister. "We hoped you'd get over Joe and develop a crush on someone else. Maybe get back together with Monroe, or meet another boy your own age."

I was only two years younger than Ruby! I fought the urge to smack her.

"We wanted you to be happy," she went on. "We wanted you to come to a place—on your own—that you would be able to look back at your silly little crush as just that. We kept the secret precisely so *this* wouldn't happen."

"What about me?" Helen suddenly asked. "What's your excuse for not telling me?"

"You're not even supposed to walk through Chinatown by yourself," Ruby answered. "I didn't think you'd want to hear that I was making love with a boy. But really, neither of you should make a big deal about this. Joe and I have been playing around. So what? It's not *that* serious."

Her excuses made me angrier. She'd lied to Helen and me. Her reasons seemed to be based on our being too innocent to accept the truth. I so hated her in that moment.

I turned to Helen. "Let's get out of here."

"We should talk about this some more," Ruby appealed to me. "Please, you need to understand—"

"There's nothing to talk about!" I screamed from a place inside me that I hadn't known existed. "I *love* Joe, and now you've ruined everything!"

"For heaven's sake, Grace. He's a man. A man doesn't want puppy love."

I thought I'd been humiliated. Now I was HUMILIATED.

Perhaps Ruby sensed she'd gone too far. "Try to forgive me—"

"Forgive you? I never want to *see* you again!"

With that, I pulled my suitcase out from under the bed.

"Don't go." Her eyes welled with tears. I'd never seen her cry before, but my usual compassion had been shredded to nothing.

I opened my dresser drawers and stuffed my purse with brassieres, panties, and the envelope with Mom's emergency money. I packed my newly bought frocks, the dance shoes and practice clothes I'd brought with me from Plain City, and the evening gown that had taken six months to pay off, but I left the trinkets Joe had given me rattling in the bottom of my drawer.

Ruby kept apologizing. Helen waited quietly. I snapped the suitcase shut and picked it up. Ruby flew to the door to block me from leaving.

"Move aside, or I'll move you." I sounded just like my father.

The steel in my voice was such that Ruby edged out of the way. Helen took my arm. Her grip was stable and reassuring as we walked through the streets, but I was a whimpering mess. When we reached the Fong compound, Helen led me through a door, up some stairs, and along a hallway. Her room was neat, fairly empty, and not all that different from my room at home: a bed, a side table with a lamp, a dresser, and a mirror. I collapsed on the bed. Helen gave me a handkerchief. I cried, and Helen kept up a commentary—which didn't cheer me any.

"First she said it was their anniversary," Helen stewed. "Then she said they'd been doing it for a while. Then she said it wasn't a big deal. Then she practically said she didn't even *care* for him. If all that wasn't enough, she then tried to make it sound like Joe was forced into babysitting you. Did she change her story because she thought that's what you wanted to hear?"

I blubbered some more.

Helen disappeared, then shortly returned with a pot of jasmine tea and a plate of cold barbecued-pork dumplings.

"I can't stay here." My voice caught—like I was being suffocated.

"Sure you can. We have plenty of room."

I shook my head. "I mean I can't stay in San Francisco."

"Just a minute! You have a job. You have friends. You have me. Don't do anything you'll regret."

But running away was how I knew to protect myself.

"Hollywood," I murmured. "I'm going to Hollywood. I should have gone there in the first place, because life is in movies, movies are life, and movies are greater than life."

"You don't make a decision just like that!"

"I do," I said as a hard protective shell came down over me. "If I didn't, I'd still be in Plain City."

I stood. *Done here.*

"At least sleep on it," Helen pleaded.

But nothing she said—and, boy, did she try—changed my mind, forcing her pleas to become more desperate. "The day we first met you promised we'd stick together."

Around four in the morning she finally accepted defeat. "All right then," she said. "Wait here."

Once I was alone, my fidgety desire to run was even stronger. It was all I could do not to sneak out of Helen's room and the compound by myself. I closed my eyes and saw Ruby and Joe naked. His *thing*. I opened my eyes and took a deep breath. Across the room on a little table was a framed photograph, fruit on a blue cloisonné dish, and a couple of candles. Grateful for a momentary distraction, I went to get a better look at the photo. It was Helen and a Chinese man, probably one of her brothers with the presidential names—Washington, Jefferson, or . . .

Helen returned with Monroe. He didn't show surprise that I was there, and he didn't ask any questions. In his mind, I'd probably come to the end I deserved, what with my *lo fan* thinking. It took only a few minutes to drive to the bus station, where Helen revved up her campaign again: "There will be consequences if you run away."

I held her hand in mine. "Thank you, Helen, for helping me . . . again. You've been a good friend, but I've made my decision."

"And your decision does not include me."

I boarded the first bus heading south. I had lived the last sixteen months with joy in my heart, but now my mind ran from the memory of seeing Joe and Ruby in bed together. I'd lived as though I would never cry again, but now I couldn't stop crying. I hoped to find refuge in sleep, but I was unable to close my eyes for fear of what I might see. All those times I thought Ruby had been out with boys from the Gayway, she'd been with Joe. And she hadn't bothered to tell me because she'd decided I'd "get over him" on my own? The bus driver stopped for gas, and I went to the restroom. I stared at myself in the mirror and saw a pale ghost. My red lacquered nails seemed morbidly alive against my dead skin.

I DON'T KNOW what I expected. Movie stars greeting me on the sidewalk when I got off the bus in downtown Los Angeles? Chauffeur-driven Packards and Auburns tooling along palm-lined boulevards? Mansions with sprawling lawns? Diamonds in the pavement? *Glamour* everywhere? What I saw as I took a local bus west along Sunset Boulevard looked drab—little bungalows with peeling paint, geraniums wilting in the sun, and regular working stiffs plodding along the sidewalks. After moving into a furnished room on Ivar in Hollywood, I taped my envelope with my mom's fifty dollars under a drawer, with a promise to myself not to spend my money frivolously as I had in San Francisco. I was nineteen years old now and determined to make myself into a star: reward for my heartbreak.

I went to Paramount Studios first. The gate looked just like it did in the movies.

"I'd like to go to your casting department, please," I told the guard.

"Do you have an appointment?"

"No."

"Then I'm sorry, miss. I can't let you in."

I went to other studios—Warner Bros., RKO Pictures, Twentieth Century–Fox, and more—but I couldn't get past those guard gates either.

I needed a new strategy. With the listings of theatrical agents torn out of the yellow pages in hand, I started with the *A*s and went to the office of a man named Abel Aaron.

"Aaron isn't my real last name," the balding man said as he waved me into his private office. "But it guarantees that young aspirants like you will visit me first. Now, please, sit on the couch."

I wasn't that dumb, but as I worked my way down the list—visiting the Bronstein Agency, Carrell Talent, and Discover New

Faces—I heard that request more times than I could count. My response was always the same—"No, thank you"—so of course I didn't get representation. My refusal to have sex wasn't the only reason I didn't make progress. I looked up casting calls in *Variety* and *The Hollywood Reporter,* but the white girl always got the job. I went to Chinatown, but it didn't have a single nightclub. My sorrow deepened. I was on my own now without a soul to help me. I had to toughen up—*grow up,* as Ruby had put it. I slept in very little clothing, trying to discipline myself to take whatever cold might come my way. I walked miles to save the nickel bus fare. And if Ruby or Joe entered my thoughts, I'd distract myself by stretching or doing a barre routine by holding the back of my chair in my room. I gave myself pep talks. I'd bounced back from adversity before. I'd do it again. But life isn't that simple or easy.

The worse things got, the more I thought about my mom and dad, and why I could never give up and return to them in Plain City. My waking hours in Los Angeles started and ended the same way: with good and bad memories of them. I'd often asked my mom how and why we'd ended up in Plain City. Her story was always the same, and it had to do with my birth. Mom and Dad had been living in San Francisco. They'd been doing pretty well, well enough to own one of the first closed Model Ts—used, of course. One weekend they drove north to Sebastopol to pick apples. "I went into labor," Mom liked to recount. "The contractions were far apart so I wasn't frightened. We started driving back to San Francisco. By the time we reached San Rafael, I had to get to a hospital. We went, but they turned us away. They said they didn't service Chinese."

What kinds of people would turn away a woman in labor? The kinds of people I now met every day in Los Angeles.

"You were born by the side of the road," she'd go on. "That's why your feet move all the time. We looked at you, our precious little girl, and your father said, 'Why would she walk when she can dance across the room?' He saw your special talent. He decided we should go where people weren't used to hating Chinese."

So we'd piled in the car and headed east. The car broke down in Plain City. Dad dropped it at the Ford dealership on Main Street and went looking for a hotel, but there wasn't one. (Because Plain City was just a place to pass through.) Reverend Reynolds at the Methodist church took us in. Dad eventually rented a two-story building on Chillicothe—the only other major thoroughfare in town. We lived upstairs; Dad opened the laundry downstairs. He was a dreamer, so he sunk a ton of money into a neon sign that blazed MR. LEE'S LAUNDRY gaudy and bright into my room all night. Dreamers are born to be disappointed. My dad was, certainly, and in this single regard I now understood him in a way I never had before.

My parents cut themselves off from their culture and replaced it with the reddest, whitest, and bluest. Some of my earliest memories were of playing with Velma, going to church on Sundays, and dancing at Miss Miller's dance studio. My life changed when I started school. It didn't happen all at once. It takes training to learn how to be a bigot. Velma dropped me and adopted Ilsa and Maude as her friends. Slowly I began to understand why they hung out together and why they always picked on me. The evil triplets were beyond beautiful with their blond hair and perfect skin, but they were just as much outsiders as I was even though they *looked* like they belonged. But how could they belong with their strange holidays—*Pikkujoulu* and *Laskiaistiistai*—and their stranger foods—*Janssonin kiusaus* and *kylmäsavu stettu lohi*? That Ilsa, for example, assumed she was going to marry Henry Billups. Didn't she understand that the minute a young man dated someone like her, his parents would become agitated?

Sometimes when I was waiting to go in for an audition, I'd run through the events of one day in particular. In seventh grade—a normal day, I'd thought at the time—I went to school and discovered Velma at the entrance, saying loud enough for everyone to hear, "Grace Lee thinks she's gonna be a movie star." Word circulated fast, and soon every kid who thought he or she was better than me, which is to say every kid from kindergarten all the way through twelfth grade, found the idea hilarious. Henry Billups pantomimed a buck-toothed, cross-eyed Chinese laundryman he'd seen in a movie . . . or maybe he was just making fun of my dad. Harold Jones followed me around for days, chanting, "Take a look in the mirror, take a look in the mirror, take a look in the mirror," and laughing cruelly. After a while, the craze faded and my classmates fell back on the tried and true: "Chinky, chinky China. Chinky, chinky China."

The evil triplets left me feeling isolated and alone, but they weren't as bad as my dad. He'd beaten my mom and me for as long as I could remember. But when I started to fill out he focused his anger entirely on yours truly, and Mom could do nothing to stop it. I never could tell what would set him off. Did I happen to glance out the laundry's plate-glass window when a man walked by? Did I spend too much time talking to a customer when he came to pick up his shirts? Did I turn up the radio when the song "Love Walked In" came on? Was my sweater too tight? I don't recall how young I was—*young,* though—when Mom told me another future lay ahead of me. "You're going to leave here one day, Grace," she'd said. "Look around church on Sunday. You'll see that all the best people have left. For you to do that, you'll need to work hard and save money."

So I did. I labored in the laundry, sorting, marking, folding, wrapping clothes in blue paper and tying the package with string, and waiting on customers. For this, my father paid me two dollars a week. "A lot of money," he griped, "when I still have to wash, dry, starch, and iron everything." At Miss Miller's studio, I earned five cents for each student I taught in my Tuesday and Thursday classes for girls from the elementary grades. When my mom was laid low with the flu, I took over selling her rice wine out our back door. The customers liked me, so I pocketed large tips. In the summer, the Methodist church ladies hired Mom and me to make paper cups for two cents a dozen for the lemonade that would be sold at the Plain City Fair. It was boring, tedious work, but I saved and saved.

I'd always planned on leaving, but that final beating was too much. Dad called me "a whore, just like your mother," which was about the worst thing he could have said. He would have killed me too, if

Mr. Tubbs hadn't stopped by for a pint when he did and pulled my father off me. That night I waited until my parents were asleep and then packed a bag by the illumination of the laundry sign outside my window. Then I quietly made my way to the door that led down to the street. When I stepped onto the landing, I heard my mom's voice.

"Grace."

She sat on a riser halfway down the stairs. I was caught. My stomach clenched.

"You're leaving," she said, rising to her feet. "I knew it was coming."

"How?"

"I'm your mother. You're the breath of my lungs and the beat of my heart. I know you very well."

"I can't stay here—"

"I understand. It's not safe for you any longer." She paused, then hurried on. "You should try San Francisco." I swallowed. Miss Miller had given me that idea when she'd shown me the advertisement for the Golden Gate International Exposition. "It's time you know the truth. I came to this country when I was five years old. I met your father in San Francisco when he was on his way to China to get a traditional wife. I was twenty-five—a spinster. I told him I wasn't familiar with Chinese beliefs or customs. He took my hand anyway. We went to the lumber camp, where I had you the next year."

I loved her, and a part of me wanted to learn more, but she was talking too long when I needed to get going. I started again down the stairs. When I reached her, she grabbed my arm.

"Wait!" she begged. "Oh, Grace, there's so much I want to tell you."

I hesitated again. If Dad heard us . . .

"Grace, always remember that a woman must take care of herself. Don't depend on a man." (Now, when I thought about what she'd said, I cursed myself for not listening or obeying.) "Never rely on a husband. You need to run away now, but I hope that one day you'll find a way to stop running."

Tears had blurred my vision. My mother was not only letting me go but giving me instructions for a lifetime.

"You'd better hurry," she advised. With that, she reached into her pocket, pulled out a wad of bills neatly folded in half, and pressed it into my hand. "It's seventy-two dollars."

Together with what I'd saved, I had one hundred and five dollars.

"Come with me," I said urgently.

Tears filled my mother's eyes. "I can't."

"You'll be free of him. We'll have each other—"

Mom shook her head. "It won't work. You barely have enough money for yourself." Her fingers caressed my wet cheek. "Now go, and don't ever look back. Don't write to me either. We don't want him to find out where you've gone." Then she walked up the stairs. She stopped at the door and turned to gaze down at me. "I barely remember *my* mother, but the last thing she said to me I'll say to you. *When fortune comes, do not enjoy all of it; when advantage comes, do not take all of it.*" Then she entered the apartment and quietly shut the door.

I hurried down the stairs and onto the deserted street, carrying my suitcase in one hand and cupping my sore ribs with the other. After a few minutes, I arrived at Miss Miller's studio. It was the middle of the night, and her lights were off. I went upstairs, knocked, and waited. She wasn't all that surprised to see me. I nervously stood with my back against the wall as she got dressed and grabbed her car keys. She drove us the twenty-four miles to Columbus. We sat together on a bench at the Trailways station until it was time for the first bus heading west to depart.

"Take care of yourself," she said. "Send me a postcard from the exposition."

We hugged, and she cried. She'd been so much more to me than just a dance teacher. She'd also trained me to focus, to think beyond Plain City, and to believe in myself. As the bus pulled out, I peered through the window, craning my neck, until she disappeared from sight. Then I turned in my seat and folded my hands tightly in my lap. I'd promised my mother I'd never look back, but I wouldn't forget a single kindness or moment of love that she'd shown me. Her courage and sacrifice were what sustained and nourished me—first in San Francisco and now here in Los Angeles.

I NEEDED TO be seen, so sometimes I tap-danced on the street outside the Brown Derby or Musso & Frank. A couple of men approached me to offer jobs in the movies. I realized right quick that they were just Hollywood smarties, trying to take advantage. I even had a couple of men saunter up to me and say things like "I have a Chrysler, cream-white, with red seats. Want to come to my place and read for me?" Ruby would have jumped at the chance to go to some man's bungalow in the hills, but not me.

At auditions, I overheard girls talk about the classes they were taking—dance, acting, singing, and locution to erase traces of accents so that they'd sound Hollywood bland. I used up the money in my wallet on four hours of classes a day. I got locked out of my room because I didn't pay the rent on time. I told the manager that if he let me in, then I could pay in full. I had the money so I shouldn't have let things get that bad, right? Except I'd vowed I wouldn't go into my envelope. Once I opened it, I easily returned to it a second, third, fourth time. I was crushed by my failure.

Twice a week, I rode the bus to Chinatown, where I could buy a bowl of soup, a salad, three pork chops, rice, vegetables, a big piece of apple pie, and a glass of milk for twenty cents at the Sam Yuen Café on Alameda. That meal could last in my stomach a day or two. (The rest of the time I ate mayonnaise sandwiches.) I learned that anti-Japanese sentiment was as strong here as it was in San Francisco Chinatown. Every time I was asked to give money to support Chinese war orphans, Ruby flooded my mind. Because no matter how much I fought it and no matter how many pliés I did, I couldn't stop myself from replaying that night again and again and again.

The worse I felt about the situation I'd put myself in here in Los Angeles, the more I held myself accountable for what had happened with Joe. He'd never seen me the way I'd seen him. He must have thought of me as Ruby's kid sister, which is why he'd taken me to see *The Wizard of Oz.* Weren't boys supposed to be nice to a little sister—buy her treats, take her to a fair, show interest in her activities—to impress the girls they were sweet on? Even at the time, I saw it, but I didn't let what was right in front of me sink in: the way Joe always stared at Ruby, the slightly weary tone in which he said, "You again. Great!" whenever I surprised him at Treasure Island, the way they sat together for *three* shows back to back at the Forbidden City. I thought he'd come to the club because of me, when it was all about her. I was still hurt, but the blame I put on myself was crushing, because Ruby had been right that night. They hadn't set out to hurt me. I'd acted like a dopey, lovesick kid and they'd both been trying to protect me, hoping I'd grow up enough so they could tell me the truth, like Ruby had said. I'd sure been unsuccessful in that department. Now I was friendless and failing—in a new city. Helen was right. *Consequences.* I never should have left San Francisco, but I was too ashamed to go back or even write to Helen. I was horribly lonely, but I refused to make new friends. *When you're so poor you don't know where your next meal is coming from,* I told myself in my fuzziness of hunger and disappointment, *you can't afford to have friends.*

In July—after I'd been in Los Angeles for five months—I fainted in ballet class. "I'm just tired," I explained to Maestro Kolmakov when I opened my eyes and found him hovering over me. *When you're poor, you don't tell anyone.*

"You're a good dancer," the maestro said as he helped me to a sitting position, "but your body is your instrument. You must take care of it. If you have a beautiful car and you don't put gas in it, it won't run. If you have a Lincoln Zepher convertible coupe and you put inferior gas in it, you'll ruin the engine. I live four blocks from here with my wife and sons. Have dinner with us tonight or you can't come to class tomorrow." He didn't want anything in return. I was reminded, once again, of human kindness.

Part Two

The Moon

August 1940–
September 1945

HELEN

Carried by the Wind

Things happened fast after Grace left. I'd always been second in the line, but Ida got promoted over me. That was all right. I couldn't see myself bringing pots of tea and kowtowing to the Lim Sisters every night as part of a five-dollar raise. And Ruby? Unemployed, and without Grace to help with the rent, she gave up her apartment and went back to live with her aunt and uncle in Alameda. We met once for tea, but it was awkward. I'd recognized what was going on between her and Joe months ago. Anyone could see—if they'd chosen to look—that they weren't exactly "in love." What they had was irresistible, wet, and uncontrollable. And *fffft*. Over. A raging fire doused. It wasn't personal or deep to Ruby, and maybe not even to Joe.

"I'm not seeing him anymore," Ruby told me, as though that would make her any less guilty in my eyes. "It burned us up to see Grace hurt like that."

I'd always been wary of Ruby. The reports coming out of China were worse every day. The barbarian monkey-people were burning, looting, and raping their way across my ancestral homeland. Maybe brutality was in the nature of *all* Japanese and therefore in Ruby's. Monroe had cautioned me: "You're going to get hurt." That it ended up being Grace instead of me made me feel like a sea slug on the ocean floor. I should have done a better job protecting her.

"Have you heard from Grace?" Ruby asked.

"No, and I don't have a way to reach her."

Grace and Ruby were like blossoms blown from a tree—carried by the wind, relying on goodness in Grace's case and wiles in Ruby's. They insisted that they'd endured so much, but I interpreted their tragedies differently. Grace's father had beat her; there were worse things in the world. Ruby's parents had wanted to return to Japan; good riddance. Grace went to seek her dream in Hollywood, Ruby would glitter wherever she was, while I had scars I would take to my grave.

"I miss the three of us being together," Ruby said.

A part of me enjoyed seeing her suffer, but later, as I watched her retreating, I was reminded just how fleeting life is. Love disappears. Friendships dissolve. I was alone once again.

IN AUGUST, SIX months after Grace left, business at the Forbidden City slowed even more. Charlie was so broke, he couldn't even change a twenty for a customer. Many of our acts moved to jobs either at other clubs in Chinatown or out on the road on what the show kids called the Chop-Suey Circuit. When Eddie got an offer to dance at the Club Casa del Mar—a private beach club and hotel in Santa Monica—he jumped at the chance. One problem: the run was for a duo.

"They want a Chinese Fred Astaire and Ginger Rogers," Eddie explained. "Now who wants to be my Ginger?"

I was quick to sign up for auditions because, first, I was looking at going back to work at the Chinese Telephone Exchange, and, second, if I got the job with Eddie, then I could search for Grace. (Ida laughed at me. "That will be like looking for a needle in a haystack.") Every girl saw this as an opportunity not just to go to Hollywood but to be with Eddie. You could practically hear the wedding gongs, cymbals, and firecrackers. Finally, he got around to me. All right, so I was last on *his* list, but when he took me in his arms I was able to follow the subtle pressure of his hand on my back, the way he leaned in to me, or he pulled me toward him. Afterward, he sat me down.

"You've changed a lot since you first started at the Forbidden

City," he said. "You used to be so shy, and you talked like you'd been raised in a moon-viewing pavilion overlooking a lake. I don't mean to insult you."

"You haven't." Because I *had* changed in the nearly two years since I'd first auditioned and Mr. Biggerstaff asked me to lift my skirt to see my legs. At the very least, I could now speak the lingo, so I sounded like I belonged in a nightclub.

"If you come with me," Eddie went on, "I won't have to deal with any goo-goo eyes coming from you, will I?"

"No goo-goo eyes," I promised.

Eddie still wasn't sure. He wanted to see if I could learn a complicated routine. *"Even metal and stone can be pierced by hard work,"* he recited, which reinforced my knowledge that he'd been raised by good and proper Chinese parents. We practiced in the afternoons before the Forbidden City opened for business. We worked on a ballroom number to "Night and Day"—a song I remembered Grace singing to herself. I soaked into my body every turn, every flick of the wrist, and every lift Eddie showed me. He wanted the dance to end with my back bent over his thigh and his head on my chest. It was a romantic and beautiful move, and it would look gorgeous when I wore a gown, which would drape on the floor around me. When we perfected the maneuver, he pulled me back to my feet, and then brought me into his arms. He stared into my face for a long moment, and then he kissed me. His lips were soft and delicate on mine. His mouth tasted like bourbon.

"You're doing a fabulous job," he said. "You look good."

"Thanks," I said, "but please don't do that again."

He hired me right then and there.

Baba made a stink, but I did my part by falling back on my tried-and-true helping-Monroe-with-his-tuition routine, which allowed us both to save face.

OUR CLUB CASA del Mar show went over big. Eddie was marvelous—his surprising height making his long lines seem even longer—and I made a solid partner, swaying around the floor by myself while he performed showy antics. The *Los Angeles Times* wrote: "Audiences were spellbound by Eddie Wu and Helen Fong's Oriental stylings. How long before we see this terpsichorean duo on the silver screen?"

A few nights into the run, I was in my dressing room pulling a stocking up my leg when I heard a knock at the door.

"Come in," I called.

The door opened, and there was Grace, holding the *L.A. Times* clipping in her hand like an offering. She'd lost a lot of weight and was now so thin that her hip bones protruded like twin ledges against the fabric of her tired evening gown. Her cheeks were hollow, and her complexion was pale and waxy. We may have been Chinese, but we were theater people now. I allowed myself to be hugged and kissed. Then we babbled about what a surprise this was, that the show was terrific, and wasn't it great to be together again? But it didn't take a diviner to see that Grace's spunk had been drawn from her.

"What's this?" Eddie stood in the doorframe, still in his tails. His big grin faded as he absorbed the changes in Grace. Without another word, he crossed the room and wrapped his arms around her. "It sure is swell to see you, kid."

She got a little weepy, but Eddie took care of that with more hugs and kisses followed by words of concern and encouragement.

"You never wrote," he said. "We all worried about you. Even Charlie."

"You mean he's forgiven me?" she asked.

"For cutting out that night? He was never mad at you. But, babe, you didn't need to do that. No guy is worth it. Believe me."

Grace blushed. "So everyone knows my business?" When neither Eddie nor I answered, she quickly changed the subject. "What are you two doing here?"

"You just saw what we're doing." Eddie scratched his chin. "The hotel wanted a novelty act, and we're providing it. They're paying good money."

"We want to get some movie work too," I added.

"Movie work." Grace frowned. "Boy, have I ever failed at that."

"Don't give us that look," Eddie chided. "No one ever said it would be easy. This business is all about breaks. Sometimes you get a good break. Sometimes you get a bad break. That's the breaks! So perk up! Laugh a little!"

"Every show business career has low points," she agreed tentatively. "It's easy to get down and beat yourself up. Even for big movie stars. You finish a movie, and then what? Will I ever work again? I love one thing about show business, though."

"Let me guess," Eddie said, game. "You work here, and you make friends. You work there, and you make new friends. Pretty soon you start bumping into those folks in clubs, theaters, and movie studios. And sometimes they pop up in the most surprising places, because our world isn't that big. See? Here we are!"

"Oh, Eddie." Grace's eyes brimmed with tears. "I've missed you all so much. Shoot! I've even missed Ida!"

WHEN THE TWO-WEEK gig at Casa del Mar ended, Grace invited me to move into her drab room in a boardinghouse in Hollywood. Eddie rented accommodations in the same building. So far, Grace hadn't asked about Ruby and had closed off any attempts by me to discuss her, but once we were roommates, the subject was unavoidable.

"We may as well get it out in the open," Grace volunteered when I started to unpack my suitcase. "How is she?"

"Ruby told me she felt terrible about what happened." I paused to get a sense of Grace's reaction. "She was heartbroken when you left."

"I was busted up too—"

"Grace, what can I say? The whole thing was horrible."

My words delivered sharp stabs into her heart. She *still* ached. I'd never realized a woman could not be married and feel so deeply.

"When I look back, Joe didn't actually do anything *to* me." I could see that she'd given this a lot of thought—months, alone, of thought. "He treated me like a smitten kid, and I was. Now I can say I've survived the agony of first love."

"And Ruby?"

"That's harder. We were friends. She should have told me. But then I think about how I reacted. No wonder she *didn't* tell me."

I took the framed photo that I'd wrapped in a sweater out of my suitcase and tucked them together in a drawer. "She'll want to hear that I found you."

"Don't tell her. Please? It's embarrassing enough that I acted like a dumb kid. It will humiliate me even more for her to know I'm down on my luck."

"All right then." I reached for her hand. "It'll be just the two of us—Grace and Helen."

EDDIE AND I made the rounds of the studios and had as little luck as Grace had. We had fun, though. Sometimes, after a disappointing day, Eddie would buy a pint and bring it back to Grace's and my room, where I'd make grilled peanut butter sandwiches on the hot plate. Cocktails and a gourmet meal! On Sundays, we splurged and had cornflakes and milk or maybe leftover rice with sugar and cream on top. Grace took us to a little place in Chinatown called Sam Yuen. The food was good and cheap, and the owner liked me because we spoke the same dialect. "If you girls ever want jobs . . ." As if I could ever be a waitress . . .

I thought we had it made when Eddie got us signed with a booking agent, Max Field, who agreed to represent the two of us as dance partners, Grace as a soloist, and Grace and me as a team. Max looked for all kinds of gigs: club dates, one-nighters, three-night stands. Grace and I got the first booking, doing a variation of "Let Me Play with It," which we'd once practiced with Ruby, for three weekends at the Florentine Gardens. Eddie and I got a couple of gigs too. One night I stayed home with a fever, and Grace stepped in as Eddie's partner at a floor show at La Rue. This gave Eddie an idea: "Let's put an act together for the three of us."

We bought time at a dance studio to work on a ballroom routine. Grace and Eddie loved Cole Porter, and they searched for the perfect tune—with a nice tempo and the right sentiment—before settling on "You'd Be So Easy to Love." Eddie took turns practicing lifts with Grace and me.

"Astaire and Rogers, Toy and Wing, Veloz and Yolanda—they all make lifts seem easy, but they aren't," Grace said one afternoon after she'd crashed on her behind for the ten thousandth time that day. How often did Eddie drop us on our shoulders, our hips, our heads, our knees? How often did we go flying through the air, slipping across the floor, banging into walls? We were covered with bruises. But no matter how often I found myself splayed on the floor, I got right up and moved back into Eddie's arms. I loved dancing with him. All the while, he stared into my eyes.

"You have to *feel* that we're in love." His voice burrowed into me. "Let the audience see that I'm seducing you and that you're weakening. The audience wants to know you're mine."

And I could play along, because it wasn't real.

Max saw the act and said we were great. Then he sat us down and pointed out the obvious: Eddie's evening dress—with the long coattails and broad lapels, the shirt with the stiff front, and the white tie—was frayed. Max was even tougher on Grace and me. "You two look kiddified. You're young, fine, but proper gowns will make you look elegant, polished, and sophisticated."

No one had ever called me "kiddified" before, and it was pretty insulting given how I'd been raised to have the nicest dresses in Chinatown and how I had so many beautiful *cheongsams* made for me in China. So Grace and I went out and I used the last of the money I'd brought with me to buy matching sequined chartreuse gowns—backless—which didn't look one bit kiddified. Max immediately got us booked to debut our act at the Vendome on Sunset Boulevard. "It isn't the Trocadero or the Mocambo," Eddie said, "but it's still a ritzy nightclub."

On the night of our show, Grace went to check the house. She returned bubbling: "Ida Lupino, Ann Sothern, and Randolph Scott are sitting at ringside tables!"

"No one would ever call them jaw-droppingly famous," Eddie sniffed, but I could tell he was pleased to have movie stars in the audience.

We billed ourselves as the Chinese Dancing Sweethearts. Grace and I wore our new sequined gowns, which caught the light and reflected into the audience. Eddie, in his new tuxedo with shimmering lapels, and his hair oiled to glisten, hoped to draw all the women's eyes to him. We flowed back and forth across the floor, embracing and releasing each other, and then coming together again. Eddie's choreography incorporated graceful arcs, sweeping shoulders, dramatic lifts, and deep knee bends. A dip here, and Eddie kissed me; a dip there, and he kissed Grace. For the finale, he put an arm around each of our waists, lifted us both off the floor, and twirled us in mesmerizing slow motion, showing not only our delicacy but his strength as a dancer and as a man. We earned back everything we'd spent on our costumes, but we were not asked to return.

"Why would one man dance with two girls?" the Vendome's manager asked after we performed. "What does it mean? Do Chinese girls do *that*?"

Max got us a few other bookings at second-rate joints, but splitting $17.50 a week between three people was no way to earn a living. The Chinese cooks in the club kitchens so pitied us that they gave us leftover ice cream and stale rolls. We'd take home our handouts, steam the rolls, and then dip them in the melted ice cream. I could have written home and asked for money, but I didn't want to give my father the satisfaction. Besides, to me, this was all still a big and fun adventure.

Then our luck took a turn for the worse. We were rejected again and again, with one kick in the pants after another. In October, Max finally managed to book a gig for us to do programmers—putting on our act before shows at the Orpheum movie palace, right across the street from where Ruby had told us she lived with her parents when she was a girl. This was the last gasp of vaudeville, and our trio was slotted between a jumping dog act and an old woman who should have abandoned burlesque a long time ago. We tried to be better than the other performers, but the audience just wanted the movie to start.

One night, after two weeks of shows, Eddie fell into a dark mood. We were backstage, the film was playing, and it reflected on us in reverse. Eddie sat on a wooden crate, put his elbows on his knees, and stared at the floor.

"I've been working as an entertainer for a long time, and I'm right back where I started," he said, his voice dry and black. "My father was a doctor, and he expected me to become one too. When I was in my first year at Yale medical school, I'd go to the local speakeasy, where they held dance contests as part of their cover. The first prize was fifteen bucks. What I'd do for that now."

I put a hand on his shoulder. "Come on, Eddie. Let's go home."

When he shrugged me off, Grace and I grabbed a couple of stools and pulled them next to him. We gathered our skirts and draped them over our knees to keep them from slipping onto the filthy floor.

"I used to go down to New York on weekends to see Fred and Adele Astaire on Broadway. I'd watch the show three times in a single weekend. I'd practice what I'd seen on the sidewalk. Then I'd go up to Harlem and watch Bill Robinson, Peg Leg Bates, the Nicholas Brothers—"

"I saw Bill 'Bojangles' Robinson in *The Little Colonel* at the Rialto," Grace interrupted. "I didn't much care for Shirley Temple, but I loved Bill Robinson—"

"I'd go in the alley behind the Cotton Club between shows," Eddie continued, "where the guys would be smoking, drinking, showing off to each other. It's 1925, and you just can't believe who's dancing there—"

Nineteen twenty-five? I was only seven years old then. If he was in medical school in 1925, he would have been somewhere around twenty-two years old. That meant he had to be about thirty-seven now. I glanced at Grace. She blinked back at me: *Holy smokes!*

Eddie ran a hand through his hair. "My dad has family connections in New York Chinatown, and he sets me up for a job in a clinic over winter break, because he wants me to get experience. Instead, I visit my buddies over at the Cotton Club. 'You gotta help me, man,' I tell them. They send me to a speak down on Fifth. When I walk in there, the headman looks at me like I've got a screw loose, but they've got a good band and I start dancing on the floor—alone, among all the couples. Pretty soon they're backing away, giving me plenty of space. They dig it! They start throwing money at me. It's raining coins and bills. I make picking up the money and putting it in my pockets part of the act. I make more dough in those five minutes than I would have made in five days working for my dad's friend. The music ends, and I'm still picking up money. The headman comes over and says, 'You dance like that five times a night and you got a job.'" Eddie lifted his chin. "Do either of you have a drink on you?"

Of course not.

"But it's a speak," he went on, "so we're raided a lot. I'm dancing in my tails, while everyone else is running for the back door. Then it was time to go back to Yale."

Eddie lifted his head. He seemed tormented by memories. "My dad wants me to shadow him as he takes care of his patients. He was one of the first Chinese to attend medical school in America. I'm proud of him, but I don't want to be a doctor. I don't want to deliver babies or lance boils. One night I ask my mom to come to my room. I open my box with all the money I made in the speak. She asks, 'Who did you rob?' Not long after that I leave for Hollywood. My first job you wouldn't believe. I'm dancing at the opening of Grauman's Chinese Theatre, and then before every movie showing. It seems like a big accomplishment, but it's actually not my big break. I get a solo in a movie. I leap off a piano and land in a split. Everyone tells me that will become my signature move. I thought I had it made."

"That is your signature move," I said, "and you do have it made. You're just going through a rough patch—"

"I understand, Eddie," Grace interrupted. "With every good opportunity that comes along, I get the sense I'll only go so far. Even if I do get a part in a movie, it will be as a maid or dragon lady. And even if I succeed, I'll always be compared to—"

"I don't want to be a copy of someone else," Eddie grumbled. "I don't want to be the Chinese Fred Astaire. There are enough imitators already. I mean, how many Chinese Fred Astaires can there be? I don't want to be the Chinese Bill Robinson either."

Grace sympathized. "Who hasn't heard of the Betty Grable Legs of Chinatown, the Chinese Sophie Tucker, the Chinese Houdini, or the Chinese Bing Crosby?"

"Isn't that just shorthand?" I asked, trying to be business-practical. "Isn't it a way for customers and casting directors to put people like us into a recognizable box—"

"Like if you can't afford Errol Flynn, you put a man in tights, give him a bow and arrow, and throw a felt hat with a feather in it on top of his head, and people will make the connection?" Eddie asked bitterly.

So I'd insulted him.

"I want to be recognized for who *I* am and for what *I* do." He sighed. "I was hired to play a Hawaiian, an Indian, and a Japanese. They never wanted me to play a Chinese, because they said I didn't look Chinese enough. I didn't look right to play a waiter, houseboy, or hatchet man. I can't win," he said, anger surfacing. "Even Charlie Chan's Number One Son never gets the girl. So here I am, flanked by two babes. But that brings the other stereotype—that Chinese men are oversexed, and we're going to rape white women and pollute the race. If that weren't enough, we'll never make what other entertainers make. Hell, we'll never make what Negro entertainers make. Back at the Cotton Club, Ethel Waters and the Nicholas Brothers earned about a thousand bucks a week. Bill Robinson made thirty-seven hundred big ones. Charlie and the other club owners will never pay us anything close to that. Never!"

On the way home, Eddie stopped at a liquor store and bought a quart of gin. When we got back to the apartment building, he didn't invite us to share it with him.

HELEN

A Tide of Emotions

By Thanksgiving, we were "on the beach"—no work, no bookings in sight. Our dinner that night: ten cents' worth of buns picked up in Chinatown. Grace and I needed jobs, but getting employment anywhere—as Americans who looked Chinese—felt as futile as plowing the sand and sowing the waves. That said, on the Monday after Thanksgiving, Grace and I lucked (ha!) into positions making hot fudge sundaes at C. C. Brown's on Hollywood Boulevard, a block from Grauman's Chinese Theatre and practically across the street from the Hollywood Roosevelt Hotel. The job allowed us to eat a little, and sometimes people left us nickel tips under their saucers. The manager, Tim McNulty, was nice. He was tall, soft-spoken, and kept his hair neatly trimmed. I'd never worked in a restaurant before, but Tim was patient and easygoing, teasing me about the deliberate way I sprinkled the slivered almonds and set the cherry just so. And really, making and serving hot fudge sundaes to people hungry for a mouth-happy experience wasn't all that bad.

When Tim asked me out just four days into the job, I surprised myself by accepting. I was lonely, and I'd been lonely for a very long time. I liked having a man take my hand when I got out of the car, hold my elbow when we walked on the street, put an arm around my shoulder when we sat in the movie theater. Hours later, Tim kissed me on the front porch of the boardinghouse. It wasn't like Eddie's performance kisses. I'd never kissed a *lo fan* before, and it made me wonder if everything would be different with him. The next day, when I went to work, he was attentive without being overbearing. A sensation of light burning the edges of my loneliness allowed me to say yes to a second date a couple of days later. We didn't do anything fancy—no big night on the town—because he didn't have much money either. He was just a sweet man, who invited me back to his apartment after dinner. His room was clean and orderly. The way he made love to me . . . His skin was so white against mine, and for a few minutes I forgot everything as a familiar warmth started to overwhelm me, washing me to the precipice . . . Then, from deep inside me, I felt darkness well up and brutally grasp my heart. Inwardly I pulled back, but I had nowhere to escape. I didn't try to get Tim to stop. I forced my body to go numb and waited for the final spasms of pleasure to shudder through him. And then, and then . . .

I began to cry. How could I have let Tim touch me at all? I knew that making love could be good and comforting for wives and mothers, but this was a terrible mistake for me. I'd been trying to quench my thirst by looking at plums, console myself with what could be, but now I felt wretched.

"It's all right," Tim comforted, but he couldn't possibly understand my feelings. I sat up, making sure the sheet kept me decent, and began pulling on my clothes. The whole time, he kept talking. "Don't go. Don't leave like this."

When I put on my shoes and stood, he slipped out of the bed too. Naked. I covered my eyes.

"I'm not this person," I said. "I don't do this."

Tim got dressed and drove me back to my apartment, even though I said it was unnecessary. He offered to come up and sit with me until I felt better. I said no. He asked if he could bring me anything. I said no to that too.

I told Grace what I'd done, and she was about as shocked as a country-bumpkin virgin could be.

"At least he's nice," she said, acting like she knew all about it. "That's how it's supposed to be, right? You do it with someone nice? Are you going to see him again?"

"We both have work tomorrow, so I guess so."

But it was hard making hot fudge sundaes with Tim coming up to me and whispering, "Are we square? I'm so sorry you're taking it this way. Can we go out later and talk about it? Oh, Helen, I thought you enjoyed it."

I wanted to stick it out, but I quit at the end of my shift. I had lasted as a sundae-maker exactly one week and a day.

"Okay," Grace said, "we'll find other jobs."

"You don't have to leave—"

"Of course I do! We're sticking together!"

We went to Sam Yuen in Chinatown that night. When the owner made his customary offer of employment, Grace and I accepted. If my father saw me, he would have died from shame.

A COUPLE OF days later, Eddie banged on Grace's and my door. When I let him in, he threw the new issue of *Life* magazine on the coffee table. The cover showed a pair of long legs that went up, up, up until they reached a giant bubble that covered . . . well, what it covered was left to the imagination. The woman's face was obscured—turned alluringly away from the camera lens—but the headline billed her as PRINCESS TAI—STAR OF SAN FRANCISCO'S HOT SPOT—THE FORBIDDEN CITY. The three of us squeezed together on the love seat and pored over the pages, looking first at the photographs.

"Hey! Irene and Jack!" Eddie's breath told me he'd been drinking. "I bet she's learned all his tricks by now."

"Seems like Ida's put on a few pounds," I observed.

"Charlie and Bob Hope?" Grace exclaimed.

The writer labeled Princess Tai the world's only Chinese bubble dancer. "She's straight from China," Eddie read, his words slurring. "When she moves that pale orb just so, visitors imagine they can see all the way to China. They don't, but the looking sure is fun."

"Everyone reads *Life,*" Grace said, "which means everyone is going to see this, which means everyone is going to visit the Forbidden City, which means Charlie's troubles are over—"

"Do you think we could go back?" I asked, hopeful.

But Eddie was like a frog at the bottom of a well, limited in his perspective and seeing only what he wanted to see. "Max is working on things," he said. "He'll get us something."

But even with all the holiday shows, Max couldn't get us a single booking. No one wanted Chinese faces ruining their holiday tableaux.

ON CHRISTMAS DAY, the weather was perfect—warm and sunny—but little cheer brightened Grace's and my room. We had a tree eighteen inches high, which we'd decorated with homemade popcorn strings, a box of miniature red balls the size of holly berries, and the cheapest tinsel we could buy. Eddie arrived with a pot of winter melon soup he'd thrown together on his burner. I gave Grace some rouge; she gave me a hat she'd knitted. I gave Eddie a necktie; Grace gave him a scarf she'd knitted. Eddie gave Grace and me a one-pound box of See's Candies to share.

It all felt bleak, but not as bleak as New Year's Eve. Eddie made plans of his own, so Grace and I got dressed up and spent the evening walking along Hollywood Boulevard. We saw happy couples swirling into the Hollywood Roosevelt Hotel for a night of dancing, drinking, and entertainment. We saw revelers weaving along the sidewalks. When midnight came, we made rosy predictions for the new year. After that, we had nothing to do but go back to the boardinghouse. When we turned onto Ivar, we came upon two policemen roughing up a man in evening dress—Eddie—while another ran down the street.

"This may be New Year's Eve, but we won't stand for any basketeers on our beat," a cop the size of an ox growled as he shoved Eddie against a fence.

Eddie started to say something, but the second cop cut him off. "You'll keep your yap buttoned if you know what's good for you."

Then he balled his fist and slammed it into Eddie's stomach. Eddie doubled over and fell to the ground.

"Brownie!"

"Fairy!"

I rushed forward, kneeled next to Eddie, searched his face, and then turned to glare up at the cops.

"What are you doing?" I demanded. "Who do you think you are?"

The ox smirked at us. "And who do you think *you* are? A pair of buttered beards?"

Grace looked thoroughly confused—like the cop was speaking in a foreign tongue.

"They're the anchors around my neck," Eddie moaned from the ground. Then, from somewhere deep within him, he managed to chuckle.

"He's with us," I said. "He had too much to drink, and we got separated. New Year's . . ."

The cops hassled us a bit more—talking way over Grace's head—before finally letting us go. Grace and I helped Eddie to his feet. We each took one of his arms and proceeded up Ivar to where we lived. I went through Eddie's pockets, found his key, and opened his door.

"Helen, you sure saved my bacon," he mumbled, thankful, as we laid him on his bed.

I left his key on the nightstand.

When Grace and I got to our room, I was scared *and* mad. "How dare they talk to Eddie like that! And did you see the way that one cop slugged him! We should report him."

"How would we go about reporting him? And what was that all about anyway? What's a basketeer?"

I cleared my throat and said what needed to be said. "Eddie doesn't like girls."

Grace shook her head, confounded.

"You know what I mean," I said. "He's a momma's boy."

Grace still didn't get it.

"He's swishy," I explained. "A fruit. A lavender." I used American slang, hoping it might help her catch on.

Grace looked like her eyes were going to pop out of her head and hop down Hollywood Boulevard, as Ruby might say, but that doesn't mean she believed me. She listed the proof I was wrong: "He went out with the ponies at the Forbidden City. He danced with our female customers. He has you as his partner. He kisses us in our routine."

"He's the Chinese Fred Astaire, but that doesn't mean he isn't a basketeer."

"What is that anyway?"

I sighed. "A basketeer is a man who likes to stare at other men's . . . baskets. They like to look at the outline of—"

Grace put up a hand to keep me from saying any more. "How do you know?"

"I grew up in San Francisco. A city. Maybe that's why I always knew what Eddie was." As an afterthought, I added, "Who doesn't have a funny uncle?"

"A funny uncle? We didn't have anyone *like that* in Plain City." Grace considered. "Well, maybe the man who ran the hamburger stand . . . Helen! Are you sure?"

I nodded.

"And you like Eddie anyway?"

"He's my friend and my dance partner. I respect him and he brought me here. And, Grace, remember all the things he's done for you. He's not any different than he was this morning when we woke up."

Grace scrunched her face like a hedgehog. Finally, she shook her shoulders, letting all the tension go. Then she gave me a frank stare. "Do you think all men in this business are basketeers or fairies or whatever? Because that would explain a lot."

THE FIRST TWO months of 1941 were desolate, unpromising, and endless. I felt forlorn and hopeless, taking the bus back and forth from Chinatown to work, going out for auditions that went nowhere, and worrying about money. Grace wasn't a bowlful of peonies either. "How many plates of rice and pork chops can you serve when your dreams are limitless?" she asked one day.

The longer the night lasts, the more capricious our dreams will be.

At the end of February, I was laid low by a stomach bug. I curled up on the love seat, slept, couldn't go out. After a couple of days, Grace began to study me the way she used to scrutinize the ponies at the Forbidden City.

"What?" I asked. "Why are you staring at me like that?"

"Helen," she said as she sat on the floor next to the love seat. "You know what's wrong with you? You're pregnant."

"Pregnant?"

"Think about it. Have you had your period?"

I made the calculations. I hadn't had a visit from the little red sister in . . . I tallied my other symptoms . . . "*Aiya!*" I dug my nails into my palms, fighting the impulse to cry.

Grace took me to a doctor, who confirmed the diagnosis. I was with child. A tide of emotions sucked me up, spinning and tossing me until I could barely think.

"You've got to tell Tim," Grace said, although I don't know what she thought that would accomplish. Still, I allowed myself to be taken to C. C. Brown's. Grace waited at the counter while Tim and I talked in the storage room.

"I can't marry you," he said. "It's against the law. I'm sorry."

"That's all you have to say?"

"Look, it's clear you had experience in this. I hate to say it out loud, but I know I wasn't your first."

I guess bailing and not taking responsibility—no matter what the circumstances—was to be expected from a *lo fan.*

Eddie offered to beat up Tim, which gave us a good laugh. Eddie said he'd find someone who could "help" me, but my soul screamed at the idea.

"I can't have a back-alley abortion," I said. "I just can't."

Grace suggested I go to an unwed mothers' home, have the baby, give it up for adoption, and then resume my life.

"Even girls in Plain City had to do that sometimes," she said.

"But did you have half-breeds back there?" I asked. Grace's eyes widened as that sank in. "The baby's going to be a mongrel. Half and half." Just saying the words made me sick to my stomach.

"What will it look like?" Grace inquired, horribly boorish.

"I have no idea. Ugly?"

Grace and Eddie stayed with me. They gave me tissues when I cried. They brought me soup and soda crackers. Despair paralyzed me. I couldn't have an abortion. I couldn't give away the baby. And I couldn't go home to the compound with an illegitimate half-breed. When Grace went to work, I unwrapped the framed photo that was folded inside the sweater I'd tucked in the middle drawer on my first day here and took it back to the love seat. I stretched out with my feet on the armrest and the photo propped on my stomach and resting against my thighs. I was alone and scared, but deep inside I felt *life*—a tiny dot, scratching, grating, growing, needing me, needing love. I enveloped that tiny dot in layers of imaginary wool, straightened my shoulders, and took a deep breath. I knew what I could do. I just needed my friends to go along with it.

A WEEK LATER, the three of us went to the courthouse so Eddie and I could get married. I wore a nice dress. Eddie looked suave in his fawn-colored sports jacket and chestnut-brown wool trousers. Grace was our witness. The ceremony was over in five minutes. When we got back to Grace's and my apartment, Eddie sat next to me on the love seat. My tiny bouquet lay on the cushion between us. None of us had much to say. It wasn't exactly wedding bells and tulle. Eddie was helping me out of a jam, and I could be a cover for his "interests."

Finally, he slapped his thighs. "I guess it's time for me to go." He stood. "We don't want to push you out, Grace. I'll sleep in my apartment for now."

"I wish this were more joyous for you, Helen," Grace said once Eddie closed the door behind him.

I jutted my chin. "It's all right."

"When you're thirty," she went on glumly, "he's going to be nearing fifty. When you're fifty, he's going to be—"

"My baba's a lot older than my mama. That's how it's supposed to be—"

"In the Chinese tradition," Grace finished for me. Then, "It's not even *his* child."

"That doesn't matter to me."

"Won't your parents figure out the baby is"—she struggled for a polite way to say what was impolite in any circumstance—"half and half? Your father has an eye for these things."

"Maybe he'll just see a grandson."

LITTLE CHANGED IN our lives. I wrote to Mama and Baba about my marriage; two weeks later, a boxed set of Canton ware with twelve place settings was delivered to our door. I let a proper interval elapse before I sent a telegram announcing my pregnancy; in the return mail I received from my mother a crisp twenty-dollar bill to use to buy maternity smocks and a note advising me to suck on salted preserved plums to settle any morning sickness I might experience.

Eddie and Grace switched rooms, but we still ate our meals together. Eddie went out for auditions and drank alone. After the lunch shift at Sam Yuen, I'd walk to the Kong Chow Temple to pray, make offerings, and beg for a son.

"But girls are so adorable!" Grace squawked.

"Every Chinese woman wants a son," I explained. "What is a daughter but a disappointment?"

"You don't mean that," Grace chided, but I meant exactly what I'd said.

"A fact is a fact." I sighed, trying to sound Chinese-practical when inside I was desperate. "A girl is a worthless branch on the family tree."

Grace listened and did her best to sympathize. "You should be happy. You have a husband. You're going to have a baby. Can't you see how lucky you are?"

We made some halfhearted attempts to revive our spirits, but the heaviness of sorrow, anger, and failure had overwhelmed us. There were things I wanted to tell Grace, but I didn't know where to begin. She wanted to run away again—I could tell—but she had nowhere to go. And Eddie? Perhaps we all wanted to go our separate ways, but as Grace put it one night—rather sullenly, I might add—"We're locked together as so many entertainers get stuck with bandmates, dance partners, and costars." As though we were nothing more than that.

AT THE END of April, a telegram arrived for Eddie from Charlie Low, whose fortunes truly had changed thanks to that *Life* cover story. He offered the Chinese Dancing Sweethearts three hundred dollars a week as headliners. It was still nothing compared to what Bill Robinson earned, but three hundred dollars a week for our trio was huge money.

"I'd give anything to return to San Francisco," Grace implored. (Unspoken: "to get away from this misery.")

"We'll never get in the movies if we go back to the Forbidden City," Eddie said weakly.

"Movies?" I scoffed, and I hoped this wasn't a sign that I was going to turn into one of those wives who belittled her husband for not planting the rice in even rows. "We have a baby coming. I want to go home. If you won't take the job at the Forbidden City, then we'll work at a different club in Chinatown."

"If I have to work at a Chinese club, then I want it to be the best." Eddie surrendered, bowing to my wishes.

Two days later, we packed our bags, took a bus to Union Station, and boarded a train to Oakland. Naturally, I worried about how Baba would react to Eddie, but I was even more anxious about how my husband would fit into the household. When we reached my family compound, we walked together through the interior courtyard to the back building. I opened the door. Baba, wearing his usual suit, sat in an overstuffed chair, reading the Chinese newspaper. Mama perched on a window seat, her bound feet resting on a small footstool. A cluster of my nieces and nephews played jacks in a corner.

"Helen's here!" one of them squealed.

Then they were all up and rushing at us from this and other rooms, proving the saying: *The house is like a marketplace.*

"Let me see this husband," Baba ordered, but fortunately his demand was lost in the whirlwind.

"You're not showing yet," Mama said, barely audible above the din.

"Did you bring presents?" one of the children asked.

"Did you meet any movie stars?" a sister-in-law inquired shyly.

"Have you eaten yet?" Mama beckoned me farther into the room with the traditional greeting. "Does your husband drink tea?"

"Will you name the baby after Ahpaw or Yeye?" my oldest brother's little boy asked.

"I doubt Helen will name her baby after your grandma or grandpa," Washington informed his son. "Just like I didn't name you after your *yeye*. Would you rather be called Jack or Do Keung?"

"Jack," the boy admitted and ran to his mother.

Monroe drifted up to Grace. I heard him whisper, "No hard feelings, I hope."

What could she possibly say to that except "None whatsoever"?

He picked up Grace's suitcase, and we went to my room, where a cot had been wedged between my bed and the window.

"The cot's for Grace," Monroe explained, "until she can find a place of her own."

With all the rooms in the compound they couldn't find a spot for my friend?

Everyone jammed around us to take stock of the new brother-in-law and inspect the girl who'd tagged along with the newlyweds.

Washington took charge. "Take a few minutes to freshen up, then please return to the living room. Dinner will be served shortly." Not much of a warm welcome—perfunctory at best—but I guess that was to be expected.

After everyone filed out, Eddie went in the bathroom to change. When he came out, he sat on the bed, pulled out a flask, and took two deep swigs.

"I don't want to go out there by myself," I said to him.

He gave me a steady look and then swiped another gulp from the flask.

"I'll go with you," Grace volunteered.

But when we got to the living room, Washington gestured to the kitchen door. I expected this too, and automatically obeyed. Grace followed me into the kitchen, where Mama directed all the activity. My sisters-in-law chopped, peeled, and obediently obeyed orders, while little kids ran in and out between their legs. Mama asked me to set the table—in Chinese so Grace wouldn't understand. Rude. But I guided Grace to the compound's dining room, which had one long table to accommodate thirty relatives plus guests. We set the table. People found their seats, and dishes started to stream out of the kitchen: almond chicken, roast duck, scrambled eggs with *char siu,* minced pork with pickled vegetables, tofu with black mushrooms, steamed fish with ginger, scallions, and cilantro. It wasn't a fancy meal—just home cooking—but the clatter of chopsticks on the sides of rice bowls, the noisy slurping of tea, and the spitting out of bones and inedible bits all made me very happy.

Eddie still hadn't appeared, and I could see Baba growing increasingly agitated, but Monroe was swell, sitting between Grace and me, putting tiny morsels from the main dishes into our rice bowls. (Could there be hope for Grace and Monroe yet? Doubtful . . . but maybe?) Baba and my other brothers talked among themselves; my sisters-in-law circulated to make sure the serving dishes never emptied, the teacups stayed full, and the children didn't do anything to upset their elders, while I fretted the edge of my napkin. Where was Eddie? Why did he have to humiliate me this way? He came from a good family. Didn't he know the effect his tardiness would have on his father-in-law?

Eddie finally appeared and took the empty seat next to Baba. My father rapped his knuckles on the table to get everyone's attention. The family fell silent as he congratulated me on my marriage and expressed "delight" at the forthcoming birth of his next grandchild through tight lips. Then Baba turned his attention to Eddie.

"Thank you for bringing our daughter home," he intoned. "Now that she's married, she won't be in nightclubs anymore."

Before Eddie could respond, I said, "Ba, the three of us have an act. I'm going back to the Forbidden City with my husband and Grace."

"Not possible!" Baba practically roared.

"I'm afraid it is, sir."

Baba turned to the man with the unfamiliar voice—my husband—and scowled. "It's bad enough I have a daughter who shows her legs and arms in public, but a *married* daughter? And pregnant too? Who do I have for a son-in-law, who would allow his wife to expose herself that way?"

"I'm not exposing myself," I said.

Baba blew air from his nose like a water buffalo trying to chase away gnats. "I might have known something like this would happen."

"Ba, I came home—"

"What use is a man who wears a coat of paint?" Baba asked, referring to Eddie. "He is a veneer with secrets inside."

I guess it was too much to have hoped that Baba wouldn't have asked around about who his daughter had married.

Baba raised his index finger. "Let me tell you what success is."

Monroe gave me a nudge and made a face which sent a message: *Here he goes.*

"It's what you accomplish over the course of a lifetime," Baba began. "You get married and you have children. Eventually, they grow up and take care of you. When you die, your children and grandchildren make offerings to you in the afterworld. Are you going to do that for me?"

"Are you asking, sir, how much money Helen and I will give you each month?" Eddie asked.

Baba stiffened. "All my children give to the family pot. It's their duty to give and mine to receive. You'll be living here, and soon I'll have to feed three of you. It's tradition—"

"Helen and I don't follow that old way of thinking," Eddie interrupted.

"You will, if you want to live with us."

"We don't want to live here." Eddie surveyed the other men at the table—my brothers—and then his eyes came to rest on my father. "I'll be earning enough for us to move very soon. We'll still send you money each month out of respect, but we won't put everything in your family pot."

We'd see about all that.

RUBY

Wisps of Clouds

A woman isn't just one thing. The past is in us, constantly changing us. Heartache and failure shift our perspectives as do joy and triumphs. At any moment, on any given day, we can be friends, competitors, or enemies. We can be generous or stingy, loving or petty, helpful or untrustworthy. Looking back, I had plenty of regrets. I'd told myself I was protecting Grace by not telling her about Joe, because I knew how hurt she'd be. I still believed my heart had been in the right place, but how the truth came out and how I handled things that awful night weren't at all sensitive to Grace's feelings. I'd been so harsh, trying to teach her a lesson about grown-ups and growing up. But teaching a lesson isn't a part of friendship. Neither is being cruel. Now, as I sat in the shadows of the Forbidden City's main room, watching Grace, Helen, and Eddie walk through the lobby and into the kitchen to go to the dressing rooms, I wondered what faces my friends would show me and I would show them. I knew *I* had changed a lot, but what about them?

A few minutes later, they returned to the main room in their costumes. Charlie came out of his office and greeted them like lost children who'd been found—as though bringing them back here had been his idea. My friends took their positions, and the band began to play the Chinese Dancing Sweethearts' music. The routine's ending was perfect, with Eddie swirling Helen and Grace, their skirts flowing like wisps of clouds around them.

"I don't get it," Charlie said as the last notes died and Helen and Grace came back to their feet.

Eddie tried to be enthusiastic. "It's great! It's unique."

"It's unique all right. It's queer, and I don't like it." Charlie pressed his chin between a thumb and forefinger. "I'll keep the married team together. Grace, one of the ponies went to the hospital last night with appendicitis. You can take her place."

She looked like she'd been slapped, but she didn't seem to have the will to put up much of a fight.

"I don't know the routines," she murmured meekly after a long pause.

"Even on your worst day, you're a better dancer than my other ponies. And fifty a week is more than you earned when you left."

"But that's a lot less than what you said I'd get paid—"

"As one of the Chinese Dancing Sweethearts," Charlie finished for her. "Now hurry along to the dressing room. One of the girls will show you the costumes." He pushed his chair away from the table and stood. "It's great to have the three of you back."

Eddie refused to surrender. "I choreographed this routine and it's good."

Charlie ignored the comment. "Come to my office when you've decided what you want to do, and we'll go over the final details."

As he walked away, Eddie turned to Helen and Grace. "At least I won't have to lift you two cows anymore," he spat out resentfully.

I understood how he felt. Within a few minutes of his return, Eddie's hopes had been crushed. But it couldn't have been a breeze for Helen or Grace either. I'd heard that Helen and Eddie were married—what a joke—and she would have to deal with his disappointment, as wives do, while Grace was out on her ear. I'd fought with Charlie about this. I'd made a plan to bring them back to the Forbidden City, he'd implemented it, and it had looked like it was going to work until that damn Lily got sick last night. Charlie asking the Chinese Dancing Sweethearts to show him their dance had been an unnecessarily pitiless ruse.

"Why get Grace's hopes up when you're going to put her in the line?" I'd asked.

"I'm the boss here," he'd reminded me.

Now, instead of being a headliner, Grace was bumped back to a pony. Tough break. The old Grace would have reminded Charlie that she'd been the head of the line, that she had seniority, or *something*, but Los Angeles seemed to have knocked the stuffing out of her.

"You're not going to be able to dance forever," I heard Grace say pointedly to Helen. "You should have told Charlie you're pregnant."

Eddie a father? That's a good one.

Eddie took Helen's arm and led her to Charlie's office, leaving Grace alone. I emerged from the shadows, put a peacemaking smile on my face, and tapped her shoulder. Grace turned. For a flash of a second her face lit up, then just as quickly went pale. She folded her arms protectively over her chest.

"Ruby," she said, her voice flat. "What are you doing here?"

"Dancing, of course."

We stared at each other, soaking up the subtle changes the last fourteen months had brought. Did I want to weep because I still regretted hurting her, because I was so relieved to see her, or because she was so clearly unhappy to see me?

"I wish you hadn't left the way you did," I said. "You never gave me a chance to explain."

"There's nothing to explain. I saw you and Joe making love. I was childish. I didn't react well."

"Grace, I'm so sorry about what happened—"

"We'll have to talk later," she said, ignoring my apology. "I have to replace one of the ponies. Will you show me the costumes?"

We pushed through the velvet curtain and into the backstage area. The two of us spoke with false politeness, jumping over weeks and months of details.

"How do you keep your figure? You're always so slim."

"Look who's talking. You're a knockout, but then you always were."

We entered the dressing room, and Grace spotted Irene, nursing her kid.

"This is Ronny," Irene said in greeting.

Grace peeked at the wiggler and made all the predictable cute-baby comments. Ida, the only other original dancer still working as a pony, gave Grace a casual salute. I quickly rattled off the names of the new ponies, but they barely acknowledged Grace.

"You're replacing Lily." I showed Grace the clothes rack. "These were her costumes. Now they're yours. Here's your first outfit." I pulled a sequined *cheongsam* hemmed to barely cover a girl's can off the rack. "As soon as you've changed, come visit me."

When I reached my section of mirror, I glanced at my reflection. My hair was piled on top of my head and my usual pair of white gardenias were pinned above my left ear. My eyes drifted across the glassy surface to see Grace shimmy out of her gown and slip into the costume for the opening number. She checked her makeup, decided it would do, and then came to the far end of the dressing room to where I was getting ready—only I wasn't putting on clothes. I was taking them off and applying makeup over my arms. I caught Grace's eyes in the mirror.

"I'm Princess Tai," I said.

Grace's mouth opened in a surprised *oh*! How could she still be so slow on the uptake?

"You're the one who was on the cover of *Life*? *That* Princess Tai?"

"Didn't you recognize me?"

She shook her head. "We couldn't see the dancer's face—"

"That was the idea. To keep the mystery." I giggled. "It's crazy, isn't it? When this place first opened, Charlie wouldn't hire me. Then he did everything he could to hire me." I chattered because I was jittery about seeing Grace. "When the exposition reopened, I went back to work at Sally Rand's. It was touch-and-go there for a while, though. Everyone still thought the exposition could go belly-up for good, but Billy Rose's Aquacade turned around everyone's fortunes. Have you heard of it?"

"No."

"Hand me my eyelashes, will ya? They're in that little box on the left. See? Thanks. As I was saying, the show starred Johnny Weissmuller. You know, Tarzan in the movies? They also hired this seventeen-year-old girl named Esther Williams. They were a huge hit. People came back to the exposition again and again to see that kid swim. Afterward, they came to the Gayway. Even Charlie came to give it the eyeball." I turned my head and confided, "The Forbidden City was dying on the vine back then. No one was coming. Here," I said, holding a sponge out to Grace. "Help me with my backside. Make sure the makeup goes on evenly."

Grace stared at the sponge. The other girls watched to see what she would do. Ida was frozen in place, probably praying that she'd be released from this task. Bringing tea to the Lim Sisters and doing little chores to make them feel special was fine for them, but I was Princess Tai! I was famous! Another performer might have asked for fresh-cut papaya and pineapple, but again, I was Princess Tai. There aren't a lot of special benefits in this business, so I took what I could get. Making another girl powder my body and glue a flesh-colored piece of silk over my fun zone seemed just the ticket. It reminded every girl in the room that I was the top-billed star. But why would I ask Grace to perform this job? I'd orchestrated her return to the club, because I missed her *and* I wanted her to see what I'd become. She'd always thought she was the better dancer, but I was a star now. How can you be a star if you don't act like one and have people love you and take care of you?

Grace dabbed the sponge in foundation and smoothed it down my back, over my rear, and along my legs like some kind of automaton. I picked up a pouf from the counter, dipped it into a yellow Bakelite container, and patted powder on my chest, breasts, and down my stomach. Clouds of powder wisped away from my naked body and drifted across the room, causing the other girls to brush at their costumes and stare daggers at me in the mirror. Maybe I deserved it, but Grace remained oblivious to the discontent around us. The kid had surrendered to me that easily and completely. I felt bad that she'd so lost her spark and fight.

"Charlie needed something—or someone—to spice things up," I twittered nervously. " 'Come back to my place,' he said. 'You'll be a headliner, but I can only pay you fifty a week, because you're . . .' " I leaned down and whispered in Grace's ear, " 'Japanese.' " I straightened. "Obviously, I wouldn't be a problem for him anymore. The Sky Room has lots of Japanese ponies, and Charlie now has girls from Hawaii and the Philippines. There just aren't enough Chinese girls to fill all the jobs, and customers see what they want to see: an all-Chinese revue."

"An Oriental is an Oriental is an Oriental—"

"Anyway, I tell him my name is Ruby Tom. Only he doesn't like it, see? 'We're going to turn you into something special—something no one else has,' he said. 'You'll be Princess Tai, who escaped from China.' If I was going to be a Chinese princess, then I sure as hell wasn't going to accept fifty bucks a week!"

"What about Joe?" she asked.

Ah! The big question.

"Joe? He still comes to the club, and I see him from time to time—"

"He's one of her many now," Ida mumbled loud enough for us to hear.

"Don't you mean he's one of *your* many now?" I shot back. The other girls laughed. I sought Grace's eyes in the mirror. "He's a long way from home, there's a lot of temptation around here, and boys will be boys—"

"Give the guy a break," Ida cut me off. "You broke his heart, and Grace here threw him for a loop. Now he's doing what he's supposed to be doing. Sowing some oats—"

Grace clenched her jaw.

"Try not to think about it, Grace," I said comfortingly. "Here, take the pouf," I ordered, changing the subject. "Make sure the powder covers everything."

Grace obeyed wordlessly.

"Now that you're here," I continued, "you can always powder me. It's good to have a real friend take care of Princess Tai. Help me with my shoes, will ya?"

She kneeled before me and slipped the uncomfortably high-heeled shoes onto my feet. The red patent leather contrasted stunningly against my powdered skin. I leaned in to the mirror for a final look-see and to test that my gardenias were firmly in place.

"I'm ready, except for my bubble." I rolled my shoulders. "You'll find it in the cubby under the stairs by the stage. The bubble needs to be perfectly clean, so use the cloth and spray I keep there. No smudges! I don't want to look like I've been manhandled! Not until *after* the show!" I winked. "Before you go, I need your help with one more thing. My patch. As you know," I said as Grace—who, it seemed, had not one ounce of feistiness left in her—awkwardly applied herself to the task, "Sally Rand worked with a fan, and so do I sometimes. But Princess Tai's specialty is the bubble."

"*Fiedee, fiedee, fiedee!* Hurry, hurry, hurry! It's showtime!" Charlie called through the door to the dressing room. The other girls began to leave. Grace started to rise, but I put a hand on her head. It was not my finest moment, but why—*why*—didn't Grace fight back? Why didn't she bat my hand away, stand up, and say, "Knock it off!" or "Eat a beet!" or "Get over yourself, Ruby"?

"At first, I was scared to death," I told her. "I was practically frozen with fear. It's hard to walk around the stage, holding the bubble just so. But ever since that article hit, we've been sold out every night. Now Charlie has to take reservations!"

"*Fiedee, fiedee, fiedee!* Hurry, hurry, hurry!"

"Come on, Grace," Ida called from the door. "You don't want to miss the cue."

As I watched Grace leave with the other ponies, I decided I'd need to try a different strategy. I'd never been too keen on Helen, but if I played her right, then I might be able to catapult Grace out of the hole she'd dug for herself and win back her friendship. Okay, so it was a long shot, but a girl has to try.

GRACE

Just a Kid

I easily picked up the first routine, which wasn't all that different from the inaugural number on the Forbidden City's opening night. As soon as it ended, I followed the other girls back to the dressing room for a quick change. Ruby asked me to stay with her once I was ready, but I returned to the curtain to watch the next act. The audience clapped and hooted when Bernice Chow—who'd replaced Li Tei Ming, who was "on the road"—appeared onstage to belt Ethel Merman's trademark ditties. Jack Mak was up next. Maybe other people didn't notice that he'd been drinking, but I did. And so did Irene, apparently; she acted the part of capable assistant except for the stinkeye she sent in his direction.

I watched, but my mind was reeling. I'd been in Los Angeles for fourteen months, and left a complete failure. I arrived here, and became an instant failure when Charlie demoted me, and Helen and Eddie stabbed me in the back by saving their own hides. Then I saw Ruby. Talk about kicking someone when she's already down! Who would have guessed it could get worse than that? But it did, because the next thing I knew I was powdering her and serving as her gal Friday. Brother! And it sounded like Ruby was still keeping up the masquerade of actually *being* Chinese. (*Princess Tai.* Ha!) But none of that really mattered, because what was happening wasn't about *her.* It was about *me.* What was wrong with *me*? For a flash of a second, I saw things very clearly: I'd been beaten down my entire life—by my father, by my skin coloring, by circumstances that seemed beyond my control. The result: I'd never had a real boyfriend, and I'd let people push me around. I'd never fought hard enough for *me*. I may have been standing at the curtain of a swanky nightclub, but inside I was at rock bottom. I needed to start thinking of myself first—*my* happiness, *my* career, *my* heart. I was going to climb up. If that meant slapping some powder on Ruby—ugh—I'd do it. Lingering there, I began to feel *fortified*, even if it irked me that it had been Ruby who had jolted me awake. Damn her.

I did great in the other numbers—for an audience more focused on girls gyrating in colorful costumes than on footwork—including the "Chinese Coolie Dance," in which we wore conical straw hats. This caused Charlie to quip to the audience, "Dancing is strenuous but better than going back to the laundry." *Very funny.* After everything I'd just heard, I figured Joe had to be here, and I looked for him in the audience. As I made a turn, I spotted him, sitting at a table with a group of guys his age—probably friends from school. My stomach drew up under my chest and my breath caught. As pragmatic as I wanted to be, my feelings for him came rushing back—my love of the sound of his laugh, the endearing way he ran his hand through his hair when he was chagrined, the strength of his arms when we danced, and the desire I'd felt for him since he first approached me on Treasure Island. I tamped all that down. I couldn't allow myself to be "in love" with him anymore, but a part of me burned with disappointment, jealousy, embarrassment, and, yes, love. No more doormat! I forced myself to keep smiling as I shuffled forward, following the other ponies to the center of the dance floor. Self-preservation first. I needed the job.

After the routine, I lingered by the curtain to stare out at him anyway. Had he noticed me? Then I became aware of a presence behind my left shoulder. I glanced up and saw the sweet and very handsome face of a young man. Out on the floor, Charlie introduced the Forbidden City's newest crooner, George Louie, the Chinese Frank Sinatra. Hearing his name, George ducked through the curtain and onto the stage. He held the microphone with both hands, closed his eyes, and began to sing "I'll Never Smile Again," sounding exactly like a recording by the heartthrob and going over huge with the women in the audience.

I rushed back to the dressing room, passing the Lim Sisters on their way to the curtain. And, boy, were they different! Instead of wearing baptismal gowns, they sported sequined, off-the shoulder, one-piece, skintight costumes. A martini glass sprouted from each sister's headdress at a tipsy angle. Their lips had been painted bright red, and their toenails gleamed crimson through their gold satin sandals.

Helen was in the dressing room when I got there, sitting as far from Ruby as she could get and still be in the same room. The tension between the three of us seemed to thicken the air. I couldn't figure out where to go or what to do. Neither of them called me over either. Helen was too busy "preparing," and Ruby couldn't stop preening in front of the mirror. I changed into my next costume and touched up my makeup. When Helen rose to leave, I managed to say, "Break a leg." She nodded in grateful acknowledgment. I heard the music for the Chinese Dancing Sweethearts, but I didn't need to see Eddie and Helen dance. I knew every pattern and variation. They must have been a hit from the roar of applause. I was straightening my hose when Helen glided back into the dressing room. Her cheeks were flushed from exertion and happiness. Her stomach was flat against her gown, but it would be only a matter of time before she was too big to dance in front of an audience. I could wait.

"Grace. Helen." Ruby slowly wended her way through the other girls, careful not to brush her perfectly powdered skin against any feathers, sequins, or flesh. "Come see my act."

Helen and I looked at each other across the room. *No thanks.*

"Aw, come on, Helen," Ruby pleaded, putting a hand on Helen's shoulder. "Don't you want to see what all the fuss is about?"

"If you put it like that—"

I ended up following them both to the velvet curtain stage right. I wasn't going to be left out. Ruby picked up her ball as Charlie began his introduction: "I promised you the mysteries of the Orient, but it's up to you to see if what they say about Oriental girls is true. The usual way or the wrong way? Please give a big round of applause for Princess Tai, our very own Chinese Sally Rand, fresh from the real Forbidden City in China . . ."

Ruby balanced the ball before her, then glided through the curtain. A single blue spot followed her as she paraded from one end of the dance floor to the other, always moving her ball, so that the so-called mysteries of the Orient remained just that. Not once did Joe take his eyes off Ruby and her blue-tinted arms and legs. As soon as her music ended, and Ruby was safely through the curtain, the rest of the cast came out to lead the patrons in a rousing Chinaconga through the club. By the time I passed Joe's table, he was long gone from it, his hands on Ida's hips, laughing, shaking from side to side, and sending out an emphatic kick in beat to the music.

Three dinner services. Three shows. Three Chinacongas. Then it was time to change, grab friends, and meet stage-door Johnnies, or move on to a bar for drinks or a late-night coffee shop for scrambled eggs. Ruby stopped by Helen on her way to the door.

"I loved your act," she said.

"Thanks." Helen seemed genuinely pleased.

Ruby gabbed on for a bit—complimenting Helen on her turns and how good she'd gotten at extending her lines—ending with "You want to come with me to Sam Wo?"

"Sure! I haven't been there in ages."

I didn't know what Ruby was up to—acting all chummy with Helen—but it surprised me that Helen could be so easily seduced.

"You coming too or what?" Ruby asked me.

"You'd better believe it." Again, I wasn't going to be left out.

Once we were seated at our old table at Sam Wo and had ordered bowls of noodles, Ruby peppered Helen with questions. I listened in wonder as Helen let out everything about Tim and her marriage to Eddie. When she said she was content to live with her parents, at least for now, Ruby turned to me.

"How about you?" she asked.

"I'm staying with Helen and Eddie, but I need to get a place of my own."

"A place of your own?" Ruby's eyebrows shot up. "Forget that! You're going to bunk with me."

"I want you to stay with me," Helen said. "There's plenty of room."

She stared at me confidently, seeming sure of a positive answer, while I considered her offer. The compound? Monroe? Her baby coming? Not one of those things appealed to me, nor did they fit with my plan to put myself first.

"I've got a two-bedroom apartment on Powell," Ruby continued, "with the works: a telephone, a radio, a full bathroom, and a kitchen, not that I use it. A lot of entertainers live in the building—Jack and Irene Mak, George Louie, and the Merry Mahjongs. They're playing over at the Sky Room. Oh, and Dorothy Toy—"

"*The* Dorothy Toy?" My idol? My inspiration?

"She lives in Apartment Seven," Ruby went on. "She's on the road most of the time, so I haven't met her yet, but once the door to her apartment was open and I saw toe shoes dangling from a curtain rod." She paused. "If you live with me, you'll have your own room."

"I doubt Grace will be able to share the rent," Helen said.

"She doesn't need to worry about that. I make plenty of dough. Besides," Ruby added, pinching my cheek, "I owe you one."

She let me absorb that, while Helen fidgeted.

"What about Joe?" I asked.

Ruby tapped her nails on the table. "I already told you. There's not much between us anymore."

"Much? What's that supposed to mean?" Helen asked.

"I mean nothing," Ruby corrected herself in an offhand manner. "There's nothing between us. We're just pals."

An image of the evil triplets came to my mind. Then I thought of the Lim Sisters and how they'd worked together since they were kids. In those sets of three, one girl was always in charge, one was a strict follower, and one was always a bit outside. But who was the leader among Ruby, Helen, and me? Ruby, because she was Princess Tai? Helen, because in Chinese tradition she had more standing than two unmarried girls? I had nothing and was at what I figured had to be the lowest point in my life, but they were fighting over *me*. In this one way I had power, and it would be my decision that would determine things now. *Think of yourself first.*

"I'd love to live with you, Ruby," I said. I wanted it to sound casual, like she was doing me a favor, but really I'd be living in the same building with other stars. Wouldn't that say something to others about who *I* was?

A MERE FOUR months later, a reporter and a photographer from the Associated Press were assigned to follow Ruby (a star) and me (her sidekick) for a spread called "Maid 'N' China." Ruby and I woke early—around noon—so we could paint our faces and apply false eyelashes. We changed out of our cotton nightgowns and into silk pajamas. We brushed our hair loose around our shoulders and dabbed Prince Matchabelli behind our ears. Then we unlocked the door, returned to our own rooms, climbed back in our beds, and were ready for the promised 2:00 P.M. knock. Ruby called, "Come in." Then Princess Tai and I took turns yawning and stretching for the photographer. Next, I sashayed into Ruby's room—the photographer clicking all the while—and sat on the edge of her mattress. The reporter asked if Ruby and I were best friends, and we answered in unison. "Of course!"

The article would eventually run in newspapers all across the country, including the *Fort Worth Journal Gazette,* the *Oakland Tribune,* and so many more. The caption for the bedroom photograph would read: "Maidens made in China say good night to the nightingale and good morning to the skylark."

Ruby and I changed into street clothes and led the boys on a walk along Grant. We waved to passersby, who either turned their faces away from the camera or smiled enthusiastically at the two no-no girls. We entered Shew Chong Tai, an import shop that specialized in toiletries from the old country made for women Helen's mother's age.

"We come here for the Chinese cosmetics," Ruby confided to the reporter. "I put them on my face until my skin looks like snow-white silk." Although we were already in full makeup, Ruby patted some cream along my jaw with a fingertip to illustrate what she meant. Then she reached for a box of *paw fah*. "We use this gel made from tree bark to glue our spit curls. See, it's a natural marcel." She stuck a few strands of my hair to my cheek with the foreign concoction.

In real life, we never went to that store or used those products. We preferred going to Union Square. We wore white gloves and hats to shop. We sat on a sofa in a large room in the store, and a saleswoman would come out and ask us what type of outfit we wanted. A day dress, a cocktail dress, a formal dress? Did we want it in mousseline de soie, panne velvet, or crepe de chine? Did we prefer georgette, poplin, or voile? We'd tell her our sizes—zero or two, depending on our time of month—and she'd go to the stockroom, bring out the clothes, and we'd say yea or nay. If we saw something we liked, we'd be escorted to a dressing room.

The photo caption for our Chinatown shopping expedition read: "Two Chinese dishes—not chop suey, mind you!—stroll along the tong-scarred streets of Chinatown, wearing fur coats over the latest Western fashions. Stylists say that dollar for dollar Oriental beauties dress more smartly than their Occidental sisters."

When we arrived at the Forbidden City, Charlie bowed to the reporter and photographer, and they found themselves bowing back. Ah, Charlie . . . On my first payday after I'd returned from Los Angeles, he asked me to close the door to his office so he could speak to me privately. I remembered how he used to run a routine to let him keep my salary or to try to short me, but these days the club was flush. "I promised the Chinese Dancing Sweethearts three hundred a week," he said. "That was supposed to be divvied up three ways, but that didn't turn out the way we planned, did it? I owe you fifty dollars, but . . . well . . . here." He pushed three fifties across the table—the same amount that Helen and Eddie were now each making.

"Is this for powdering Ruby?" I asked.

"If it will keep her happy, then I'm happy."

"Did you pay this much to Ida?"

"Hardly, but Ruby wants you. If you don't want to help her, that's your decision. But a word of advice. She brought you here. She can get rid of you just as easily. Divas, you know . . . Now take the money."

His gesture, which he continued to do weekly, changed my life. Otherwise, I wouldn't have been able to afford to patronize shops with Ruby, buy a three-quarter-length seal coat on layaway, use Western Union to start sending money once a month to Miss Miller to slip to my mother, and still have enough left over to save twenty dollars a week. (I still abided by my mother's wish that we have no actual contact. Wiring money through Western Union also protected my privacy. I didn't want my father to come looking for me.) Charlie paid Princess Tai a lot more than either the Chinese Dancing Sweethearts or me. Ruby earned five hundred dollars a week at a time when office workers were lucky to make forty. Eddie would have gone out of his gourd if he'd caught wind of that. But he didn't hear, because I didn't tell Helen. As for the news that Ruby had brought me here and had control over me . . . I couldn't exactly hold my nose in the air and act all hoity-toity, because my intention had been to use her too. But something unexpected happened along the way. Ruby courted me with her generosity, her humor, and her giddiness. She reminded me how to have fun. She forced me to remember why we'd liked each other in the first place. The makeup job was still pretty unpleasant from my perspective, but what's ten minutes out of twenty-four hours for one hundred and fifty bucks a week? Besides, she'd tell jokes and keep me amused while I dabbed, dabbed, dabbed, and tried not to stare at what was in front of my face. And she continued to help me in other ways, like insisting I be part of this interview.

The reporter and photographer remained outside the dressing room while Ruby slipped into a kimono. I let the men in and watched as they tried to keep their eyeballs in their sockets. Sitting before them was a stunningly beautiful woman with just the thinnest silk between them and her naked flesh. Funny, isn't it? Men see us every day. They see us in our clothes every day. We're naked under our clothes every day. But present them with a different picture—a girl wearing nothing beneath her kimono—and they can think about only one thing. And in her own way, Ruby was shrewd. As soon as she came offstage, she covered up. She never paraded around so the guys in the band could see her, but, boy, did they ever try. All anyone actually *saw* was her twitching derriere as she ducked through the velvet curtain at the end of her act.

"I started out using fans, just like Sally Rand taught me," Ruby chirred. "But using fans is hard work. Each one weighs twenty-five pounds and—"

"They keep more of you covered," the reporter finished for her, his voice predictably gruff.

"Do I look like I could heft all that weight?" Ruby asked, oblivious to his tone. "I still dance with the fans, but I much prefer my bubble."

"What advice would you give to our female readers to attract a man?"

"A woman should always look elegant," she answered.

"What's the fun in that?" he asked.

"Not everything is about fun." A tiny frown crinkled the space between her eyebrows. When I first met her, she'd said she wanted glitter in her life. Since then, she'd figured out not only how to have glitter but also how to "sell" glitter and glamour to an audience. "Grace, the other performers, and I do all sorts of things to help our community," she continued. "We've performed at charity shows in Santa Cruz, Salinas, and San Jose to benefit the Rice Bowl Campaign. None of us Chinese like what the Japanese are doing in China." This was her story, and she was sticking to it! "And once a year, before the big game, Cal alumni rent the Forbidden City for a night to raise funds. Charlie stacks five hundred people in here. We've got the Cal band and Cal glee club, but we give them our regular show too. Go Cal!"

The reporter scribbled all this in his notebook. Then he glanced up, serious. "Our readers would like to know if you're truly naked behind your bubble."

Ruby's laugh filled the room like tinkling crystals. "That's for me to know and you to find out! You boys need to go to your table now. The other girls have to get ready and"—she leaned forward and caressed the reporter's knee with a red-lacquered fingernail—"so do I."

After the show, the boys from the Associated Press wanted to see what we did next.

"I'm not the kind of girl who *needs* to be taken to expensive joints, but I sure like them," Ruby confessed.

Actually, if Ruby and I had been alone, we probably would have gone somewhere for noodles. Or, if we wanted to spend a little more money, we would have joined up with a group of show kids to go to other clubs.

"What's happening tonight at Bimbo's 365?" someone might ask.

"Shall we go to Finocchio's? Or would you prefer the Italian Village?"

"How about Andy Pond's Breakfast Club on Kearny? We can eat bacon and eggs and listen to jazz at the same time."

"If we're having breakfast, let's go to Coffee Dan's." (The café was open twenty-four hours a day, and you could get a shot of bourbon in your cup of joe.)

Or the kids at the Sky Room might throw a party, and we'd all go to that. (No one brewed bad blood about which club was more popular or classier.) Some nights everyone came over to Ruby's and my apartment. Oh, maybe fifty people in the living room, sometimes more. I played an upright piano while others sang. Pretty soon, the guys were bringing their ukuleles and their guitars. Or we'd put on a record and dance until we couldn't breathe.

We took the newspaper boys to an all-night coffee shop that served Chinese dishes and American food like custard pie.

"What about stage-door Johnnies?" the reporter asked Ruby as the photographer snapped a few more shots. "Are they a nuisance?"

Ruby laughed so long that I stepped in.

"You've got it wrong, mister," I said. "They bring her flowers and chocolates. They write fan letters—"

"And love letters," Ruby added. "Those boys are so sweet. I treasure them all."

Yes, Princess Tai had plenty of beaus, and she enjoyed their company. All except for one fella named Ray Boiler, an Occidental short-order cook twice her age, from Visalia, who visited once a month after he received his paycheck. "Something isn't right about him," she told me one night after he'd followed us home. "He gives me a bad feeling even when he smiles at me. Especially when he smiles at me!" But, as she pointed out, we worked in a nightclub, where the mix of men like Ray Boiler, booze, and scantily clad women was inherently dangerous. She didn't tell any of that to the Associated Press fellas. She just smiled and laughed and flirted. That's what made her Princess Tai.

NOTHING WITH RUBY would have worked if things hadn't gone well between Joe and me. He didn't come back to the club for a month after my return to San Francisco. By then, I'd stopped searching for him in the audience. I was on my way to have drinks between shows with a couple of cattle brokers from Omaha when I bumped into him. He blushed, sheepish. No wonder. The last time I'd seen him, I'd seen *a lot* of him. Only I could put that behind us. I gave him a friendly hug, and he instantly began to loosen up. He pulled out a chair and I sat down. (So much for the cattle brokers.) He talked at me a mile a minute—still nervous, of course. I looked great . . . I was still the best dancer in the line . . . He'd missed me . . . He had so much he wanted to tell me . . . When his speech finally slowed and he gave me that lopsided grin I so loved, I was relieved. It seemed he could forget that embarrassing night, if I could, and be the person he'd always been. When he invited me to lunch, I readily accepted.

The following Sunday, he took me to a little Italian place in North Beach. "I hope we can take walks together, like we used to," he told me, and we did. "We'll talk, like we used to," he said, and we did. He said he was sorry that I'd seen him making love to Ruby, because I was "just a kid" and shouldn't have had to see something like that. I reminded him that on Treasure Island he'd told me I was too young for him; now I saw that he was too young for *me*. He laughed and laughed. He apologized for running out that night instead of sticking around and explaining things to me. "Water under the bridge," I said, and we made it so.

He started coming to the club on weekends regularly again, and we fell into a pattern—one almost identical to what we'd followed on Treasure Island: I kept Joe amused, while Ruby—naked—entertained other men. He still liked her, and she kept him on a string—meeting with him sometimes before the club opened, dancing close to his table, even having an after-hours meal with him on occasion. They were strangely locked together, but from day one I'd been the third corner of the triangle. Many nights, as soon as I finished putting on my makeup and applying Ruby's powder, I'd go out front and talk to him. Or later—after the last show—I'd quickly change and go sit with him. But I wasn't some stray pup nosing around for attention anymore. We spent time together because we liked each other's company. I often told him things I'd never tell the girls, and he confided in me. He'd graduated the previous year and was now at Boalt Hall at Cal, studying law. His dad had offered him a job once he passed the bar, but Joe wasn't sure he wanted to go back to Illinois or be a lawyer. Flying was still his passion, he said, and he'd talked to the folks at Pan American to see what it would take to fly a Clipper ship. Mainly, though, I listened when he got wistful about Ruby.

"She was my first love," he told me. I could sympathize with that. "Did she love me as much as I loved her?"

"Of course she did," I answered steadfastly.

"Our relationship never would have lasted anyway," he admitted one night as the busboys cleared the last of the tables in the club. "We don't have miscegenation laws in Illinois, but marriage to Ruby would have been impossible. There's prejudice, and then there's prejudice. A bubble dancer is"—he struggled to find the right words before settling on—"a different kettle of fish."

"But you always knew she performed bare," I pointed out.

"No one in Winnetka would have known about *that,*" he responded. "But the cover of *Life* changed everything. I mean, *look* at her. If you had a brother and he brought her home, what would your parents say?"

I didn't have a brother, but if *I* returned home and my father knew what I was doing, he would have beaten me to death. Pure and simple.

"What about someone like me?" I asked. "I'm a dancer. I've had my photo in lots of Sunday supplements thanks to the Associated Press story. I was in that newsreel. What if you brought home someone like me?"

"You don't dance buck naked," he said. Just then Ruby approached our table. Joe patted my hand. "Don't worry, hon. One of these days there'll be someone like me waiting for you."

He didn't love me like I loved him, but I preferred to be his friend rather than not have him in my life.

HELEN NEVER GOT very big. She was Chinese, she performed every day, and she was one of those blasted gals who's blessed with not looking all that pregnant. Still, in May, six months into her pregnancy, her stomach popped out. After that, Helen stayed home, and I took her place. The customers loved Eddie and me. We may have looked great, but his melancholy had deepened since our return to San Francisco, and he ironed it out with drink. Helen had never complained about it, but I did. If he had a martini between the first and second shows, I pestered him. If he bought a round for everyone in the bar between the second and third shows, I hounded him something fierce, because he'd been boozing too.

"I don't want your breath in my face." I seethed indignantly when we performed. "You reek of liquor down to your shoes."

"Am I making any mistakes?" he asked as he tipped me back for the dip over his thigh. And of course he didn't, because he was a flawless entertainer.

On September 8, 1941, Helen got want she wanted: a son, born in the early evening when the rest of us were at the club. The baby was full term, although he arrived just seven months after Helen and Eddie's wedding. The Fongs went ahead and threw a huge one-month banquet for their new grandchild at Shanghai Low. (Anything to save face.) Helen's father even invited Ruby. As a leader in Chinatown and a member of the Chinese Six Companies, he was showing how important *he* was to have the "Chinese princess" featured on the cover of *Life* attend his party. Ruby, wearing a day dress in emerald shantung with navy trim and a matching hat with a net veil coming down over her eyes, handled it all like a star—shaking hands, posing for photographs, and smiling, smiling, smiling.

Bowls of dyed red eggs symbolized happiness and the renewal of life. Ginger added a touch of *yang*—heat—to the nutritional needs of the new mother, who was tired and weak after giving birth. The infant didn't yet look like much of anything one way or the other, which was a good thing. Mr. Fong announced his newest grandchild's name publicly for the first time—Thomas Bo Yu Wu. The baby's milk name, Bo Yu, meant *firstborn fish*. Helen said she'd call him Tommy, which wasn't all that far off from Tim for those of us in the know. The banquet? The very best, with bird's nest soup and every delicacy imaginable.

After the party, Helen invited Ruby and me back to the Fong family compound. When I told Helen she handled Tommy like a pro, she laughed lightly. "Have you seen how many little nieces and nephews

I have?" I stared down into his face, searching his unformed features, touching the tiny wisps of fuzz—not brown, not black—on top of his head. He seemed like every other baby to me, but Helen was besotted, adoring him with eyes of love. "*One joy shatters a hundred griefs,*" she recited, and I nodded like I understood what she was talking about.

Ruby tired of the baby-staring party first. "I thought you and Eddie wanted to get your own place."

"It's better to be in the compound," Helen responded. "We'll be safer here."

"Safer?"

"The four walls. The family. The . . ." Helen gestured around her at the implied wealth.

"What about Eddie?"

Helen looked startled by the question, and she adjusted the baby in her arms. "What about him? He's never around."

Ruby tilted her head, considering. "He leaves right after the last show—"

"And he doesn't come home," Helen finished, but she didn't seem perturbed. "He stays out all night. He won't tell me where he goes or what he does."

"You need to come back to the club," Ruby suggested. "Keep an eye on him."

"I know, and I'll do it," Helen said.

She tightened her arms around the baby, and he greedily took her breast. She appeared content. At peace, in a strange way. But when I looked ahead at Tommy's future, I couldn't imagine how he, as a half-and-half child, would be treated in Chinatown, outside Chinatown, or any place he went. It would have to be far worse than what I'd experienced in Plain City. I saw that each of us, and now Tommy too, was cursed—not in the Chinese manner of bad fate or inauspicious destiny, but in the very Western way of being weighed down by the blood that ran in our veins, the secrets we kept and the lies we told, and the things that we, with our American know-how, had the greatest capacity to deny to ourselves and others. But at this moment, as Helen stared into her baby's face, she glowed—blissful, a heavenly mother.

WHEN TOMMY WAS three months old, Helen reluctantly returned to the club to be part of a new holiday show. It had a novelty number for the chorus girls in which we carried kittens in net muffs. (Those little fluff balls would pop their heads out of the muffs and the entire audience would ooh and aah.) Naturally, Helen brought the baby with her. She was crazy about the kid and couldn't go anywhere without him. She hated to be parted from Tommy for more than the few minutes it took the Chinese Dancing Sweethearts to do their routine. And, from the moment of her return, she bickered with Eddie nonstop. They danced beautifully, though, and I was colossally jealous. Helen was in the spotlight again. Her breasts were large and creamy with milk, which made her more luscious than ever, while I was, once again, a pony.

RUBY

The Jimjams

Grace and I could sleep through just about anything, but not the neighbor's brats running up and down the hall, banging on everyone's doors, and shouting, "Turn on the radio! Turn on the radio!" I rolled over and squinted at the clock. It wasn't even noon yet, and a Sunday to boot. I'd give those kids what for later. I closed my eyes, letting darkness suck me back into slumber. The sound of someone thudding across the room upstairs jolted me awake again. Through the walls, I heard panicked voices. I forced myself out of bed—only five hours' sleep—and shuffled out to the living room, where I found Grace, tousled and groggy, leaning against her doorjamb.

"I'm going to kill those kids," she muttered sourly.

The room was littered with empty glasses that oozed the smells of brown liquor and ashtrays overflowing with cigarette butts left from the party the night before. A wave of nausea swept over me. I can't speak for Grace, but I may have had one drink too many. I steadied myself and turned on the radio. I heard President Roosevelt's voice. The Japanese aggressors had just bombed Pearl Harbor in a surprise attack. Ships were sinking or on fire. Hundreds, maybe thousands, were dead. I started to shake. Grace grabbed me, and we staggered to the couch. We held hands, bent our heads together, and cinched our shoulders. Grace was trembling as badly as I was.

"What does it mean?" Grace whispered, terrified.

"War," I answered numbly. "We'll be going to war."

"Do you think my mother's heard yet? Should I call her? My father . . . Could the Japs reach Ohio?"

Under my skin, my muscles rearranged themselves until my face was mask tight. I'd never heard her use that word before.

"My parents and my brothers *live* in Honolulu." My words shot from my mouth like iced bullets. "I'm a little more worried about what might have happened to *them* than I am for people who live thousands of miles away from the attack. And what about *me*? I'm Japanese."

Grace recoiled. *She's a Jap.* The hairs on the back of my neck stood on end.

"Oh, Ruby. I'm so sorry," Grace managed with some effort. "What can I do? What can we do?"

I called the Chinese Telephone Exchange and asked to put a call through to Hawaii, but already the lines were clogged. With each unsuccessful attempt, I became increasingly frantic. The radio was no help either. News of civilian casualties and the extent of the damage—whether in the harbor or in Honolulu—trickled out impossibly slowly. Each passing hour brought more frightening news: the FBI had been watching "certain Japanese nationals" around the country for a year, and now rounded them up. In Nashville, the Department of Conservation put in a requisition for six million licenses to "hunt Japs" at a fee of two dollars each. The purchasing department vetoed the requisition with a note: "Open season on Japs—no license required." Every tear that fell from my eyes, rolled down my cheeks, and dripped off my chin was a physical reminder of the love—and fear—I felt for my mother, father, and two brothers. *Were they all right?* I dialed the telephone exchange again.

"We'll put the call through to you as soon as we get a connection," the operator told me tersely.

In the afternoon, we heard someone in the hall, banging on doors again. Chilling terror. *What now?* We opened the door to find Jack Mak announcing to all our neighbors that Charlie had canceled the show for the night. Around eight, Grace heated a can of soup. We stayed glued to the radio. I called the telephone exchange every fifteen minutes, with no result. At midnight, Grace and I crawled into bed. We slept together, hanging on to each other, believing that somehow the warmth of our flesh huddled in a cocoon would save us from our drowning fear.

The next morning, we immediately turned on the radio. President Roosevelt announced that we had declared war on Japan. All members of the armed forces in the area were called to duty and sent to battle stations.

Around noon, Joe arrived, wanting to check on us. He looked just as unsettled as we felt: *This is bad, very, very bad.*

"If the Japs could strike Pearl Harbor, could they hit San Francisco too?" I asked. The inside of my head was ringing. I'd succumbed to the same apprehensions as Grace, and I'd crossed a line by uttering the word *Jap*. "Is that possible?"

"No way," Joe answered staunchly.

"Why can't they come here?" Then I repeated something I'd heard a commentator warn on the radio. "Submarines could be submerged just offshore."

"Do you think New Yorkers are worried that Germany, which is only three thousand or so miles away from them, will mount an assault?" He spoke in his college voice—determined, smart, and encouraging. He answered his own question. "Of course not. So we shouldn't be worried that San Francisco—or any city on the West Coast for that matter—will be attacked by Japan five thousand miles away."

That boy was full of more shit than a Christmas goose, because the United States wasn't *at war* with Germany, nor had the Nazis mounted a sneak attack on us.

At 8:00 that night, the lights in our apartment went out. We were plunged into darkness. *This is it!*

"Grace, are you there?" My voice shook.

"I'm here," she answered, sounding as if that father of hers had his hands gripped around her throat.

"Joe?"

"Do you have candles?" he asked. Never before had I heard a man sound so petrified.

Peeking out the windows, we could see that our neighbors in Chinatown—and maybe the whole city—had also lost electricity. We had no idea about what had happened or what was about to happen. Maybe we had only minutes to live. We stayed inside, too afraid even to go into the hall. The entire building was silent with people preparing to die. When the lights came on three hours later, I burst into tears. Grace tried to comfort me, but I was in too much turmoil—worried about my parents, and afraid of what could happen tomorrow or the day after that. I stared at Joe, wishing he would *do* something, but there was nothing he could do. We stayed together in the living room. None of us slept. The entire city had a bad case of the sweats and the jimjams.

Joe went home at dawn. Not long after he left, the radio reported that the previous evening two squadrons of fifteen enemy planes had left a carrier off the coast and entered U.S. airspace above San Jose. From there, some flew north and some flew south. After midnight, they returned. Just before dawn, they came again. We were scared out of our pants, especially when Lieutenant General DeWitt, who was in charge at the Presidio, declared, "You people do not seem to realize we are at war. So get this: last night there were planes over this community! They were enemy planes! I mean Japanese planes!" His panic increased our panic. In response to the sortie, over one thousand households in Santa Cruz, Monterey, and Carmel were evacuated and moved inland. Some reporters claimed that the planes flew too high to have dropped bombs. The Japanese aggressors must have been on a reconnaissance mission. Other reporters dismissed the whole thing as a hoax, calling the citywide blackout and the stories that had swirled around it an example of "invasion fever," to which DeWitt angrily responded that the planes had been tracked out to sea. "You think it was a hoax?" he demanded. "It is damned nonsense for sensible people to assume the Army and the Navy would practice a hoax on San Francisco." And still, I hadn't reached my parents.

A little after two in the afternoon, the phone rang. An operator told me to hold for my call. I waited and waited. Grace came to me. *I'm here with you.* Then I heard Yori's voice.

"Kimiko?"

"Yes, it's me," I answered in English.

My brother didn't say anything, but I could hear him breathing. Even over so many miles, I felt myself in our house by the shore. Behind the sound of my brother raggedly drawing air into his lungs as he tried to collect himself, I heard an empty well of silence. He shouldn't be the one speaking to me.

"Yori?"

"*Sumimasenga*—I'm sorry but . . ."

I sucked in a breath and held it as Yori choked out the story. As he spoke—a phrase here, followed by a rush of words, then pained silence—I saw images in my head as familiar as snapshots from my childhood. My family usually stayed home on Sundays, but my father told my brothers they'd be taking the boat out anyway . . . Yori asked if he should start letting out the nets . . . I'd seen Pop and my brothers do that chore a million times. But as Yori continued, my mind struggled to absorb—*see*—what he was telling me.

The Japanese dive-bombers and pursuit planes whined in from the southeast over Diamond Head . . . Yori heard bombs thudding in the distance and the rhythmic *clack-clack* of machine guns . . . Hideo and Pop were by the controls . . . Pop turned the boat to pilot it back to the docks . . . Hideo hurried to the stern . . . A lone American plane buzzed overhead, swooped down, and sprayed the sampan with bullets . . .

"Hideo . . . was . . . ripped . . . in . . . two." Yori sobbed so hard I could barely understand him. "I saw it, Kimiko. I saw it. He's *dead.*"

My legs buckled, and I collapsed on the floor. "What about Pop? Where's Pop?"

"Men came that night. They confiscated the sampan—"

"Where's Pop?" I whispered into the phone.

"They barged into the house. They searched our drawers and closets. Then they took Mom and Pop away. I don't know where. No one at the FBI will tell me anything except that they're convinced Mom and Pop helped with the attack."

"What happened?" Grace kneeled by my side. "Tell me."

I waved her away. On the phone Yori shifted from tears to anger as he told me that in just a few hours the rumor had started that fishermen, Japanese-language teachers, and Shinto priests were spies. My parents fit the first two categories, and it must have seemed extra damning that my father and brothers had been at sea during the air strike. Aware that Grace was next to me, I asked several questions in Japanese. Yori answered, *"Hai, hai, hai."* Yes, yes, yes. The last thing he said was "They'll be coming for me soon. I know it. Take care of yourself. And beware." I stared at the receiver for what felt like a full minute before dropping it in the cradle. I covered my face with my hands and began to weep. Grace wrapped her arms around me. I told her some—but not all—of what Yori had told me.

Through my tears, I rasped, "I can't believe my brother's dead. What's going to happen to my mom and pop?"

"I'm sure your parents will be fine," Grace said, but it couldn't have been a more useless comment.

"What about Yori?"

Of course Grace didn't have an answer.

"Will they come for me next?"

Before Grace could answer, someone pounded on the door. Double fists! Terror shot through my body as my woman parts constricted, yanking in fear up to my heart.

GRACE

Extreme Joy Begets . . .

You don't know how your life can change. You go to sleep one night, you wake up the next morning, and something unimaginable has happened on the other side of the world. It may be far away, but it ripples over all those miles and comes right into the rooms where you live. War, I had already learned, creates extremely strange and complicated situations. Ruby was facing devastating family losses, which were made even more difficult by the uncertainty of what it might mean that she was Japanese. Now, listening to the knocking at the door, I watched Ruby go white with fear. She was too scared to move. When I peeked through the keyhole and saw Helen, relief flooded through me. I opened the door, and she stalked into the apartment. She didn't say hello to me or Ruby, whose face was wet with tears. Helen scanned the room, didn't find what she was looking for, then moved to peer into Ruby's bedroom before acknowledging us.

"Where's your suitcase?" she asked, sidling over to Ruby and tapping her on the shoulder.

"Suitcase?" Ruby sounded bewildered.

Helen turned to me. "Has she packed? Did you help her?"

"What are you talking about?" I asked.

"Are more planes on the way?" Helen went on, once again addressing Ruby in an eerily calm manner. "When are they coming? Did they tell you where to go to be safe? That happened in Shanghai. The Japs who lived in Shanghai got word before their friends invaded—"

"Helen!" I exclaimed, thoroughly shocked.

"I always suspected Ruby hid a dagger behind her smiling face. Has she told you anything? I've got to protect Tommy."

Her strange demeanor confused me. Worse, I didn't understand *what* she was saying.

"Where is Tommy?" I asked.

"I left him with Mama. I made her promise to take care of him in case I don't come back."

That seemed a little melodramatic when all she had to do was walk a couple of blocks from her family compound to our apartment and back again. But to be fair, I was so scared I hadn't even gone outside yet, and neither had Ruby. If I had a child, maybe I would have left him at home too. Still, I had to make Helen understand that her suspicions were misplaced and that she had something far more serious to consider. I said, "Ruby's brother was killed in the attack—"

"And my parents have been taken away somewhere," Ruby added. "The FBI could be coming for me next."

This scenario seemed like a real possibility. The idea was beyond frightening, and yet, I'll admit it, a tiny part of me had doubts about her. Ruby was Japanese. I was living with the enemy. But she wasn't *the* enemy, I argued with myself. She was my friend. But was she, really? The insidiousness of fear and distrust kept trying to worm its way inside me. In my head, I repeated, *She's my friend, my friend, my friend.*

"Come for *you* next?" Helen asked in that same unsettling monotone. "What about *us*? What's going to happen to Tommy and me? To my family?" She pointed at me. "They could come and kill you, Grace. Have you thought about that? Rape and kill you."

"For God's sake, Helen. We're all scared, but Ruby's brother was *killed.*"

At that, Helen's composure crumbled. "So was my husband. The Japs murdered him right in front of me."

The news was so overpowering I couldn't take it in. I didn't know what to say or do, but Ruby, momentarily shaken out of her despair, managed to mutter, "Your husband?"

Helen and Ruby gaped at each other—two women who'd suffered unbelievable losses.

"Tell me what happened," Ruby said.

I was still a few paces behind, processing the information. *Husband?* I conjured up the photo I'd once seen in Helen's room. I'd always assumed the man beside her was one of her brothers, but now I realized he had to be her husband, and all the oranges and candles must have been part of an altar to him.

Ruby reached for Helen's hand. Surprisingly, Helen allowed herself to be led to the couch. Now that she'd revealed her marriage, the rest flooded out—urgent and wretched.

"We were hiding in the rice paddies. All of us," she began as tears pooled in her eyes. "Lai Kai, my in-laws, his brothers and sisters, their children, the servants. We heard the Japanese splashing around us. Lai Kai whispered, 'Stay still. Don't run.' He was my husband. I obeyed." She covered her eyes with her hands. "He tried to lure the soldiers away from us. They killed him with bayonets. And then they found the others . . ."

Her moans of grief were almost too much to bear. Ruby held Helen tight and looked at me. *Now what?* I had no idea.

Needing a moment, I went to the kitchen. I was numb as I filled the kettle, put it on the burner, and waited for the water to heat. I took a quick glance out the kitchen door; they hadn't moved. I had thought Ruby had suffered the worst thing possible, but Helen had witnessed true horror. Their experiences were beyond me. Never had I felt so confused or lost for words.

I made tea, put the pot and cups on a tray, and returned to the living room. Helen lay slumped against the couch's back cushions, her hands splayed with every finger as white as bone, her legs open and limp. I poured the tea and handed cups to Ruby and Helen. Tears still ran from Ruby's eyes—beyond her control. Helen chewed on her lips and sucked air in through her nose in tormented breaths. I pushed aside the coffee table and sat on the floor between them, tucking my legs beneath me.

"I'm sorry for your loss, Helen," I said, yet the words sounded small and insignificant compared to what my friend had been through. "And yours too, Ruby."

I rested my head on Ruby's thigh and put a hand on Helen's knee, letting them feel through my skin and my warmth that I was part of this too. But they were so locked into their own grief that I doubted they were aware of me or could even *hear* what they each said.

Over the next hour, Helen told us that when she turned sixteen her father had arranged her marriage into the Kwok family in Soochow. "Baba informed me that Lai Kai's family was wealthy and that I would live a comfortable life. My future mother-in-law sent me his photo. He was so handsome. The story I told you about my family going back to China during the worst of the Depression was true, but they would have gone anyway for my wedding. I was married on my eighteenth birthday. Lai Kai and I had a traditional ceremony. I wore all red and a traditional headdress with beading that hung down so Lai Kai and I wouldn't see each other before we reached the privacy of the bridal chamber. Baba threw some water on the ground when I left our family compound in the home village, saying, '*Marrying out a daughter is like tossing out a cup of water.*' I loved Lai Kai from the first moment he removed my headdress."

The family celebrations continued for another three days.

"After the festivities ended," she went on, "my family stayed in the home village near Canton, while Lai Kai and I began our married life with his family in Soochow. He was an architect, and he had a special practice, restoring large private gardens."

As she dabbed her eyes, I remembered all the times Helen had talked about China: how she'd traveled everywhere (probably on her honeymoon), how Hangchow was the most romantic city (and of course it was, because she was in love), how she'd adored Soochow's beautiful gardens (because she'd spent a lot of time in them with her husband). But there were the other stories: the Japanese invading, the plane strafing Helen and Monroe, only it probably hadn't been Monroe. She'd been married, and she was a widow, which was why she'd dressed the way she did . . .

"When we first met, it had barely been a year since I lost Lai Kai," she said. "The two of you saved me."

Helen had kept all this a secret from Ruby and me for *three* years. It was unbelievable. But I didn't have time to sort that out in my mind, because it was Ruby's turn.

"Hideo was only twenty-seven years old," she told us. "He was not only my mother's best student but he was good at judo and fishing and laughing too. Grace, you would have liked him. He loved movies. Any kind. Gangsters. Cowboys and Indians. War pictures. He was the eldest child and the best of us. My mom and pop must be heartbroken . . ." More tears. "I'm so scared. Where are my parents? Do you think the authorities have taken Yori already? What will happen to me?"

We had no answers, so Helen resumed her story: "Lai Kai took me with him everywhere, even though it wasn't traditional for me to be *out* like that. He said, 'You have learned a lot from watching your father and brothers. You have a good business mind. You can help me with my clients. You can negotiate with contractors, gardeners, and artisans. You can balance our books and make sure we don't waste anything on our projects.' "

"He sounds perfect," Ruby said.

"He was. We were like a pair of chopsticks—always in harmony. I expected we would be like that forever, even if chaff-eating days should come upon us. We were that happy. But you know what they say. *Extreme joy begets sorrow.*"

They went back and forth, sharing their sadness. It felt like they were behind a wall and nothing I could say or do could reach them.

Helen told us about the invasion itself. Four years ago, Japanese troops landed on the shores of Hangchow Bay for the march to Nanking. They killed everyone and everything they saw. At the same time, other Japanese—supposedly living peacefully in China—launched balloons in Shanghai and other cities around the country emblazoned with Chinese characters which read: ONE MILLION JAPANESE TROOPS LAND NORTH OF HANGCHOW.

"We heard the message was designed to ruin the morale of the Chinese troops," Helen said. "But what if it was true?"

Separately, another Japanese force entered Soochow. Helen put a hand over her breast. "The scar you've seen. That didn't happen in a car accident. It was made by a bayonet. I wish I'd died."

"But you didn't," Ruby said. "You lived, and you got out."

"They left me for dead. I stayed in the rice paddy until night, then I slipped from one paddy to the next, slithering through the muck like a water snake. I slept during the day. I lost track of time. I was a walking corpse. I had to get to Shanghai, where I'd be safe in the International Settlement. I don't know how long it took to cover the seventy-five miles or so. I went to the American Embassy. At first they wouldn't let me through the gate. You can imagine how I looked. But when I spoke, they heard I was an American."

She was put on a boat and sent to her family in the south.

"A Chinese widow is at the mercy of her husband's family," Helen continued. "They can care for her, or they can throw her in the street. But my husband's family was gone, so they couldn't determine my future. My parents took me in and brought me back to San Francisco. I was shunned by everyone—girls I'd gone to school with and the women at the Chinese Telephone Exchange—because no one wanted my bad fate to leave dust on them. All because of the Japs. They did this to me." She paused before adding, "That day, Grace, when you asked me to go upstairs with you into the Forbidden City, I went because I had nothing to lose. You rescued me from decades as a proper Chinese widow—"

"I had nothing to do with what happened to you, but how could you ever tolerate being around *me*?" Ruby asked. "You must see me and—"

"What about your family? Your father?" I cut in before Helen could respond to Ruby's worries. This wasn't about *her*.

"Since Lai Kai's death, my life has been an abyss of suffering, filled with deep water and hot fire. I became a pariah even in my own family. They all ignored me. My parents, my brothers. Everyone except Monroe. Baba believes that a wife *belongs* to her husband, even in death. *Marrying out a daughter is like tossing out a cup of water,*" Helen repeated bitterly. "No life lay ahead of me, because no proper Chinese man would ever marry me. I truly was a worthless branch on the family tree and a reminder to all those in the compound that I'd survived while so many others had died. Baba said that, as a widow, my only purpose in life was to linger on before dying. Back then I thought—I *hoped*—there would be something I could do that would make him acknowledge my existence again. But after he found us that day outside the club . . . well, you saw what happened. He didn't care enough about me to stop me from working there, although later he said I had no bottom to the depths I would go to embarrass and humiliate the family. I had disgraced myself as a widow, who would have been better off committing suicide. If I couldn't do that, then I should live as a chaste widow. I slipped just once. I thought Tim would be a comfort. He wasn't, and now I have Tommy." Her eyes glistened wet again. "Eddie gave me a way to be a chaste widow for real."

It was close to one in the morning when Helen got up to leave. Such sad things had happened to her, but it seemed she wouldn't let them, or even this crisis, rupture our relationship. We had to go on.

"I'm sorry about your brother," she said to Ruby.

"I'm sorry about your husband," Ruby replied.

Helen gave Ruby a hug and departed, with barely a word to me. I wanted to talk to Ruby—about the terrible tragedy of everything Helen had experienced and the emotional consequences that had so affected our friend—but her face was set in grim determination.

"You'll want me to move out," she said. "I'll start to pack—"

"No." I shook my head, adamant.

"Grace, I'm the enemy now." She stared at her feet. "The FBI has to come for me after what they think my parents . . . I don't want you to get in trouble for harboring an outlaw."

I reminded her of what she'd said to Helen earlier: she was innocent of what had happened to Helen, her husband, his family, and their retainers. And she was certainly innocent of the attack on Pearl Harbor.

"You're not an outlaw. You're my friend."

Ruby looked up, unsure but hopeful.

I reflected for a moment before going on. "I've run away from a lot of things, so I'm telling you this from experience. Don't do anything hasty. Let's wait and see what unfolds."

With that, Ruby sank to her knees and covered her face with her hands.

THREE DAYS AFTER the bombing of Pearl Harbor, a China Clipper landed at Treasure Island pocked with bullet holes from a strafing at Wake Island. The day after that, San Francisco and the West Coast were named the Western Theater of Operations. Lieutenant General DeWitt was put in charge. The city became a citadel with antiaircraft guns, searchlights, and radar receivers dotting the tops of the hills overlooking the Golden Gate Bridge. China Clippers were given new duties: flying military personnel and medical supplies between San Francisco and Pearl Harbor. Treasure Island became a docking station for special blimps, which went on antisubmarine patrols along the coast. Over four hundred mines were placed in the waters around San Francisco. A special net was extended from the marina in San Francisco to Sausalito, which was opened and closed by a heavy-duty tugboat to allow friendly ships and subs in and out of the bay. Ruby and I made blackout curtains and tacked them over our windows. A midnight curfew was instituted, which cut into business not only at the Forbidden City but at every club and bar on all sides of the bay. Helen used one of her many proverbs to tell us what we all felt: *Every bush and tree looks like the enemy.*

Persons of Japanese descent living in the city were asked to turn in their flashlights, cameras, and knives from their kitchens—just in case. The Native Sons—and Daughters—of the Golden West launched a campaign: "Get rid of the Japs! They're all spies!" At the club, Charlie handed out pins that read I AM CHINESE to all his employees to wear. "I want everyone to be safe," he explained. "If any of you is Japanese, who cares? You're my glamour girls. You work for me." He wasn't the only club owner to take this approach. Most of the proprietors who had Japanese dancers and musicians decided to turn a blind eye for the time being, because there were customers to entertain and money to be made. The audience accepted those pins and that willful blindness. They applauded when Charlie started and ended each show with "Let's nip the Nips." As for Ruby, she performed—enticingly lit by her blue spotlight—laughed and joked with the boys, and generally kept up her Princess Tai façade, but she was inconsolable at home. She hadn't heard from Yori, yet she resisted trying to track what had happened to him or her parents.

"The Japanese share something with the Chinese," she announced one night. "My face is my family's face. Whatever I do is a reflection on them. But whatever they do is a reflection on me too. If I disgrace myself, I also disgrace my family. If my family is disgraced, then I am also disgraced."

I hated to see her so frightened and sad, but I didn't know how to handle the shame and embarrassment she felt about her own family. Confused, I went back to my room and shut the door. After that, when I heard her crying, I stayed put. Perhaps I should have gone to her, but I didn't want her to lose even more face by seeing me.

And Helen? She'd kept the secret of her husband a long time, and that story got sucked right back inside to where it had been hiding. "I don't want to rehash all that," she'd say if I tried to get her to talk about her husband. "You're getting so nosy, you're worse than Ida." Helen brought Tommy to work, but she'd nearly have a fit every time she had to leave him to perform. In other words, she could shift from cool as a cucumber to jittery wreck in minutes. She wasn't the only one to run cold and hot.

Passions were wild and immediate. A sense of we're-going-to-get-them filled the air. Several Forbidden City busboys, janitors, dishwashers, and second cooks, who'd long harbored bitterness against Japan for invading China, quit their jobs and enlisted. Not long after, more men in the kitchen received their greetings from Uncle Sam and were called up.

Ten days after the attack on Pearl Harbor, Joe brought issues of *Time* and *Life* to our apartment. Here, at last, was information we believed we could trust, but, oh, brother. The magazines offered diagrams and photos titled "How to Tell Japs from the Chinese" and "How to Tell Your Friends from the Japs." *Life* encouraged its readers to overcome their "distressing ignorance" on this "delicate question." So . . . Chinese were tall, averaging five feet five, while Japs topped out at five two and a half. Chinese tended to put on weight to show they were prosperous, while Japs were seldom fat (except for sumo wrestlers). Chinese were not hairy, while Japs could grow mustaches. After decades of being labeled inscrutable, suddenly Chinese could be identified by their placid, kindly, and open expressions, while anyone—armed with the information provided in the magazines' pages—should be able to spot a Jap by his dogmatic assertions, his insistence on pushing his arrogance in your face, and the way he could be counted on to laugh loudly at the wrong time.

"It says here that Chinese have parchment yellow complexions," Ruby relayed to Joe, "while Japs have earthy yellow complexions. Japs also have flat noses, massive cheek and jawbones, and short faces."

That stuff was nonsense, but to hear Ruby read those things aloud? It was chilling. I caught her eye. When I saw *nothing* there, I understood the absolute terror she must have been feeling. It all made me ill—the lie itself, the disquieting apprehension of what would happen if her secret was revealed, and the concern over what Joe—our *friend,* for heaven's sake—would do if, and when, he found out.

As Christmas approached, the phone company ran ads—"Long distance helps unite the nation"—and promised to use every circuit and every operator on Christmas Eve and Christmas Day. I wanted Mom to know I was safe. I wanted to hear her say, "We're fine too.

We love you, honey." But a part of me was so terrified my father might answer the phone—what if he didn't let me speak to her?—that I didn't even try to put through a call: I hated myself for being such a coward, so some nights I, too, cried alone in my room.

At the end of January, the Justice Department announced that all strategic locations, which included San Francisco, needed to be cleared of enemy aliens. On February 2, registration would begin.

Ruby didn't seem concerned. "I'm not an enemy alien. I was born here, and I'm an American citizen."

I was scared for her.

GRACE

Dancing on the Edge

Our lives changed quickly in those first few months of the war. We still had air-raid sirens and blackouts, but the curfew was abolished and the immediate danger dissipated. San Francisco became a liberty port, and the whole city buzzed with activity. In Chinatown, the world rushed in. Servicemen moseyed up and down the streets, going from bar to bar. They jammed nightclubs. They spent money like there was no tomorrow, and for some maybe there wasn't. No one wanted to stay home—although business at the Forbidden City went up and down, as it did in nightclubs across the nation, depending on news from the war front, whether in Europe or the Pacific. A writer for *Variety* called this phenomenon "escapology." Clubs like the Forbidden City gave people a place to blow off steam, celebrate, share experiences and trade stories, and laugh away their staggering dread of what might come. Charlie had a hard time keeping ponies, because soldier boys—total strangers—married our girls on what seemed a lark. The fear of death is a powerful aphrodisiac.

Helen and Ruby were tied together by tragedy, yet remained wary of each other. Often I'd find the two of them sitting together in a corner of the club before we opened, conversing in low voices about who knows what. Now that Helen's secret was out, her deep-seated distrust and hatred of the Japanese could spark on occasion. Ruby responded to Helen's rare outbursts the same way she did when one of our boys talked about going overseas to kill Japs—by accepting another drink, jitterbugging until she exhausted her partner, and sleeping around. Unlike the rest of us, she was not only dancing on the edge of a volcano, she was looking down into its fiery center. I don't know if she was afraid, thinking about jumping into it, or daring it to erupt. Maybe all three.

One evening in early '42, I sat at a table with some Navy officers stationed on Treasure Island, listening to them talk about how the place had changed since I'd last been there. The band was playing "The Japs Won't Have a Ghost of a Chance" when Joe entered the main room and spotted me. The sureness of his gait and the way he held his shoulders told me he'd enlisted. I thanked the sailors and walked toward Joe, meeting him in the middle of the dance floor.

"The United States Army Air Forces," he said in greeting.

Of course! What had previously been called the Army Air Corps was now the most active service of the military in recruitment, because Japan had large reserves of pilots, and we did not. The air forces wanted and needed educated men, and Joe was a college graduate, with two years of law school under his belt. The air forces was considered *the* elite service, and it was meant for him.

"When do you report?" I asked.

"Not for another couple of weeks," he answered.

Charlie gave Joe dinner and drinks on the house. All the girls came out to congratulate him. Ida sat on his lap like she belonged there. Joe nonchalantly accepted the attention like the glittering flyboy he'd become just by signing his name to a piece of paper. Ruby regarded him with an expression I recognized. Glitter attracts glitter, and no one was more entranced than Ruby. The heat that was always between them—even during these past months, when it had been reduced to mere embers—once again ignited. In minutes, Ida was out on her ear, and Ruby had Joe completely in her thrall. Even after all this time, it was excruciating for me to see because once again the game had changed. There was something about the way he reacted to her that was elemental, primitive, sexual.

That very night, Joe proposed to Ruby, and I couldn't help but wish he'd chosen me instead. None of it made sense, but we were all scared of the future and hanging on to "normal" life in whatever way we could. I think—I *believe*—Joe mistook Ruby's seductiveness, and how it made him feel, for love. And, of course, he was caught up in the moment as so many boys were. For Ruby's part, Joe was a possible bridge to safety. That she would even consider marriage was the first dent in her armor—the rash fearlessness with which she faced the hatred around her. We were now at war, and my heart seemed insignificant compared to what Joe and Ruby were each facing. That didn't mean they could get married in California, though.

"Let's drive to Mexico to tie the knot," Ruby suggested.

Joe vetoed the idea, saying it would be foolhardy to leave the country now. Instead, he wrote to the State Bar of Nevada, asking if he could marry an Oriental girl there, and received a letter denying the request on the basis that it was a crime for a Caucasian to "intermarry with any person of the Ethiopian or black race, Malay or brown race, or Mongolian or yellow race." He next wrote to the second nearest state, Utah, and was informed that "marriage between whites and Mongolians, members of the Malay race, mulattos, or quadroons" was prohibited there as well. Each rejection infuriated Joe and further demoralized Ruby.

"You've got to tell him the truth," Helen insisted one night as the three of us sat together in the apartment on Powell, with our blackout curtains trapping all light within the four walls of our living room, Tommy asleep in a basket on the floor, and the radio playing in the background.

"That I'm *Japanese*?" Ruby whispered the last word. "Not possible."

"What will happen when he finds out you've lied to him?"

"If anyone told him, he'd be snowed under," she admitted. "But who's going to tell him?"

"Oh, honey, you don't want to live a lie," Helen said, but she didn't sound all that sincere to me. "It's not worth it. If he loves you, your ancestry won't matter."

If true, this was a stunning leap for Helen, who was always so against mixing. Or maybe she was just trying to comfort our friend. But Ruby's case was different even from those of other *Nisei*. Her family had been suspected of signaling to Japanese bombers, her older brother was killed on a fishing boat in the minutes after the attack, her parents were accused of being fifth columnists. She was in a terrible and dangerous spot. That she hadn't been picked up or reported already seemed miraculous.

"Joe is so American." Ruby spoke haltingly, as though she were afraid to reveal her true motives. "He's the *most* American person I've ever met. If I marry him, won't that prove I'm American too?"

But wouldn't Ruby still have the same black mark against her as her parents? Wouldn't she seem especially suspect because she'd masqueraded as Chinese, dancing in a nightclub frequented by servicemen? If she were caught, wouldn't that reflect badly on Joe as well? Maybe even ruin his chances for flight school?

On February 19, President Roosevelt signed Executive Order 9066, which authorized the secretary of war to designate certain areas as military zones and said that he could exclude any or all persons suspected of being enemies from those places. The next day, 250 enemy aliens, mostly Japanese, were rounded up in San Francisco and sent to Bismarck, North Dakota.

"Where the hell is Bismarck?" Ruby asked, sassy as could be.

On March 2, General DeWitt issued instructions that all people of Japanese ancestry living in San Francisco would be wise to voluntarily evacuate inland. Instantly, posters appeared on telephone poles—even in Chinatown—addressed "To All Japanese." The instructions didn't distinguish between alien and nonalien. (It hit me then: *alien* and *nonalien*. Whether citizens or not, all Japanese were now considered *alien*.)

"Why should Princess Tai move?" Ruby asked.

The next day, we went with Joe to the Port of Embarkation in Oakland. He was going to the newly opened Santa Ana Army Air Base for basic training, which would last for nine weeks. He chucked my chin and said, "Keep your nose clean, kid." I blubbered like nobody's business. Then he turned to Ruby. "I'll get our marriage problem ironed out," he promised. They kissed right in the open.

JOE SENT POSTCARDS to Ruby and me every few days:

> *This is an overnight city of thousands of men in the middle of bean and tomato fields. Hey, isn't Hollywood supposed to be around here?*

> *I want to fly, but we don't have planes, hangars, or runways. All we do is march, salute, and learn to obey orders.*

> *We're taking tests nearly every day to see how book-smart we are, analyze our eye-hand coordination, and evaluate how we react under pressure, so the brass can decide where to assign us. Some guys will be lucky to become bombardiers, navigators, or mechanics. I only want the pilot's seat. Keeping my fingers crossed for aviation training.*

We taped these to the mirror in the dressing room.

We had our own concerns, minor though they were. The government ordered a 15 percent reduction in the allotment of yardage to be used for women's and girls' apparel. Dolman and leg-of-mutton sleeves became no-nos, as did tucks, pleats, plackets, hoods, and belts wider than two inches. We went along with the rules because we wanted to help our boys, but we suffered less than other women across the country, because theatrical costumes—along with bridal wear and religious and judiciary robes—were exempt from the new restrictions. In other words, we looked crummy by day and fabulous by night.

Helen took her patriotism seriously. The next time she ordered a costume, she asked the seamstress to leave out the midsection to save a little fabric. Although she'd regained her shape, she'd still had a baby. To hide the imperfections, Eddie had her oil her midriff so it would shine. Now her midriff caught the light, but it could be slick. Eddie's vanity wouldn't allow him to admit he was wrong. Backstage we could hear the audience utter a collective *"whoops"* whenever she slipped a little through Eddie's hands on a lift.

Joe had been gone three weeks when, on March 27, General DeWitt made internment and relocation mandatory for all people of Japanese ancestry, beginning in April.

"I'm not worried about that," Ruby declared.

Four days later, *The San Francisco News* reported that Joe DiMaggio's parents might be evacuated from the city as enemy aliens of Italian descent. If Joe DiMaggio's parents could be rounded up, then what would happen to my friend?

"I'm Princess Tai," she said, unabashed. "No one knows I'm Japanese."

But I did. Helen did. Charlie did. And some of the ponies did too.

On April 1, Doolittle's raiders sailed west under the Golden Gate Bridge, "bound for Tokyo." Evacuation of the Japanese in San Francisco began five days later. Ruby's Aunt Haru and Uncle Junji closed their store in Alameda and boarded a bus to the horse stables at the Tanforan racetrack in San Bruno to be housed with several thousand other Japanese. Their bank account had been frozen, and they'd been forced to sell their business, car, and most of their possessions for next to nothing, but they were allowed to take bedding and linens for each family member, toiletries, clothes, cutlery, dishes, and personal items as long as they could carry everything. Ruby made no attempt to contact them. On April 21, Japanese were ordered out of more Bay Area neighborhoods, with the result that several dancers from the Sky Room disappeared and had to be replaced.

In May, Joe finished basic training and had a few days off before he started flight school. He came up to visit Ruby. He didn't mention marriage, because he was completely focused on flying and the next stage of his training. "I'm going to Minter Field," he announced to a group of us. "It's in Shafter, near Bakersfield. Even though I already have my pilot's license, they have guys like me start right back at square one with an open-cockpit Stearman. If I don't wash out—and I won't—then I'll move on to a four-hundred-fifty-horsepower canopied BT-13."

Ruby didn't seem to mind that her wedding had been put on the back burner. "Maybe I don't need to get married after all," she said.

SERVICEMEN MIGHT TAUNT—AND sometimes rough up—the Juggling Jins, our waiters, bartenders, and busboys, mistakenly accusing them of being "yellow-bellied Japs," but they had a different attitude toward the girls in the club. Ruby, the other gals, and I spent God's own time trying to appeal to our boys, doing what we could to manifest glamour in our suddenly unpredictable world. We developed a new hairstyle: teasing, piling, pinning, and spraying our hair until it looked like a cross between the Empire State Building and how the Mexican girls down in Los Angeles built their tresses into mile-high pompadours for Saturday night dances. We bought extra-long false eyelashes. We painted our lips to look bee-kissed. We attended to all our boys—whether soldiers, sailors, or airmen. A bunch of the show kids—like Helen and Eddie, Irene and Jack—were married, but there was a lot of fooling around. I mean a lot.

And then there was Ida. She had loads of admirers, but she always saved time for Ray Boiler, the creepy short-order cook from Visalia who used to follow Ruby around. Even though Ruby had warned Ida about him, she saw him anyway. I guess she thought she was one-upping Ruby. Since Ida was more receptive to Ray's attentions, he gave her bracelets and earrings. He bought her scarves and hats. He brought her sugar and other rationed foodstuffs stolen from the coffee shop where he worked. When she sat with him between shows, he slipped her fifty-dollar tips. Whenever she dared to treat Ray like dirt, or brazenly dance with one soldier boy after another in front of him, he'd go nearly crazy with desire and jealousy, which caused him to fixate on her all the more. She was playing a dangerous game, and she liked it.

Finally it came time for me to get my feet wet. Almost a year to the day after the bombing of Pearl Harbor, this boy in uniform came to the club. He was a woesome thing, trying to act courageous, on his way to the Pacific. I felt sorry for the kid. We drank beer. We danced to "On a Little Street in Singapore."

"Where you from, soldier?"

"You wouldn't know it," he said.

He swung me under his arm. His jitterbug was awkward, and I had to be nimble to keep him from crushing my feet.

"Try me."

"I'm from Darbydale, Ohio."

"Darbydale!" I exclaimed. "That's close to where I grew up. I'm from Plain City."

His parents were farmers. He and his family had gone to the Plain City Fair for as long as he could remember, although he didn't recall seeing me win a dance contest.

"I never went to that part of the fair," he admitted bashfully. "I was 4-H all the way."

We drank a few more beers and danced a few more times. He clapped and smiled during my numbers. He reminded me of home when the world was conspiring to make me yearn—longingly and unrealistically—for the consolation and security of the town where I'd grown up. I got caught up in the moment so many ponies had before me with the soldier boys who came to the club before shipping out and might never come back. I took him to my apartment after the last show. Jeremy Scott was his name, and I was twenty-one years old. I wish I could say it was a big deal, but it was the first time for both of us, and it wasn't anything to rave about. Grope. Poke. Bump. Grunt. Sigh. It hurt like the dickens, and it was over so fast I was flummoxed. *That's it? I've been pining and worrying and saving myself for this?* He slouched out of my apartment at five in the morning. He promised to write, but he never did. For all I know, he got killed in his first firefight. Very sad if true. But from the moment he left I was scared down to my toes. What if I was pregnant? I looked for symptoms everywhere. Did the smell of food turn my stomach? Was I sleepy? Did my breasts hurt? The girls at the club peppered me with advice.

"Try douching with olive oil," Ida recommended. "That's what I do when Ray comes to town."

"I prefer Coca-Cola," Irene said. "It's fizzy, and Jack doesn't mind the taste."

The idea made my head swim, but the other girls laughed.

"You could try spreading pomegranate pulp down there," someone else suggested.

"Or fresh ginger."

"Or tobacco juice."

"You're making me sick," I said.

The girls stared at me sympathetically. Ida voiced what they were thinking. "That probably means you're knocked up for sure."

Which made my eyes go black with dizziness.

"If you are knocked up," Ruby said, "none of those things is going to help you. They're only good if you use them before you do it."

"A friend of mine has a trampoline," one of the girls suggested helpfully. "I heard that if you jump a lot, the baby will come loose."

"You could throw yourself down some stairs—"

Ida said, "I know a man who can take care of it—"

"Stop, all of you," Helen ordered. "You're frightening her half to death."

Literally, because death from exsanguination or sepsis was what I was looking at if I got a back-alley abortion. My father had accused me of being a whore, and now I burned with shame and fear. All this from a few minutes with some kid . . .

"I'll help you," Helen vowed. And she did, although I probably shouldn't have put my faith in her when she herself had gotten pregnant and ended up with Tommy. Helen put me in a bathtub with steaming hot water. She sat on the floor and kept me company while I massaged my stomach and prayed for whatever was in there to come out. About a week later, while I was dancing the Chinaconga through the club, something warm and sticky leaked between my legs. My period had arrived . . . right on schedule.

"You were lucky this time," Helen lectured. "You and only you will have to suffer any mistakes you make in connection with one of our boys."

"You don't have to worry," I promised. "I'm never going to do it again."

Helen took me to a doctor anyway. "Just to be on the safe side."

The doctor—as white as his coat, but not nearly as judgmental as I expected him to be—fitted me with a diaphragm. When he was done rummaging around in there, he said, "This isn't all up to you. Our boys have seen films and they've all learned the slogan: Don't forget—put it on before you put it in."

As crude as what he said was, at least now I was prepared. And even though I'd vowed never to do it again, over the next few months I sometimes got caught up, once again, in the moment. Making love got a lot better too. Fun! I wasn't the only one to see it that way. Young women, whether at our club or working as waitresses near munitions factories or in bars outside bases, came to be called Victory Girls, although some people dubbed us Khaki-wackies, Cuddle Bunnies, and Good-time Charlottes. We were doing our part for the war effort—even if that meant we had to deal with a lot of busy hands. And when the boys shipped out, we presented them with signed photographs—"Dreaming of you, forever yours, Princess Tai," "To a swell guy, love always, Grace," or "May you stay as sweet as you are, love and kisses, Ida"—so they'd have something to hold when they got lonely. We gave them our address at the club so they could write to us, and many of them did—sad, homesick notes. Sometimes we never heard from them again, and we wondered if they were dead, injured, or had just forgotten us. But the next day, a new batch of boys would come through, and the cycle would start over. I didn't get pregnant, and no one got too rough. (That doesn't mean I didn't count the days each month, though. One mistake would destroy my life.)

As for Ruby, she'd gone fourteen months without being identified, and either her fears had vanished or she did a great job of hiding them, because Princess Tai was the most popular of all the girls. The ponies complained that her gardenias intoxicated the men in the audience. And they did seem intoxicated, but it wasn't from her gardenias. You should have seen the way they leaned forward in their chairs, waiting for Princess Tai to drop her fans or her bubble. She never did. They bought her dinner and drinks. They sent flowers to the dressing room. She showed the youngest ones how to dance. She taught them how to use chopsticks. When some smart mouth would tease her with the old myth about which direction an Oriental girl's privates went, she'd laugh merrily. "Oh, sweetie, you should try it. It's just like eating corn on the cob."

One night at the beginning of March '43—a full year after Joe went to Southern California for training—a wiseacre in dress blues popped Ruby's bubble with the tip of his cigarette. People went crazy! After that, Ruby deliberately stayed in the middle of the dance floor, sashaying only once a night close enough to some lucky boy, who'd paid to have the honor of popping her bubble. "It's all in good fun," Ruby always said after she'd scampered Eve-style back to the dressing room. The new showstopper made Charlie happy too, because he could put an inflated price for the bubble on the patron's check.

Through it all, Ruby remained true to Joe, but the more risks she took and the more daring and flamboyant she became, the more I lay awake at night, anxious that one slip and it would be all over for her.

GRACE

A Succulent Dish

"Cripes! Get a load of this!" Ruby beamed as she held a telegram out to me. "It's an offer to be in a movie!"

I read the telegram inviting Princess Tai to dance in a Paramount Studios film called *Aloha, Boys!,* starring Deanna Durbin, with music by Kay Kyser, who'd recently had a big hit with "Praise the Lord and Pass the Ammunition." These were not top-top stars, but the ponies in the dressing room flipped their lids. It hadn't even been four weeks since that guy first popped Ruby's bubble and already she was reaping big dividends.

"It's beyond exciting!" Ida said.

"Stupendous!" Irene whinnied.

"Can I take your place while you're gone?" asked Esther, a new girl, who, it now became apparent, had bigger ambitions than any of us realized. "I've been working on a routine."

Ida jabbed Esther with her elbow. "Stop it already. We've all heard about your girl-in-a-gilded-cage act. Charlie doesn't want it. This is about Ruby, not about you trying to steal her spot in the show."

Ruby and I left the gals to their arguing and went to Charlie's office so she could call the casting director. She held the phone to her ear and repeated pieces of the conversation so I could hear. She'd be required on the Paramount lot for a day, but with train travel and time for her to relax before and after filming, she'd be gone for five. As I listened, I grew angry with myself. I'd become lazy. I'd forgotten ambition. I'd let Ruby jump far ahead of me, because it was easy to float through as a pony, earning $150 a week with my extra powdering-and-gluing job and living on the edges of her bounty.

By the time she got off the phone, Charlie had opened champagne and was pouring it for everyone—from the lowliest dishwasher all the way up to his prized princess. "I promise a raise to anyone else who gets a part in a film," he proclaimed as he lifted his glass.

"I'd kill to be in your place, Ruby," I confessed, truthful as can be.

She flushed with joy as she announced, "They told me I can bring someone with me. You and Helen are closest to me. I wish I could bring you both."

I'd sat through enough of Reverend Reynolds's sermons back home to recognize that the greed and covetousness raging through my body were sins.

"I can't go. I've got Tommy," Helen said, giving me the best gift of my life.

I hugged Ruby and thanked Helen. I was grateful and ecstatic. Then something occurred.

"Isn't this trip dangerous?" I asked when we were alone. "What if you're caught?"

"Give it a rest, will ya?" Ruby snapped.

After that, I kept my mouth shut.

Ruby and I needed clothes for the trip, so we went out and spent a fortune. We bought outfits in wool, cotton, and rayon, because those fabrics were produced in America. Not only had the amount and types of fabric been dramatically cut to help the war effort, but the range in colors had also been reduced, since the chemicals used for dyes had shifted to military purposes. What hues remained had all-American names: Victory Gold, Gallant Blue, Valor Red, and Patriot Green. My favorite skirt had a pattern of *V*s done in Morse code—three dots and a single dash—to symbolize *V* for *victory.* We splurged and used our entire ration of three pairs of shoes for the year in one day.

Joe was to be the cherry on top. He'd finished half of his training and had managed to swing a couple days off to meet us. When Ruby asked the production folks if Joe could come to the set, they agreed, saying, "Anything for our boys."

Charlie arranged for newspaper photographers to see us off, so Ruby and I planned our travel ensembles accordingly. We were entertainers; we needed to appear alluring yet approachable. Ruby wore a knee-length skirt, a twin set, and a pair of wedges. I wore a ruffled blouse and a cotton dirndl skirt printed in a red, white, and blue pattern, and red canvas platforms with brass studs. We painted our nails with Cutex's Alert varnish and applied Elizabeth Arden Velva Leg Film to our legs to give us the appearance of wearing stockings, even though the cream stained the insides of our skirts an awful yellow. We used eyebrow pencil to draw lines up the backs of our legs for seams.

A car and driver met us at Union Station in Los Angeles, and we were sped west along Sunset Boulevard. We made the jog over to Hollywood Boulevard and arrived at the Hollywood Roosevelt Hotel like we were real movie stars. (Big change since the last time I was here!) Once we got to our suite, we dressed for a night on the town: Ruby in a black crepe gown and a black snood (like Hedy Lamarr), I in a royal-blue crepe gown shirred at the waist with my seal fur thrown over my shoulders. We both used Tussy Jeep Red lipstick—"Lovely as a Jeep; attention-getting as a Major." When the front desk called to notify us that Joe had arrived, we primped for a few more minutes, then rode the elevator to the lobby.

Joe wore his uniform, and he sure looked good. A cool sip of water. A man with the world by the tail. He grinned as he strode toward us. He stopped just before Ruby so he could give her the full head-to-toe. "You're a succulent dish, baby," he said, and she was.

He took us to the Coconut Grove. Princess Tai was a very big fish in the minuscule pond of San Francisco Chinatown and a pretty big fish in the moderately sized wartime pond of the San Francisco nightclub scene, but even here—at the apex of glamour and class—she turned heads. She wasn't a movie star yet, so we were seated on the first tier above the dance floor. "Second-best seats in the joint," Joe pronounced as he happily surveyed the room.

He was besotted with Ruby, and she was thrilled to see him too. The way they had their hands on each other, I bet they wished they could whisk off to someplace private, but I was there and they did their best to include me. He danced with each of us, and, as usual, other couples made room for Joe and me as we swung through some of our special moves. When we returned to Ruby, he topped off our champagne glasses and told us what was coming next for him in training. Ruby and I plastered interested expressions on our faces, but what in the heck was he talking about? He had us back at the hotel by midnight. Ruby needed to be rested for her big day, but Joe came in for a while and they spent some time alone in her room. I put up my hair in curlers and tried not to listen.

The next morning, Ruby kept her face clean of makeup, as she'd been told to do, but I dolled up. I was going to a movie studio; I wanted to look fabulous. I swept up the front and sides of my hair to form a waved pompadour, using a foam doughnut to increase the volume.

Joe was waiting with the studio car when we got downstairs. He put a hand on the small of Ruby's back as he helped her into the backseat. It was a short drive to Paramount Studios. A tall blond woman carrying a clipboard greeted us. Her name was Betty, and she managed to come across as both authoritative and stunning. "The director wants to meet you before you go to Hair and Makeup," she explained. She ushered us through the soundstage—cavernous and dark, with a sensuously lit set of a nightclub built in the center—where David Butler was going over blocking details. Famous! He'd directed a few Shirley Temple movies and had just wrapped *Road to Morocco*. He shook hands with Joe, nodded to me, and eyeballed Ruby as though he were checking the freshness of a fish.

"I've heard great things about you." He motioned for Ruby to turn so he could get the 360-degree view. "I haven't seen your act, so can you show me both dances—the one with the bubble and the one with the feathers?"

"They're fans," Ruby corrected him.

He gave her a wink, pleased with her spunk.

"How much of me is going to show?" she asked, her rotation complete.

"How much can I get?" he asked mischievously.

Ruby tipped a finger at him. "You're the one who has to deal with the decency codes, not me."

He laughed. "Don't worry about a thing. You'll be plenty decent."

He asked Betty to escort us to Ruby's dressing room. We went back outside and strolled down a path lined with perfectly cut box hedges. When Gary Cooper and Ingrid Bergman walked past us, I practically had to pinch myself. Ruby fluttered her eyelids at me, delighted. It felt like we'd arrived in heaven. Joe beamed too. He'd have plenty of stories to tell when he returned to Minter Field.

The dressing room was small but elegant. Betty pointed to a carton that protected a pair of flawless gardenias for Ruby to wear. Then Betty whisked us to Hair and Makeup, and we watched as folks painted Ruby's face and squeezed a wig over her head with hair that came down past her rear end.

"They must be going for a Godiva look," Ruby commented.

Betty shrugged. Apparently no one had bothered to inform her.

"We'll have the body makeup girl take care of you in your dressing room," Betty said. "Can you two make it back by yourselves? I've arranged for someone to take Joe on a tour of the studio."

Joe docilely allowed himself to be led away by Betty, and Ruby and I wandered back to her dressing room. A few minutes later, the makeup girl arrived, and I showed her how Ruby liked her powder applied. After the girl left, I helped Ruby into a silk robe and pinned the gardenias over her left ear. Then we stood—because Ruby didn't want to smudge her makeup—and waited. Finally, we heard a knock at the door. I answered it to find Betty nervously scrutinizing her clipboard. Two men in dark suits with gray felt fedoras pulled low over their foreheads loomed behind her. Mr. Butler had tagged along too.

"These men are from the FBI. They're searching for . . ." Betty glanced at her clipboard then back at me. "They're calling her Kimiko Fukutomi."

The men impatiently pushed Betty aside. One of them put his meaty palm on the door and shoved it open against my pathetic resistance. What did I think holding it closed would accomplish? That I'd give Ruby a chance to climb out the window in her robe? Where could she possibly have escaped to?

The FBI agents planted themselves in the middle of the room, their legs spread to hold them solidly to the ground, their fists clasped in front of their privates. Betty and Mr. Butler crowded into the dressing room too and positioned themselves a little to the side. Ruby's gardenias, warmed by the presence of so many bodies, sent forth their stiflingly sweet scent.

"Are you Kimiko Fukutomi?" the taller of the two men asked.

Ruby stared ahead, her eyes seeing nothing. I held my breath as terror welled inside me.

"Ma'am?"

Ruby blinked and looked at the man. "I'm Ruby Tom," she answered, her voice even. "My professional name is Princess Tai."

The man pulled a telegram from his inside breast pocket. He glanced at it and then back at Ruby. "We received word from San Francisco yesterday. It says here you're Japanese. My partner and I did a little digging and, ma'am, your family—"

With that, Ruby's composure crumbled. *Caught, caught, caught.*

He turned his attention to me. "What about you, miss? Are you a Jap too?"

I shook my head no. Actually, my whole body shook. He was more than a foot taller than I was, so just his physical presence was menacing.

"Were you aware she's a Jap?"

I opened my mouth.

"No!" Ruby's voice was knife sharp. "Miss Lee is not Japanese. That will be easy to prove. And she doesn't know anything about me." She shifted her focus to me. "I'm sorry I didn't tell you. I'm sorry for any trouble that you might be in because of me—"

"Hey, we can't have any Japs in our film," Mr. Butler cut in, stating what must have been to him the most important issue.

"Kimiko Fukutomi won't be in any films," the second agent added. "Not where she's going."

"You need to come with us." The first man rolled his neck as though he had a pinched nerve.

"May I put on some clothes first?" Ruby asked in a small voice.

"Five minutes. We'll be right outside the door."

As soon as the two men, Mr. Butler, and Betty left and the door closed behind them, Ruby dropped her robe. I needed to thank her for protecting me, but we had so little time. I hurried to rub off as much makeup as I could.

"Someone ratted me out." The words came out of Ruby's mouth, but somehow they didn't sound as though they'd emanated from her. She stood there like a child as I lifted her left foot and put it through the leg opening of her step-ins. I repeated this action with her right foot and then pulled the fabric up her legs.

"Hey, fellas, what's the dope?" A cheerful voice came through the walls.

"Joe . . ." Ruby breathed.

From outside the dressing room we began to hear the mumbling of three men in intense conversation. I slipped Ruby's dress over her head and zipped up the back. Already she moved like an echo.

"Draw your own conclusions, pal" came through loud and clear. The door opened. "It's your headache."

Joe looked like a kid who'd had his ball taken from him. No. That's wrong. He looked more like Freddie Thompson back in Plain

City when the kids teased him after they discovered I was wearing his hand-me-downs—hurt and more than a little disgusted. If an eight-year-old can feel like that, imagine those emotions multiplied in a young man, who's been trained to kill someone of your race and has not only slept with you but proposed to you as well.

"Is it true?" The words seemed to hitch in his throat.

"I'm not ashamed of who I am," Ruby stated flatly.

"You aren't?" he asked. "Then why didn't you tell me you're Japanese?"

"You wanted a China doll. I gave you a China doll," Ruby said with a toss of her head.

I knew she was trying to protect herself from her own emotions and failures, as well as Joe's reaction, but the impact of her mocking words on him was brutal. Color sped up his neck—anger . . . and humiliation. He clenched and unclenched his fists until his knuckles shone like ivory. He suddenly looked like he did the day he almost got into the fight on Treasure Island—out of control. Everything that had happened to the country was focused into hate for one person—Ruby, the woman who'd led him on, lied to him, betrayed him, and made him a sucker. He drew back his arm. Without thinking, I jumped in front of Ruby. Joe's fist hit me square in the jaw. I felt the familiar lift into the air, but Joe was a lot bigger and stronger than my father, so I was thrown up and back with tremendous force. I slammed against the wall. My rib cage cracked on a table edge on the way down. Searing pain shot through me when I hit the floor.

Ruby remained as beautiful and still as a statue—the long hair of her wig trailing down her back, her skin as pale as the gardenia petals, her eyes set like stone. I whimpered in the corner, tentatively touching the places where I hurt as I had so many times when my father beat me, but I wasn't paralyzed by fear. I'd learned how to act in a crisis, and I felt all my senses sharpen to be ready for what might happen next.

Joe's eyes widened with the horror of what he'd done. He looked frantically from me to Ruby and then back at me again. He shook his head. No to hitting me? No to Ruby? He loosened his fists, tightened them again when his eyes met Ruby's, and then he bolted from the room.

Ruby rushed to my side. "I can't believe you did that for me. Are you all right?"

I bit my lips to hold back the pain. Ruby helped me into a chair then kneeled before me.

"We don't have much time," she whispered urgently.

I took a breath to speak and winced as my lungs pushed against my ribs.

"Go after him," she implored as the FBI agents entered. "Please go after him. *Please* . . . He's going to need someone . . ."

She squeezed my knees then rose to face the agents. I got up and lurched toward the door.

"Goodbye, Grace," I heard her say.

"Goodbye, Ruby." The words felt like dust in my mouth.

With my right arm cradling my throbbing left side, I limped down the pretty little pathway outside the dressing room. I found Joe next to a fountain, doubled over, his hands on his thighs, his whole body shaking.

"I was a prize sap." He spat out the words, disgusted with himself. "I guess I had that coming."

I was in such physical agony that it was hard for me to speak. "You aren't a sap, and you didn't deserve that."

"Did you know?" He pulled himself up to face me. He sighed. "Of course you did. Helen too, I'll bet. You three—"

"We begged her to tell you."

He stared at me, weighing what I'd said. He didn't apologize for hitting me, and he didn't ask if I was in pain. He was so blindsided by Ruby's lies—and mine too, I guess—that he wasn't thinking straight. When he came to himself again he'd feel dreadful remorse. For now, though . . .

"A woman can tell a lie a mile long, and a man will believe it's the truth."

There was nothing I could say. Ruby had lied to him, and he *had* believed it. I'd kept her secret, knowing it would devastate him if he ever found out. I'd protected him and her. Now I was seeing the painful results.

He then made a crisp turn on his heel and strutted in the direction of the gate. Hurt radiated from his shoulders. I could tell that he *still* hadn't registered that he'd hit me.

My jaw burned. It was going to swell if I didn't get some ice on it quick. I'd also landed on some old injuries. I'd either fractured or broken a couple of ribs on my left side, so every breath burned like a hot poker twisting between my bones. When I got back to the dressing room, the two FBI agents were gone and so was Ruby, but David Butler was waiting for me. He held Ruby's wig in his hands. The gardenias lay crumpled on the floor.

"I've got a scene to shoot, and I need an Oriental dancer," he said. "Can you do it?"

"Absolutely!" I rubbed my jaw. It hurt like hell, and my side was killing me. Too much was happening for me to process my feelings—I was worried spitless about Ruby, sad for Joe, and sick with guilt that my opportunity had come at such a terrible price—but this was my chance. I had to embrace and accept it, didn't I? "But we'd better hurry. I'm going to bruise up pretty soon."

"Don't worry about a thing," he said, repeating what he'd told Ruby earlier. "This is Hollywood. We've got makeup for that, and with the right lighting I can make anyone look good."

"I'm feeling pretty woozy too. Do you think I could have a couple of aspirin?"

"Aspirin? Betty will get you something a lot stronger than that."

Mr. Butler handed me Ruby's wig and robe, and sent me to Hair and Makeup. When I got there, I put in a quick call to Max Field, the agent Helen, Eddie, and I had used when we were in Los Angeles. He agreed to reschedule his day, come to Paramount, work out a quick contract, and watch the filming so he could book me elsewhere. I forced myself to push away thoughts of Ruby and Joe and handed myself over to the nice ladies. They began by pulling apart my hairdo and then pinning the strands as close to my head as possible to fit the wig over my skull. When they were done with me, I was transformed. For the first time, I wasn't just a China doll. I was an extraordinarily beautiful woman. Mr. Butler studied me and decided against new gardenias.

"You don't need them," he pronounced. "You're exquisite as you are."

With that compliment lifting my spirit, I found my mark. This was my dream, but working on a soundstage is not the same as working in a club. You don't have an audience, wanting to be entertained. You don't have the feeling that people are *with* you. You want to express yourself and sell the number, but you're basically playing to an empty room—with cameras aimed at you—and it's very, very difficult. No matter what I did, Mr. Butler didn't like it. He asked me to use Ruby's fans. She'd always said that what she did was a lot harder than it looked, and she was right. I was naked except for a patch, and I had to walk around for three choruses, which is a long time in music. At least one rib was broken or fractured, and those feathered fans were heavy. I was also scared silly, because I'd never done anything like that. I lost my balance and heard a couple of men on the crew snicker.

"Let's try the bubble," Mr. Butler suggested.

But it wasn't easy to turn with the bubble and not have my fanny flash in front of the camera. I heard "Cut! Cut! Cut!" too many times to count. I was humiliated and ashamed of my poor performance.

"Do you have anything else?" Mr. Butler asked in frustration.

"I might," I said. "Give me ten minutes and I'll come up with something that will work with your music. I can show your audience the world," I promised.

I went to a corner of the soundstage and began to count in my head. *One, two, three, four. Five, six, seven, eight.* Mr. Butler had just made his first Road picture, which probably meant he wanted something "exotic," so I took hand gestures from Siamese and Burmese dance routines I'd encountered at the exposition on Treasure Island, hula I'd learned from Ruby, and bits of Chinese opera movements I'd seen with Monroe, and then brought them into ballroom styling. When I showed the dance to Mr. Butler, he said, "Perfect! I love it! Let's shoot it!"

Someone slapped some very long false fingernails on me, powdered me for shine, and blotted my lipstick. Since I needed a last-minute costume, they tied me into a sarong like Dorothy Lamour and had me take off my shoes so I could dance barefoot. I performed the routine several times as Deanna Durbin and another actor wisecracked their way through a scene in the foreground.

I was going to be a motion-picture star.

RUBY

Whirlpool Valley

"Who's going to win the war?" Agent Parker asked in a harsh voice.

"The United States," I answered.

"Are you pro-Japan?"

"No."

"Then why did your father and brothers go fishing on a Sunday?"

"I don't know."

"Were they sending signals from their boat to the Jap planes as they flew into Pearl Harbor?"

"I'm sure they didn't," I answered.

"Are you aware that your mother made her language students sing the Jap national anthem before every class?"

"Yes, but you're making it sound worse than it was. Her students learned Japanese faster when they had a melody to follow."

Agent Parker exchanged glances with his partner, Agent Holt. We were in a windowless office somewhere in L.A. I was angry at myself for being caught, livid that my big Hollywood chance had been lost, and more furious at whoever had reported me than I was scared of the men, but I was working overtime not to let them see my emotions.

"This is the first time I've heard about my parents since the attack on Pearl Harbor," I volunteered, flashing Agent Parker my pearly whites. "Where are they? And what about my brother? His name is Yori Fukutomi—"

"We're the ones asking the questions, sweetheart," Agent Holt notified me.

How I would have liked to have biffed him one right then, but I needed to keep my head about me.

"Did your parents take food or oil to Jap ships at sea?" Agent Parker resumed.

"No."

"Did they hide any Japs in their house?"

"No."

They grilled me for two days. They asked the exact same questions, and I gave the exact same answers again and again and again—always with my best Princess Tai smile. My inquiries, on the other hand, were met by stony silences, flip ripostes, or threats. When I asked if I could go to the powder room, they pursed their lips and looked away. When I asked who'd turned me in, Agent Holt quipped, "Lies, betrayals, and disappointments. That's what friendship's all about, sweetheart," which narrowed the field down to . . . who? Ida? Charlie? Eddie? One or all of the Lim Sisters? A band member? Maybe Monroe? One of the many men I'd dated since becoming Princess Tai who'd gotten suspicious about me and made a lucky guess? When Agent Holt got tired of my answers, he warned me: "There are people a lot tougher than us. You want to be in a room with them?" Was the threat real? I didn't want to find out, so I tried to elaborate a little bit. When Agent Parker pressed me on why my family had always lived near naval facilities, I replied, "No one else wanted to live in those neighborhoods, so the rents were cheap." He didn't like that response. "Just how long have you and your family been spying on America?" he bellowed only inches from my face.

At night, I was locked in a cell and given a tray of food. I wasn't allowed to telephone anyone. I wasn't given clothes, a toothbrush, or a hairbrush. I didn't cry, because inside I was boiling. Someone had given me up and robbed me of my opportunity for real fame. I kept going over and over it in the night. When I got to the end of my loop, I'd repeat something my mother used to say to me. *Sakki naita karasu ga mo warau. The crow that was crying a few minutes ago is already laughing now.* In Japanese, Mom explained, the word for *crying* sounded like *birds making noise* even though the written characters were different. "Crows are smart, stubborn, tough survivors," she told me. "But also remember, Kimiko, that the *gaijin*—the white foreigners—can't hear the difference if we are crying or laughing because they don't see us as human. You will forever trick them. And tomorrow you will fly and laugh your way across the sky again."

On the morning of the third day, I was brought again to the windowless room. My body—my mouth especially—felt foul. I prepared myself for another day of questions. The agents entered—all business.

"We're going to lay it out for you straight," said Agent Parker. "We've got a special internment camp in Arizona called Leupp. It's where we keep Japs we suspect are traitors to the United States. Two of those internees are your mother and father."

"They're alive?" I was incredulous and grateful but also wary.

"What do you think we'd do? Take them out and shoot them?" Agent Holt scoffed.

Maybe.

"The War Relocation Authority has your brother in an internment camp in Utah," Agent Parker went on. "If it were up to me, we'd keep you here until you told the truth—"

"I've told the truth," I said.

Agent Parker kept going. "But we've been ordered to give you a choice. Do you want to be sent to your parents or to your brother?"

Both men leveled their peepers at me to see how I'd answer.

I WAS LOADED onto a train with a handful of other straggler Japanese: some single men and a couple of families, who had, like me, managed to avoid being detected and caught until now. One family had suitcases and packages around them—all the worldly belongings they could carry. The father wore a business suit. The mother had a hand-knit cardigan draped over her shoulders. Their teenage daughter wept into a handkerchief, while her younger siblings jostled and wiggled on their shared bench.

I was still in the dress I'd worn to the studio. No bed linens, no toiletries, no clothes. I had my purse with me and about fifty bucks, which wouldn't get me far. Everything else I owned, including all my savings, was in my apartment. (What I hadn't spent on clothes and other extravagances was in a box under my bed. Neither Grace nor I trusted banks.) I was alone and unprotected. The others regarded me wordlessly. Armed guards at either end of the car kept watch over us. I heard a little girl ask her mother almost the same question I'd wondered about my own parents: "Are they going to shoot us?" "If they were going kill us," her mother answered, "they would have done it already." When we passed through train stations, we were commanded to pull down the blinds, because the guards couldn't guarantee what would happen if locals saw us.

Hours later, we stepped off the train and into a nighttime dust storm. I couldn't breathe. I stretched my arms in front of me, but the dust was so thick I couldn't see my hands. Me, in that! And it was freezing. I didn't have a coat, and neither did the others. We were herded into trucks covered with canvas and driven over bumpy roads. Dust and sand continued to swirl around us. I covered my nose and mouth with a sleeve, and closed my eyes.

The truck bumped to a stop. Below the howl of the wind, I heard men yapping at each other, then the driver put the truck into gear. We crept along until we once again jerked to a stop. Rough hands yanked us out of the truck. The dust and sand created a stinging, pitting, merciless tempest in the midnight darkness. My traveling companions—who had previously kept to themselves—and I now clung to each other, moving as a mass up some stairs toward a dim yellow light and through a door. As soon as it closed behind us, I gulped my first full breath since disembarking from the train. We tried to brush the grit from our faces and clothes. Eyeballing us, I saw that we looked filthy, exhausted, and strained.

We were in some kind of administration building. A sign read: TOPAZ WAR RELOCATION CENTER. One of the little boys grabbed the front of his dungarees and announced he had to go pee-pee. That set up a chorus from the other tykes. And to tell the truth, I also had to go so bad my back teeth were floating. A couple of guards escorted a group of us back into the dust storm. We followed the beams from the flashlights to a communal latrine. The stalls had sides but no doors. The mother wearing the cardigan started to cry. It wasn't a big deal for me after so many years sharing a dressing room with a bunch of girls, but how could the people who ran this place expect a proper Japanese woman to do her business in front of everyone? But she—and we—had no choice. Then it was back into the storm to return to the administration building.

One by one we were fingerprinted and processed. I tried flirting with the officer, attempting to keep things light and breezy. Didn't go over well. I was assigned to a barracks: 24 3-D. An older Japanese man—clearly *Issei*—approached me. He bowed, and I automatically bowed back more deeply. He spoke to me in Japanese. "I am your block manager."

I thanked him in Japanese, using the proper honorific for his age and station, although I didn't know what a "block manager" was.

At the sound of my voice, the creases in his face furrowed even deeper.

"You talk white," he noted, and I couldn't deny it. I inquired about my brother. He said, "You can look for him tomorrow." Then he gave me a kerchief to cover my face, turned on a battery-powered lantern, and took me back into the horrors of the night. I saw nothing in the lantern light except dust, dust, dust. I had no sense of where I was or where I was going. After walking for ten minutes or so, he dragged me up some stairs, through a door, and into a minuscule foyer.

"Welcome to your new home," he whispered in his heavy accent. He studied my clothes disdainfully. "We'll get you something useful to wear tomorrow. We have a lot of families here, so be quiet as I show you to your area."

I took off my shoes and followed him down a dark hall past what looked like separate rooms for the family groups he'd mentioned. He opened one of the doors and motioned for me to enter. Sheets and blankets hung from clotheslines to divide the space. Heat came from a potbellied stove. He pulled open a sheet and motioned for me to enter. There was a cot, a pillow, and two folded Army blankets. When I turned to thank him, he was already gone. I peeled off my dress and draped it over the end of the cot. Then I lay down in my slip and panties. The curtains around me shivered like ghosts. On the other side of the curtain, I heard breathing. Other people—total strangers—were sleeping just inches from me without any barrier or protection beyond the sheets. Someone snored softly. Nearby, one of my roommates rolled over, and her—his?—cot's springs groaned. I should have been scared out of my wits, but I was madder than mad. I was bone-tired too, but I had a hard time falling asleep.

Early the next morning, I was dimly aware of a bell ringing, people talking in hushed voices, kids running through the hall, and the stomp of boots. When I opened my eyes, I saw that the ceiling was covered in tar paper and a single bare lightbulb hung from a cord. *Jesus, what a pit.* Dust and sand had come into the building while I slept and were all over my blanket, my face, and my arms. I reached for my dress and wrestled myself into it under the covers as quickly as I could to keep the chill out. When I stood, the floor creaked. I could see through the cracks between the floorboards to the ground. I needed to find my brother, but I had to do other things first. A woman hurried purposefully down the hallway. I asked where to find the bathrooms, and she told me in perfect English that individual barracks didn't have toilets.

"Our block has a special building for that and for washing up," she explained. "You've missed breakfast, but I can give you directions to our block's mess hall too, if you'd like. The bell will announce lunch."

Outside, the wind had fortunately settled. I walked down the dirt street to the corner of my barracks, where I stopped to get my bearings. Row after row of barracks stretched in every direction. This place was like a small city, and the men—some dressed as though they had business to attend to, while others wore casual slacks and sweaters—all seemed to have somewhere to go. I found my way to the latrine, where a line extended onto the road and around the corner. I saw grandmothers draped in big Army coats that hung down to the ground and young women with their hair tied up in kerchiefs. Mothers held infants in their arms and scolded their little ones for not staying in the line. I waited my turn. After I used the toilet, I entered the washroom. Showers lined one wall. The center of the room was filled with big tubs to do laundry by hand. A few mothers had commandeered the tubs and were dropping their kids in one after the other for quick baths. I washed my face and hands and went back outside. Now I felt a tiny bit presentable.

I asked for directions to the administration building. I walked about a half mile, passing barracks lined up in groups or "blocks" like anchovies in a tin. Topaz was so big that there were street names and addresses, but there wasn't a plant in sight. The desert had been scraped clean to create the camp. In ten minutes, I saw more Japanese than I'd probably seen in my entire life. I wanted to shout at them, "How could you let them do this to you?" Suddenly before me was a barbed-wire fence. Clearly I'd missed the turn to the administration building. I saw a guard tower to my left and one to my right. Armed guards patrolled with trained German shepherds. Outside—flat, flat, flat, to a distant mountain range with one especially high peak. Dust devils swirled in the distance and not a sign of civilization in sight.

"How ya doin' up there, soldier?" I called to the young man in the guard tower.

He lifted his rifle to his shoulder, aimed, and shouted, "Step away from the fence!"

All right, then. I walked back the way I'd come. I found my correct turn and in minutes arrived at the administration building, which in the light of day I could see was just another hastily built structure with plywood walls and a tar paper roof. I was given a khaki shirt, some green trousers, and an old Army coat—like the ones I'd seen the grandmothers wearing—and mine, too, came down to my ankles. When I asked for my brother, a woman flipped through some files, found Yori's folder, and told me he was the coach for the Rams baseball team. She gave me directions to the "high school." For the first time in days, my smile was sincere. Yori was truly here!

I found the baseball field and spotted my brother huddling with a group of kids. The last time I'd seen him was on the wharf when I left Honolulu for San Francisco. He'd had an island-boy quality back then—with a loose gait that carried him from the beach where he surfed with guys from his school to my dad's sampan to the temple where we worshiped. In the last four years, Yori had grown up. He had broad shoulders, high cheekbones, and the authoritative but friendly manner that seemed just right for a coach. When the boys took their spots on the field and started playing, I approached. Yori's eyes lit up in stunned surprise when he saw me.

"Sis!"

None of that bowing stuff for us. He put his arms around me, and we held each other tight.

"You look like shit," he said when he released me, and we laughed.

"Mom and Pop?" I asked.

He nodded toward the boys. "Let me finish up here. I'll tell you what I know later."

I sat on a bench and watched him coach the team. A bell rang. Yori dismissed the boys.

"I haven't seen Mom and Pop since that terrible day," he said as he sat down. He stared out across the field with a faraway look, telling me how he'd been detained and questioned for hours. His interrogators had wanted to know if Pop had been signaling to Japanese planes.

I shook my head. "I know the drill."

"I told those bastards I'm a *Nisei,* born in Los Angeles," he went on. "I said they were talking out of their asses. I let them in on the fact that someone in an American plane shot and killed Hideo—also an American citizen." He fought his emotions. "Kimiko, I've never seen anything so horrible in my life. What they did to him . . . And Pop and I still had to go back to shore . . ."

I burned for Yori and my father, helpless at sea with someone whom they'd loved, dead—in pieces—on the deck. There were no words.

"Mom and Pop have been sent to a special camp—"

"In Arizona," I finished for him. "I know. Have you heard from them?"

"No, and I haven't written to them either. I don't want guilt by association. You?"

"I haven't written to them either. I only just found out where they are."

"Well, don't start now," he ordered, but the regret in his voice felt heavy. "*Shikata ga nai.* It cannot be helped," he added, and I could practically hear my mother reciting those same words.

We sat in silence for a few minutes. This place was so desolate, our family had been so broken, and my life was so destroyed that I wondered not only what hideous thing could happen next but how—if ever—we could recover what we'd lost individually and as a family.

Yori sighed, then asked, "Lunch?" I was starved, and dwelling in self-pity wasn't my way. He took me to the mess hall in his block. "I've got a surprise for you," he said. We grabbed metal trays, waited in line, and food was dropped on our plates, whether we wanted it or not. *Plop, plop, plop.* Then we walked through the long rows of tables, with Yori scanning the room until he saw what—or whom—he was searching for. He set his tray down on a table already occupied by a husband, wife, and a bunch of squalling, brawling, shoving brats. Yori beamed, but I didn't ken to why until the two adults stood and bowed. Aunt Haru, Uncle Junji, and their kids! They had all changed so much I hadn't recognized them at first. My aunt and uncle both seemed careworn—thinner and shorter than I remembered. The kids had all grown, though, and they certainly hadn't lost any of their spunk. Overall, the family looked healthy despite what they'd been through. We had only a few minutes to catch up, because my aunt and uncle had to get back to work. Before they left, they asked if I'd like to move to their barracks and live with the rest of the family. Everything was happening so fast that I was shaken down to my toes. A few days ago I was in a movie studio; today I was in a hellhole. Being united with other Fukutomis offered some comfort at least.

After lunch, Yori guided me to his block and introduced me to the other residents in the barracks. A couple of people gave me things they could spare—an extra toothbrush, a small men's T-shirt, a pair of socks, a sweater. Once my new belongings were piled up next to me, Yori said, "We were taught never to ask anything directly, but . . ." He motioned around the claustrophobic space. "Life is different now, and Mom and Pop's rules don't make sense here."

"What do you want to know?"

"Where were you, and why did it take so long for you to join us?"

He knew me, so it didn't surprise him all that much that I'd tried to pass as an authentic Chinese princess, dancing in a San Francisco nightclub. "I thought I could get away with it for the duration." I shrugged. "I was wrong."

"Things might have been different for me too. Most Japanese were allowed to stay in Hawaii and continue to live their regular lives." He gave a short but bitter laugh. "The *haoles* need us to keep the island economy going, and there's a lot of new work there with the war and all. But I had our family problem. The authorities shipped me to Angel Island, where I was photographed, fingerprinted, and examined for infectious diseases like I was a goddamn coolie laborer."

"I'm sorry."

"Nothing for you to be sorry about. It's not your fault. And listen, I'm lucky. Topaz isn't great, but it could be worse."

I gave him a questioning look.

"This place was originally called the Central Utah Relocation Center," he continued. "CURC sounds like *curse,* so they decided to name it for the nearby town, but the Mormons got all up in arms about it. So now this is called Topaz for the big mountain that—"

"I saw it."

"But we call it Whirlpool Valley, because of the dust storms. Anyway, this is now the fifth largest city in the state. How do you like that? About nine thousand people live here between the internees and the staff."

"So where's the lucky part?" I asked.

"Last month the government decided to let people like me fight," he answered, "but first everyone was required to take the loyalty oath. We had to answer certain questions. Would we swear allegiance to the U.S. of A. and faithfully defend it from any and all attacks by foreign or domestic forces, and forswear any form of allegiance or obedience to the Japanese emperor, and so on? The answer was easy for me—yes—but it was terrible for the old-timers. *Issei* don't have the right to become American citizens, they can't vote, they've spent years being picked on, and now they were asked to forsake the emperor? They would be without a country! Stateless! Then we were asked if we were willing to serve in the armed forces of the U.S. on combat duty. I answered yes to that too."

"Have you lost your marbles?"

His response was not one I wanted to hear. "I'll be leaving soon for basic training at Camp Shelby in Mississippi—"

"You can't leave! I just got here!"

"Sis, no one told me you were coming . . . Anyway, the Army is putting together an all-Japanese unit called the 442nd Regimental Combat Team. I hear there's gonna be a bunch of other *Nisei* from Hawaii—"

"Yori! *We*'re finally together! Isn't that more important than fighting with some guys you went to high school with?"

"*Sumimasenga,* I'm sorry, but you never even tried to get in touch with me," he said sternly. "Why do you suddenly care?"

"I guess I deserve that, but you're going to fight for them after everything they've done to our family? After putting you in *this* place?"

He gave me his best big-brother you-don't-know-squat look. "It's our country, Sis. Don't ever forget it."

I loved the United States. It was my home, but inside I was so angry. So angry about *everything*.

He watched my face, and I could nearly hear him thinking, *Too much emotion*. After a long pause, he added, "You know as well as I do that Germany and Japan have to be defeated."

He was right, of course.

"They're going to ask you those two questions as well," he informed me. "A word of advice. If you answer no to either of them, you'll be labeled a no-no girl."

"No-no girl?" My mind went to Grace and Helen. Sorrow welled in my chest. But Yori had a very different definition.

"Those who answer in the negative are taken away. They're sent to special camps like the one where they're keeping Mom and Pop."

We talked awhile more. He told me that Topaz's rules had loosened, so that now people could leave to hike, work in the nearby town, or take jobs on neighboring farms.

"We have everything and everyone here—teachers, scientists, artists, businessmen, even performers. There's a guy, Goro Suzuki—"

"The comedian? He used to play the Sky Room in Chinatown!"

"Well, he's gotten clearances to play clubs in Cleveland, Akron, and Chicago. He's changed his name to Jack Soo so he'll sound Chinese."

I knew all about that.

"You just have to get past the loyalty oath," he added.

After I left Yori, I walked straight to the placement office.

"How in the hell do I get out of this joint?" I asked, momentarily slipping and letting the truth of how I felt show, which was probably not the most diplomatic way to introduce myself to the man in charge.

"You can't just arrive one day and expect to leave the next," he huffed in response. He told me that most girls my age had to wash laundry or work in the nearby sugar beet fields. Maybe he saw me for what I was—a girl with a scrapbook past—because he gave me an inside job as a file clerk, earning sixteen dollars a month, for which I acted grateful. But, clearly, becoming a file clerk wasn't going to work for Princess Tai.

GRACE

Good Luck, Bad Luck

I'd been home ten days, and I was just beginning to come to terms with what had happened. By the end of filming, it had been clear to everyone that I was seriously hurt. The studio had offered to take me to the hospital, but I just wanted to go home. The trip back to San Francisco was sad and lonely. I had no idea, however, that I would feel even worse when I entered my apartment. It echoed hollowly without Ruby's vibrancy, but her presence was everywhere: a pair of shoes left helter-skelter by the bathroom door, her perfume bottles on the dresser, her robe draped over a chair. I took it all in then loaded up on aspirin and whiskey. I tried to sleep, but I hurt too much.

The next day I went to my doctor. "The physical blow rarely causes injuries. Instead, it's what happens on your way to the floor," he informed me, as though I hadn't lived with that knowledge for a good part of my life. "The bruise on your jaw won't win you any beauty contests. It's these other injuries that are of more concern." He gently palpated the swollen green, purple, and yellowing splotches that ran from my armpit down my side and along my left hip. He verified my fractured ribs from my encounter with the table edge and diagnosed a hematoma on my hip from my hard landing. I also had vertigo that came as a result of a slight concussion. "It looks like you've been down this road before, my dear. Is there anything you want to tell me? I'd like to help." When I thanked him but said no, he sighed, advised me to rest for a month, and ordered me to drink milk to build myself up and heal my bones.

On my third day home, I received a delivery of roses and candy. The card read:

I'm sorry.
Please forgive me.

Joe

All the emotions I'd needed to push aside to deal with the events of that day—and get home—now surfaced. I cried when I thought about Joe and how he must be feeling—his guilt for hitting me and his anguish over Ruby. My sympathies for her were deeper still. If I listened to the radio and "You're a Sap, Mr. Jap" or "We're Going to Find a Fellow Who Is Yellow and Beat Him Red, White, and Blue" came on, I turned the music right back off and sat in silence. My closest friend was gone, and there was nothing I could do about it. I gathered up her things and packed them in a trunk. I took her box of money from under her bed and hid it with mine.

I couldn't afford to keep the apartment by myself, so on my fifth day home I invited Ida to live with me. We'd never gotten along that well, but she seemed as eager to move in with me as I originally had been to share the apartment with Ruby. A few hours later, she bumped her way into Ruby's old room with two suitcases, a lamp, and some knickknacks. And really, Ida wasn't so bad—small and cute, and all the boys loved her, but she still kept up with Ray Boiler, despite the warnings about him, and they made a ruckus in her room all weekend. He scared me, but she reminded me that he only visited every four weeks. The prospect was about as appealing to me as the monthly visit from Aunt Flo, but I'd tolerate his presence because I couldn't bear to be alone.

On my eighth day, Helen visited, bringing Tommy. Our conversations ran in circles.

"Who could have done that to Ruby?" Helen asked.

"I have no idea. It just doesn't make sense," I replied.

"Some people can be so cruel . . ."

And then we were back at the beginning and not one inch closer to an answer.

This morning, my tenth day back in San Francisco, Charlie dropped by with a pot of his mother's soup and to inquire when I'd return to work, reminding me that he'd promised a raise to anyone who got a part in a film.

In the afternoon, I received a short letter from Joe:

Dear Grace,

I will never be able to apologize enough for what I did to you, but I hope you will allow me to visit. What I need to say, I need to say in person. Will you meet me at noon on the 12th at Foster's? Please don't say no, although I will understand if you do.

Joe

He could have called. In fact, he could have called at any point during the last week and a half. That he hadn't told me just how twisted up he was inside.

ON THE APPOINTED day, I got dressed, fixed my hair, and put on makeup—enough to cover the last bit of yellow from the bruise on my jaw yet still subtle for day and somber for the occasion. I grabbed a taxi to Foster's, the same place Joe had taken me after the incident on Treasure Island. I didn't know how to feel about that. Was this part of a pattern or did he want to confine his mistakes to one place by turning Foster's into his confessional?

A waiter pointed to a corner table. Joe stood when I approached, literally with hat in hand, looking about as hangdog as a man can look. He didn't hug me or give me a peck on the cheek as he usually did. Maybe he was afraid of how I'd react. He didn't even give me a chance to say hello before he started with his apologies.

"Can we sit?" I asked, interrupting him.

That jarred him and he appeared even more ashamed, if such a thing were possible. He came around the table, pulled out the chair for me, and gently pushed it in after I sat down. Once seated across from me, he stared straight into my eyes. That was the kind of man he was. He'd done something wrong, and he would take responsibility for it.

"I've gotten in fights before, but I've never hit a girl," he said. "I'm a heel, and I'm very sorry that you had to take the brunt of my anger." He hung his head. "But honestly, if I saw Ruby again, I can't say what I'd do. I hate myself for that."

"Joe, I don't want to talk about Ruby. I want to talk about being hit—"

When he started to apologize again, I put up a hand to stop him.

"We've been friends a long time," I said, "but there are things you don't know about me. If you can be honest with me, then I should be honest with you. But, Joe, this is hard—"

"Just tell me. Whatever you have to say, I can take."

This time I was the one who stared him straight in the eyes. "My father used to beat me. I ran away from home because of the things he did to me."

"Oh, God, Grace," he said, shocked and even more horrified by what he'd done to me. "You must have looked at me like I was your dad."

"You're nothing like him, but that doesn't mean your temper doesn't scare me. So I'm only going to say this once. What happened on Treasure Island and what happened in Hollywood were partly my fault. I jumped in front of you when you were angry. I understand that. But I won't do it again. I *can't* do it again. And I can't be around someone who would *ever* hit me *ever* again."

"If I even thought something like that could happen, then I'd stay away," he said.

"Promise?"

"You have my absolute word."

With that, I reached across the table and put my hand over his. We sat connected, yet in silence, for a long while.

AFTER I RECOVERED, I replaced Ruby as the headliner at the Forbidden City. Charlie billed me as "The Oriental Danseuse featured in the soon-to-be-released motion picture *Aloha, Boys!*" Customers were entranced by my new fake scarlet fingernails. Reporters wrote about their grace and expressiveness. When asked how they got that way, I cracked, "Exercise!" Readers ate it up. Customers did too. The dressing room filled with bouquets. Charlie paid me a ton of money, and I was able to afford Ruby's apartment on my own, but I let Ida stay because I was lonely, and she made me laugh. One of Ida's aunts had taken her to see *Oklahoma!* back in high school. Ida loved to twirl around the apartment singing "I Cain't Say No." I called her I Do Annie instead of Ado Annie. We both got a kick out of the silliness. Ida was earning her label as a Victory Girl the old-fashioned way—by latching on to Marines and martinis with equal enthusiasm. She toned it down when Ray came to town, but he was mistrustful, cagey, and menacing nevertheless.

Just as bad luck sometimes masquerades as good luck, good luck can also masquerade as bad luck. My big break had come at the expense of my best friend, so someone started the rumor that I'd reported Ruby. I became a bull's-eye for target practice, but definitely.

"You always wanted to be the top performer," Bessie, the eldest of the Lim Sisters, sniped.

"You're the one who glued on Ruby's patch," Esther pointed out. "You must have hated her for that."

Once I walked into the dressing room and heard Helen confiding to a cluster of ponies: "Grace would do anything to be a star. They say she tricked Ruby into taking her to Hollywood."

"You know it wasn't like that!" I exclaimed.

"I'm just repeating what I heard," Helen admitted, more than a little embarrassed.

"I'm still shocked, Helen, that *you'd* get caught up in gossip."

"You're right, and I'm sorry," she said, but the damage had been done. I could see on the faces of the other ponies that none of them believed me.

The only person who truly came to my defense was Ida.

"That's because you live with Grace in her fancy apartment," one of the newer ponies jibed.

Actually, Ida, who'd never been my biggest fan, had seen me every day and knew how devastated I was by what had happened to Ruby. Either that, or she was a better performer than I imagined. Still, the other girls tormented me, but the last straw was Irene.

"You're the only one of us who goes to Western Union once a month," she said, wily as a rat.

"I send money to my mother," I explained.

"Sure you do."

I lost control. "Stop it! Stop it, all of you!" The others took my outburst as proof of my guilt. After I regained my composure, I asked, "How do I know one of *you* didn't do it?"

But the allegations against me continued and were impossible to fight. I was known to go to Western Union; Ruby and I had traveled to Hollywood together and only I had come back; I got the big break, not Ruby. I became a headliner, and my friends dropped me like a hot rock. They stopped asking me to parties, for drinks, or to go out after the show for scrambled eggs. And still no one knew what had become of Ruby. She was constantly on my mind, though. And Joe's too, with his memories of her still painful:

Grace, even now when I think about Ruby— How could she have lied to me like that? If she'd jilted me with another guy, maybe that would have been easier to take. Now I play things in my head again and again. The level of deceit, and for so long. And what does it say about me that I couldn't tell? Maybe she was right. I saw what I wanted to see.

I didn't bother him with my troubles. Instead I tried to distract him, writing newsy items I hoped would amuse him:

The War Production Board has ordered all of California's wine grapes to be made into raisins for the troops. When you and your friends eat them, you can think of our sacrifice!

And:

A Navy blimp spotted an enemy submarine outside the Golden Gate Bridge today. Dropped depth charges; sank a whale.

I wanted every smile I gave him to lessen his heartbreak.

ALOHA, BOYS! WAS released. Here's a Hollywood truism: even a bad movie with a mediocre performance can sell a song, a new fashion, or a novelty dance. Almost overnight, everyone wanted me to perform the routine I'd made up on the spur of the moment. I had wanted to be the new Eleanor Powell—the *Chinese* Eleanor Powell—with all her finesse and charm. Instead, I became famous for a Siamese, Hawaiian . . . Aw, what the heck. Let's just call it what it was: an Oriental mishmash. It was not at all what I'd had in mind for myself, not when Eleanor Powell, Ginger Rogers, or even Ann Miller was the ideal.

But no matter how popular I was or how many boys asked me to sign photographs for them, the suspicions about me wouldn't go away. I could have been back in Plain City, with people whispering about me in the dressing room, avoiding me when I walked backstage, ignoring me if I asked a question or said someone looked nice that day. Eventually, the animosity started to overflow into the audience.

Then Charlie fired me. I couldn't believe it, not after he'd come to my house with soup, put my name in lights, and was raking in plenty of cabbage *I* had earned for him.

"You're giving me the bounce?" I asked. When he nodded, I tried to defend myself. "You know I didn't do anything, Charlie. I'd never hurt Ruby."

He jutted his chin.

I went on. "It could have been someone in the audience or from one of the other clubs. It could have been Irene. Or Bessie. The ones who talk the loudest are the guiltiest."

"You're causing too much trouble," Charlie said.

"But I'm a hit! Who are you going to get to replace me? First Ruby. Now—"

"Esther's going to do her girl-in-the-gilded-cage act."

"Are you kidding? Maybe *she*—"

He cut me off. "You're a doll, Grace, but I'm tired of all the name-calling and bellyaching. You've made me a lot of money, but I have a business to run. I can't afford to have bad blood spill out to the front of the house. I can't risk queering all my hard work."

"*Your* hard work—"

"You'll land just fine, because there are plenty of other clubs in Chinatown . . ."

I walked out of the Forbidden City with my tail between my legs and a big guilty sign on my back. And there wasn't one goddamn thing I could do about it. I wrote to Joe, and he called me right away from the pay phone on the base. He was livid, but it didn't scare me because his anger was on my behalf. He was defending me. Soon his words became more comforting. "You'll get through this, Grace. You're a resilient woman, and you're going to come out of this stronger than ever." He was so convincing that even I, who'd been feeling pretty darned sorry for myself, believed him.

Max Field didn't let me down either. "Charlie Low's shortsightedness will be Chinatown's gain," he said. "We'll make him sorry he ever let you go. You watch. When he comes begging with hat in hand, we're going to sock him one good."

Max booked me two weeks here, four weeks there. Maybe I was resilient, like Joe said, because I'd finish a run at Andy Wong's Sky

Room and open at Eddie Pond's Kubla Khan the next night. I did six weeks with the Lim Sisters, who joined me at the Lion's Den. They'd refashioned themselves once again. They'd discarded their martini headdresses and now dressed in modified military uniforms and sang from the Andrews Sisters' repertoire: "Strip Polka," "Don't Sit under the Apple Tree," and "Here Comes the Navy." I played with the Merry Mahjongs at the Club Shanghai, and even ran into Li Tei Ming at a one-nighter at the Club Mandalay. I did my Oriental Danseuse routine and my fame grew. I could walk into a department store without Ruby at my side, and the salesladies recognized me right away.

ALL THROUGH THE summer, Joe sent letters to me from Minter Field—sometimes once a week, sometimes more. His missives still had lots of technical information. He'd just finished his advanced pilot's training in the 650-horsepower AT-6, which had retractable landing gear. "I don't know yet what assignment I'll be given—transport, bomber, or cargo plane—but I'm still hoping for a fighter," he wrote. "Those are the most dangerous and exciting for a guy like me." As the weeks passed, he stopped mentioning Ruby. The tone of his letters changed, too, as he peppered me with questions: Did I have a five-year plan for my life? What did I want to do after the war? Should he become a lawyer or follow his heart and become a commercial air pilot like he'd always dreamed? I couldn't imagine that he and Ruby had ever had a single communication like the ones he and I had regularly.

Since that first phone call, he'd gotten into the habit of buzzing me every Sunday morning as well. I'd be as sleepy as all get-out, having been at the club until just before dawn, but he'd be bright and chipper, having just come back from mess hall, chapel, or an early-morning training flight. We talked about nothing, really. Would I ever think about attending a college class? He thought I might enjoy American history or drawing. "Or you could take kinesiology," he suggested. "It might come in handy if you ever want to teach dance." Soon we were even able to talk about Treasure Island, and it was as though

Ruby had never existed. We searched for and found only good memories, because that's all that mattered. "I'll never forget the nylon stockings you gave me," I told him. "What I wouldn't do for a pair of those now." He liked to remember how we used to swing-dance together. "I've always enjoyed dancing with you," he said. "We sure know how to cut a rug." And it was true. We'd always made a great couple on the dance floor.

JUST BEFORE THANKSGIVING, an envelope arrived with a return address I didn't recognize. Inside was a letter from Ruby:

> *Grace!*
>
> *I'm sorry it's taken me so long to write. I wanted to forget myself, forget everything. I have not been a good friend. I hope you'll forgive me.*
>
> *I'm in an internment camp in Utah. The other night after dinner, they showed* Aloha, Boys! *What a surprise! But I'm happy for you, Grace. You looked great.*
>
> *There's a lot I could say, but I'll boil it down to this. I'm stuck in a sandpit. No one has come to our aid. Not the Red Cross, Salvation Army, nor the ACLU. Maybe you can do something to get me out of here now that you're a big star.*
>
> *Help!*
>
> *Ruby*

When I showed the letter to Helen, she said she'd received something similar: "Everyone at the club got a note from Ruby, and some of the customers too."

"I should write her . . ."

"Why? What can you or any of us possibly do for Ruby?" Helen asked. "No one wants to get in trouble, but *you* should be especially careful. Either you housed a Jap or you turned her in. Better to toss the letter and keep out of that mess."

I agreed a little too quickly, but how had I become such a coward? What was I afraid of? I mean, I'd *lived* with Ruby after Pearl Harbor. I'd protected her secret, and—if not for her—I could have gotten into serious hot water for that. I loved her, she needed a hand, and I wanted to help her very much, but I was paralyzed by fear—scared out of my pants to get involved or act in a manner that might be perceived as unpatriotic. I wasn't the only one to abandon a friend. Plenty of people had neighbors or business associates who were sent to internment camps, and they didn't do a thing for those folks either. We weren't proud of it. It was just a fact.

I followed Helen's advice and threw out the letter. I mentioned none of this to Joe either. I didn't want to upset him.

ON DECEMBER 17, 1943, in the spirit of one ally honoring another, the U.S. government overturned the Chinese Exclusion Act, which had barred the immigration of all Chinese to our shores except for students, diplomats, merchants, and teachers. At last, Chinese could become naturalized citizens. Helen's parents, however, refused the offer. "We don't want to lose our rights to return to the home village," Mr. Fong told me when I visited Helen and Tommy in the compound. "We don't want to go home and be called barbarians or foreign devils." But most folks considered the repeal an act of forgiveness.

That same day, Charlie called Max Field to invite me back to the Forbidden City "in honor of the current spirit of forgiveness," but actually Esther had run off with a sailor. Max—smug as can be—immediately phoned me to present Charlie's offer, which included a gigantic salary bump. No hard feelings. I gladly accepted. The club was booming, and Charlie was now making money hand over fist. Consumer goods were scarce, courtesy of rationing, so money flowed into entertainment. The ponies were making as much as $60 a night in tips. And that was on top of their $50 a week. I earned a lot more than that, and the money ran through my fingers faster than you can say *snot.* I bought a mink coat for $2,250, and my first car—a used Chevrolet sports sedan for $659, all cash. Of course, I didn't get to drive it much. Gas rationing. So I rented space in a garage and parked the car there most of the time.

"Have another drink," Charlie appealed to the crowd each night. "If you get a hangover, what the hell? You can always buy an aspirin."

AT THE END of the year, nine months after Ruby was sent away, Joe wrote me a letter that changed everything.

> *For the longest time I thought of you like I would a kid sister. Turned out I was blind to what was right in front of me. Do you think you could see me another way? Might I have a chance?*

I'd waited for him for so long, and I was as ecstatic as a girl with her first crush. Of course, he *had* been my first crush. Now he wanted *me.* But was it real? This time I didn't write back right away. I needed to think, and protect myself.

His next letter went further:

> *How do I spend my time when I'm not training? Dreaming about coming to see you. I might as well admit it. I've gone for you in a big way.*

His words made me happy, but I had to be clear about one thing. I wrote back:

> *I want you to be sure. I don't want to be anyone's rebound girl.*

I received a letter in the return mail:

Dear Grace,

This is the last time I will ever mention Ruby, but I need you to understand this. She was all razzle-dazzle, and she didn't have integrity. You are beautiful on the outside and the inside, and I know I will always be able to trust and rely on you. I'm only sorry it took me so long to figure it out.

You're very different than when we first met, and now I see you in a whole new light. Let me tell you something, Grace. I'm learning more and more about courage every day down here, and you have it. But it's more than that. When I think about the past and the times we've spent together, I see that you always listened to me. On Treasure Island. In the club. These past months. I hope you know that I listened to you too. I heard you for who you are as I think you heard me for who I am. That is more meaningful to me than I can ever express.

You are not my rebound girl. You are the girl I should have bounded to in the first place.

Love, Joe

Finally! Finally! Finally!

HELEN

Sequins, Top Hats, Chiffon

Early on a Friday in mid-April 1944, Grace and I stood on a train platform at the embarkation center in Oakland to say goodbye to Monroe, who'd been called up and was being sent to basic training in Memphis. Baba had invited Grace, since she was the closest thing Monroe had to "a girl to come home to." Our group should have been the biggest on the platform, since my brother was a local boy with a large family, but not everyone could come. Lincoln, my dentist brother turned chauffeur, had enlisted and was attached to the 54th Signal Battalion, where he was finally getting to use his dental skills. Madison and Jefferson couldn't take time off from work at the Benicia Arsenal, where they made ammunition in assembly lines. My sisters-in-law? Before Pearl Harbor, they'd "stayed inside the gate," cooking, taking care of their children, and obeying Mama. Now a couple of them had jobs as Rosie the Riveters at the Kaiser shipyard, where a new ship was christened almost every day. Another worked at the converted Ford factory, preparing tanks for deployment to the Pacific. One sister-in-law had been promoted to welder at Bethlehem Steel. For China-born women, like my sisters-in-law, this work was an act of double allegiance: they were helping the country where they were born and where their parents and siblings still lived, and they were supporting the land of their husbands, sons, and daughters.

So only three brothers, their wives, and children were on hand for farewells. Mama stood on her bound feet, gazing up at Monroe, a hand on his sleeve. During the past year, no one had surprised me more than my mother. She'd organized a group of women of her same social standing not only to cook for the Chinatown Canteen at the YWCA every Thursday evening but to have boys in the military of Chinese descent over for dinner in the compound on Sunday nights and for special holidays. Now Mama was trying so hard to be brave about Monroe leaving that she nearly broke my heart.

My brother bowed to Mama and shook hands with Baba. My tears stained my blouse as I said goodbye. He was the person I was closest to in my family, and I couldn't handle the thought that he was going into danger.

Monroe turned to Grace. "Having you here is a bit like what families did back in China when their sons sojourned to the Gold Mountain," he told her. "A married son would be duty-bound to return to his wife in the home village. Mama and Baba would be happier if we were married. Then they'd know for sure I was coming back. Filial duty and all."

Even though Mama and Baba were standing right there—*because* they were there—Grace wrapped her arms around his neck. "Write to me, and I'll write back."

He put his hands on her waist and pulled her close.

The conductor called the all-aboard. My brother joined the other men as they climbed onto the train. He craned his upper body out an open window. The train began to pull out of the station. A woman standing near us started to trot next to the car, wailing, "I love you," to her husband—brother? boyfriend?—who stretched down a hand.

"Be brave," he said back to her as their fingers touched.

Such public displays were not my family's custom, but our reserve fell away. We might not ever see Monroe again.

"Kill some Jerries," Washington, our eldest brother, encouraged.

"Be safe, Son," called Baba.

"Come home," Mama cried out.

We stayed on the platform until the last waving hand disappeared from view. Baba and my brothers set their jaws. Mama wept. My sisters-in-law broke down. I sobbed into a handkerchief. The children, not old enough to understand what was happening, caught the mood and joined in the misery.

My family piled into three cars, though Tommy and I went with Grace to her apartment. I wanted her company. She grabbed a stack of envelopes out of her mailbox, and we went upstairs. Grace made tea while I worked on my puffy eyes in the bathroom. When I came out, Tommy was sitting on the couch next to his auntie Grace as she sorted through her mail.

"A letter from Joe," she announced, ripping open the envelope. "'Dearest Grace,'" she read aloud, "'I'm sorry you couldn't come down for my graduation, but you're doing a lot for the war effort where you are, cheering up guys, putting grins on their faces, and leading them in the Chinaconga. I've got some time off before I ship out. I was able to get a seat on a transport to Chicago, so I'll visit my mom and dad for a couple of days. Then I'll hitch a ride to Frisco. Please don't make any plans. I'll take care of all the arrangements. I want everything to be perfect when I see you. Loads of love, Joe.'"

Grace put the letter back in the envelope and held it to her chest. "What do you suppose will happen?" she asked.

"He's a man. You're a girl. You've both waited a long time. What do *you* suppose will happen?"

Grace started to laugh, and I laughed right along with her. She was very happy. It felt good to think about love on so sad a day.

After a few moments, she said, "I just don't want him to think I'm a Victory Girl, like Ida."

"That's right. You're exactly like Ida. She has Ray Boiler, and all the boys on the side. You have Joe Mitchell, and . . ." I raised my eyebrows. "Grace, he could never think of you that way. To him, you'll always be that sweet kid he met on Treasure Island."

"I don't want him to think of me like that either!"

That sent us into another spasm of laughter.

We spent the rest of the afternoon playing with Tommy. There is only one perfect child in the world and every mother has him. He was as precious to me as the underfur of a fox. His hair was the softest brown with just a hint of a curl, so there was no getting around the fact that he looked different than the other kids on the playground and in the compound. Baba had noticed, of course, but Eddie insisted that he had a grandmother with brown hair.

"A carrot of a different color," Baba had responded. "What else could I expect from a son-in-law like you?"

When Baba said things like that, I understood that our time in Chinatown was limited. Eventually, he'd put it all together. I'd have to protect my son from his grandfather's disdain—and the dirty leers and taunting Tommy would receive from our neighbors—but not yet . . .

At 4:00, we walked to the Forbidden City. Servicemen wandered Chinatown's streets in undulating herds. Already a line—populated with boys eager to meet the Celestial maidens of their dreams—snaked from the club's entrance down the street. When we got to the dressing room, Tommy went to his corner—where I'd set up a child-size cot—lay down, and began humming to himself, while I oiled my midriff.

Ponies billowed in. Many of them had babies, toddlers, and little kids in tow. The older boys were lucky little monkeys, getting to hang out in the dressing room, zipping girls into their costumes. I'll say this for Charlie: he loved kids. He was patient with them too, as long as they kept quiet. Quiet? What a joke!

"Fiedee, fiedee, fiedee."

Charlie had perfected the art of "dressing the room" by putting celebrities, movie stars, and beautiful women in long gowns accompanied by the most successful men at ringside. I'd met and had my photo taken with lots of movie stars, and I now could recognize most of them. That night, we had Captain Ronald Reagan and his wife, Jane Wyman, as well as Errol Flynn, in the audience. My husband, who'd gotten into the habit of drinking a martini before the first show, bought one for Mr. Flynn as well.

Charlie opened with his usual patter. "My mother is half-Indian.

Fortunately, I didn't come out orange!" The soldier boys guffawed. Charlie went on, recounting that he was only eight years old when his father died. "I received an eighth-grade education in a one-room schoolhouse with Indian kids from the nearby reservation. You'd have to say I've done pretty well for myself."

He was hugely successful given his background. Sometimes customers would say to me, "Look what Charlie Low has done for Oriental performers." But I'd picked up enough about business from Baba to recognize that Charlie hadn't given us a chance for altruistic reasons. He did it because he believed he would make a killing. And he did. Eddie Pond, Andy Wong, and the other club owners who'd come out of the Depression lived like the boom was going to last forever. They *all* went as wild as mandarins, Charlie especially.

"Have you heard the one about the three sisters? Tu Yun Tu, Tu Dum Tu, and No Yen Tu . . ."

The soldier boys loved that one, no matter how many times they heard it, but they were easy to please. They needed to forget about the things that had already happened to them and bury the dread of the unknown that lay ahead. Tomorrow or the day after, they'd ship out to do their own brand of business with Hitler, Hirohito, and a whole shooting match of international gangsters.

The floor show began. The ponies still carried "kitten" muffs, but kittens grow up, and those cats sure didn't like being confined. In the middle of the number, Ida's cat clawed out of his muff prison and hit the floor. He arched his back, hissed, and scrammed for the Catskills. The boys hooted and yuk-yukked.

Next up: Eddie and I did our routine, but the minute we came offstage we were at each other's throats. I complained to him about drinking before our act; he snarled at me to stop nagging. Then the girl we'd hired to be the new Chinese Sally Rand had a hard time with her fans. She lost her balance, dropped a fan, and ended up with her fingers in a G.I.'s chow mein. After that, Mabel, one of the ponies, caught her son behind the stage, peeking through the curtain to catch the back side—the *naked* side—of that fan dancer. Mabel yanked her boy back to the dressing room by the ear, and I'm sure customers could hear him yowling—even worse than the cat—all the way out front.

"What the hell's going on tonight?" Charlie asked, irritated, as we went out to talk with customers during the first break.

Our boys wanted to dance with Chinese girls, and we did because it was part of our jobs, but plenty of women—fabulous and rich, with orchids splayed on their shoulders—in the audience wanted to dance with our Chinese men. But Eddie didn't feel like it that night. Instead, he collared Jack Mak, and together they made a beeline for the bar. Jack threw down a hundred-dollar bill and asked the bartender to pour as many drinks as he could for the customers around them, including Errol Flynn. One drink too many prompted the star to eat the orchids off women's shoulders—one by one throughout the club.

Charlie started the second show with one of the stalest jokes in the book: "Have you heard that Kotex paid Maxwell House for their slogan? Good to the last drop."

It went downhill from there. Eddie's hands slipped on my midriff. It wasn't any worse than usual, but I bet there wasn't a single person ringside who didn't hear Eddie muttering to me through clenched teeth: "You're suffocating the kid. Give him a chance."

And me, biting back, "He's only thirty-one months old. *I'm* his mother."

"And *I'm* his dad! Let the kid breathe."

George Louie tried to turn the tide with "I'll Be Seeing You." He circulated around the edges of the floor, sometimes kneeling before a woman so he could sing directly into her eyes, when one—and I can only call her this—dame threw her skirt over his head and held him between her knees to show him what was under there. George kept singing, though. "I'll be seeing you in all the old familiar places." Our boys in uniform laughed so hard they barely managed to stay in their chairs. When that dame finally let George out, his face was as red and shiny as a Christmas ribbon.

After the second show, Eddie and Jack returned to the bar. "I want to buy *everyone* a drink." Eddie brought out two hundred-dollar bills and slapped them on the bar, outdoing his pal. "Let's see how far this will go."

When the third show started, Eddie and Jack were pickled. From opening night, Jack had done a trick in which he shot into a box, opened the lid, and a dove would fly out. Only tonight he opened the box and feathers flew out. He'd actually *shot* the bird!

Then Eddie and I returned to the stage. As he lifted me to spin me over his head, his hands slipped—once again—on my oiled midriff. This time, he dumped me on my rear end, and I skidded across the floor. People shrieked in surprise, and then howled until they held their sides. They thought it was part of the act, but Eddie was in no shape to be laughed at. When we came backstage, he leapt up the stairs toward the dressing rooms. I followed right behind him. When I reached the landing, he turned and bumped into me. I tumbled back down the stairs. Eddie fell too—sprawled out, drunk as a skunk. Was it an accident? Or had Eddie *pushed* me?

"He's my son!" he screamed at me.

The ponies averted their eyes. Mabel put her palms over her boy's ears. Grace was so much stronger now, but she stood stock-still. A deer confronted by a hunter, or a warrior on alert? Charlie swung through the curtain, furious, bouncing his open hands up and down, trying to calm the situation. "Pull yourself together," he said to Eddie. "Get some coffee. Are you going to make me fire you? Is that what it will take to get you to stop drinking?"

Eddie got to his feet, elbowed past Charlie, and shoved through the kitchen door.

Grace ran to me. "Are you all right?"

I was so dazed that at first I didn't notice Grace squeezing my arms and legs. I pushed away her hands in embarrassment.

"I'm fine," I bleated, though I felt bruised and sore.

Grace walked Tommy and me to the compound. She was awfully silent. I had the feeling she was remembering her father and maybe even Joe. She could change all she wanted, but a part of her would always be that scared little runaway from Plain City. I was too overwhelmed to speak either. I loved Eddie, and I was grateful to him. I never wanted to be afraid of him.

The courtyard was eerie in the middle of the night. We tiptoed into the back building and edged down the deserted hallway to my childhood room. After we put Tommy to bed, the two of us sat up, eager for Eddie to come home. We waited and worried, but my husband didn't barge through the door still bristling and drunk or contrite and bearing forgiveness gifts. What had first been fear about him coming home turned into fear about why he hadn't come home.

As the sun came up, Grace dozed off. I bathed Tommy, took him to the dining room for breakfast, and then sat in the courtyard watching for my husband to stroll through the gate. I finally gave up, went back upstairs to my room, and shook Grace's shoulder.

"What time is it?" she asked, sitting up, rubbing her eyes.

"One in the afternoon." I stifled a sob. "And he still hasn't come home."

"Now, Helen, you've told me yourself that sometimes he stays out all night."

But her reasoning didn't help. We went to the club at 4:00, but Eddie wasn't there either. Charlie, worldly as he was, looked particularly anxious.

Around 6:00, Eddie arrived with a black eye and other contusions, some of them serious. I drew the back of my hand to my mouth. The ponies' eyes widened. The guys in the band hung their heads as though they'd expected something like this might occur for a long time.

"What happened?" I rasped.

Eddie rubbed his forehead. "I got caught in an alley by a group of sailors. It's my own damn fault."

But that wasn't the worst of it. In a rage or in despair, he'd staggered into an Army recruiting office and enlisted.

"Those places are open twenty-four hours a day, so they can take you any time you want." He laughed hideously. "Uncle Sam wants you!"

"Oh, Eddie," I sputtered. "You could get killed."

He put a hand on his hip and turned to Charlie. "You can't have a black-eyed Chinese Fred Astaire after all," he said, flippant but resolute.

"Jesus, buddy, what have you done?" Charlie shook his head, deeply troubled. Then he turned to me. "Don't worry, Helen. We'll take care of it."

By the end of the first show, Eddie's anger and humiliation had burned off. The reality of his situation began to crinkle his edges, yet he continued to act the matinee idol.

"You babes all love a man in uniform," he uttered with false bravado.

During the one-hour break after the second show, he and Charlie paced backstage, talking in low voices. By the end of the third show, Charlie had a plan. "Helen, get Tommy. Grace and Ida, we're going to need you too." His eyes brushed over the other show kids. "If any of you want to come, that would be great." As we started to move, he added, "Don't change—not your costumes, your shoes, or your makeup. I need you all just the way you are."

What a spectacle we were—a troupe of performers in skimpy costumes with coats or jackets thrown over our shoulders—drawing the utmost attention to ourselves, like we were acrobats going from village to village, eking out an audience and a few *yuan*. We reached the Army recruiting office, and it was open just as Eddie said it would be. The weak-jawed sergeant and the skinny lieutenant working there seemed both surprised and wary as we filled the space with our sequins, top hats, chiffon, hosed legs, and rouged cheeks. Charlie did the talking, explaining that we were patriotic, that we were Americans, that he'd sent more than half his staff to war, so he was asking for one small favor.

"Could you tear up the paperwork my star here was fool enough to fill out last night?" he asked, pointing to Eddie, a tall man, dressed in a tuxedo, with powder on his face, and surrounded by a zoo of colorful performers.

The lieutenant made little grunting sounds, which translated to "You've got to be joking."

Charlie went on. "Mr. Wu has a wife and a baby."

The lieutenant shifted his eyes to Tommy and me, then motioned to the sergeant, and said, "So do we."

"And," Charlie continued undaunted, "Mr. Wu has a contract to fulfill. I've got it right here." He reached into his breast pocket and pulled out a sheaf of papers folded into thirds.

The lieutenant paged through the document. "He's only got two weeks left," he said. "Sure, we'll give you that."

Two weeks? For all Charlie's plotting, he hadn't bothered to *read* the contract. On to the next idea:

"As you can see, we're performers. We've all"—here Charlie motioned to the rest of us—"done our bit for the war effort. I'd like to recommend that you put Mr. Wu in the Special Services to entertain."

Even the sergeant got a kick out of that one.

Charlie took umbrage at their attitude, straightening his back and setting his face. "We've performed at war bond drives, for the Red Cross, and at Chinese Rice Bowl celebrations. We've also done USO tours to the local bases for all the different branches of service."

We nodded in agreement—little dolls in a penny arcade.

"No dice" came the verdict. "Everyone has to do their part."

"Of course they do," Charlie agreed, "but the Special Services—"

"He's an Oriental. No one wants to see an Oriental when we're at war with the Japs."

"We aren't Japs," Ida got up the nerve to say.

"And we've entertained thousands of boys already," Charlie added. "Come by the club tomorrow night. We'll"—and here, again, he gestured to us in our costumes—"show you. You should see Eddie dance—"

But *no dice* meant *no dice.*

There was one sure way out, but Eddie would have to speak it himself.

TWO WEEKS LATER, a group of us were at the Port of Embarkation in Oakland, saying goodbye to Eddie as he set off for boot camp in Tennessee. We stood on the platform with so many other women and children, bawling our eyes out. He picked up Tommy and kissed him. Then he pulled me into their embrace. He whispered into my ear, "Give the boy a chance to grow up properly. Loosen the reins a little. *You cannot refuse to eat just because there's a chance of being choked.*"

He boarded the train.

"I love you," I burst out.

Eddie's voice cracked as he called down to me. "I love you too. And be good to your mom, Tommy."

We waved our goodbyes, and then Grace, Tommy, and I returned to the car, drove back across the bridge, and went to work.

"I'm all alone now," I said, although I was tied more than ever to my family.

Grace promised that she'd stick by me until Eddie came home, and Charlie was a prince. He invited me to stay on as a soloist—doing the exact same routine I'd done with my husband, only he was missing. My dancing solo was like my trying to draw a portrait of a dragon and ending up with a doodle of a dog, but Charlie was too softhearted to demote me back to a pony.

GRACE

Every Particle of Happiness

At the end of March—a year after Ruby was picked up—Ida packed a bag and went to stay with one of the ponies. I went downstairs and waited on the street for Joe to arrive. Soon enough, he hopped off a cable car and swept me into his arms. There was nothing brotherly about his kiss, let me tell you. He held me close as we walked to the Mark Hopkins Hotel, where an elevator whisked us to the nineteenth floor. The Top of the Mark had once been an exclusive nightspot for San Francisco's café society. Now it catered to the elite-of-the-elite servicemen. Since it was wartime, not only was I allowed in but I was permitted to enter on the arm of an Occidental. Joe slipped the maître d' a tip, and we were shown to a window table, which had a spectacular view of the city, including the Navy base on Treasure Island and the lights in the Berkeley Hills.

After a waiter took our order, Joe and I studied each other. He'd finished his two years of training, and the way he looked in his uniform—with the wings on the flap of his jacket pocket—was very impressive. His face had formed angles. His sandy-colored hair was trimmed and neat. His smile was still a bit crooked, but he was clearly a man now.

"It's good to see you, Grace—"

And that's as far as he got before a flyboy with a floppy mess of hair and the radiating energy of a kid on his last night of leave approached our table. "What squadron?"

When Joe answered, "The Flying Knights," a gang of guys grabbed him and hauled him out of his chair.

"We're Flying Knights too!"

"Come with us!"

One of the men sized me up. "Don't forget the little slant-eye!"

Joe put up a hand. "Hang on there, bub. This is Miss Grace Lee, and she's my girl."

The flyboys took that in, decided to accept me as Joe's sweetheart, and herded us to the bar.

"Let me buy the drinks," Joe offered.

The band of young men hollered and whooped.

"Forget it!" someone brayed.

The man with the floppy hair called to the bartender. "Bring our squadron bottle!"

I was told that anyone in that squadron could come to the Top of the Mark, ask for the squadron bottle, and drink as much as he liked for free. Whoever finished the bottle had to replace it. Joe exchanged vitals with the guys. We drank shots. It was a good way to start our time together, because what were the alternatives? *Let's have a long chat about Ruby? Let's go over everything that's gone wrong between us in the past? Let's talk about the war and where you'll be going?* Instead, we experienced the moments as they came. I was nuts about Joe. He laid on the flattery, but it never got too sticky.

I danced with one after another of his squadron buddies. Latin bands were just coming in big, and I was twirled across the floor for hours to the sounds of Carmen Cavallaro and his orchestra. When Mr. Cavallaro slowed the tempo, Joe cut in with a jolly "Hey, bub, quit bird-dogging my girl." Joe swung me away, holding me in his arms, bringing me slowly into his rhythm.

When we left the club, a light rain drizzled. Joe offered to hire a taxi, but I wanted the fresh air, some time to find quiet between us, and to prolong the anticipation—even after all my months and years of desire for him—a little longer. As we walked back to my apartment, we encountered some rowdy servicemen, who made the predictable rude remarks about an Occidental being with an Oriental. A fight could have broken out, but Joe pulled me away before things went too far, saying in a husky voice, "We have other things to do." His doing that made me want him all the more.

We reached my apartment around three in the morning. Both of us had drunk a fair amount, but we knew what we were doing. I took him to my bedroom. Rain pattered against the window, soothing, lulling, beautiful. We were both eager and filled with desire as we tantalized each other with touch: his hand on my naked breast, his fingers slipping into wetness, my tremulous palm around something hard and proud.

"Neither of us wants to get in trouble," Joe said, pulling away from me.

I promised, "Nothing will happen. It will be all right. Don't stop."

I had a sense of my breath being sucked into his lungs and his breath being inhaled back into mine, of his flesh skimming against mine, of him reaching that part of me that so longed for love.

"Grace." He arched his back and pushed himself up on his hands so he could look down at me. "Grace, baby, I love you." Then he drove himself into me and let me watch the pleasure I brought him shudder across his face. When it was over, we lay curled together, happy, sated, his finger tracing circles around one of my nipples and my hand resting on his chest. We forgot time. We forgot our responsibilities. We forgot everything except that in that moment we loved each other more than two people had ever loved each other.

The next few days felt leisurely and blissful—with nothing to do except stroll the streets, hold hands, and sneak a bit of time alone to monkey around in my room. But every particle of happiness has a price. All too soon I was at Fort Mason, saying yet another goodbye, begging another young man to write, kill the enemy, be careful, and promise to come home. The difference this time was that I loved this boy with all my heart, and he loved me too.

• • •

HELEN AND I grew closer. She told me she hoped one day to have her own house and garden. She wanted to live a "normal" life with Eddie and Tommy when the war was over. Joe and I hadn't made plans, but I didn't want what Helen wanted. I couldn't imagine not performing. Maybe I would never be a Hollywood star, but I was a star in a jewel of a city. Helen and I comforted each other when news from one or the other front was bad, and together we did what we could to help the war effort.

We read all the pamphlets—"Make It Do Until Victory" and things like that—to teach us how to cut a man's suit into a smart (if boxy) suit for a woman and how to shop and conserve in our households, but suits wouldn't work for us and we didn't have households of our own. We easily accepted the rationing of meat, coffee, and butter, because we didn't buy meat ourselves, didn't drink much coffee, and rarely—and in my case, never—cooked. I had my car, which I barely drove because of rubber and gasoline rationing. I suppose we could have gathered newspapers, scrap metal, bacon grease, rubber bands, and milkweed pods, but we didn't know where to start.

"I don't even *read* the paper," I said one afternoon. I was a long way from writing reports on current events for social studies class in Plain City.

"Where am I supposed to find scrap metal?" Helen wondered. "Hasn't it all been turned in already?"

We were sitting on Helen's bed, propped against the wall. Tommy climbed back and forth between our laps.

"Mama's in charge of all grease in the compound," Helen went on. "She takes it to the reclamation center herself. It makes her feel like she's helping Monroe."

"I have rubber bands," I said, "but they're so darn small. It's hard to imagine they'll make a difference."

Helen visibly ransacked her mind. "What do you suppose the government wants with milkweed pods?"

I shrugged. "You got me."

We volunteered our time to sell bonds, but there were other jobs—more important jobs—women could do to help. After Congress passed a bill establishing women's corps in the Army, Navy, and Marines, one of the ponies joined the WACs, but Helen couldn't do that.

"Not with Tommy so young," she said. "I don't want you to enlist either. Whatever we do, we'll do together, like you said."

All around us, Chinese were getting jobs we never dreamed possible. Even a woman who didn't speak a word of English could leave the sweatshop, where she'd done piecework, to sweep floors at a shipyard. Mabel's sisters worked as draftswomen and flangers. Instead of making 25 cents an hour, they were now making $1.25 an hour.

"A gal in my building works as a file clerk at the Naval Auxiliary Air Station in Oakland," I said. "I wouldn't mind doing something like that."

But later, when I mentioned my idea to Charlie, he scoffed. "My Oriental Danseuse spending her time filing? You're already doing more for morale than most women."

Maybe Charlie was right. Then Irene Mak volunteered as a Gray Lady. Once a week, she hired a sitter for her kids, put on her uniform—a gray dress with a white collar, white cuffs, and a white hat embroidered with the Red Cross insignia—and went to the Oak Knoll Naval Hospital, where she escorted injured boys to the X-ray department, took amputees to a nearby golf course to get them "back in the swing of things," and helped some of those with grievous injuries write letters to their girls back home breaking off their relationships so they wouldn't be "a burden." It wasn't long before Helen joined Irene—two mothers helping the war effort. So much for sticking together, but I didn't let it bother me. I was glad she'd found something to make her feel useful.

In late April, I received a letter from Joe. He was stationed at Henderson Field on Guadalcanal, and he'd just flown his first mission:

I got assigned a P-38 Lightning. Just what I wanted. The Germans call it "the fork-tailed devil." The Japs say, "Two planes, one pilot." It's great for dive-bombing, level-bombing, and ground attacks. I'll be flaming Jap bastards out of the sky. My first time up, I inflicted damage on the enemy, but I wasn't able to shoot down the plane. That's all right. This little fighter is responsible for destroying more enemy aircraft than any other. We're cleaning up the Pacific one island at a time. I'll get mine next time. Grace, baby, I'm coming back to you an ace. I promise you that.

He added that he loved me and wrote words I would hold in my heart forever.

In May, Charlie and Mr. Biggerstaff began putting together a new show to carry us through the summer. Ida had been at the club since the beginning, and I pushed her to create a solo to get her own spot at the bottom of the bill. We practiced in our apartment, and I helped her design a costume: skintight, rose-tinted satin shorts and jacket, cream-colored peep-toes, a matching top hat, and a walking stick. The night before she was to audition, her boyfriend came to town. She visited with Ray during the breaks at the club, but she also chatted with servicemen, sitting on their laps as she typically did and signing napkins for boys to take with them to battlefields. Ray seemed more steamed than usual, which only egged Ida on to act even more devil-may-care. After the show, Ray and Ida went their way, while the rest of us went to the Variety Club. Around 5:00 A.M., I headed home.

I should have suspected something when I saw the door to my apartment was ajar, but I figured Ida and Ray had just come in, or he'd just left to drive back to Visalia. Police sirens wailed in the street. Didn't the cops realize folks were sleeping? I shut the door behind me as I turned on the light. Something that looked like red paint spattered the walls and blinds. A horrible rusty smell filled my nostrils and the back of my throat. Blood smeared across the floor to Ida's bedroom. Suddenly, there was Ray holding a long knife wet with blood. I was too terrified to scream or run.

"Maybe I've lost," he said in an oddly calm voice, "but at least the other guys won't win."

He stepped toward me. I closed my eyes. Then something crashed through the door.

"Police! Drop the weapon!"

Officers tackled Ray to the ground. I sprinted into Ida's room. Her head was twisted back, and her neck was slit. The rest of her body lay splayed at unnatural angles, with her legs and arms askew. Her glassy eyes stared unblinking at the ceiling. Her blood was slick on the floor. I skidded and fell, then groped my way to Ida's side and touched her hand. It was still warm.

"Ida!" But it was useless. She was dead.

Jack Mak and Chan-chan, one of the acrobats from downstairs, elbowed their way through the phalanx of cops and into the room.

"We heard fighting—"

"I called the cops—"

"So did I—"

"Ida," I said.

That shut them up. Chan-chan looked like he might keel over. Jack grabbed the acrobat's arm and helped him back to the living room. "Put your head between your knees—"

The policemen handcuffed Ray to a chair. I made myself stay with Ida. Jack returned to the bedroom and hovered over us protectively. Ida had always been so ready with the wisecracks. She'd made me laugh and cringe with her "I Do Annie" song. And now all that vibrancy was gone, leaving an empty shell.

"Look through her dresser drawers," Ray kept repeating. "You'll see I've done the country a favor."

The detectives—one burly, one stout—arrived, did a quick survey of the scene, and then motioned to the police officers to join them in a corner. The cops spoke in low voices; the detectives scribbled into notebooks, lifting their eyes occasionally to glance into the bedroom at Ida, Jack, and me, over to Ray on his chair, and to Chan-chan, who sat on the sofa. Finally, the four men nodded in agreement and started to break apart.

"Search the girl's room," the burly detective ordered. Then he beckoned to me with a finger. "Come here."

Jack followed me out to the living room. The stout detective glowered at him; the other shot his thumb. *Scram.* They waited until Jack and Chan-chan had slouched out of the apartment.

"I'm Detective Collins," the burlier of the two men said. "This here's my partner, Detective Flynn. Can you tell us what happened?"

My story was short. I came home, saw Ray with the knife, concluded I was going to die . . . When I finished, Detective Collins asked, "How well were you acquainted with Miss Wong?"

"We're roommates. We met about six years ago," I answered. "We're dancers at the Forbidden City—"

"So the two of you were close," Detective Collins prompted.

I nodded.

"Do you know the suspect?"

"His name is Ray Boiler."

"And you say that you and Miss Wong were close."

"I already said that."

"Have you met her parents?"

"No, but she hasn't met mine either."

"What do you imagine Mr. Boiler meant when he said"—here the detective read from his notebook—" 'Maybe I've lost, but at least the other guys won't win'?"

"Ida had a lot of admirers," I explained. "Ray was jealous."

"Would you say Miss Wong had a penchant for servicemen?"

Penchant? I wasn't a college girl, but I got the drift. "We try to keep up our boys' spirits. If they ask us to dance with them, we dance with them." Then I emphasized, "*I* dance with them, because it's my duty. My boyfriend isn't jealous. Ray was different. He was obsessed with Ida. He gave us the heebie-jeebies and we tried to warn her, but—"

One of the policemen came out of Ida's room, holding a packet of letters. "Take a gander at these, Detective."

Detective Collins studied the envelopes before directing his gaze back to me.

"We get mail from servicemen stationed overseas," I said, trying to be helpful. "They write to us, and we write back. It's our duty." Even to my ears that explanation was starting to sound weak.

Detective Collins opened one of the letters, scanned it, and then sauntered across the room to where the killer sat in his chair. The detective leaned down and spoke quietly with Ray. A few minutes later, the two detectives put an officer in charge, and then they left the apartment. Ida still lay on the floor, growing colder. I shivered from shock, afraid to move from my spot on the sofa. An hour later, the detectives returned. Detective Collins ordered the policemen to "see what else you find in the girl's room. Make it thorough, boys." I watched as the cops opened Ida's dresser drawers and pulled out the contents, letting her panties, bras, stockings, and nighties sail—like leaves torn from trees in an autumn storm—into her blood on the floor.

Detective Collins approached me. "Let's start again," he requested. "What do you surmise Mr. Boiler meant when he said he didn't want the other guys to win?"

As I repeated what I'd said before, Detective Collins ran a hand through his hair. When I came to the end, he said, "Well, we've just interviewed your neighbors. It seems you have a history of harboring Japs."

My stomach clenched under my rib cage.

"What's this all about?" I asked.

"Your roommate, or should I say your *second* roommate, was a Jap. We need to figure out just how active she was for the Jap cause, and if you were helping her."

"I don't know what you're talking about," I retorted indignantly.

"Take a look at these."

He handed me the letters from Ida's room. They'd been written to

Ida by her parents from the Japanese internment camp at Manzanar and sent to a local post office box. Her real name was Ume Otsuka. I had held on to my emotions—frozen from shock—but now tears welled in my eyes. I cried—not because I'd been deceived, but because I knew the terror Ida must have hidden all these years. She must have been petrified that she'd be caught, hated, vilified, sent to a camp, and, yes, beaten or murdered. It chilled me to think she might have lived with me—the person folks believed had ratted out Ruby—as a way to deflect suspicion from herself.

THE PRESS DUBBED the incident the Triangle of East and West, which didn't make a lick of sense but it sold a ton of newspapers. The public defender painted Ray as a heroic patriot, while I was called in for questioning by agents from the FBI and the War Relocation Authority on six separate occasions.

"Did Ume use her job at the Forbidden City to get information from our servicemen to send to Japan?"

"I knew her as Ida."

"Was she sympathetic to the Jap cause?"

"Not that I know of."

"Are you sympathetic to the Jap cause?"

"No!"

I barely slept. My nerves were wrecked from the questioning, the reporters, the way my neighbors stared at me, and, worst, the memory of Ida's gaping throat and the lingering stench of blood and death that permeated my apartment. I hadn't been physically hurt, but I felt broken. My old habit of squeezing my legs, arms, and ribs to feel for injuries returned. Things let up once Ray confessed that he'd "known Ida was a Jap all along," but that he'd killed her in a jealous rage—just like I'd said. Before he was sent to jail, he gave a final interview in which he proclaimed, unrepentant, "She got what she deserved." All this was followed by predictable chest beating about the insidiousness of the enemy and reminders that loose lips sink ships, even though Ida's only crimes had been trying to pass and bad judgment.

I hadn't done anything wrong, but the news about Ida being Japanese—and my roommate—went over at the Forbidden City like a dented can of Spam. The ponies and other performers gave me the cold shoulder but good. They couldn't decide if I was a traitor because I befriended Japanese or if I'd somehow orchestrated Ida's death in the same way I'd ratted out Ruby for my own gain. I was exhausted. My eyes were swollen and my cheeks blotched from crying. I lost weight. I looked so bad that servicemen didn't invite me to their tables to chew the fat. Either that or they'd read about me in the newspapers and didn't want to be seen anywhere near a "Jap sympathizer." My same old desire to flee—that phantom itch—was overwhelming. But before I could run, Charlie lowered the boom. He fired me. For the second time!

I called Max Field. My agent had wrung out his guts trying to get me another film role without an ounce of success. Now he failed at getting me a gig in San Francisco. "You're famous," he allowed, "but I can't book you in a mainstream nightclub like Bimbo's because you're Chinese."

"What about in Chinatown, like last time?"

"Not after all that's happened."

"But I didn't do anything!"

"Look, first Ruby, then Ida—"

"But I'm innocent!"

"Whatever you say . . ."

Which wasn't exactly an endorsement.

I'd lost a job I loved. My friends high-hatted me. My agent didn't believe me. I was blackballed by clubs in Chinatown. Even Helen, who had helped me so many times before, was at a loss. My career and my life were in ruins.

"What am I going to do?" I cried to Max.

"I might be able to get you some gigs on the Chop-Suey Circuit. You won't be making anything close to what you're used to making, but you'll be out of town. People will forget . . ."

The Chop-Suey Circuit was an idea I hadn't considered. Jewish performers traveled the Borscht Belt through upstate New York, going to hotels and bungalow resorts during the summer. Black entertainers had the Chitlin' Circuit, and they cruised the blues highway through the South, playing clubs and dance halls. We Chinese had the Chop-Suey Circuit. Clubs across the country—mainstream nightclubs—invited us, meaning the Chinese "This" or the Chinese "That," to perform as novelty acts. It sounded good to me, because there was nothing and no one keeping me in San Francisco. No one, that is, except Helen.

"You promised you'd stick with me," she said when I told her my plan.

"I did, and I'm sorry."

"But I went to Los Angeles to find you. We came back here together—"

"Helen—"

"What will I do without you?"

"Move out of the compound? Get your own place?" I suggested.

"I could never go out on my own."

"You went to Hollywood," I reminded her.

"To find *you,*" she repeated. "Anyway, that was with Eddie and before I had Tommy." After a pause, she asked, "Are you really going to desert me?"

I could have said she'd already deserted *me* when she went to work as a Gray Lady with Irene, but I knew how she'd respond. *She* was helping the war effort, while I was breaking my promise to stick with her until Eddie came home.

"I love you, Helen," I said, "but Ida was murdered not ten feet from where I sleep. Every time I close my eyes, I see her face."

"We could get an apartment together—"

I gave her a sad smile. "How will I pay for it? No one will hire me. They all think—"

"*Don't let the worst thing about a person become the true thing.* You've got to stay and fight!"

"The worst thing is already the true thing. I don't have a choice."

"All right," she said, seemingly yielding. "Then let us come with you. Tommy's old enough now."

But I was running, and I needed to change the current path of my story. I couldn't have a mother and child in tow.

"Ruby wouldn't desert me," Helen protested, laying on the guilt. But that was Helen all over, playing Ruby and me against each other. Besides, wasn't she the one who'd said I shouldn't respond to Ruby's letter? "Please don't leave me," she begged.

Helen was a good and loyal friend, but her neediness felt selfish to me. I reached over and squeezed her hand. "This isn't about the three of us," I said.

"It's about your career," she said as she began to weep, which was darned insensitive, considering the circumstances.

For the second time, I had to pack my roommate's things and, again, it was excruciating. I put Ida's belongings in storage to give to her parents once the war ended, but what were they going to do with her polka-dot blouses, hairnets, or the dried corsages soldier boys had given her? I sold or gave away most of my possessions, including my car. I took Ruby's money and my savings and hid the cash in the lining of my makeup case. I promised Helen that I would write to her at the compound and told her she should send her letters to Max Field, who would forward them to me wherever I was. I wrote to Joe, telling him to do the same. I didn't give him any details about Ida, the gossip, or losing my job. I needed to buck up and take care of my own business. He had enough on his plate.

LETTERS

Topaz War Relocation Center
June 3, 1944

Helen!

Grace sure left you high and dry. Some friend! But it doesn't surprise me. If she can't bring herself to write to me, why would she help you? Ugh! If I ever get out of here, I hope you and Tommy will come and meet me. We could have some real adventures together.

I finally heard from Yori. The 442nd shipped out last month and landed at Anzio on the 28th. It sounds pretty bad over there. The 442nd's motto is <u>Go for Broke</u>, but I hope Yori doesn't do anything foolish.

It's already an inferno here—well over 100 degrees. The ground is so dry that the surface has cracked and now looks like brown icebergs. Each step—<u>crack, crack, crack</u>.

These past fourteen months have been god-awful. Winter—snow, icicles, a potbellied stove, and a government-issued coat. Spring—sudden cloudbursts, flash floods, the bare earth of the camp turned into one big mudhole, and so much gunk sticking to our boots that we teased each other about being as tall as Occidentals. <u>Ha, ha, ha!</u> Now we're back to dust storms—sometimes as many as three a day. And this damn heat.

Oh, how the mighty have fallen! From nightclub to crapville. The worst part about being here is that I've gotten used to the rou-

tine. I was never an early riser, but now I try to wake up early enough to be one of the first in the shower line to get the limited hot water. After that, a bell announces breakfast. Then lunch— Then dinner— Other people gab to me about the beauty of the landscape—the silhouette of a cactus against a twilight sky, the appearance of wildflowers after a cloudburst, the shifting reds of sand, the way the stars glitter with few lights to dim them. Blah, blah, blah. I know they're trying to make the best of a bad situation, but they're out of their gourds. I'll always prefer champagne glasses and stage lights. I've been robbed of all that. I've been robbed of my life.

Okay, so we do get movies. (Most have been out for a long time, but they're better than nothing.) We have dances. (But sometimes five girls are wearing the exact same dress ordered from the Sears, Roebuck catalog.) Variety shows. (Remember Goro Suzuki? He's here, and he still does a good comedy routine.) Favorite song in the camp? "Don't Fence Me In." Gotta keep smiling and laughing, I always say!

I honestly don't know what I would have done if you hadn't written back to me all those months ago. You were the only one, Helen. That still eats me up. No Grace— No Charlie— Not one of the ponies, guys in the band, or customers who used to drool over me— Only you.

I was finally allowed to fill out an Application for Leave Clearance. The War Relocation Authority has been releasing about a thousand people from different camps each week. All I need now is a job and a sponsor on the outside. Some girls have been sent to Maine and Vermont, but I don't want a dumb job as a secretary somewhere practically off the map, and I never want to file again as long as I live. I've written to all the people who've written about me in Life, Variety, The Hollywood Reporter, and so many more. I've mailed letters to the big-deal night crawlers in New York—Ed Sullivan, Lee Mortimer, and Walter Winchell. A lot of folks have written back to say they can't or won't help me. I'm still hoping—

Yours till Austria gets Hungary and fries Turkey in Greece, Ruby

P.S. Thanks for the cash. I'll use it to buy some shampoo and conditioner. Sure will beat the baking soda mixed in water I've been using to clean my hair! Trying to stay positive, but man, oh, man.

San Francisco
June 10, 1944

Dear Ruby,

Feeling a bit blue today. I was up all night with Tommy, who has a fever. And I'm so worried about Eddie. Have you seen the pictures in the paper of the invasion of Normandy? Our boys wading through the water to shore— Those photos scared me. I know the situation's different, but it reminds me of what happened to me in the rice paddies. I look at those pictures and I hear the sounds of death in my ears. And the water— I remember that so clearly— Being cold and terrified— The splashing— Seeing my father-in-law floating facedown— When I think of Eddie in something that— This morning, the papers showed photos of injured soldiers. Some of them had their entire heads wrapped in gauze except for little slits for their mouths and noses. Could Eddie be one of them?

Good iron should not be made into nails nor gentle men into soldiers.

Sorry to be low, Helen

Train to Denver
June 17, 1944

Dear Helen,

Greetings! I'm sitting in the lounge car on a train heading to Denver, and I'm surrounded by boys, boys, boys—all in uniform. They're playing cards, drinking beers, and doing their darnedest to distract me from my letter writing. Outside the window, I see salt flats—nothing to write home about, although I'm writing about it to you. I hear it'll be beautiful when we start climbing into the Rockies.

Remember when Eddie used to tell us that all troupers are born tramps and that when you're in show business, you'll go east, west, north, and up the hill to get a job? That's me now! I broke in my act at the Mapes Hotel in Reno. Then I traveled to El Rancho in Las Vegas, the Ranch on the Everett Highway in Seattle (where I broke the theater's record for highest attendance!), and the Clover Club in Portland. I'm seeing America all right. Everywhere I go folks are 100% behind the war. People are pulling together and doing their parts. I'm doing my part too by giving my ALL!

After a tiring show, I can knock off a sixteen-ounce sirloin, but I'm still holding my weight under a hundred pounds, because I dance so hard and travel all the time. The other day, when I was interviewed about my figure, I said, I eat like a bird—like a bird who eats cats. (Big laugh.) Dancing is strenuous work, I told another reporter, but it's better than going back to the laundry. (Remember when Charlie used to crack that one? Well, it's true for me!)

I'm copying this from one of my reviews—

If not for the Oriental Danseuse's race, she would undoubtedly be in New York's Rainbow Room or some other first-line cabaret. She is that beautiful, witty, and talented.

I'll get there too!

I'm really happy I did this, but, Helen, I miss you tons. Please give Tommy a kiss and a hug from his special auntie. When you have a chance, will you write to me about Eddie? I'd sure like to know how he's doing.

Your gal pal, Grace

P.S. I almost forgot to mention that I ran into the Merry Mahjongs! In Las Vegas! Crazy, huh? They're out on the road too—kicking that gong around!

P.P.S. Why haven't you written? You aren't still mad at me, are you?

Somewhere in the Pacific
June 23, 1944

Grace, baby,

I've seen more, done more, and learned more in the past few months than I imagined possible. Have I told you about the guys on our ground crews? We've got Chinese, Mexicans, Poles, Irish, and Negroes all working together. We may not look alike, but we eat the same bad food, follow the same crummy orders, are bitten by the same damn mosquitoes, and suffer the same blasted heat and humidity, because we all fight under the same flag to defend the same land. When this thing is over, our country will be very different. But don't you go changing! I want my girl just the way she was.

I wish the two of us were back in your apartment, if you catch my drift. When I get home, baby, we'll never leave the bedroom.

Loads of love, Joe

Topaz War Relocation Center
June 24, 1944

Helen!

You'll never guess what came in the mail today—a letter from Lee Mortimer, the night-life editor for the New York Daily Mirror! He wrote, All the Japanese dolls are vanishing, leaving playful gentlemen like me to fend for ourselves— Funny, right? Turns out he's quite fond of Oriental girls— He's already married and divorced a couple of them— He wrote that he's long been an admirer, thanks to Life, and complained that I've been too far away for him to enjoy the pleasure of my company. He's going to sponsor me and bring me to New York right away. Right away in camp lingo could mean months, but I'm excited!

Please forgive me for sounding like I'm only thinking about my-

self. Here's the most important question— How's Eddie? Have you heard anything from him since D-Day? I know he's all right— He has to be— He'll dance around any and all bullets! Yes, I'm making light, but it's the only way I know to get through these days.

Yours till the kitchen sinks, Ruby

Somewhere in the Pacific
June 27, 1944

Dearest Grace,

Have I told you how hot it is in a P-38? HOT! The guys and I strip down to our skivvies, tennis shoes, and parachute packs to fly at low altitude. We can't outrun Zeroes when we're close to the ground, but we've got superior rate of climb and our firepower is hands-down better and more effective. Grace, I want you to trust that if an engine fails or I take flak, I can drop fuel tanks and outrun the Japs all the way back to base. What I'm saying, baby, is don't worry about me. But I sure as hell worry about you out there on the road. What if you meet some guy who didn't get called up or maybe has flat feet? I bet you have tons of rich guys lining up to see you too. Just don't forget about your old boy out here. Every flight I take, I'm carrying you in my heart.

Loads of love, Joe

P.S. I've received all your letters and packages. You sure know how to remind a guy what we're fighting for.

Train to St. Louis
July 10, 1944

Dearest Joe,

I'll take your heat and raise you some. I had to sleep in a tornado shelter the other night. I'd forgotten the Midwest's humidity.

Yuck! You must have forgotten it too, or is it really hotter than blazes flying over the ocean? Seems crazy to me, but what do I know? I miss you. I pray that you'll be careful. Promise you'll come back to me.

Forever yours, Grace

Train to Chicago
July 12, 1944

Dear Helen,

Is there anyone besides you and Tommy left in San Francisco? I've run into George Louie, the Lim Sisters, Jack and Irene Mak and their two kids— I hate to say it, but our friends are still doing a bang-up job of putting the chill on me. The Merry Mahjongs and the Lim Sisters mostly ignore my presence, but George has become the road king of spite. (He's sleeping his way across the country, just in case you want to know. The guy goes bananas for that you-know-what place between a girl's legs. I've seen him arrive in town, date one, two, three girls, and then hit a dry patch, so to say, which means the gossip mill has gotten going and he's plumb out of luck. He doesn't worry about it, because a new crop of girls is just a town and a gig up the track.) Anyway— He can't decide which accusation he likes more—that I ratted out Ruby or that I hid two Japanese in my apartment. I've tried to wave him off. "Aw, tell it to someone who cares." If he blabs on, I say, "Run along now, Georgie. Your mother's calling you." Jack and Irene tolerate me, though, because I'm a good babysitter. Thank Tommy for teaching me the ropes!

You haven't written to me. What's up?

Your gal pal, Grace

Somewhere in the Pacific
July 13, 1944

Grace, baby,

I only have a few minutes. I had a wild day! Shot down two Zeroes! Lots of great pilots out here. I need to measure up. I miss you like mad. Why didn't I have you meet me in Winnetka when I visited my folks? We could have borrowed my dad's car and gone to Niagara Falls. You never know what can happen in this world. I miss you, baby.

I love you, love you, love you, Joe

Train to Cedar Rapids
July 23, 1944

Dearest Joe,

The words you wrote make my heart soar. Maybe that sounds corny, but that's how love is supposed to sound. I love you too. I've loved you from the moment we first met. Then we went through all that rigmarole— So much wasted time— But now I'm yours and you're mine— Niagara Falls! Oh, Joe! I'm so happy!

I just finished a gig in Omaha with Dorothy Toy—the first, and still the truest, Chinese Ginger Rogers. Did I ever tell you she's my idol? I used to watch her in the movie theater back in Plain City. Her partner—Paul Wing—was called up four months ago and is in a tank in Europe, so Dorothy and her sister came out on the Chop-Suey Circuit to kill time—just like me. I told her, Even though we never met, we lived in the same apartment building in San Francisco. I should have said something about what an inspiration she's been all these years. She's the nicest gal. Dorothy has encouraged me to broaden my act to incorporate some patter and a couple of songs. I now start with "I came from a town so small it didn't even have a Chinese restaurant." That always gets a chuckle.

I'm blabbing on like a fool when all I want to do is kiss you and tell you how much I love you. I LOVE YOU! I think of you every minute of every day.

Love, Grace

Train to Cedar Rapids
July 23, 1944

Dear Helen,

Joe loves me and I love him, but I'm not being totally honest with him. He can't understand what it's like for me out here. I'm alone most of the time—traveling from club to club, city to city, sometimes playing shows near military bases. I've come across a lot of Victory Girls, who'll sleep with any man in uniform. I'm not one of them, but I worry that Joe might start to take what I'm doing the wrong way—

I don't have much in the way of companionship, so I have loads of time to read magazines and go to movies. I see a lot of ads begging women to work for the war effort while remaining feminine for when our men come home. Don't those magazine people know we're changing? I've watched movies that praise brave widows. If, God forbid, something happens to Eddie, I know you'll be brave, but what will happen to your heart after all you've already been through? Those movie people don't think about that. Then there's the battle against Victory Girls. It's led by another bunch of men—this time in Washington—and it's downright sneaky. Women—like us—who work in clubs and bars that cater to our boys, are being accused of being patriotic amateurs. They accuse us of staging orgies in the barracks. That's ridiculous, and a long way from being labeled a Khaki-wackie! And it makes me sick. Rumors have been circulating that some Victory Girls average fifty or more encounters a night. (Come on!) And did you see that Life article? The reporter wrote that a diseased Victory Girl can do far more damage than a

500-pound bomb dropped right in the middle of an Army camp. It's not fair, and it makes me fighting sore every time I think about it, because aren't our boys making love too? They're the instigators for heaven's sake! You think they get in trouble or in trouble? No! They're told they need sex to be good soldiers! But if a girl is rounded up and found to have a venereal disease, she can be held for the duration. Exactly how long might that be? Months? Years?

So that's one thing. The other is that I kind of lied when I wrote to Joe about Dorothy Toy. (Yes! I finally met her!) I left out that the Chinese Ginger Rogers isn't Chinese. She's Japanese. She and Paul were doing a show in New York when Ed Sullivan, a gossip columnist at the New York Daily News, broke the news— You know, ratted her out— She's hightailed it to the Chop-Suey Circuit, playing towns and cities where, she says, they haven't met many Chinese or Japanese. She's just Oriental. I never could have written that to Joe, but I never want him to consider me a liar like Ruby either.

Max called to say that he's having a hard time getting me good bookings. (Cedar Rapids and Des Moines are up next. I ask you!) After I pestered him about why, he finally spilled the beans. Turns out George Louie's bad-mouthing about me has moved from our dressing rooms to the front office. Club owners have enough to worry about without entertainers fighting backstage. I said I didn't do anything. Max said, Yeah, yeah, yeah, and then he hung up on me! If I can't work in San Francisco and he can't get me bookings, what am I going to do?

I keep writing to you, but you never respond. What have you heard from Eddie? And Monroe? He also promised to write, but I haven't heard from him either.

Sorry to make this so darned long, but I sure could use your advice.

Your gal pal, Grace

Topaz War Relocation Center
July 30, 1944

Helen!

You wrote to me not that long ago that a tree may prefer calm, but the wind will not stop. Things will take their own course regardless of what I want. The thermometer hit 120 degrees yesterday! I spent the afternoon lying on the cement floor in the latrine. It's the coolest place in the camp— The little girls like to hang out there too— They got me to play jacks with them, if you can believe it. (Believe it!) When you want to do your business, it's a good idea to kick the toilet first. Scorpions! I've tried every mess hall, looking for something decent to eat— No luck— We're served things that make no sense— Spaghetti and rice at the same meal. People around here are gaining weight, but not me. I can't eat that stuff.

Sometimes I go to the fence and stare at the desert. There's nowhere to hide out there, no place to go, and no way to survive, even if I got out. I ask myself, why do they hate us so much? What did I do that was so dreadful or unforgivable that they need to lock me up in a place like this? There is no lower helplessness than realizing you've lost control over every aspect of your life— And you want to hear something? When I walk by the schools in the morning, I hear the kids saying the Pledge of Allegiance and singing "God Bless America." But if we ask the authorities how long we'll be in here, the answer is NO ANSWER! (Go ahead, Mr. Censor, black that out!)

Yours till the toilet bowls, Ruby

P.S. Thanks for the Pond's cold cream, Camay soap, and petroleum jelly! They're going to do a lot for my beauty regimen. You're a pip.

San Francisco
August 4, 1944

Dear Grace,

I'm sorry to be the one to inform you, but I've got bad news about Monroe. He caught lobar pneumonia—the worst you can get. He's dying, bed-slow, at Walter Reed Hospital. The Army doctors are experimenting with him—giving him something called penicillin. They've written to Mama and Baba that there's little to no hope. And it could take months for him to die, even with that new drug. All we can do is pray—

The mood in the compound is very sad. We are a large family, but the idea that Monroe won't be coming home— I— We— Baba stays at his office. Mama is out all the time. Since there's nothing she can do for Monroe when he's so far away, she's taken my place as a Gray Lady. Caring for other mothers' sons gives her faith that there's a mother out there taking care of Monroe.

Best, Helen

Topaz War Relocation Center
August 6, 1944

Helen!

GREAT NEWS!!! I finally got my release from camp after seventeen months in this pit hole! Lee Mortimer has sent money for my train ticket, and he's lined up an agent for me in New York. Everyone here is full of advice and warnings. Don't speak Japanese when I leave the camp. Not a problem! Don't gather in groups of two or more Japanese. Really not a problem! Don't call attention to myself and ruin it for others. Well, they got me there. I plan on calling plenty of attention to myself, but I hope I don't ruin it for others.

Want to know what I'm thinking about? New clothes! Making real money again! I'm getting out of here!

Will write from the BIG APPLE!

More soon, Ruby

Fox Theatre, Detroit
August 10, 1944

Dear Helen,

Your first letter finally reached me, and it contains such sad news. I'm very sorry to hear about Monroe. I feel just terrible. And it seems so unfair. Monroe was always so full of life. And opinions! Remember when he took me to the protest against sending scrap metal to Japan? At the time, I thought he was stuffy, but he was right. Now I wish the whole country had paid more attention to what Monroe and others like him were trying to warn us about. You're surrounded by your family, but please write to me if there's anything I can do.

You're in my thoughts, Grace.

San Francisco
August 14, 1944

Dear Ruby,

That is great news. I'm happy for you.

Did you get my note about Monroe? Maybe it got lost in the mail? Or have you already left the camp? If so, you won't even receive this. Monroe's got lobar pneumonia. They say he won't make it. I keep thinking about the word worse. Is his pneumonia worse than if he'd been maimed or died alone on a battlefield somewhere? Is it worse that I'm more worried about Eddie than I am about my own brother? Is it worse that I want to stay home, get all the kids off to school, and make sure they complete their homework than go back to volunteering with the Gray Ladies with Mama? I just couldn't take it anymore. I'd seen too many boys who'd lost limbs or had been burned.

I'd better quit now before I feel too *sorry for myself.*

Helen

Train to Buffalo
August 15, 1944

Dear Helen,

I suspect this is going to be another long one. Sorry about that. But I have so much to ask you and tell you. I wish you could know how lonely I get out here by myself. I wish even more that I could come home to San Francisco, the Forbidden City, my friends, and YOU!

First things first. I still haven't heard back from you. I don't know what that means. Is there something more about Monroe you haven't told me yet?

All right. On to me and my problems. It didn't seem appropriate to ask in my last letter, but I was really hoping you could give me some advice about what I should do about Joe. You weren't too happy when he proposed to Ruby. I'm Oriental too, and he's still an Occidental. Are you upset that our kids will be mongrels? (Your word!) Maybe you worry I've turned into a no-no girl. As you can see, I'm feeling very insecure.

Last night didn't help me any— The last straw— I just finished my gig at the Fox in Detroit. I was exhausted after the show and didn't bother to remove my stage makeup before I left for my hotel. As I walked, I heard someone following me. I haven't been that scared since Ray came out of Ida's room holding the bloody knife. Petrified! Every time I stopped, the person following me stopped too. I pulled my guts together and ducked into an alley. I hid behind some garbage cans and prayed no dogs would start barking. I waited until the man ran past, and then I waited some more. I took off my heels and sprinted barefoot to the hotel. When I got to my room, I locked the door and wedged a chair under the knob. I checked my whole body to make sure I wasn't injured. The man hadn't touched me, but I ached everywhere, and my feet were cut pretty bad. I didn't sleep a wink, and I cried buckets.

Sorry my writing is so squiggly today. Bad stretch of track. The train is nearly empty. Makes me feel even more alone.

Anyway, this morning I packed to shuffle off to Buffalo. I ran into George Louie in the lobby. He was coming in to play the Fox as I was leaving. I was still so upset that I told him what happened. I wanted sympathy, but he blamed me! "It's your own damn fault for leaving the theater in your stage makeup. If you look like a Victory Girl, a guy will treat you like a Victory Girl."

My own damn fault? I've heard some version of that my entire life. When my father apologized for beating me, he used to say I made him do it. Did I ask him to kick and hit me? Did I ask to be punished for something I didn't do to Ruby? George is an ass. He doesn't know anything about me or my life. Still, I pledge right here and now on this train never to leave a club in stage makeup again, even though that won't protect me from someone like my father, Ray, or even—God help me—if Joe ever loses his temper again. (You see why I need your advice?)

We're pulling into the station. Gotta go.

Here I am again. Checked in to my hotel. Just did an interview with a kid from the local paper. He was sweet, but he asked the same question I get at every stop—what's it like for a young woman like me to be on the road, away from my family and friends? Usually, I answer that this is my way to help build unity on the home front, but I told that kid that every night is a job. I go out there. I start the show. It goes well. The next night, I lay a bomb. I forget things. But how can I forget my routine when I've done it night after night for weeks? I forget because I'm anxious about the train I have to catch tomorrow and that I need to wash my undies before I go to sleep. I think about my mother, who I haven't seen or spoken to in years, the war, or how nice the gown the woman sitting at the second table on the right is wearing and how much it might cost. I just forget. Then the next night I go out there, start the show, and maybe it's great. I told that kid I can't worry about it too much, because if I did, I wouldn't last long in this business—

I've been thinking a lot about my mom, though. I'm spending so much time in the Midwest, how can I not think about her? I wonder if she might like to see me, but what about my dad? I don't want to be hurt— Makes me sad—

Please give my best to your mother and father and tell them that I'm praying for Monroe. Kisses and hugs to Tommy.

Your gal pal, Grace

Somewhere in the Pacific
August 20, 1944

Dear Grace,

Sorry I haven't written in a while. The other pilots have gotten a kick out of the photos and clippings you send. "You've got the most famous doll in the squadron, you lucky stiff." They've decided you're something you're not, and they won't stop rubbing my nose in it.

I'm an ace now. I shot down my fifth Jap plane a couple of days ago, and today I knocked another out of the sky. I saw the pilot's face when he realized he wouldn't be able to bail out. The other day bullets ripped through the right wing of a B-17 a pal of mine was flying. It caught on fire. He crashed in the jungle not far from here. No one made it. Good guys, all of them.

I've been thinking about it, Grace. I love you, but I need to concentrate on getting the job done out here.

Sincerely, Joe

Train to Altoona
August 30, 1944

Darling Joe,

Are you embarrassed by me? What we have is special. Don't let the guys tease you. I know it's tough out there and things are hard, but always remember that I'm right here—waiting for you. So please write. You're scaring me.

I'll love you forever, Grace

Somewhere in the Pacific
September 15, 1944

Postcard:

Just shot down number seven. You're a good egg, Grace, and you always will be. I look forward to seeing you when the war's over.

Train to Fort Wayne
October 1, 1944

Dear Helen,

I'm sobbing as I write this. Joe sent me a Dear Jane postcard, and he didn't even bother to sign it! Oh, Helen, I love him so much. What should I do?

Grace

New York
October 2, 1944

Helen!

Nothing ever turns out like I hope it will. I beat it to New York, and it was great. Lee Mortimer was grand too. Sam Bernstein, my new agent, booked me in a club, where I did my bubble routine. I must be rusty, though. I didn't measure up against the other performers. I can't believe how much I lost of myself in the camp. And those New Yorkers? I guess they've seen everything— Or think they have, because what a bunch of boobs, drinking their martinis and not even looking at me. Sam and Lee want me to hit the Chop-Suey Circuit to get back in the swing of things. I can't go out west, for obvious reasons. They say I'll be safest in the south, where few people have seen a Japanese. I'll be making $400 a week! Not half bad for someone who's been out of sight as long as I've been. I promised that we'd be together once I left Topaz. How about coming on the road with me as my dresser?

Tipity tops, Ruby

Train to Flint
October 3, 1944

Dear Helen,

Life sure throws some curveballs. Max called yesterday with an offer to join George Louie and a comedy duo called Ming and Ling for an all-Chinese holiday revue in Atlanta. I automatically thought of Eddie—east, west, north, and up the hill. He always left out the south, admitting it made him nervous. He'd say—I'm not black, but I'm not white either. Same here! So I told Max no, but he just kept talking. He said they'll call it something like the Chinese Follies or

Chinese Extravaganza. The club owners will run ads along the lines of—It's Oriental! Gay and exciting! Spiced with song, comedy, and dance thrills! I said no, no, no, no. I told him I won't work with George Louie. I don't want to hear his snotty comments about me. He must be as hard up as I am if he's willing to work together—thrown together by necessity is how Max put it. I still said no.

Then Max bowled me over. Guess who else is going to be on the bill. Ruby! She's out of the camp! I'm so relieved. She's going to be performing as Princess Tai. I guess they figure she's an actual Chinese princess. It'll be great to see Ruby, and teaming up with her will also be a way for me to start clearing my name.

Any good news about Monroe? Any news, period? Now that I'm going to be in one place for a while you can finally write me back.

I haven't heard one word from Joe, in case you're interested. I can't believe I let him break my heart again.

Your gal pal, Grace

P.S. I almost forgot. The club has offered to drop George from the bill if I'll take the top spot. Hmm— Hard decision— Take that, George!

Western Union Telegram. October 5, 1944.

Max, I'll do it. Stop. Can you do me a favor first? Stop. Book me something near my hometown. Stop. I want to see my mother. Stop.

Grace

GRACE

A Wind-Chime Voice

The best Max could find for me was three weeks playing programmers before film showings in Cincinnati. After that, he sent me to Columbus, where he booked a one-nighter for my solo act. "Enjoy it," Max said. "Because I don't see much for you after the Atlanta holiday run." The news was so scary, I didn't know how to begin to process it. Once I reached Columbus, I was only twenty-four miles from home. I hired a car and driver to take me to Plain City. I'd been gone for six years. I'd wired money to my mother, but I'd kept my promise never to write. I'd never corresponded directly with Miss Miller either. Here was my chance to show them that I'd made something of myself, even if Atlanta might be my last hurrah. I was terrified, however, about seeing my father. The years hadn't changed my feelings about him.

The land—at that time of year—was still as flat, empty, and brown as ever. Piles of dirty snow edged the highway or lay in shady spots created by low berms and wedges of earth. I passed through towns—each looking much like the last—with clapboard houses, dignified churches, and predictable shops. I'd forgotten the echoing loneliness of deserted central squares and empty sidewalks. I sat in the backseat of the car, wearing my fur, my makeup perfect, and so, so nervous. Railroad tracks, a grain elevator, a service station, and signs advertising Orange Crush, Quaker State motor oil, and a trailer camp marked the outskirts of Plain City. I sat up and clenched my hands in my lap.

"Pull up over there by the bank," I told the driver. "I'll walk the last couple of blocks."

He parked, came around to the passenger side, and opened my door. Things like this don't happen in Plain City, and I felt eyes peering out of windows. My breath came out in billowy clouds. My fur shielded me from the wind, but my shoes were slippery on the snow and ice. *Snow and ice*—I hadn't missed those for one second. I put my head down and pushed onward. I passed the Ford dealership, still in business. I saw Thanksgiving decorations in store windows: cornucopias overflowing with autumnal vegetables, a sign to "order your turkey now" in the butcher's window, and a poster advertising Miss Miller's winter recital.

Up ahead, the neon sign for Mr. Lee's Laundry glowed in the twilight. I glanced over my shoulder and saw the car, creeping along the road, following me. Then I took the final steps and positioned myself directly in front of the laundry's window. I expected to see Dad pushing an eight-pound hand iron across a shirt. Instead, I saw a strange man—an Occidental—working a steam presser and singing with great animation. He pulled the presser's head down, locked it in place with his foot, steam swirled around him, and then he lifted the head again, bobbing in time to "The G.I. Jive." The place was completely different—updated. My parents must have sold the laundry. But if they'd sold the place, why hadn't the sign been changed?

I took a deep breath and entered. The radio blared. The man caroled along at the top of his lungs. "Roodley-toot. Jump in your suit. Make a salute." When he saw me, he broke into a grin. He reached over and turned down the radio. As he came around the presser, I saw he was an amputee—probably a veteran.

"Grace?" His grin broadened. "Grace!"

I nodded, unsure.

"I'm Henry Billups. Remember me? From school?"

Ah, Henry Billups. Ilsa, one of the evil triplets, had once been sweet on Henry. Now look at him—minus an arm and working a presser in a laundry. So sad.

"Of course I remember you!" I said, always the cheerful performer. "But what are you doing here? You own the place now?"

He gave a good-natured snort. "You're quite the joker, Grace. You always were." He paused. "I'm not much good to my dad out on the farm these days. Your mom hired me."

My mom hired him?

"All this"—Henry gestured around him—"is because of her. Right after Pearl Harbor, your mom donated most of her irons during our first scrap-metal drive. She could have gone out of business, but she squeaked through. Then she gave me a job when no one else would. The whole town was grateful. Now business is growing. Who has time to do their wash these days?" He stared at me, waiting for a reaction, but my mind was so muddled I didn't know what to say. "But you're the real kicker. Quite apart from the money you send, you've helped the business more than anything your mom or I could ever have done."

"Me?" How did he know so much about my family? How did he know I'd sent money? How did he know anything about anything? Creepy.

He jerked a thumb to the wall behind the cash register to where a poster for the show I'd be doing in Columbus hung. The image was of me in my Javanese-inspired costume with the wacky headdress: THE ORIENTAL DANSEUSE—STAR OF STAGE AND SCREEN. I was astonished.

"We're set to see your show on Saturday night. Your mom planned the whole thing. Practically everyone in town is going. Reverend Reynolds got folks to donate their gas coupons so we can all ride in buses together. Your mom wanted to surprise you. I guess you'll surprise her instead."

I barely took in his words. "Where is she?" I asked.

Henry jerked his thumb again—this time to the ceiling.

I thanked him, and then went upstairs and knocked on the door. I was excited to see my mother, but a knot of terror gripped my guts when I contemplated coming face-to-face with my father. The door opened. My mom looked . . . younger.

"Grace, dear. I always hoped you'd come home, but I never expected it."

When I heard her wind-chime voice I burst into tears. She drew me to her and hugged me tight. Finally, she released me, held me at arm's length, and searched my face. I scrutinized hers too. She wore a gingham blouse tucked into trousers. Her hair was tied up in a bandanna. She appeared strong, healthy—like one of those Rosie the Riveters back in San Francisco—and, again, so much younger. Happier, I realized.

I peered over her shoulder and into the main room. It looked exactly the same, except my dad wasn't sitting at the table, his anger ready to fly at me.

"He's not here," Mom said. "He passed away. Come in. We have so much to talk about."

She pulled me into the room, gestured for me to sit, and poured us cups of coffee into which she stirred fresh cream and sugar—treats, when everything was inhibited by the austerity of rationing. She sat across from me, and we stared at each other again, soaking in every change.

"I want to ask you so many things," she said.

"I have questions for you too." I bit my lip. "I guess you'd better tell me about Dad first."

"We had dinner right here a little over a year ago," she recounted in a steady voice. "He said he was tired and went to the bedroom. By the time I got there, he was gone. Doc Haverford said his heart gave out."

The news left me confused. Dad was the biological vessel who helped put my soul into this body, but he'd hurt me so many times.

Mom's hand covered mine. "The doctor said I should be grateful he didn't suffer."

I pondered that, then I said, "I'm sorry, Mom, but I can't forgive him."

She withdrew her hand, sliding her fingers back across the surface of the table and spidering them into her lap. "You never understood your father. You never knew how much he loved you or how proud he was of you."

"How can you say that? You were *here.*" I gestured around the room. Memories of being bashed into furniture and walls battered my mind. It still deeply hurt that my mother couldn't or wouldn't defend me.

"I want to show you something," Mom said. She went to a cabinet, pulled out an album, and brought it back to the table. "It's a scrapbook. Your father put it together after you left."

I opened the cover. On the first page was a photograph of the ponies at the Forbidden City on opening night. I quickly flipped through the book. Somehow my father had found almost every review and notice that had been printed about me.

"How?" I asked.

"We saw you in the newsreel," Mom answered. "Your dad made sure everyone in town knew that you'd gotten out of here and that your dreams had come true."

I cast my mind back to that day on the beach when the other ponies and I had danced in the sand, and tried to imagine my father seeing it in the darkness of the Rialto.

"No." I shook my head, refusing to accept what she was telling me. "You're wrong. Dad couldn't have been proud of me. I became exactly what he hated."

"Do you remember the night you left?"

"I'll never forget it. He called me a whore . . . 'just like your mother.' "

Mom's gaze was steady and her eyes clear. "He told you the truth. A long time ago, I was a willow flower—a prostitute. Once those words came out of his mouth, I realized he couldn't keep them buried any longer. We never wanted you to learn about all that and, of course, he worried that somehow you would follow my path."

Nothing she could have said would have stunned me more.

"There's no point in keeping the secret any longer," Mom continued matter-of-factly. "I was born in China, like I always told you. My parents sold me when I was five. Maybe younger, maybe a little older."

"Did you come through Angel Island?" That was my first question? I blame it on shock.

"I came before Angel Island opened." Her eyes darted to the ceiling as if the past were projected there. "Back then, no one paid much attention to who was coming in, but I have a vague memory of some kind of interview. Then I was sent to Idaho, where I worked for a shopkeeper and his wife. They were Americans, which is why I speak the way I do. Like you, I didn't see another Chinese until I was older. The Johnsons were like parents to me, but they died of typhus when I was twelve. The townsfolk sent me to San Francisco, because no one wanted a Chinese orphan."

"I was scared when I went to San Francisco," I said, still trying to absorb what she was telling me. "And I was a lot older. Where did you go? The YWCA?"

"They didn't have that then. This was just one year after the earthquake and fire. A gang swept me up. I was put in a crib on Bartlett Alley."

"Oh, Mom. I'm so sorry."

"It was a hard life." She angled her head and smiled wanly.

"How did you escape?"

"The man in charge of the brothel said I could buy my freedom for five thousand dollars, or he could sell me to a tong gunman or professional gambler. But I knew I'd be dead from a willow-flower disease long before either of those things happened." She saw the look of horror on my face. "It could have been worse. I could have been working in that life since I was five. I met other girls, little girls, who had that fate." She paused and took a breath. "I was rescued by Donaldina Cameron."

Donaldina Cameron? Incredible. I knew from Helen that she worked out of the building right around the corner from the YWCA. She'd rescued hundreds, maybe thousands, of Chinese slave girls and prostitutes. My mother had been through hell and yet she'd suggested I go to the very city where she'd suffered.

"How could you encourage me to try San Francisco after everything you'd been through?" I asked.

"I couldn't see him hurt you again. Letting you leave was the only way I had to save you . . . I paged through your magazines. I saw Treasure Island, and I saw the city. San Francisco—the *world*—had to be different."

I reflected on all the stage-door Johnnies I'd met over the years; the ponies who'd gotten in trouble after nights of goodbyes to servicemen only to be labeled Victory Girls; Helen, who was left high and dry by Tommy's father; the way Joe dumped Ruby when he found out her background, and now had dropped me. Men weren't perfect and what they did to us could be thoughtless and cruel, but none of that compared to what my mother had experienced. I ached for her.

"I lived with a lot of shame," Mom admitted. "Miss Cameron took care of me for many years. I changed back to the girl I had once been. She promised to help me get a husband, but nothing could erase the black mark against me. No good man would take me."

"Is that why Dad married you? Because he was a bad man? And he saw you as a bad girl?" I didn't mean to sound unkind, but I needed to know.

Mom sighed. "You still don't understand."

"Is his story different too?" I asked. "Was he actually born here?"

"Yes. I'm sure of it. He lived with his father in a mining camp—"

"Why did he always say it was a lumber camp?"

Mom shrugged. "What does it matter now? He did laundry and cooked for miners. He was on his way to China to find a wife when Miss Cameron introduced us. She sold him on the idea that I was reformed and a good Christian woman. He convinced her that he could make an honest and righteous life for me. Miss Cameron consented to his proposal. Your father and I were married. He took me back to the mining camp—"

"But the two of you lived in San Francisco—"

Irritation flitted across Mom's face. "Will you listen? We were in the mining camp. I got pregnant. We had a car. We drove to Sebastopol to pick apples . . ."

I recognized this part. Mom went into labor, was turned away from the hospital, and I was born by the side of the road.

"When you came out, everything ripped down there," she recalled. "When your dad finally got me back to the mining camp, one of the men stitched me together. I couldn't walk upright for a month. I felt like my insides were going to fall out. That's not so different from what many women feel, but I was the only woman in the camp. You have to understand that back then there was—what?—about one Chinese woman for every twenty Chinese men in this country? Most of those women were willow flowers. The miners started to gossip about me. They made guesses about me, and they guessed right. They were our people. *Chinese* people. Your father was ashamed."

"So you ran away and came here—"

"Where we hoped we'd be safe."

"But where we would *all* be humiliated. Dad had it the worst. He was a laundryman. He was a joke."

"Your father suffered great loss of face in this country, where a Chinese man is considered less than a man. And yes, your father was forever a laundryman, doing women's work."

As she spoke, I couldn't help thinking of Eddie, who'd endured so much disgrace not only for being a dancer who preferred boys but for being a *Chinese* man, and even Monroe, who'd graduated from Cal but couldn't find work because he was Chinese. Both of those men—like my father—were *enthusiastically* American, but what had it gotten them? I could see it and understand it—and I felt terribly sorry for my mother—but even so my parents had systematically betrayed me.

"Did you and Dad ever tell me anything that was true?"

"Grace!"

"Well, did you?"

"I always told you I loved you—"

"But he didn't." I began to weep.

"When we saw *Aloha, Boys!,* your father cried and cried. Everyone in town saw you in it." For a moment she exuded joy and pride. "That was the longest running movie ever at the Rialto. From the time you were a little girl, you were a star in your dad's eyes. That movie just proved it to everyone else."

"That doesn't change the fact that he beat me."

"He was ashamed of me. He was ashamed of himself. Grace, maybe you haven't yet met a man who's been shamed, but he'll do crazy things. Unforgivable things."

Like Joe, when he learned about Ruby.

"Your dad loved you and wanted to keep the truth about me a secret."

So which one was it? That he was afraid I'd stumble on Mom's secret? Or that he'd been humiliated as a man? For every man who hits his wife or his children, there are a hundred excuses. My team didn't win . . . You didn't clean the house . . . I don't like this meal . . . I had a bad day at work . . . The kids won't shut up . . . But what did it matter in the end? My father beat me, and the reasons—however real or misguided—didn't change that. I loved my mother, but she hadn't protected me. But by allowing me to leave, it finally dawned on me, she took his full beatings on herself. The realization of that shook me to the core. I could pity my father at some level, but it didn't alter what had happened in that room over many years. The aches and stiffness in my ribs, fingers, and spine from injuries my father gave me would be in my bones forever. The terror I experienced whenever I felt threatened was deeper still.

I looked at the scrapbook my father had composed—saw all the obsession and work he'd put into it—and knew I'd never understand him, his life, his choices, his shame. No matter what my mother said, I would always be my father's measly girl. But I had a choice about what might happen next—hold on to bitterness or try to forge a different kind of relationship with the one blood relative I had left in the world.

"Tell me about Miss Miller," I said, and that was that.

Mom caught me up on my dance teacher, who was still single and still carrying a torch for the manager of the Farmers National Bank, and she still let him walk all over her. All this was news to me!

"You were a little girl," my mom said. "What do you expect?"

I told Mom about life on the road. "I pour my heart out to lonely boys in base towns, mothers missing their sons, lovers who might never be reunited." I recited something Eddie had once said: "If I *feel* a song, then the audience does too, because music purges the soul of tragedy. It's the vehicle by which we can express our deepest human emotions and our spirits."

"What highfalutin talk," Mom said, and we laughed.

"It's not always like that," I admitted. "Sometimes I can command an audience to watch me; other times they ignore me because they're putting on the dogs for their girlfriends or they've had too many drinks. But when I become the Oriental Danseuse and showcase my routine from *Aloha, Boys!,* I put customers in the movie with me."

"Oh, honey. I'm so proud of you."

I didn't tell her about being blackballed or that I had no jobs lined up after Atlanta. Mom and Dad had run away from her past. I was running from lies that had been told about me, but would she believe me? So I asked about kids from school. Mom told me that Freddie Thompson, who'd teased me when I wore one of his old shirts, had died in the war. Henry, who now worked for my mother, had gone against his family and married Ilsa—"even though she was Finnish"—when he was drafted.

"But that girl never was any good," Mom said. "As soon as she heard Henry lost his arm, she hightailed it out of town."

Frankly, plenty of girls "abandoned ship" when they heard their husbands or boyfriends were maimed, blinded, or badly burned in the war. I'd also heard of servicemen who refused to answer letters or allow hospital visits from their girls. No man wants a woman to see him as anything less than strong and able.

"And you, honey?" Mom asked. "Is there someone special in your life?"

I told her everything about Joe, ending with "I haven't heard from him in a month."

"He's in a war, Grace. He faces death every day. That will change a man."

"I don't want him to change."

"Maybe he understands that about you," she reasoned. "Maybe he realizes he won't be the same in your eyes when he comes back."

My mom was giving me advice on my broken heart. Incredible. No matter what had happened in the past, she was my mother.

"I love him," I confessed.

"Then fight for him. Don't run away. Stand your ground and fight."

"How can I do that, if he won't answer my letters?"

"Keep writing," she counseled. "Stake your claim. That's what your father and I did. We were both flawed, but we found this place, and we built a life for ourselves and for you. Maybe in this one way you can learn from us. Fight for him, Grace. Fight for him because you love him."

THE NEXT SATURDAY, the theater was filled with familiar faces: Miss Miller, Doc Haverford, my mom's friends from church, a couple of my teachers, and Mr. Tubbs, who'd pulled my father off me that last night. There are many ways you can measure success, but none is more meaningful than having folks who've known you forever see your rise in the world. They "knew you when." They celebrate what you've accomplished. And yes, there are some—like Maude and Velma, the remaining evil triplets—for whom your success is a knife in the gut, making it a triumph all the way.

As a girl, I'd believed my family and I would be outsiders forever. We'd washed people's dirty laundry. We looked different, but my family had struggled just like all the other families did in Plain City. At the

Forbidden City, total strangers asked if they could touch me, because they'd never touched an Oriental before. In Plain City, everyone had known me, and they hadn't wanted to touch me. In Chinatown, I'd learned from Helen the importance of family over the interests of the individual. In my hometown, maybe the individual took precedence. Maybe that was what had allowed me to run away in the first place. When I took my bows and saw those faces in the audience, my heart brimmed with pride. But I also remembered what my mother used to say to me: *When fortune comes, do not enjoy all of it; when advantage comes, do not take all of it.*

RUBY

Dying Ashes Will Burn Again

The taxi went in fits and starts down Atlanta's Peachtree Boulevard. The next few hours were going to be momentous for me, and I was having a difficult time lining up my feelings. I wasn't at all sure how I'd react when I saw Grace. Last night, Helen had told me a lot of strange things about her. Interesting, chilling things, really, about how she'd turned me in, stolen my part, wheedled her way into Joe's heart, and then been dumped by him. It was hard for me to believe she could have done all that but, as Helen said, everyone couldn't be wrong. Two and two always add up to four, but my mind reeled away from the possibility that *any* of it could be true, even though I knew that at least *some* of it must be.

My taxi dropped me off in front of the theater, where a man on a ladder was placing letters on the marquee. Top billing: GRACE LEE, THE ORIENTAL DANSEUSE, STAR OF STAGE AND SCREEN. Below that: MING AND LING—TWO HILLBILLIES FROM THE BURMA ROAD. And at the bottom of the bill: PRINCESS TAI, FRESH FROM HER APPEARANCE IN HAVANA. (Ha!) My agent made it sound like I was lucky to hook up with these performers. I hadn't heard of Ming and Ling, but as far as I was concerned, Grace wouldn't be the headliner for long. I *had* to become better and bigger than she was. I had to get my career and life back. Like I said, momentous.

The man climbed down the ladder, paid my driver, and offered me his arm. "Your trunk has already been delivered, and your dresser is arranging things. Right this way, Princess."

Princess. It gave me chills to be called by my title again. I followed the man through the theater until we reached a door with a big gold star and PRINCESS TAI written in red glitter. I entered, and there were Helen and Tommy.

"Your bubble is polished." As Helen spoke, I noticed that she'd put two framed photos on my makeup table: one of Eddie doing the flying splits, the other of Helen and Lai Kai in China. "I've fluffed the fans, in case you chose to use them tonight. I'm ready to do your makeup."

Aah—the cold of the foundation followed by the pouf, pouf, pouf of the powder against my naked skin ignited physical pleasure in my body. I stared at myself in the mirror. I looked pretty damn good, considering. Just as Helen kneeled before me to glue on my patch, someone knocked at the door.

"Answer it, sweetie, just like I taught you," Helen told Tommy.

He went to the door, opened it a crack, and delivered a well-rehearsed statement in a tiny yet clearly bossy voice. "No visitors allowed."

The door swung open anyway. Grace whisked into the room, wearing a gorgeous fur coat, hat, and gloves, and acting like a big star. It was hard to believe she'd once been such a hick.

"Ruby! Gosh, am I glad to see you! Helen! Tommy! This is a surprise! What are you doing here?"

It had been a little more than a year and a half since I'd heard Grace's voice, and I can't say it gave me a big thrill.

"I wondered how long it would take the weasel to say 'Happy New Year' to the chickens," Helen mumbled. "This is like opening the door and saying hello to the bandit."

Helen and her sayings! Gotta love her!

"I hardly know where to start," Grace babbled on. Was she really that oblivious to the ice in the room? "Ruby, you have to tell me everything. Tommy! You've grown so much! How old are you now? Three? Oh, Helen, I can't believe you're here! How's Eddie?"

"He's fighting in France," Helen said.

"And Monroe?"

"Still hanging on."

"Fifteen minutes, people," someone called. "Fifteen minutes."

Grace did an exaggerated roll of her eyes. "All right, then. Hey, why don't the three of you come to my suite after the show?"

Her *suite*?

After Grace left, Helen finished my makeup. We didn't talk about the Oriental Danseuse. I was tense. I wanted to be better than perfect. I walked alone to the curtain, because Helen's only request had been that Tommy not see me perform, which didn't make a lot of sense when he'd just watched her powder me, but what the hell. I'd promised that we'd be together when I got out of the camp, and I'd come through on that promise. Good thing too. That boy of hers . . . The way he looked she *needed* to get away from her family.

My music started. I placed my bubble just so and glided into the blue light. My skin prickled to have all the men's eyes on me. For a few moments, the room turned raw and hot. It gave me confidence that I would get back to my full form a lot sooner than Lee and Sam imagined. When I came offstage, the Chinese hillbillies whirled past me. Ming and Ling, who were actually a half-Filipino and half-Irish father-and-son team, wowed the audience with their "Yangtze Yodel." Those ding-dong daddies had the audience rolling in the aisles. Helen—with Tommy—joined me by the curtain, relieved me of my bubble, and handed me a robe. The hillbillies came offstage—higher than kites from the adrenaline that comes when you go over big. Coming toward us was a jingling, jangling creature in a goofy getup with gilt and bangles and I don't know what else. It was Grace. Everyone moved aside for her, like she was the Queen of Sheba. She nodded at us. *Thank you, peasants, for your adoration.* Cripes!

She smacked a fake smile on her face, raised her hands up to her head and her fingers into rigid sticks, and then shuffled onstage on bare feet. I stayed by the curtain to watch. What a cockamamie routine! Her style had evolved from her performance in *Aloha, Boys!* The dance now had every stereotype in the book, but the audience ate it up. And those long nails? Kooky. I may have liked to float above and removed from the earth, but I *lived* in my body. That's why I could dance naked! Grace may have been technically better, but my dancing was filled with passion. All right, I'll call it what it was. Sex! No wonder Helen didn't want Tommy to watch me.

"I guess it's going to be like old times," Helen muttered, and I could hear the jealousy in her voice.

"Not at all." I squeezed her arm. "It's you and me against *that* out there."

"Dying ashes will burn again," Helen recited.

Another saying! And it was perfect for us.

"Jeez, Helen, it's good to have you here." My grin cut all the way across my face.

HELEN DIDN'T WANT to visit Grace in her suite after the show.

"Why should we go groveling?" she groused. "Let her come to us."

"No, we're going to accept her invitation. I want to hear what she has to say."

"Fine," Helen said, but she didn't sound fine. "That's just fine."

Five minutes later, we were standing at Grace's door. She was as beautiful as ever, even with her hair in curlers under a scarf. She wanted us to sit on her bed, propped against the pillows with me in the middle, like we were still best friends. Ugh, but we did it. Tommy tried to stay awake, but he fell asleep stretched across our laps.

"We have so much to catch up on, but first tell me how you got on the Chop-Suey Circuit," Grace said. She may have presented herself as more sophisticated than when we first met, but she was no less stupid if she thought we could pick up where we'd left off.

"I wrote to all my friends," I answered, trying to stay bland, "hoping someone would help me."

A shiver ran through Grace.

I went on. "I wrote to people we'd worked with, gossip columnists like Ed Sullivan—"

"The skunk who ratted out Dorothy Toy?" Grace sneered.

"Can you believe we lived in the same building with her and didn't know she was a *Jap*?" I asked.

Grace winced. It killed me to use that word, but I wanted to see her reaction.

"Anyway," I continued, "most people wrote back to say they couldn't help me. Some didn't bother to reply. Helen's the only one of our old gang who wrote to me when I was in Topaz."

"We've been writing to each other all along," said Helen. "We're very close friends."

Grace leaned across me and tapped Helen on the arm. "You told me *not* to write to Ruby. You said we could get in trouble for writing to her—a Jap, as you put it. Especially me, since I'd lived with her."

"If you say so," Helen said, pulling away from Grace's touch.

"I say so!"

"A story about a tiger can only be accepted as truth when told by three people," Helen retorted.

Grace pushed herself off the mattress. Tommy's slippers fell with two soft thuds. She planted herself at the foot of the bed. "You're saying it's my word against yours?"

Helen looked away. Grace's face sagged. What a good actress.

"I can't believe this. What did I ever do to you?" she asked.

Helen set her jaw. "You hurt our friend—"

"I didn't—"

"Keep singing that song, Grace," Helen said. "It seems to be working well for you."

"What's that supposed to mean?"

"I think you know."

"Are you talking about the rumors?" Grace asked Helen, disappointment dripping from her voice. "Is that why *you* never wrote to *me*?"

"I wrote you a letter," Helen replied. "That's more than you wrote to Ruby."

"You told me not to write to her!" Grace repeated, practically shouting. She pressed her lips together and tried to compose herself. "And in case you haven't figured it out yet, I'm as much a victim in all this as Ruby. Do you have any comprehension of what I've lost? Our friends stopped speaking to me. I was blackballed—"

Helen cut her off. "Victim?" She spat out the word indignantly. "You promised you'd stay with me, but you deserted me—"

"What did you want me to do? Sit in my apartment until I went broke?"

"You were protecting your own skin—"

"As usual," Grace finished for her bitterly. "Jesus, you're worse than George Louie."

"Let's not fight," I said. So all of a sudden I'm the peacemaker, when *I* was the one who was chiseled out of Hollywood, lost Joe, and was sent to a camp. Maybe they thought they knew everything about me, but there was one thing they hadn't counted on . . . I was down but not out.

I turned to Grace. "I wrote to Helen when I was released from Topaz and asked her to be my dresser," I bragged.

Grace's mood changed in an instant. "How can you afford it?" she asked, competitive as ever.

I blurted the answer. "I'm making four hundred big ones a week."

Grace frowned. She might have had top billing and a suite, but I was making more money than she was!

"Who's your agent?" she asked.

"Sam Bernstein. He's in New York," I answered, one-upping her again.

"How nice for you," Grace said. "Well, look, I should be getting to bed. I hope you don't mind . . ."

I was glad to be free of the camp, but the idea of spending the next month—and however many shows—with these two was about as tantalizing as being tied in a burlap sack with a bunch of wailing cats. Then Grace did something that really yanked my knickers. She opened her makeup case, rummaged around, pulled out an envelope, and tossed it in my lap.

"Your savings," she said. "I've kept them for you all this time. Now good night."

WOULDN'T YOU KNOW it, a week later Grace dumped Max and got Sam to take her on as a client. Cutthroat bitch. Her fee jumped above mine, to which Helen commented, "It doesn't surprise me. Does it surprise you?" Not one bit, but it didn't jibe with her taking care of my money or putting my things in storage either.

Sam called to ask if I'd like to be booked on a whole new way-down-south production with the Oriental Danseuse, Ming and Ling, and Jack and Irene Mak's magic show for an Oriental Fantasy Revue, "singing, dancing, laughing, and magic in one fun-packed hour."

"Don't do it," Helen advised when I told her about the offer. "Grace acts like she's taken the ladder to the clouds, but I have her letters. She can't get any other work."

But when I called Sam back, he laid it out for me straight. "So? Grace has a problem up north. You have a problem too, but not in the south—at least I'm hoping that's the case. Besides, you're new to the road. The Oriental Danseuse and the others have recognizable names. You'll do more shows and get more fans if I book you together. Neither of you is in a position to be choosy."

"Are you sure Grace wants to do it?"

"She's the one who suggested it!"

So she was giving me a hand like I did for her when she came back from Los Angeles, but I wasn't sure I wanted it. I told Sam I needed to talk to Grace before I made my decision. After I hung up, I waited until Helen took Tommy downstairs to the hotel coffee shop for lunch, then I changed into a day dress of blood-red crepe, pinned a pair of gardenias above my ear, and went to Grace's room. She answered wearing a towel around her dripping body.

"I'm taking a bath," she said, waving me in.

I followed her to the bathroom and watched as she slipped back into the bubbles.

"Do you mind if I open the window? I get claustrophobic nowadays." I shrugged, embarrassed. "Ever since the camp."

Grace let that sink in. Then she asked, "Will you tell me what happened after those men came for you at Paramount?"

My eyes narrowed.

"You don't have to talk about it if you don't want to," Grace added.

"Will you tell me about Joe?" A challenge. "Helen tells me the two of you became an item."

Grace shifted in the bath, and water sloshed over the edge. I tossed a towel on the spill and dabbed at it with the tip of my shoe.

"You don't have to talk about him if you don't want to." I mimicked her perfectly.

Her eyes darkened. "All right. Tit for tat," she said. "What happened after those men took you away?"

"You got my job."

A tiny muscle under Grace's right eye twitched. "I don't know how many ways I can say this or how I can make you believe me, but I didn't report you."

I held her gaze, considering. Aw, what the hell. "Do you have any idea what it's like to have everything gorgeous and perfect, and then suddenly have it all taken from you? That's what Topaz was like."

I told her some details about life in the camp and how ashamed I was to be there; she murmured sympathies. When I came to the end, she pulled the plug and stepped out of the tub. Not a wrinkle. Not a bump. Not an ounce of unwanted fat. Not an inch of skin that wasn't the color of cream. She was still flawless, but then she hadn't been through what I'd been through. I handed her a towel. As we were about to leave the bathroom, she put a hand on my arm and asked, "What about your parents?"

"I honestly can't say what they did or didn't do. I want to believe they're innocent—"

"What I meant was, have you been in contact with them?"

"It's not like I can call them."

"You could write," she suggested.

"I don't want to remind them"—and it didn't take a brain surgeon to figure out I was talking about the FBI and the WRA—"I exist. I don't want to risk being sent to Leupp to join my parents. I want to forget all that. You left your mother behind. Now I've left mine."

"These aren't the same things."

"Aren't they? You want an American life. I want an American life. Even Helen wants an American life."

And all of us, in our own ways, were doing the best we could to erase who we were.

We went to the bedroom. I perched on the edge of her bed. Once Grace was dressed, she sat next to me and told me about Joe. Just when I thought she'd reached the end, she went on: "I'm following my mother's advice. I've been writing a letter or postcard to him every few days with messages like 'Never forget I love you' and 'When I did my routine, I thought of you.' His replies have been halfhearted at best."

I'd asked her to tell me about him, but now I wasn't so happy she was doing it.

She went to the dresser and returned with a bundle of letters and postcards. "Listen to what he wrote two weeks ago," she said. " 'By now I've seen every kind of death imaginable. All death is bad. Being shot down over the big briny and being lost *in* the sea is terrible, but the worst are the guys whose planes catch fire.' " As she spoke, I could practically hear Joe's college-boy voice. " 'Some pilots manage to fly their planes and their crews, if they have them, back to base, but the agony and destruction onboard is bad. Lost limbs. Faces gone. Flesh burned. No one wants to go on living looking like that. Better to check out fast.' " She stopped reading and met my eyes. "I wrote back to say that wasn't going to happen to him and asked him to promise me that he'd stay safe and come home to me." She handed me a postcard. "Here's what he sent."

I turned over the postcard. It read: *I'll never make a promise to you that I can't keep. Goodbye, Grace.*

"I love him," Grace said when I gave her back the postcard. "And I'm not going to give up."

I wasn't particularly busted up about losing Joe as a lover, but my heart ached anyway. Was there no end to what Grace had stolen from me? And yet, if Sam was right, I *needed* to find a way to spend time with her. What she next said gave me an opening.

"I didn't go into entertainment for job security or to make friends, for heaven's sake," Grace went on, going right back to acting like the big noise she thought she'd become. "I am the Oriental Danseuse. I'm giving you an opportunity. Take it or leave it."

"Thanks for laying your cards on the table," I said, rising to leave. "Now we can go on the road together with nothing between us."

The Oriental Fantasy Revue hit the road at the beginning of 1945. I'd been in San Francisco and then Topaz for most of the war, so traveling from town to town to places I'd never been before was new to me. Servicemen were everywhere. Military convoys created endless columns on the roads. We were asked to lead our audiences in "The Star-Spangled Banner" and the Pledge of Allegiance before our shows. Sometimes women's organizations invited us to visit their victory gardens. The mood in the south: we're gonna win this thing. The news from overseas seemed positive for the most part. In Europe, American troops had repelled German forces at Bastogne in Belgium. Allied forces were advancing from Paris to the Rhine. In the Pacific, tens of thousands of imperial Japanese soldiers had been killed in the battle of Leyte. But for every positive development, there were sad news items. A month earlier, right in the midst of our holiday performances in Atlanta, Glenn Miller's plane had disappeared in the English Channel. He was declared missing in action. How many times had I been swung around a dance floor to "In the Mood" and "Moonlight Serenade"? How many times had I listened to the radio at Topaz and chimed in to "Pennsylvania 6-5000" and sung "Chattanooga Choo Choo" with the kids? His death—because what else could have happened to him?—was tragic and hit us all hard, because if a star like him could die, then it could happen to anyone. All three of us had people to lose and that colored every moment of the day, but then there wasn't a woman in America who didn't fear the arrival of a telegram or a knock at the door.

Our revue brought cheer to every town we visited. Grace sang, emceed, and appeared as the Oriental Danseuse. She always opened the show with "Good evening, ladies and gentlemen. You're my kind of people . . . all drunks." *Har, har, har.* The Maks pulled out all the tricks and illusions, ending with shooting the dove in the box. I did my bubble routine *and* my fan dance—*above* Ming and Ling. Helen and Tommy tagged along too, of course. Helen, business-minded like her father, fell into the job of handling our logistics, telling us where and when to show up, checking us in and out of hotels, and getting us to and from train and bus stations. Tommy was as spoiled as they come, whiny and impossible, but Helen loved the kid. I'll admit, though, that he and the Mak imps *looked* precious, and they learned fast how to ham it up as adorable mascots, sometimes attracting more attention than the rest of us. (Although Helen took a different view: "The five fingers are not the same." Yes! We get it! Your kid is better than the rest!) If people hadn't seen a Chinese man or woman before, they certainly hadn't encountered darling Chinese kids. Of course, you had to be the kind of person who liked kids . . .

When we got off a train, people walked blocks to stare at us. Sometimes they called us Chinks. On a few occasions ruffians threw stones and taunted Grace for being a Jap, which secretly made me laugh my insides out. In any event, she didn't seem to mind. She was more worried about being picked up in one of the sweeps of Victory Girls, because women with no families, who appeared to be strangers in town, were automatically suspect. Once, on a day off in Mobile—a port town known for building Liberty ships for the war effort—we took a stroll and saw two white women dressed in shiny satin get arrested by a pair of policemen and put in the back of their cruiser. Those women had been walking along just like we were. They hadn't looked all that different from Grace and me, since we were performers and made sure we "dressed" no matter where we went. What saved our cans that day was Helen and little Tommy. Grace and I just seemed like two friends keeping a well-dressed mother, whose husband must be overseas doing his duty, and her child company.

"Sure, I'm scared," Grace confessed when we got back to the hotel, not that anyone asked her. "Sometimes I'm scared to death, but what am I going to do? Stop touring? If I'd allowed myself to become paralyzed every time I felt fear I wouldn't have left Plain City when I was seventeen. I wouldn't have done a single thing."

She wouldn't have either, just like I wouldn't have. I didn't need to like Grace, but I could admire her. In her own way, she had as much guts as I had.

So there we were—four women, three men, three small children, cages filled with cooing doves, and trunks loaded with costumes, toys, and Jack's props and other magic paraphernalia—traveling through the south from booking to booking. Irene was pregnant with her third child. Helen, Grace, and I often had to share a room—with a double bed for Helen, Tommy, and me, and a double bed for Grace. One of the best things about being in show business is staying up all night, having drinks, laughing, dancing, but we practically lived like nuns. We had dinner at four o'clock, two hours before we had to arrive at the theater or club, because Tommy was much better behaved if he had a full stomach. And we went to bed early, because if Grace and I didn't get enough sleep, we made mistakes *and* we looked terrible. We'd all done some hard living, and some days it showed.

"If you're a stenographer, and your work is good, you don't have to prove yourself every day," Helen chided us. "But as performers, your bodies have to be maintained at all times. If a secretary gains ten pounds, so what? If she gets wrinkles, who cares? But for an entertainer, these things can mark the end. Lotions, potions, and creams won't return youth."

Thank you, Helen, for reminding us.

HELEN

V for *Victory*

Often, when I waited in the dressing room for Ruby to come offstage, I daydreamed about my beloved Lai Kai. If he were still alive, we would have had many children by now and lived in our own compound, *always together under the full moon, always bathing in a river of love.* But if he were alive, I never would have met Grace or Ruby. I never would have danced in clubs. I never would have gone to Hollywood with Eddie. I never would have seen so many American cities. I would have traded all those experiences to be still married to Lai Kai. I didn't deserve to be either happy or alive, but *a silkworm will only stop providing silk when it dies and a candle will only stop crying when it turns to ash.* I could live as a chaste widow, who happened to be married to another man, as long as I had Tommy. If Chinese people could have seen us together, they would have offered the supreme compliment for motherhood—that I loved my son like a cow licking her calf—but we never encountered proper Chinese. Just Chinese hillbillies!

The Oriental Fantasy Revue played Corpus Christi, Houston, and Memphis. We did shows at the Baker Hotel in Dallas and the Washington-Youree Hotel in Shreveport. All the while, the war raged on. We did our best to help, even on the road. When the Navy issued an urgent plea for type O blood, I arranged for the entire troupe to go to the local Red Cross in Birmingham to donate. When we were in

Montgomery, I spotted a booth selling war bonds and volunteered the troupe to sing and dance on the sidewalk to attract buyers.

In March, we traveled with the Ink Spots. When our bus stopped for gasoline, I'd go to the coffee shop and pick up sodas and sandwiches for Hoppy, Deek, and the other Spots, because they couldn't get served. A lot of states had curfews for Negroes, and the guys couldn't cross a certain line after midnight. Can you imagine the irony of headlining in a town and not being able to get a meal or take a stroll after dinner? But once we played a black venue, and Ruby and Grace were assigned the smallest dressing room on the third floor, where all the heat collected. It was only fair. But I told Grace she'd have to help Ruby with her makeup that night so I could take Tommy outside for some fresh air.

What a mistake! After everything I'd done for Ruby, she started *speaking* to Grace. Jealousy skulked from its hiding place, but how could I be jealous, truly? Except that Ruby was more of an equal to Grace, while I was like a road manager . . . or a maid.

"Maybe we should put together an act for the three of us," I suggested one night in the dining car as our train chugged from Jacksonville to Savannah.

"I don't think so, Helen," Ruby said. "We already have our own acts."

A bramble finch can never understand the lofty ambitions of snow geese.

ON APRIL 13, WE woke in Charleston to the sound of church bells. We hoped the war might be over. Instead, we heard President Roosevelt had died. We could hardly believe it. He'd only just been elected for a fourth term. He had brought us out of the Depression and now was our leader in wartime. The realization that we would no longer have him to guide us was crushingly sad. Our show was canceled that night. The next day we moved on, doing one-nighters as the Oriental Fantasy Revue's tour began to wind down, but our audiences were slight and the mood somber. It felt like the entire country was in mourning.

On April 30, we arrived in Norfolk for a five-night run at a club called Pieces O'Eight. Soon we'd need to decide what to do next: keep the revue together, find others to travel with, or go our separate ways. I spoke directly to Sam Bernstein now, and he warned me that Norfolk was a rowdy port town—or, as he put it more directly, "the worst war town"—with a volatile mixture of military bases, plenty of liquor, and an abundance of vice, but it didn't seem so bad in the light of day as we were driven from the train station to our accommodations.

I checked us in to the hotel, where I had to accept a two-bedroom suite with a shared bathroom. Once we unpacked, we put on clean clothes—Grace in her skirt with the Morse code pattern that spelled *V* for *victory,* Ruby in a blood-red dress that looked stunning against her hair, and me in a simple skirt and blouse—and then went downstairs for a late lunch. The Maks were already there, and they waved us over to join them. After we ordered, Jack announced, "Irene and I have been discussing things. We're going back to San Francisco after this gig."

"What about the revue?" I asked, the practical one, running the show with no thanks from anyone.

"You'll find someone else to fill in for the rest of the tour," Jack said. "What about the Lim Sisters—"

"They don't do magic," I protested. "Please don't leave us!"

"Helen, look at me. I'm as big as a house," Irene pointed out.

I couldn't deny it. At our last one-nighter, I'd tried to zip Irene into her costume and the whole thing had split apart. I'd rigged together a replacement out of a kimono and a Spanish shawl, which made her resemble a gigantic fringed lampshade.

"I can't go onstage like this," she went on, rubbing her belly. "Besides, our elder boy will be starting kindergarten next year."

"I've agreed to be the house magician at the Forbidden City," Jack informed us.

"And I'm going to stay home," Irene added. Listening to her, I couldn't tell if she was happy or sad about it. "It will be a circus at home, I guess."

"I'll go on alone tonight," Jack said. "If you'd like, you can leave Tommy with Irene and the kids here at the hotel."

My heart raced like hummingbird wings. "I've never left him alone."

"He won't be alone," Irene said. "He'll be with us."

"All right. Just this once." I forced a smile, but I noticed Grace and Ruby regarding me as if I were pathetic. They weren't mothers. They couldn't possibly understand.

Ruby, Grace, and I left the hotel a little before six and walked through streets already teeming with sailors. Catcalls. Whistles. "Hey, baby, want to join me tonight?" It was nothing new. We entered Pieces O'Eight, which was down by the docks. A busboy pointed the way to the dressing room. I went through the door first so I could open Ruby's trunk and get straight to work setting things up for her. I'd barely crossed the threshold when I came to an abrupt stop. A Western Union telegram, taped to the mirror. My heart dropped. *Eddie. Monroe.* But I wasn't the only one who had someone to lose. In the mirror's reflection—around that tiny yellow rectangle—stood three women whose faces had drained of blood. We approached the mirror together. The telegram was addressed to Ruby. Relief cascaded through me. I wouldn't be a double widow, and my brother was still breathing.

Ruby peeled the envelope off the glass and held it in her hands for a few agonizing moments before ripping it open. In cold official language she was informed that Yori had been killed. Grace put a hand on Ruby's arm.

"I . . . I . . . I need to get ready," she stuttered. "Helen, where are your sponges? Hurry along now."

I could only repeat again and again how sorry I was and respect her wishes. We got ready in silence. Ruby kept her emotions hidden under an icy-white enameled shell. I thought about Eddie and my brother. I'm sure Grace was thinking about Joe.

"Curtain! Five minutes!"

We did our usual three shows, but the news about Ruby's brother had affected everyone. Grace was a clumsy wreck, Jack was inept, but Ruby gave the most beautiful and entrancing performance of her career. The bubble seemed to float before her. When she did her fan dance, she looked like a swan skimming across the smooth surface of a pond.

As the headliner, Grace had the last routine of the evening. When she returned to the dressing room, I was trying to convince Ruby to let me remove her body paint before leaving the theater.

"No, no, no!" Ruby pushed me away and then caught Grace's eye in the mirror. "Let's get out of here."

Grace jumped at the chance. She hurriedly changed out of her costume and threw on her skirt and sweater. We emerged onto a street that vibrated with activity—all those men on leave, swaggering in little groups, buddies in war and onshore. They'd been drinking for a while now and were even more rambunctious and unruly than they'd been earlier. More catcalls and whistles. Some had women on their arms—girlfriends, Victory Girls, no-no girls, a sister or mother here and there.

Ruby led the charge, swaying down the sidewalk. The lights from neon signs gave a festive glow to her skin. Her limbs swung like a doll's broken arms. She dragged us into a bar at the end of the block.

We Chinese have a blood understanding of *yin* and *yang*. *When a good thing comes, it comes in a pair; but bad things never walk alone.* She had placed us in a situation as precarious as stacked eggs.

"What's the house drink?" Ruby demanded.

A few minutes later, three Mandalay moons sat before us. The combination of white rum, white crème de menthe, sugar, and lemon juice was sickly sweet. Ruby drank hers before I had my second sip. She ordered another round and proceeded to gulp down all three drinks. Of course, Grace and I tried to stop her. Of course, we tried to comfort her. But she ignored us, favoring the hardened sailors who gathered around us, sniffing like dogs.

I paid the bill. Grace and I—united for the first time since San Francisco—pulled Ruby out of there. The scene on the street was wilder still. To any catcall, Ruby grinned and waved. A couple of the men from the bar had followed us and tried to chat us up. Ruby shimmied before them. Grace and I kept drawing her forward.

We were a block away from the hotel when a van braked at the curb next to us. The door on the passenger side opened, and a policeman bounded out.

"Ladies." He seemed welcoming as he gestured to us to come to him.

I thought he was there to help us, but once we reached the van he roughly shoved us into the back, where another eight women sat. We'd been caught in a vice sweep. Grace and Ruby sat across from me. Grace's face was sickly green. Ruby tried to talk to the other women, but they were too terrified, too busy crying, or too bored to listen to her.

When we got to the jail, we were herded into a holding cell, which looked like it should have held about twenty-five people, but we had to be almost seventy. The walls were lined with benches, and the floors were covered with stained mattresses and filthy blankets on which dozens of women sat. One toilet—totally exposed—occupied a corner. One disgusting toilet for seventy women. And the smell! From the toilet, from the heavy perfume, and from sanitary pads worn too long. I pushed my way through the undulating mass of women to the bars and tried to get the guard's attention.

"There's been a mistake," I called. "My friends are performers."

"I bet they are." He laughed scornfully. "And what are you?"

I straightened my shoulders. "I'm Princess Tai's dresser." But I doubt he knew what a dresser was. I tried again. "My son is at the hotel. I need to get back to him."

"Did you leave him alone?" he asked.

"He's with a friend," I answered.

"A 'friend,' in the hotel?" He'd heard it all before. "Then you have nothing to worry about."

"Can I at least make a phone call?" I asked.

"Later, honey, later."

I squeezed back through the others until I found Ruby, who was too drunk to realize the seriousness of the situation. I sat next to Grace, who stared at the floor in despair. "My father always said I'd end up in a place like this. Picked up like a goddamn whore."

Every few minutes, a group of three to five of our cohorts was called from the holding cell. "Where are they going?" I asked a woman, who let's just say had been around the block a few times.

"You know how it is," she drawled, road-weary. "We have to be tested for the clap and whatever else they're looking for."

I sat back, horrified. Grace began to weep. A girl of about sixteen wailed, "I got separated from my brother. You have to help me find him." The guard showed no sympathy, and Grace and I were too scared about ourselves to console her.

"Don't worry," Ruby slurred. "Sit by me." She scooted to her left, creating enough space for the girl to squeeze in beside her. "Try smiling. Maybe they'll let you out." She seemed dazed. "If that doesn't work, you can start a letter-writing campaign. It may take months, years even, but you'll get out of the camp eventually."

There's nothing like a loquacious but confused drunk.

After a couple of hours, a guard came to the cage. "Hey, you three," he grunted. "Slant-eyes, your turn."

Grace and I helped Ruby to her feet, and we wedged ourselves through the warm hips, pillowy breasts, and perfume as thick as cheese. We were taken to an examination room. A table with stirrups sat in the middle of the room, as ominous as a torture device run by demons in the afterworld. I tried to explain our situation to the doctor, but I was thrown off by Ruby, who had a hand on her hip, her drunken chatter silenced, her whole being ominously still.

The doctor glanced at his chart, then back at us. "What you're doing is unnatural for women. You should be married—"

"I *am* married," I spoke up. "My husband is in France right now."

"And this is how you behave?" He gaped at me as though I were the most repellent creature on earth. "The surgeon general has called venereal disease the number one saboteur of our defense, and I agree."

"We aren't like that," I objected.

He harrumphed and shook his head. "You gals are finished. When I find what I'm looking for, you'll be sent to an institution to be treated. Now who's first?"

Grace and I stared at the table with the stirrups and then at each other. I'd given birth. It wouldn't be the first time a doctor had poked around down there.

"I have nothing to be afraid of," I volunteered in a shaky voice.

I slipped off my step-ins, got on the table, put my heels in the stirrups, and then used my hands to hold my skirt in place. The doctor lowered himself onto a stool with wheels and rolled between my legs until his head was all the way under my skirt.

"Well, I guess we've proved it once and for all," he snickered. "Your slant-eyed twat goes in the same direction as every other."

Ruby went next. She looked so bad she could have scared the ass off a brass monkey. Her hair was a mess, and her makeup was streaked. One of her false eyelashes had peeled half off her eyelid. To me, she was a woman in terrible grief; the doctor took her for our ringleader.

"I don't even need to examine you to know what I'll find." The corner of his mouth curled in distaste, but his tone conveyed sickening pleasure. "Someone who's as infected as you're bound to be is facing forcible detainment until the end of the war."

"So what?" Ruby smoothed her hair and tried to straighten her wilted gardenias. "I've been detained before. It's nothing new."

What she said and how the doctor heard it were two different things. The result was bad. He roughly examined her, probing and prodding with his instruments. Again and again, Ruby cried out in pain. By now, Grace and I were a puddling mess of tears. I was frantic to get back to Tommy; Grace was petrified to be next. She sobbed as she pulled down her step-ins. She got on the table, and the doctor rolled his stool across the floor.

"*V* in Morse code," he observed, noting the pattern on Grace's favorite skirt. "*V* for *Victory Girl*! Ha! Haven't seen that before."

"*V* for *victory,*" Grace mumbled as his examination began.

We were required to be held for a minimum of seventy-two hours, when our test results would come back. More women were thrown in the cell with us. Grace kept going on about how courageous I was, saying, "You're so brave, Helen. Brave!" Well, I'd had experience. After eight hours, Ruby started to come around, although she had a terrible hangover. I knew she was back to herself when she asked, "Have you offered a bribe yet?" Crackerjack, our Ruby. And it only took ten dollars for the guard to let me call the hotel. Ten minutes later, we heard Jack Mak arguing with the sergeant at the front desk, who asked, "You their pimp, or what?"

Jack slammed out the door and returned a few minutes later with Irene, their kids, and Tommy. "Those women are traveling with me. They're my responsibility." (First I'd heard of it.) "Here's our playbill for the run we're doing at Pieces O'Eight. How do you expect me to do three shows a night without them?"

"Shout all you want," the sergeant said. "No legal procedures exist to get these dames out of the fix they're in."

Later that afternoon, around the time I should have been having dinner with Tommy, a guard came through to tell us that he'd just heard on the radio that Hitler had committed suicide. The news rippled through the ninety or so of us in that crowded holding pen but just as quickly subsided. We had our own concerns. The next morning, several women were released, but a dozen or so were declared infected and carted away to a detention facility. They had no way to fight back, no legal recourse. Jack came to tell me that Tommy was fine, bring us food, and update us on all he was doing to get us out. He even brought the manager of the club to talk to the officer in charge, but "rules are rules," and we had to wait. Grace bore up remarkably well, considering, but Ruby was in a dark mood. She still hadn't cried about Yori's death nor had she once tried to flirt with a guard to get out. I worried she might be infected.

That night, new women were brought in, some of whom claimed, like us, to be completely innocent. "I'm here to visit my son before he ships out." "My fiancé will go mad when he hears what you've done to me." We also heard, "I got separated from my brother" several times, too many times perhaps, so it came as no surprise on the morning of our fourth day that the sixteen-year-old girl we'd met on our first night was pronounced infected and sent away for the duration. We, fortunately, were released.

"Make sure you keep clean down there," the sergeant at the front desk cautioned as we pushed out the door, "and don't come back to Norfolk."

We went to the hotel and took long baths to clean the grime, germs, and the memory of the doctor's hands off us. I hugged Tommy and promised never to let him go. He buried his face in my neck and cried. Ruby wept in her room, beginning, finally, to deal with her brother's death. Grace jammed her *V* for *victory* skirt into the trash bin under the desk. I considered myself to be the tour manager, but Grace picked up the phone and called Sam Bernstein to cancel the rest of our bookings.

"I don't give a damn about penalties," she said into the receiver. "I've got money. I'll pay the penalties." She listened to Sam, nodding. She glanced in my direction so she could communicate to both of us at the same time. "You're telling me Charlie still says the weather isn't good?" she asked, which meant that the show kids hadn't forgiven her yet and didn't want her around. She sighed. "Doesn't matter anyway. We can't take Ruby to California." Then, without asking me, she announced, "We're going to Miami to rest for a couple of weeks and get Ruby back on her feet. Then you're going to find a gig for just Ruby and me."

Later that day, we said goodbye to Ming and Ling. Then we saw Irene, Jack, and the kids off at the station. An hour later, we boarded a train to take us south. In Miami, we found a nice hotel right on the shore, checked in to a two-bedroom suite with a shared living room, ordered room service, and vowed to keep life as simple as possible for a while. After lunch, we walked to the beach, sat under an umbrella, stared at the ocean, and let Ruby grieve. We watched Tommy dig in the sand. We let the sound of the waves wash over us. The warmth helped us to heal. The soughing of the palm trees soothed like a mother—*shh, shh, shh*. A few days later, Germany surrendered. Now all that remained was to finish off the Japs, but how long would that take? I pushed that out of my mind and concentrated on planning our future.

BAD LUCK MAY have brought us to Miami, but all we found there was good luck. After a month of rest, Sam booked Ruby and Grace into Winnie's Riptide. On opening night, a well-heeled rubber king with vast holdings in Singapore sat in the audience. Ruby performed with her fans, expertly manipulating them until she threw caution—and her feathers—to the wind and stood there, quite unashamed, dressed only in her blue spotlight and that single tiny piece of silk. After that, Ruby and Grace took turns topping the bill each night. The next thing we knew, the rubber king hosted a party for us. The Club Bali—"with South Seas charm and toe-teasing tunes played by two orchestras"—hired Ruby and Grace away from the Riptide. Sam got them substantial raises, and Ruby increased my salary. Six weeks later, they got a gig at the Colonial Inn.

The rubber king bought Ruby a white ermine fur worth thousands of dollars, which she wore for grand entrances. He gave her diamonds—and rubies, of course. He had his chauffeur polish one of his cars—a prewar Cadillac convertible, mint green with white-wall tires—and presented it to Ruby to drive for as long as she liked. Tommy spent his days playing on the beach. Things were going so well that we decided to take the summer off and stay with the rubber king in his mansion in Coral Gables through Florida's quiet months. I was relieved to see Ruby so happy. Was she "in love"? Hard to say, but she was back to her old self—giggly, chatty, flirtatious, always with a pair of freshly cut gardenias tucked above her left ear. We lazed, danced at parties, shopped, and drank icy daiquiris.

Then, at the end of the first week of August, the United States bombed Hiroshima and Nagasaki. We studied the photographs of the mushroom clouds with a mixture of awe and horror. I thought the Japs deserved what they got, but I didn't say that to Ruby. Japan surrendered a week later, on August 14. In Miami, people flooded the streets and carried on all night—making love, breaking windows, and overturning cars and trash cans. Church bells rang. Strangers hugged each other. Confetti fell on us like snow, and fireworks lit the sky. Eddie would be coming home soon, and so would Joe. Over breakfast on the veranda, Grace read to us from the letter she'd written to him. " 'I'm so looking forward to seeing you, kissing you, and making love to you.' " Two weeks later, she received his response. The envelope didn't have a return address, but the postmark showed that it had been mailed in the United States.

"He's home already!" Grace said excitedly as she tore open the envelope and pulled out a single sheet of folded paper. She began reading aloud. " 'Dear Grace, You've tried hard these past months to keep me interested, but it's finally come time for me to be frank with you. I can't see you. Please stop writing to me. Joe.' "

It is difficult for a snake to go back to hell when it has tasted heaven. That night, I caught her stuffing clothes into her suitcase. I woke up Ruby and together we stopped Grace from running away. She'd been there for me when I found out I was pregnant, and now Tommy and I let her sleep in our bed, where I could keep an eye on her. Grace had helped Ruby through her grief by taking her to Miami after Yori died, and now Ruby sat with Grace on the beach for hours on end as she stared out at the ocean so still under the hot and humid sky. The world was at peace again, and the three of us had reached our own truce.

Part Three

The Truth

December 1945–
June 1948

RUBY

Sunny-Side Up

We'd been in Miami for eight months. I dumped the rubber king after he proposed. (No one would tie me down.) So we were back in our beach hotel—happy with our suite of rooms and attentive doormen. Grace and I were playing the Beachcomber. We had a group of harmless stage-door Johnnies, and we basked in the glow of our mutual success. Grace's body—skinny legs and big tits—had finally caught up to the time and place. Every magazine and newspaper wanted to photograph her, even more than they did me. I didn't let it bother me too much. Tommy had recently turned four and would be going to kindergarten the following year. Helen started to plan. "Soon Eddie and I will be a broken mirror rejoined—a husband and wife together again. I don't want to return to San Francisco, and none of us wants to be on the road again. I'm going to look for a house." It sounded good to Grace and me, and we asked her to look for something for us too.

Club business was bigger than ever as men returned stateside. *We survived. Bring on the drinks! Bring on the girls!* I took up with a Cuban sugar king, and he introduced Grace to a pineapple prince—also Cuban—named Mario, who was sweet enough. (He and Grace sure could mambo.) The sugar king proposed to me, so I immediately gave him the boot. "I'm not the marrying kind," I said, and I meant it. A week later, Mario proposed to Grace. "Nothing wrong in marrying for money," Helen advised. "You'll be set for life." Helen had once said something similar to Grace about marrying Monroe. Grace was never going to marry this guy either. Mario wasn't a bad sort; she just didn't love him.

On Christmas Eve, Helen packed away her photo of Lai Kai, and then off we went to the airport. When she spotted Eddie, she swooped up Tommy and pointed. "There's your daddy!" Eddie looked as cool as ever. He'd been mustered out of the Army with a standard suit, a pair of shoes, an overcoat, and an old-fashioned trilby. He moved just like he always had—with inimitable grace—but somehow he seemed a little lost. He hugged us one by one. He shook Tommy's hand, careful not to scare him. We climbed into the rubber king's convertible—I wasn't about to return it!—and drove to our hotel. In the rearview mirror, I saw Eddie's eyes shifting from side to side. A horn blared next to us, and he jumped so high he nearly flew out of the car.

A small tree with white flocking and red balls sat on the table in our shared living area. Helen was obviously thrilled Eddie was home, and he acted happy to be with all of us, but the poor guy just wasn't the same. He tried mightily to put up a good front, though. When Tommy worried that Santa wouldn't find him because we didn't have snow or a chimney like he saw in his picture books, Eddie hammered five nails into the windowsill, hung our stockings, put some cookies on a saucer, and promised, "Santa will come right through this window." That night, Tommy slept with Grace and me so the married couple could have some time alone—to talk. The next morning, Helen opened our door and called, "Merry Christmas!"

Eddie gave us French perfume, Hermès silk scarves, and the softest kid gloves you can imagine. Grace, Helen, and I had shopped together, so we didn't have a lot of surprises: straw purses embellished with appliquéd tropical fruits and flowers, earrings, bangles, and—now that shortages and rationing were over—brightly colored skirts with fluffy petticoats. Grace and I gave Eddie bathing trunks, shorts, a Panama hat, and sandals—to welcome him to Miami. Helen's present: a stylish tuxedo. "So you can dance again," she said. Eddie stared at it for the longest time before trying it on.

Tommy had to be about the luckiest little cuss that year. His mom and his aunties gave him clothes, coloring books, and toy trucks. In France, Eddie had bought a set of antique tin soldiers for his son to play with backstage. Tommy, overcoming his initial shyness, climbed on Eddie's lap and pronounced this "the best Christmas ever." Maybe for him, but I thought his dad might burst into tears.

AT THE CLUB, while Helen was backstage with Tommy, Eddie danced the bolero, tango, and rumba with customers to try to get back in the swing of things. Soon he and Helen (and the kid too, of course) started staying after the last show so they could practice their old routines and come up with some new ones. (They didn't have a traditional marriage, but they did love each other, and they'd always been fabulous dance partners.) Eddie was sober and physically strong, but Grace and I could hear him prowling around the suite's living room all night. In the morning, Helen, Eddie, and Tommy would emerge from their room looking exhausted. Helen said Eddie often woke up shivering and drenched in sweat. He was nervous and jittery, cringing any time he heard a loud noise and during the fireworks on New Year's Eve. By now my friends and I had all suffered. Time, love, and companionship had helped each of us. I hoped the same would happen for Eddie, and his anxious state would pass.

In February 1946, Grace and I headlined the Miami branch of the Latin Quarter. A week into our run, the manager came backstage after the second show and told us two men at table ten—the best in the house—wanted to see us. Grace and I dressed in gowns, fluffed our hair, reapplied lipstick, and then went out to see just who they were. My body was as slippery as an eel under my sequined gown as I slithered through the tables. My skin was translucent. A sparkling rhinestone clip held my gardenias in place.

"It's Lee Mortimer!" I squealed in surprise and delight, grabbing Grace's arm. "He's the one who sponsored me to get out of Topaz!"

Lee looked just the same: tall forehead, bright white teeth, a cigarette held between his forefinger and middle finger with an air of casual sophistication. Next to him sat a big Irish ape of a guy with a half-chewed cigar clamped in his mouth. His name was Tom Ball.

"I wanted Tom to see you, Ruby," Lee said. Once a sponsor, always a sponsor? "And of course everyone's heard of the Oriental Danseuse—"

"Show business," I interrupted before he could get too carried away with Grace. "One minute you're up . . ." I slowly lifted one of my legs up, up, up until my sequined skirt slipped into my crotch and my leg extended above my head. ("All the way to high heaven" is what Lee would later write about that move.) "The next minute you're down," I purred as I brought my gold-satin high heel back to the floor. "I ought to know, darling. My career has truly been a roller-coaster ride."

Yes, even after all we'd been through, I still wanted to outshine Grace.

Lee gulped. "You gals have been in Miami long enough," he managed to get out. "You're ready for New York, and New York is ready for you. Tom here is opening a club called the China Doll. We're down here to lure you up there."

I sat up in my chair. Return to New York? Finally!

"We want to build the whole show around the two of you," Tom added in a voice that grated like a cement mixer. "We're calling it Slant-Eyed Scandals. It's going to be the biggest, costliest, most elaborate Oriental floor show seen anywhere, and it will stand up to any all-white show on Broadway. We open in eight weeks."

Grace signaled to a waiter, whispered in his ear, and then slid her chair closer to Tom. "Who else do you have?"

"We've got Keye Luke, Charlie Chan's Number One Son, to emcee."

Grace and I arched our eyebrows. *Charlie Chan's Number One Son? So trite. So stereotypical.*

"He's a terrific singer, for your information," Tom said. "I'm getting the best of the best." He was also negotiating with the Lim Sisters, the Merry Mahjongs, Bernice Chow, George Louie, and Ming and Ling.

"We've played with all those folks," Grace said with a shrug. "You make it sound like just another Oriental follies."

She could be quite the smart aleck, and she peppered him with questions, but I could see she wanted this as much as I did. Her delay tactics were explained when she announced, "Ah, here's Helen, our road manager. Let's see what she has to say."

Helen assessed the situation and explained that she would handle logistical details that couldn't be left to Sam Bernstein. Her first question was where would Grace and I reside.

"Wait a minute! You're coming too," I blurted.

"I can't go," Helen said. "Eddie and I are putting our act back together."

I turned to the men. "You can't have an Oriental theme without the Chinese Dancing Sweethearts."

"Haven't heard of them," Tom growled.

"Then call Charlie Low at the Forbidden City," Grace said.

But Tom, bullheaded, took a hard line. "We've already got a father-son comedy duo," he said. "I don't want another family team. It's a nightclub. People go to nightclubs for fantasy, not to see husbands and wives."

"They don't dance like a husband and wife," I assured them.

"He's been off the stage for too long," Lee objected.

"He was in the war!" Grace exclaimed. "Where's your patriotism?"

"Lee, Tom, sweet ones, let me give this to you straight," I declared. "Grace and I won't go to New York unless you hire Helen and Eddie too."

The two men exchanged glances. Could we really be such prima donnas? YES!

"All right," Tom sighed. "We'll check them out with Charlie. If everything's on the up-and-up, then we'll call Sam to work out the financial details."

Sam negotiated $1,000 a week each for Princess Tai and the Oriental Danseuse. The Chinese Dancing Sweethearts would earn $750 a week. We'd be rolling in dough. Oh, and no George Louie. Grace still held a blood grudge against him and didn't want him around. That was fine by me. I'd purposely locked away from my mind what had happened to me—the internment camp and who might have turned me in—and I'd continue to do it. No questions, no bitter accusations, no arguments; a thousand bucks a week, New York, stardom. Brighter stars ahead.

We arrived in New York City on February 11, seven weeks before the China Doll's grand opening. We settled into a three-bedroom suite with a small living room at the Hotel Victoria at Fifty-First and Seventh. Lee Mortimer swept Grace and me on a champagne-bubble tour of the Stork Club, Copacabana, Leon and Eddie's, and the Rainbow Room. We met Clark Gable, Noël Coward, Hedy Lamarr, Lena Horne, Betty Grable, and Gene Kelly. We listened to bands play "Brazil," "You'd Be So Nice to Come Home To," "That Old Black Magic," and "Avalon." We saw Milton Berle (who we heard made ten thousand dollars a night), Danny Thomas (the nicest guy), and Jimmy Durante (a hoot and a half). We danced purely for fun and showed those big-city folks what was what.

And, man, were we *dressed.* We shopped like maniacs, throwing out our tropical prints and exchanging them for sophisticated city dresses. When Lee asked us, "How much do you need to buy new shoes?" and we answered, "Three dollars," he laughed. "You can't buy a pair of shoes in New York for three dollars." He opened his wallet and gave us each fifty bucks. We bought black satin ankle-strap sandals and black suede platform pumps. He gave us even more money to buy frocks with hemlines that covered our calves.

"You've got the look, baby," Lee told Grace. "You're a perfect piece of cheesecake in the city that invented cheesecake." He encouraged Grace to drop her neckline to showcase the cleavage that had once embarrassed her. He gave us the skinny on what to do with our handbags. "Dames who carry their purses while dancing demonstrate that they're more at home in a dance hall than a nightclub." He taught us the ropes: don't go to a dressy place wearing day clothes; don't go to a dump in evening togs; don't complain about the bill, because you were a sucker to go there in the first place. He showed us how to spot and then steer clear of out-of-towners.

When he took us to Sardi's, he suggested we speak loudly, so other patrons could eavesdrop on us. Dorothy Kilgallen, the gossip columnist, wrote: "What two lovely denizens of the night are building reputations for their biting repartee and devastating treatment of 52nd Street wolves? Lee Mortimer calls the enchanting Princess Tai his 'little minx.'" Then, on to Grace: "Never one to pick a single bloom when she can have a bouquet, the Oriental Danseuse is known to attend many First Nights on the arms of different lucky gents. Those swells better watch out for her nails, though. Meow!" As a result of that squib, Grace's nails became so famous that Sam got her a contract with a cosmetics company as the first Chinese nail model in the country. I said I was happy for her, but it was a bitter pill to gag down.

Of course, I cut my usual wide swath. I spent time with Xaviar Cugat, who was between wives, before moving on to Louis Prima, who was married. Under the headline ROMANCE, Walter Winchell scribed: "What unfortunate bandleaders have had their hearts broken by a girl who should change her name to Jezebel?" When I read that, I laughed and laughed.

Where were Helen, Eddie, and Tommy while we were tearing up the town? Either in our hotel, where Eddie could avoid the grinding gears and honking horns of prewar taxis, or at the studio space they'd rented to work on their act. Grace and I stopped in one evening to see the new routine Eddie had choreographed to "It's Been a Long, Long

Time." It was typical Eddie—beautiful, intricate, and graceful. He still suffered from sweats and nightmares, but I was convinced he'd knock the socks off those New Yorkers once they saw him onstage.

In mid-March, and completely out of the blue, I received a phone call from my mother. I hadn't spoken to her in ten years. She skipped the "I missed yous" and "how have you beens," and got right to it. My parents had been released from Leupp and had decided to go back to Japan immediately. "You can't do that," I told her in Japanese when I saw Grace listening. "We haven't even seen each other yet."

"We will have a long voyage together—"

"I'm not going to Japan."

My mother balked at that. "Have you forgotten who you are?" she asked. "Have you forgotten that the Americans killed Hideo, and Yori is dead because he fought for them?"

"Yori was in the most highly decorated regiment in the history of the armed forces," I told her. "He earned the Medal of Honor. You should be proud of him."

She said, "Your father and I and the others in the camp celebrated the emperor's birthday. We ate our eggs sunny-side up, because they looked like the flag of Japan. When we were told the war was over, your father asked why the Japanese flag wasn't flying over the camp."

By the time I hung up, I was sobbing. Grace put her arms around me.

"Do you want to go to San Francisco and see them off?" she asked.

"No," I replied with a sharp shake of my head. "I can't get it out of my mind that they might actually have been spies."

"But you can't be sure about that—"

"They never got a trial, but I'm no closer to the truth about them."

"Other people were sent to camps, including you," she pointed out, trying to comfort me, "and it was terrible. Maybe they're going home because they're fed up. Maybe they're going home because they *always* wanted to go home. You told me that the first day we met."

"True, but I can't honestly say if my parents are innocent, can I? I want to believe they are." I dabbed my eyes with a handkerchief. "You and Helen are all the family I have left."

I went to bed and wept for hours. But the next morning . . . New York!

What else could I do? I needed to survive.

GRACE

Woo Woo of the Week

Two weeks before the China Doll opened, all the headliners met for blocking and dress rehearsals. The club was just a half block from our hotel. Where the Forbidden City played up an imperial China décor with plenty of red, gold, and clutter, the China Doll, a few steps below street level, was sleek, modern, and first-class all the way. The walls were pale blue with simple Chinese scenes painted in white. Dark blue lanterns hung from the ceilings.

The ponies and showgirls shared one dressing room; as headliners, Ruby, Helen, and I each had our own dressing room. Settling in, I heard a familiar voice at my door: "Hi, Grace. What's cooking?" It was Bessie, the eldest of the Lim Sisters. Ella and Dolores stood on either side of her, and one foot back, just as they did when they performed. Soon, others arrived: the Merry Mahjongs with their whirling acrobatics, Bernice Chow with her big voice, Ming and Ling with their hillbilly act. It was great to see them all.

We met the director, Donn Arden—gayer than a sweet potato and famous for mounting extravaganzas with snazzy costumes. Ruby was given a new bubble and fans made from ostrich feathers. The fabric for Helen's gown was dyed in tea until the color matched her skin, then seamstresses covered the dress in rhinestones. My costumes were the most glamorous and expensive of my career, including one made from fifteen yards of monkey fur imported from Hong Kong. Real diamonds were sewn onto the tips of my shoes, so my feet would sparkle when I danced.

The China Doll was to be a regular United Nations. Mr. Ball, an Irishman through and through, hired Jewish choreographers, composers, and writers to come up with good—fresh—material. We had two bands: one to play the show and a Latin band to pack the joint for dancing on weekends. A young guy named Lenny Bruce would do a comedy routine after the last show. Mr. Ball found Chinese cooks, a Jewish maître d', and Puerto Rican waiters, dishwashers, cigarette girls, and hatcheck girls, who would all pretend to be Chinese. The ponies? It was just as hard as, if not harder than, it had been in San Francisco to find local Chinese girls willing to work in a club. More Chinese lived in the area, but that also meant the community was more conservative, so Mr. Arden and Mr. Ball poached a bunch of gals from Charlie and other club owners out west. Although Charlie had once labeled his glamour girls "Chinese" to protect them, all the entertainers at the China Doll were labeled "Chinese" so no one would be reminded about the dropping of the atomic bombs.

On opening night, the place was packed with Broadway and Hollywood celebrities, critics and press agents, and Manhattanites and suburbanites. Our first show was clicking. Ming and Ling clowned and crooned. "Lee Mortimer's China Dolls"—as the ponies came to be called—were sharp. Backstage, Eddie—slick as a cat's whiskers in his evening dress—listened warily as Helen reassured him. He truly was one of the most handsome men ever to walk the earth, but I could see he was nervous.

I recited the usual good wishes. "Break a leg!"

As their music started, my heart was full. *Kiss me once, and kiss me twice, and kiss me once again . . .* Was there anyone in the audience who didn't respond to that postwar ballad—so romantic it made you want to cry every time you heard it? Helen floated onstage, her gown flowing, her arms extended. Eddie was supposed to be right behind her. Instead, he stared out at her, slack-jawed, his body shaking. Helen completed the circle that would bring her and Eddie face-to-face with the audience. When she realized she was alone, her smile wavered.

"Eddie," I urged in a whisper, "you've got to get out there."

He shook his head.

"Come on, Eddie," I prodded. "Helen's alone."

But he was paralyzed. He'd survived the war, but he wasn't the same. Shell-shocked. He'd done well during rehearsals, but now he was crippled by stage fright. Onstage, Helen kept dancing—Ginger minus her Fred. I remembered back to my final audition at the Forbidden City, when I froze and Eddie helped me.

"We'll do our old routine," I whispered. "Two girls and one man. Hear it? The tempo is a little slower, but we can do it."

"No."

"It's easy, Eddie. We practiced this ten thousand times, and we've got that neat trick at the end. All you have to do is count in your head: Say it with me. One, two, three, four."

"Five, six, seven, eight," he mumbled.

I took his hand. "One, two, three, four. Ready? Here we go."

Together we glided out. The audience applauded. The Oriental Danseuse was making an early appearance! I heard Eddie counting under his breath. I whispered through my stage smile, "You're doing great." I prayed that Helen would decipher what we were doing. Eddie and I did a couple of turns from the old routine, slowly moving closer to Helen. When she changed her steps—awkwardly to be sure—to fall in with us, I relaxed a little. Eddie released me and took Helen in his arms. Back and forth we went, weaving together and apart, but Eddie was terribly stiff, his face expressionless. Our grand finale, when Eddie lifted us off the ground and spun Helen and me, was a huge success. We took our bows, with Helen and me each putting a hand on Eddie's back to push him down.

When we came offstage, almost the entire cast was there. They parted to let us through. Everyone loved Eddie, and they offered congratulations. "That was great!" "You still have your magic!" "You slayed it, buddy!" Eddie kept his head down, refusing to acknowledge the sympathetic lies. Helen tried not to cry.

Then: "A Chinese Fred Astaire and Ginger Rogers act won't work if Fred is a clod." It was Mr. Ball, and he proceeded to berate Eddie in front of us. But there was no time to defend Eddie, because it was opening night. The show must go on! The Lim Sisters were a smash with their new fruity Carmen Miranda headdresses and full ruffled skirts and sleeves, and the audience went ape for Bernice's rendition of "Let's Do It." Our reviews were over the top. The Merry Mahjongs earned "Wow of the Week," Ruby grabbed "Best Undressed Doll of the Week" (with a special note about her "gorgeous chassis"), and I snagged "Woo Woo of the Week." That skunk columnist Ed Sullivan, who, it turned out, worked at the same paper as Lee Mortimer, wrote in his "Little Old New York" column: "It's a slant-sational show. The wolves brayed wolf whistles at all the China dolls." Mercifully, no mention was made of the Chinese Dancing Sweethearts.

THE MORE WE tried to help Eddie, the worse he got. He forgot how to lead. He forgot his lines. He forgot how to count in his head. It was heartbreaking to see, and, after six weeks, Mr. Ball notified Eddie and Helen that he wouldn't be renewing their contract. "It's just as well," she said in resignation. "These new people can't get Ruby's makeup right." Then one of those darned Merry Mahjongs volunteered to help, saying, "I'll dance with you." Chan-chan and Helen, with assistance from Mr. Arden, put together an endearing routine, in which Chan-chan's only role was to partner Helen, lifting and whirling her so she looked like an angel. Helen, never one to trust good fortune, decided to work as Ruby's dresser as well. Eddie reacted to all this by going back to dipping his bill, staying out all night, and coming home in the morning still boiled to the eyes. Helen was worried sick, and Ruby and I worried about both of them.

The club was rocking, though, jammed wall-to-wall with customers. The line to get in went around the corner. We hummed with one-shot business as servicemen, many of whom had first been enchanted by the charms of Oriental girls in Japan, the Philippines, and China, returned to the States and sought out those same beauties before going back to Florida, Kentucky, or Maine. Even the Smart Set got a kick out of seeing Oriental girls swinging, shaking, and jiggling to Latin rhythms—so much so that some wags began calling the club "El Chino Doll." And Ed Sullivan? Like most Americans, he put his suspicions about Japanese Americans behind him and became a reliable chronicler of Ruby's every move.

And I was living the life I'd dreamed of in Plain City. When I stepped onstage, everyone in the club stopped to watch me. I demanded attention, and I got it. I had lots of admirers. They sent so many flowers that sometimes my dressing room smelled like a florist shop. I shunned the special house drinks for champagne and developed a love of caviar. I went to parties until the sun came up. I slept most of the day. The next two years were a helluva ride, but it can be lonely at the top without someone special to love you.

HELEN

A Camellia Drops

It was 1948, and the China Doll had been open twenty-six months. On the surface, things still seemed to be clicking, but champagne living had lost its fizz. The China Doll—"New York's Favorite Rumba-vous"—and other nightclubs were drying up, because people stopped spending money like there was no tomorrow. Our boys had come home, married their sweethearts, gotten jobs, and moved to the suburbs, where they drank martinis, bounced children on their laps, and watched television. Those people were mortgage poor—and they had to save for washers, dryers, lawn mowers, and power tools—so some nights we performed our hearts out, giving everything we had, to a half-filled house.

Reporters began to ask our ages. We always gave the same rehearsed reply: "Age is a number, and I have an unlisted one." In truth, Grace was twenty-seven, Ruby was twenty-nine, and I was thirty. A female performer is a lot like a camellia, which doesn't fade, wilt, drop petal by petal, or brown on the stem. At the height of its beauty, a camellia drops whole from the bush. You can't escape aging no matter how talented you are. We still looked beautiful—perfectly ripe—but after ten years as entertainers, we weren't young or naïve anymore. We were like carps stuck in a dry rut—or, as *lo fan* might say, world-weary showbiz broads.

You cannot wait to sink a well until you're thirsty nor can you wait to make a cloak until it starts to rain. When Mr. Arden announced he was leaving New York for Las Vegas, where he promised to stage the splashiest productions in that town's history, he asked us to join him. Mr. Ball, not to be one-upped and possibly taking advantage of his rumored "connections," proposed taking the China Doll floor show to Las Vegas too. That gave Ruby the idea of putting together her own small Oriental revue and trying the gambling city as well. "I'll call it Ruby and the Dancing Chopstix," she said. I'd always seen her as bird-like, but by now I understood she was more like a hawk than a skylark. I couldn't imagine her ever slowing down or retiring. As for Grace . . . Mario, the pineapple prince, had recently come up from Miami, bearing a thirty-thousand-dollar platina fox fur and an engagement ring. She'd never been all that faithful to him—and, let's be honest, she didn't love him—but after all this time, she considered his offer.

"Beggars can't be choosers," she said, which made me sad for her. The burdens of her mother and father had been lifted from her and she'd achieved great success, but she was still missing the one thing she'd longed for since the day I met her: romantic love. It seemed all her hopes for a true happily-ever-after had faded after Joe broke up with her. "I sure don't want to be alone down there with just Mario," she said. "Why don't you and Tommy come too? You could go into real estate," and it seemed like a great idea, because I had long handled our living arrangements and could spot a defect a mile away. "I bet in six months you'll be riding around in your own Rolls-Royce."

Ruby enticed me with a different plan. "The Mahjongs have agreed to be in my revue. Wouldn't you rather keep dancing with Chan-chan than go to Miami?"

"I love you both," I said, "and I want to be with both of you, but I need to think about what will be best for Eddie and Tommy."

At the beginning of June, my parents came to New York to meet up with Monroe, who'd finally been released from Walter Reed, and to see Tommy, Eddie, and me. Through the miracle of penicillin, my brother had survived his lobar pneumonia. However, he'd been sick a long time—so long that he'd fallen in love with and married his nurse, a girl from Indiana, who happened to be an Occidental. *Aiya!*

Mama, Baba, and the newlyweds reserved a table for the show. They ordered dinner and clapped at all the right places. Grace, Ruby, Tommy, and I peeked out of the curtain to stare at the bride, who was as white as white on rice, or however that American saying goes. My parents did their Chinese best to pretend she wasn't at their table. My marrying Eddie—who also sat with my relations—was nothing compared to marrying a *lo fan*.

When the first show ended, Ruby and Grace changed into gowns and came to my dressing room. They'd promised to stand by me when I met the family. Baba entered, followed by the others until the room was jammed. Eddie pulled the bench out from under my makeup table, took Mama's elbow, and helped her to the bench, where she sat down and tucked her bound feet out of view. Baba congratulated us on the show, but mainly he gushed over me, telling me what a great performer I was. Maybe I truly had risen above my brother!

Then Baba spotted my son. He stiffened as he took in Tommy's hair and complexion. He went on to handle the introductions anyway, ending with "And this is Maryanne Lively—"

"Baba, her name is Maryanne Fong now," Monroe cut in good-naturedly. He put a protective arm around his pretty wife's waist and pulled her close. He was corpse-thin but so happy. "She's your daughter-in-law now."

Into the subsequent silence, Mama finally spoke. "We want you to come home, Helen. We want to reunite with Eddie and our grandson too."

"Yes, it's time for you to quit this life," Baba agreed. *"A man does not travel to distant places if his parents are still alive."*

He may have been trying to display generosity and forgiveness, but his words were like nails in my eyes. "I'm not a man. I'm only a daughter—and worse, a widow—as you've forever made very clear."

"Considering you're a daughter, you should be grateful we want you to come home." Baba bristled. "This is an opportunity for us to be a family again. To live in the compound—"

"I agree with your father," Mama picked up. "You can't spend your life powdering some woman's rear end and dancing around. When you have a child, you can't live like a vagabond."

Mama had a point, but then Baba went on. "You need to be a proper mother to Tommy. It's true, he might be more comfortable in another family. He's a mongrel, but at least he's a son."

Baba had made a tactical error. He could treat me as a worthless daughter for all eternity, but I'd never allow him to hurt my son. *Always place righteousness above family loyalty.*

I turned to Eddie. "Let's go to Miami and buy a house through the G.I. Bill."

Grace smirked (she'd won), Ruby looked peeved, but Eddie shook his head no.

"I want to go to San Francisco," he said. "Charlie will take me back. Maybe I'll be fine at the Forbidden City." He paused to let me digest the idea. Then, "I saw too many people die to be anything other than who I am. I can be myself in San Francisco."

My lungs emptied of air. "I don't want to lose you, Eddie." In an abrupt reversal, I added, "I'll even go back to the compound, if we can stay together. I'll do anything for you, Eddie, because you did everything for me."

For a second, I stepped out of my body and sensed how strange it had to be for the others to witness such an intimate moment—my husband practically announcing his preference for men and my trying to hold our marriage together, even if it was in the oblique manner of a proper Chinese couple, in so tiny a room. And I'll say this: nothing that was said came as a surprise to my relatives, but that Maryanne sure didn't know what had hit her.

"A family without a woman is like a man without a soul," Eddie recited. My parents nodded, happy that they had him on their side, and recognizing, at last, that he had come from lineage as good as, if not better than, ours. "I love you and Tommy, but you don't need to stay with me out of duty or obligation. I'll buy a house for the two of you. What city you choose is your business, but you might want to consider Los Angeles, where you'll be closer to—"

Tommy's real father . . .

"—me," Eddie finished. He may have been humbled and shell-shocked, but he would forever be a gentleman in my eyes. He'd never let me down when I needed him the most.

"I don't want you to be alone." My voice cracked.

"He won't be alone," Baba declared, breaking into the conversation. "Your husband will live with us. We have enough disgrace with you being a widow and a big-thigh girl, but at least you aren't divorced."

I couldn't believe what I was hearing. It was better to have Eddie as a son-in-law than me as a daughter? The realization was excruciating yet oddly freeing. I felt like a balloon that had been released from a child's fingers—up and away . . .

"I wanted to give your father eight sons," Mama murmured. "Eddie can be our eighth son. He needs loved ones to take care of him. Maryanne is a nurse, which is even better than having a doctor in the family. I promise you, Helen, that I'll cherish him as my own."

All eyes turned to Eddie. He was a man of elegant grace, but his defeated shoulders and bowed head illustrated more than any words how broken and fragile he was. Still, he was better than a daughter, a widowed daughter, or a divorced daughter.

Eddie lifted his chin and spoke directly to Baba. "I'm not going to change who and what I am."

"So? I won't be changing who I am, and it's clear Monroe hasn't changed who he is," Baba replied. "The gossips will do what they do, but you are part of my family and that will never change."

Mama reached up and took Eddie's hand, which wordlessly seemed to seal the deal. Perhaps the most overused Chinese curse is *May you live in interesting times.* With the addition of Eddie and Maryanne, the people who lived in the compound were about to experience some "interesting times." I was glad to keep my little Tommy out of it.

A FEW DAYS later, Eddie departed for California with Mama, Baba, and the newlyweds. Even though he was leaving, I didn't feel he was abandoning me. He was doing what was best for me, for Tommy, and for himself. In that regard, we would be forever partners in the true sense of the word. When Tommy and I returned from Grand Central Terminal, our suite felt empty. Tommy missed Eddie already, but I'd always be number one in my son's eyes. But the separations were hardly over. Miami awaited Grace, and Ruby would be heading to Las Vegas, but what about me? Never have I heard so much crying up the virtues of wine to sell vinegar.

Ruby pressed me to go with her: "That way you'll be close to San Francisco *and* Los Angeles. Don't you want Tommy to see Eddie and meet his real father too?"

"What? Do you expect me to show up on Tim's doorstep? *Here we are*. Forget it," I pronounced with finality.

Eddie called and repeated his suggestion that I move to Los Angeles—close, but far enough for us to lead our own lives: "We'll always be like a pair of mandarin ducks—forever an affectionate couple. And I don't want to lose Tommy." I promised that, no matter where I decided to live, I'd make sure Eddie saw Tommy at least twice a year.

Grace put the screws to me too: "Come with me and you'll be the first millionaire among us."

They all *wanted* me. I was being given a chance for a new beginning. I could release the bad things that I'd done and that had been done to me, which meant goodbye at last to my natal family, goodbye to the compound, goodbye to Eddie, goodbye to Ruby, and goodbye to so many sad memories, resentments, and jealousies. I would no longer let my history determine my destiny. I would go to Miami with Grace.

I had made it this far without revealing my deepest secrets, and, for a moment, I forgot that to believe in dreams is to spend half your life asleep.

GRACE

Movie Talk

A week later, as we were finishing our contractual obligations to the China Doll, scouts from a new television show called *Toast of the Town* visited the club. Ed Sullivan, who'd written so much about us in his column since we'd come to New York, was to be the host. "He's looking for an Oriental act," Sam Bernstein said when he called to discuss an offer.

"I'll do it!" I practically shouted into the receiver.

"I bet you would, but it's for a trio. Would you be willing to work with Ruby and Helen?"

Helen rejoiced when I told her about the opportunity. "This could be the beginning of Heaven and Earth! Epoch-making! Finally, after all these years, we're going to perform together . . . and on national television. Think of where that could lead . . ."

We didn't have a lot of time to prepare, Helen had never been much of a hoofer, and Ruby's specialty was walking around with a bubble in front of her. Ruby spoke to Mr. Arden on his last day at the China Doll, and he came up with all sorts of cockamamie concepts for what we could perform. Helen called Eddie to get his ideas.

"Be the girls you've always been," he told her. "Be yourselves."

When Helen relayed that message to us, I pictured something in my mind.

"We'll do 'Let Me Play with It,' " I said. "We can update the original arrangement by dropping the country sound and going with all strings. We'll do the routine we taught Helen back on the Waverly Playground but all in soft shoe. If we keep it simple, then we'll still have enough breath to sing. Of course, everything will need to be squeaky clean for Mr. Sullivan, but it could be fun . . . and unexpected."

Helen and Ruby loved the idea.

"What should we call ourselves?" Ruby asked.

"That's easy," Helen said shyly. "The Swing Sisters, like I suggested all those years ago in Sam Wo."

Ruby and I loved *that* idea.

We worked on the routine in the afternoons, and then we went to the China Doll for our three shows. I'd rarely been so exhausted, but excitement and anticipation buoyed all of us.

Several nights later, I left the China Doll early, hoping to spend a few quiet minutes alone going over the details of our *Toast of the Town* performance before Ruby, Helen, and Tommy returned to the hotel. I waded through the usual stage-door Johnnies, waving them off as the endearing nuisance I'd grown to accept. A tenderly thin man, wearing a fedora pulled low and leaning his weight on a cane, stood a little removed from the other Johnnies. He was tall and his shoulders were broad, but the message he sent with his body was one of frailty. His eyes pulled mine to his.

Joe.

Next to him, an older woman—wearing practical walking shoes, a decidedly non–New Look dress, and a mink stole wrapped around her shoulders—pulled on her fingers nervously. A worried expression creased her forehead.

Struggling with my emotions, I glanced at the cane and then back into Joe's eyes. At last, I lifted my chin and strode forward purposely. "Joe," I said, professional yet friendly. "This is a surprise. How good to see you."

"Grace." He drew out the syllable like it was wine being poured into a goblet.

"What are you doing here?" I asked, all good cheer.

"My mom and I have come to look at NYU and Columbia. I need to finish law school. My parents would like me to be closer to Chicago—"

"We're in New York to see you," the woman, who had to be his mother, interrupted.

I absorbed that, and then asked Joe in my most chipper tone, "How did you know where to find me?"

"It's a cinch Winchell knows!" he answered, reciting the popular tagline.

That told me he'd read about Mario and all the others, and yet here Joe was on the sidewalk in front of the China Doll. The stage-door Johnnies edged closer.

"I'd like you to meet my mother." Joe gestured to the woman beside him. "Mom, this is Grace. Grace, this is my mom."

"Mrs. Mitchell." I extended my hand.

"Call me Betty." Instead of shaking my hand, she held it in both of hers. "I came with my boy, because I wanted to make sure he didn't turn chicken. He's got all sorts of medals now—the Bronze Star, the Air Medal, and a Purple Heart," she recited proudly. "But he's always been a bit of a scaredy-cat when it comes to girls."

"Mom." Joe stared at his shoes. I felt for him, because no one can embarrass you more than your own mother. Despite my best efforts to protect myself, I could feel my defenses crumbling and my heart opening.

"Are you set now, Son?" Mrs. Mitchell asked. When he nodded, she returned her gaze to me and squeezed my hand. The message couldn't have been clearer. *Don't hurt my boy.* Then she embraced Joe. "I'll see you back at the hotel."

After she left, we stood silently, searching each other's faces. His was wan—from lingering pain? From months as an invalid? His eyes looked as though they'd seen too much. I wondered what changes he saw in me. Finally, I said, "Let's go somewhere we can talk without all the ears." I cocked my head to the stage-door Johnnies, but I was actually fretting that Ruby would emerge from the club any second.

Joe and I walked, slowly, slowly, because of his limp. He had always seemed invincible, but to me he felt almost ghostlike. It hurt me to see him so frail. We found an all-night diner and slid into a booth. The waitress served us coffee. He pushed his cup back and forth in front of him nervously. I fought to regain my resolve: *I can't help him. He dumped me.*

"No reason to make this long," he began, his voice slower and more deliberate than I remembered.

"Take as much time as you'd like," I said.

He didn't seem to want to do that either.

"I had a rough go, Grace." Joe struggled to get out the words. "My plane and I got shot up pretty bad. My right lung was pierced, and my leg took a lot of shrapnel. I barely made it back to the airfield. By the time they pulled me out of the wreckage, I'd lost consciousness. I didn't wake up for a long time. When I did, I had gangrene."

I sucked in a breath through clenched teeth. The side of his mouth ticked up at my reaction.

"I fought them hard, but they took my leg," he went on. "I can't tell you how angry I was . . . at myself, at the world. That's when I first told you to stop writing back to me."

Whatever backbone I'd hoped to have went to mush. "Oh, Joe. That's just awful. I wish you'd told me. I would have helped you."

"At first, I didn't want you to worry about me," he admitted. "And, of course, you're Grace. You kept writing anyway. But later, when it looked like I was going to die, I didn't want to hurt you. I wanted you to be free of memories of me—"

"That's the most preposterous thing I've ever—"

"After they amputated my leg," he continued, speaking right over me, "I didn't want to come back to you as less than a man."

What was he telling me exactly? I blurted out my first crass notion: "It's just your leg, right?"

A long moment passed. Then he threw back his head and laughed.

"Then all is perfect." I tilted my face and gave him my best China doll smile. "After all, your manhood isn't measured by your leg."

He laughed even harder at the audacity of my comment.

"A lot of guys got it worse than you." I thought of Yori and all the waiters, busboys, and servicemen, who didn't make it back.

"But I was an ace." Joe hesitated before trying to explain himself. "I thought, when this thing is over, I'll forget about law school and become a commercial air pilot. Remember how we used to talk about that? I won't be able to fly commercially now," he stated with grim finality. "You need all your parts—"

"So you'll fly for fun."

He gave me a wry smile. He didn't need to explain. What if I'd never been able to dance professionally?

"Anyway," he went on, "it took a long time before I was stable enough to be sent back to the States. Even when I got home, I didn't want to see you. I felt sorry for myself, but my anger was what kept me from getting in touch. I'd promised I wouldn't be around you when I was like that."

Disappointment still radiated from him, but I didn't sense fury or bitterness. His fighting days were over.

"What changed?"

"Time. Home. My mom and dad. I told them about you. And they—my mom especially—have been working on me. But I'll be honest with you, Grace. I'm not who I was."

"Neither am I."

That hung heavier in the air than I expected. Outside, night was melting into dawn. The clock on the wall read 6:34. I needed to get a little sleep before meeting the gals at 2:00 for our last rehearsal before *Toast of the Town*, and then I had three shows tonight. I still had no idea what Joe wanted, but I needed to be firm for the sake of my friends.

"I'm really sorry, but I need to go to my hotel and get some sleep. The next two days are big for me, Joe."

He didn't ask why. Maybe this hurt him. But if he wanted to say something or ask me something, then *he* needed to act. I wasn't going to help him, not after everything we'd been through. Yet the look on his face pushed me to ask, "Will you come and see me tonight at the China Doll?" As soon as the words were out of my mouth, I regretted them. "Ruby will be there."

"I know," he responded. "I had a lot of time in the hospital and even more time in Winnetka to read the gossip columns. But why would I care where she is? I came to see you." He shook his head. "What I mean is, I've come *for* you. My life is no good without you."

Romantic words, and I so wanted to believe him, but a part of me was in turmoil. He was the love of my life, but could I trust him after he'd left me high and dry and broken my heart? And what would he do when he saw Ruby? She was so beautiful, and he'd always been entranced by her. My insecurities went even deeper than that. Even if he no longer cared for her, was he just falling back on someone he thought would take him now that he was crippled?

While all this was batting around in my head, Joe was watching me, bemused, taking in, I felt sure, every questioning emotion that must have been playing across my face. Even after our long separation, he knew me so well.

"I'll come to the last show," he said finally. "That's always been your best."

A FEW HOURS later, Ruby woke me out of a sound sleep. "You look like hell," she quipped after I sat up and put my feet on the floor. "Hurry up. We need to rehearse."

Over the years, I'd learned that people deceive each other in many ways. By hiding: secreting clothes and money under the bed so you can escape, as I had done. By destroying: tearing up receipts so your husband doesn't see what you spent on that new pair of shoes, as Irene had done. By changing the topic: "Good show tonight, dear?" as Eddie had asked Helen after he'd spent a night carousing. By outright lying: "I'm Chinese," when actually you were Japanese, as Ruby and Ida had done. But the best—and easiest—is simply to keep your mouth shut. You tell yourself, "This isn't a good moment" or "We'll talk about it later." People recite those inanities, but that doesn't make them any less liars, cheats, or deceivers, which is how I managed to get dressed, ramble five blocks with Ruby and Helen to the studio to practice our routine for the last time, then walk to the China Doll and get ready for the night's shows without mentioning that I'd seen Joe, what he'd said just a few hours earlier, or that he'd be in the club for the third show when we performed.

My omissions left me jumpy and on edge. After the first show, I went to Helen's dressing room. Eddie had sent Tommy a new set of tin soldiers, and he was lining them up in neat rows on the floor. I sat on a stool to watch, but I nervously clicked my Oriental Danseuse nails against each other to the point that Helen said, "Stop worrying. We're going to be great tomorrow."

The second show was swell. When Ruby's cue came for the third show, I followed her to the curtain. I watched as she slipped off her kimono, picked up her fans for her last performance of the night, and sidled onstage into her blue light. I peeked out at the house and spotted Joe. He appeared mesmerized by Ruby and her feathers. The smell of her gardenias seemed to waft through the club like a dark vapor. Could that same old triangle of Ruby, Joe, and me ever be broken? Would I ever be able to forget that they'd been together? I was a grown woman—a famous woman—but an impulse to flee gnawed at my insides. This time I was determined to stay and fight.

Ruby's act ended, and she swept offstage right past me—her ostrich feathers caressing my face, arms, and breasts. I needed to tell her about Joe—he was mine—but there wasn't time. I heard the music for my routine. I lifted my hands, extending my absurdly long nails, and let my feet carry me onstage. My mind churned with visions of Ruby and her feathers and Joe's expression as he'd watched her dance. Now it seemed as though all the things that made him the man I loved had drained from his face. Through the laughter, the clink of champagne glasses, and the happy sighs of the club; above the band, cutting through the sound of my feet padding across the stage, my breathing and the beat of my heart—but surely it was my imagination—I heard Joe's chair scrape across the floor as he pushed himself away from the table. He lurched from the room. Was he running from me again? Or was he running *to* Ruby?

Onstage, all I could do was keep counting in my head—*one, two, three, four*—and finish my number. I didn't stay for my second or third bows. Instead, I ran to Ruby's dressing room. I opened the door to find Helen wiping off Ruby's makeup and Tommy on the floor with his toy soldiers. I shrugged as if I'd made a mistake.

"Don't bother with me. I'll see you in a couple of minutes." I retraced my route, feeling confused and worried. Where had Joe gone? Had seeing Ruby dance changed his mind about *me*? I entered my dressing room, and there he was, sitting on the bench before my mirror, holding a rose he'd plucked from one of my bouquets. I felt like I was able to breathe again—from relief . . . and gratitude.

"All the husbands are returning to their Rosies," he began. "Those women don't realize that the men who went away are not the same as they once were." He glanced past my shoulder into the hallway, struggling with his emotions. "Grace, the things I saw. The things I did."

The years without him completely fell away, as did my doubts. Whatever he'd done—or not done—to hurt me in the past no longer mattered. He was my future. He'd *always* been my future.

"Whatever you have in you, I can take," I said.

"This thing"—he tapped his artificial leg—"isn't good enough for what I'm about to ask, so I hope you'll accept me where I am." He inhaled. Held it. Then, "I've made a lot of mistakes, and I've wasted a lot of time. I love you. I don't want another minute to go by without you. Grace, will you marry me?"

I didn't hesitate. I'd been waiting for the question for so long. "Yes."

"Are you sure?" he asked, unwilling to accept my answer so readily. "Are you willing to give up everything for me when you've already seen my weaknesses and stupidity?"

"Yes," I said as I kneeled before him.

"I'll never be able to dance with you, Grace. Not like we danced before."

"We'll do the box step."

"If we get married, neither of us can ever run away again—emotionally . . . or otherwise." He rapped a knuckle on his leg. I saw him then as so vulnerable. He was telling me he was committed, but he needed me to be as well.

"I love you, Joe. I always have."

He took that in. Then, "We won't have the moon, Grace, but we can be happy—"

Such movie talk!

"Let's get out of here. Let's never look back." He whistled the opening bars to Kay Kyser's newest hit. *I'd love to get you on a slow boat to China, all to myself alone.* "Come with me now. Don't pack. Don't say goodbye. We'll get out of here and go to San Francisco. I'll go to Stanford or back to Cal to finish up at Boalt."

In that moment, I knew I'd won the prize I'd always wanted: love. I loved him so much I would suffer anything for him. I loved him more than my own life, I realized. Yet this was the moment when the two things I'd dreamed about for so long—love *and* stardom—collided. And I wasn't willing to give up either.

"I didn't have a chance to tell you this morning, but Ruby, Helen, and I are going to be on a television show tomorrow. I can't back out now. I need to be there for them."

He had just proposed and asked me to run away with him this instant, but now his eyes burned with disappointment.

I tried to explain. "They're my friends . . ."

"And *you* want this."

I bowed my head and nodded. But how could I be ashamed when this opportunity might be the greatest of my life?

I got up, opened my purse, and handed Joe a ticket for tomorrow's show. "I hope you'll come."

He held the ticket in his hands and stared at it wordlessly. Finally, he reached up to me with his eyes. What I saw in them was sure and true. He was happy for me. "I wouldn't miss it for the world."

"I love you," I said.

"I'm nuts about you too, Grace."

With that, he used his cane to stand, and he limped out of my dressing room.

I took a deep breath, sucking in happiness, releasing worry. I loved Joe more than dancing, but what about Ruby? I didn't want to hurt her in case she still had feelings for him. *Play it light, and it might go easier.*

I didn't bother to change. I walked down the hall to Ruby's dressing room, hesitated before the closed door to brace myself, and then entered. Helen wore a pale pink cotton sweater set with a light gray skirt that came midcalf. She was on her knees, having just finished removing Ruby's body makeup. Ruby leaned in to the mirror, smoothing cream under her eyes. She was dressed in her kimono and gardenias. Tommy sat in the corner, making his first battle moves with his soldiers. I swallowed and clicked each of my nails from the pinkies to my index fingers once against my thumbs as the three of them turned to look at me.

RUBY

The Dark Shadow Side

"Joe is here," Grace announced as she entered the room.

My neck stiffened. Below me, on the floor, Helen sighed.

"He's asked me to marry him," Grace went on, "and I've said yes. We're moving to San Francisco—"

"What about the Swing Sisters?" I asked with seemingly dead calm, calling on all the rules my mother had taught me about not showing my emotions.

"I'm staying for the show," she answered breezily.

"Great, but what about the Swing Sisters?" I repeated.

"The Swing Sisters?" Grace looked confused. "I was worried you'd be upset about Joe."

Joe, Joe, Joe. She'd always been stuck on that guy—like I cared. Joe was one thing; my career was quite another. "What about our plans?" I persisted. "What about our new lives?"

"What about your revue?" Grace asked unperturbed. "What about Helen taking Tommy to Miami?"

"Don't be ridiculous." I put my hands on my hips. "*Toast of the Town* changed all that. This is our gold ring."

When Helen cut in to say, "Besides, we said we'd never let a man come between us," I knew this was going to be a two-against-one disagreement that Helen and I would win.

"I'm sorry," Grace said. "I love him."

We'd gotten along pretty well since Yori died, but this news and her attitude about it caused something to rise up inside me. I'd thought I'd done a pretty good job burying my anger and suspicions about her these past years. Turned out they were right below the surface of my skin, ready to pop, all along. As that stupid dam people are always going on about burst, I was shaken by the rush of my emotions. Didn't stop me, though.

"How can you do this to me?"

"To you?" Grace asked, taken aback.

"You *owe* me."

At which Helen sat down fully on the floor and muttered one of her idiotic Chinese sayings. "*Predestined enemies are fated to meet in a narrow alleyway.*"

"This isn't about fate," I said to Helen. "It's about loyalty and friendship." I turned back to Grace. "You've never honored either."

Grace feigned lightness. "What is this? Target practice?"

"You didn't comfort me when Hideo was killed or when my parents were detained," I began, as all the injustices she'd inflicted on me began to flash through my mind.

"Of course I did—"

"You let me cry alone in my room—"

"That was seven years ago!"

"I needed a friend, but you liked hearing me suffer."

"I didn't want you to lose face," Grace explained, still trying to remain unruffled. "And *you* didn't want to talk about it. You wanted to make believe nothing had happened. You wanted to pretend you weren't Japanese—"

"You showed who you were even then." Anger was not my deal-e-o. I knew I had to try to pull myself together, but I just couldn't. "Later, you stabbed me in the back by stealing my part in *Aloha, Boys!* But that still wasn't enough for you. You had to steal my fiancé too."

"How can you possibly say that?" Grace now visibly struggled to stay cool. "You *invited* me to go to Hollywood with you. How was I to know that people would come and take you away or that the director would ask me to fill in for you? If you knew how painful all that was for me, you never would accuse me. And do you really believe I *stole* Joe? I understand you're upset, but you aren't remembering things correctly."

"Oh, I remember. You pinched my part, then you became the Oriental Danseuse."

"Is this about fame?" Grace asked. "Why *me* and not *you*?"

"Stop acting so coy," I shot back.

Helen put a hand on her forehead and closed her eyes.

"I don't see why you're so mad," Grace said.

"You don't? Well, try this on for size. Why did you turn me in?"

"I didn't turn you in," Grace said placidly. "I've told you that before."

"Admit it." I prickled.

"I won't. Because I didn't."

"Helen told me all about it." It felt surprisingly good to be confronting Grace, but why had I waited so long? "She said everyone at the Forbidden City looked at the clues and figured out it was you. *You* were the one who sent Western Union telegrams all the time. *You* were my friend and *you* reported me, so *you*'d get my part in the film."

Grace's brow furrowed. "Why did you tell Ruby that?" she asked Helen. "Why would you say those things about me . . . ever?"

From the floor, Helen regarded Grace. "You've never accepted responsibility for what you did."

"If you really thought that . . . In all these years, you never told me . . ."

"Has your conscience been eaten by a dog?" Helen asked.

Grace returned her gaze to me. "Is this what you truly think?"

I held my ground. "I said it, didn't I?"

"But all this time we've been together—traveling, sharing clothes, sometimes sleeping in the same bed . . . If you thought I'd betrayed you, how could you have stood to be near me at all?"

After the attack on Pearl Harbor, I'd said something similar to Helen, but Grace had cut me off. Now I did the same.

"Helen said it was best to keep an eye on you. *Keep your enemies close—*"

"The direct translation is *Know the other, know the self, hundred battles without danger,*" Helen murmured.

I liked Helen all right, but she was bugging my teeth right out of my gums. Why didn't she stand up and fight at my side? Maybe it wouldn't matter anyway, because Helen was so easy to ignore. Sure enough, Grace spoke directly to me.

"I didn't report you. You're my friend—"

"You would have done anything to take my part." My eyes bored into her. "Can you deny it?"

"That doesn't mean I reported you."

"Then who did?" I demanded.

"It could have been anyone," she answered. "Maybe it was Ida."

"Yeah, blame it on a dead Japanese girl." I jutted my chin. "I'm not a fool."

"Charlie," she tried again, her voice cracking. "Maybe it was Charlie—"

"Right. Charlie would report his number one moneymaker."

"What do you want me to do? Make a list of everyone we knew back then? It could have been anyone—"

"It was you!"

An intense silence fell over us. I wasn't going to budge, and neither was she. Then, a small but authoritatively businesslike voice spoke.

"You're not a loyal person, Grace," Helen said from her spot on the floor. "I went to look for you in Los Angeles. I lived with you in that horrid little rooming house. But when we went back to San Francisco, you moved in with Ruby."

This accusation Grace willingly accepted. "I wanted to get ahead."

"You *chose* Ruby. You cut me out entirely. I had a baby, but you didn't even visit."

Grace glanced from Helen to me and then back to Helen. "You didn't want visitors. You were obsessed with Tommy."

Wow. Another truth from Grace. Maybe Helen was getting somewhere.

"You dumped me when I was no longer useful to you," Helen went on. "You got rid of Ruby when she stood in your way. You did your best to have George Louie blackballed—"

"He lied about me!"

"Sounds like he was saying things you didn't want to hear," I had to throw in.

But Helen continued, as persistent as my FBI interrogators. "You even fired Max Field when you saw Sam Bernstein could get you up the ladder faster. You did whatever you could to have your name in bigger lights. You'd do anything to get to the top. And now we have this opportunity. Have you—either of you—imagined for just one moment what this means to *me*?"

Actually, I hadn't. And, as much as I hated to admit it, what she'd said about Grace's ambition could just as easily have been addressed to me.

"Everything you say is accurate," Grace also agreed, "except that I didn't report Ruby."

"*Ha!*" I exclaimed, like I was a five-year-old.

The room went quiet again, but it practically vibrated from the intense emotions. I'll admit it. Right that second, a part of me wanted to laugh. The three of us in such a crazy fight. My blowing my top—so not my usual style. Helen going all samurai on Grace, who, in turn, was suddenly acting the part of placating queen. Toss a little Joe into the mix for fun. Ridiculous.

Oh, and Tommy, too. Where was he? Over there in the corner. He'd been hearing all this, but Helen hadn't done a single thing to protect him. She hadn't covered his ears or rushed him out of the room. She'd temporarily *forgotten* about him. That was so singularly shocking that my thoughts suddenly shifted in a frighteningly new direction. I blinked several times as memories skimmed across my mind: how Helen had reacted after the attack on Pearl Harbor, the way she wouldn't meet my eyes when she repeated George Louie's gossip about Grace, the way she instinctively clutched at her breast when the subject of Japan or the Japanese entered the conversation, and, farther back, the way she'd said that Charlie hadn't hired me because I was Jap (when actually he didn't like that I'd made a pass at him), and the way she'd always called attention to my race when I could so thoroughly pass that no one had suspected until . . .

I backed away. My spine hit the wall. "You reported me, Helen," I said from a place so deep inside that my words came out a bare whisper.

The accusation shuddered in the air. Helen stared up at me. Cornered . . . Then, accepting . . . Then, proud . . .

"Yes, I did." Helen owned up in a chillingly matter-of-fact tone.

Grace shook her head like some disbelieving cartoon character. "What?"

Helen remained utterly still, except for her eyes, which moved to Grace. "I did it for you. Ruby broke your heart first by sleeping with Joe and then by saying yes to his marriage proposal. Getting rid of her gave you a chance to be with him."

I could see Grace struggling to catch up as she seemed to replay those days in her mind. Then she said, "That doesn't make sense. I accepted that Ruby and Joe were going to be married. I didn't do a single thing to slow or stop it."

Helen's lips quivered as her reason instantly fell apart. She tried another excuse. "You can't tell me you didn't want to be in *Aloha, Boys!* I gave you what you wanted."

But we'd already covered that territory.

Helen's eyes now searched the room until they came to her son. She reached out to him, beckoning. He ran across the room and put his arms around her neck.

Take pity on me.

Maybe her ploy worked, because my anger was gone and I was weirdly back in my body. Of course, all this was a lot more self-awareness than I was used to, which meant I was unnerved as hell. Still, I needed to know *why* Helen had turned me in. With some effort, I pushed myself away from the wall, moved to Helen, and put a finger under her chin to lift it. "During the war, it was our national job to hate the Japs," I said, trying to speak her language. "We wouldn't have been Americans if we hadn't hated them. They attacked us, and we dropped atomic bombs on their country. But why hurt me, Helen? What did I ever do to deserve what you did to me?"

Helen suddenly jerked her body and pushed Tommy away from her. He scrambled to a corner. She sat as still as death, her head hung low. I don't know about Grace, but I felt like my heart was in my mouth.

"They killed my baby," Helen murmured.

"Baby? Honey, Tommy's right here," Grace said.

Helen's head moved from side to side—*no, no, no*—as she slowly rose to her feet. "I knew love once."

"Yes, your husband," Grace prompted softly.

"Lai Kai," Helen said. "We were so happy. I got pregnant. I had a son. His name was Dajun."

"Oh, Jesus," Grace rasped.

"Dajun was three months old when the Japs invaded." Helen's eyes seemed to focus on a scene about a foot before her face that only she could see. "Like everyone else, we ran. The whole family. We couldn't believe that the soldiers would kill civilians, but we passed bodies everywhere—women with their pants pulled off and sticks shoved up inside them, babies tossed in ditches, men with bullets in their heads, people burned and still smoldering, limbs blown from torsos. We heard gunfire and screams."

I covered my mouth with my hands. Next to me, Grace shut her eyes and held her two closed fists against her cheeks. Tommy whimpered in the corner. In a way, Helen was like I was earlier—unleashed.

She didn't need us to ask questions. Her secret was out, and she was going to tell the whole story. Another one of those godforsaken dams broken. Shit.

"We saw smoke billowing from a village and the bodies of its inhabitants—shot and bayoneted—dumped in an open trench for dogs to eat," Helen intoned relentlessly. "Beneath our feet, the ground shook with thousands of boots pounding the earth. We dropped down into a rice paddy. After the soldiers killed Lai Kai, they found the others one by one. They used bayonets and swords to slash and stab. They killed my mother-in-law and father-in-law. They killed my sisters-in-law, brothers-in-law, and all their children."

I listened in horror as the enormity of what had happened to Helen ruptured for good the silly way I'd chosen to the view the world, even when "bad" things happened to me.

Helen sucked in a breath in an attempt to steady herself. "I tried to run, but I tripped over bodies. One of the soldiers . . . He held his bayonet before him . . . Blood covered his face . . . His mouth was open wide . . . I could see the white of his teeth. I held Dajun to my heart. I could do nothing to save my son, but at least we would die together."

Tears streaked down her face as she opened her blouse to expose the scar on her breast.

"The blade went through my son and into me. The soldier yanked his bayonet back. He took Dajun on the blade." She collapsed to her knees. "My baby died to save me, and I failed as a mother. After that . . . The soldiers ruined me . . . One after the other . . . They left me for dead. Except I wasn't dead. I had to live with what had happened."

Grace and I stared at each other—mute, paralyzed. She moved first, putting a hand on Helen's shoulder. I felt soul-sick.

"You are so courageous, Helen," Grace said. "I don't think I could have survived what you went through."

"Me either," I said gently. "I probably would have killed myself. But I hope you realize none of that was my fault. And I wish more than anything that I could have done something to make you hate me less."

"I don't hate you," Helen said, and I thought that despite the terrible—and unwarranted—punishment she'd inflicted on me, I could forgive her because she'd suffered the worst losses a woman can endure and in the most horrific and terrifying ways. Then she went on. "Being around you was like picking at a scab and sucking the blood."

Jeez. But I could see it. She'd taken perverse pleasure—from the first moment we met—in attaching herself to me.

"I never had much in the way of inner strength." Helen wiped her eyes with the back of her hand. "I didn't need it. I was raised to be cared for by my husband and his family. I was taught that my son would look after me when I became a widow. All that changed the night my husband and baby were killed. After that, I had no family protection and no purpose. I was lucky Mama and Baba allowed me to come home, but I was an embarrassment to them. *When you are held under water, you only think of air.* I needed air, and you gave it to me. I needed help, and you took me in. But I also wanted to destroy you as my husband and son were destroyed."

"You did a pretty good job," I said, attempting buoyancy, trying now to find a path back into the light for her.

"When Grace came back alone from Hollywood, I didn't feel one drop of guilt," Helen went on. "And I now had Grace to myself."

I know Grace had been devastated by all we'd just heard. Nevertheless, the comment sent her, with unexpected speed, straight up onto her high horse. But then none of us was acting normally. "Me? Don't throw me in with what you did to Ruby!"

Did this mean she might be able to forgive me for accusing her?

"I love you, Grace," Helen said. "You are my true-heart friend."

"I love you too—at least I thought I did," Grace replied. "And I'm sorry about what happened to you. I really am. But what does any of that have to do with what you did to Ruby . . . and to *me*?"

"I loved you, but you always preferred her," Helen said, going back in time. "We'd all barely met when the two of you got an apartment together . . ."

"*You* found the apartment for us. *You* orchestrated that." Grace shook with anger and frustration. "And that was ten years ago."

I'd flipped and shown my true emotions, and look what it had let loose. Alliances were shifting and battle lines were being redrawn. But what else could have happened? I mean, this was Grace, Helen, and me. Had it ever been otherwise between us? Still, now that I was back to myself, it was startling to see Grace get het up on my behalf when only a few minutes ago I'd been accusing her of such terrible things.

"I saw you, Grace." Something ravenous scuttled below the surface of Helen's skin. "I picked you. Yes, I found the apartment for the two of you. I knew it would only be a matter of time before you'd see Ruby for what she is. So again, yes, I figured out about Ruby and Joe and what it would do to you if you discovered the truth about them. But I didn't guess that you'd run away and leave me. I went to Los Angeles with Eddie to find you. And later, when Ruby was sent away, you *still* thought about her."

"How could I not?" Grace asked. "She'd disappeared and—"

"But we were supposed to be true-heart friends at last—just you and me."

"True-heart friends?" Grace repeated the words like they were poison in her mouth. "Did you start the rumors about me?"

"You were right about George Louie," Helen answered. "He's a bad man, but the more those rumors damaged you, the more you needed me. Then you deserted me again by running away to the Chop-Suey Circuit. In your own way, you hurt me as deeply as Ruby did."

As I listened, I understood at last that the dark shadow side of love had been much stronger among the three of us than it had ever been among Joe, Grace, and me.

"But what about later?" Grace asked. "When we were all together again, you ganged up with Ruby against me."

"I couldn't let Ruby learn what I'd done." Each word Helen spoke came out a jagged shard. She had planned and plotted from a place of such misery that looking at her was like looking at a mortally wounded animal.

I'd never been one to put the welfare of kids at the top of my list, but I glanced over at Tommy. He'd coiled his arms around his calves and pulled his knees under his chin. His eyes were twin black pools.

Helen now appealed to me. "It wasn't until you wrote from Topaz that it finally sunk in what I'd done to you. I felt guilty and knew I had to atone. Once I joined you on the road, I arranged your travel and your hotel rooms." Her voice darkened. "I'm from a good family—one of the best in Chinatown—and yet I lugged your suitcases, cleaned your bubble, and served as your maid. Every night I stared into your private parts to glue on your patch."

"I paid you to do that," I said, as though that would make a difference. I glanced at Grace. She'd gone pale. Yes, I'd made Helen and Grace share the same indignities—the puffs, the powder, and my vagina just inches from their faces. My shoulders slumped.

"I thought all that was finally over," Helen stammered mournfully. "I was going to find Grace the perfect house in Miami. We were going to be neighbors. We were going be together. Now what am I supposed to do?"

"You can still come with me to Vegas," I offered in a true display of friendship . . . or did I just want to prove once and for all I was the best and most desirable?

"I don't want you," Helen said, which had a deflating effect on me, as you might imagine. She appealed to Grace. "Even after everything I've done for you, you never once saw *me*. I only wanted a true-heart friend, who would be all mine. I didn't want to share you." Her voice cracked as she began to weep again. "But how could I have a best friend when there was someone like her"—she inclined her head toward me—"who was funny, beautiful, talented, and always trying to keep you for herself? You two always left me out."

Helen stared at us so piteously that Grace sunk to the floor and embraced her. There were no secrets left between us. Despair over the terrible mistakes each of us had made and the cruelties we'd inflicted on each other swam through my body. Tommy finally got up his courage to approach his mother—tears rolling down her cheeks, her entire body emanating sorrow, grief, and guilt. I reached out, grabbed him by the shoulders, and held him to me.

THE NEXT AFTERNOON, a car picked us up at the Victoria to take us to the Maxine Elliott Theatre at Broadway and Thirty-Ninth, where *Toast of the Town* would be filmed live. We sat together in the backseat, staring straight ahead, our arms and thighs touching, Tommy on Helen's lap. None of us spoke. I'd lived much of my life by my mother's saying: *The crow that was crying a few minutes ago is already laughing now.* Not this time. We were exhausted from restless sleep, nervous about how the day would unfold, and still undone by last night's revelations. The car pulled to the curb in front of the theater. Helen cracked open the door. Without looking at us, she said, "I'm sorry. I'm sorry for everything." Then, she swung the door wide, set Tommy on the sidewalk, and slid out behind him. They headed for the entrance. Grace scooted across the seat, hesitated, and turned to me.

"Are we really going to do this?" she asked.

"Of course, we are. We'd better catch up, or she'll go on without us," I said, trying for a joke. Could Grace hear the depth of my remorse for suspecting and disbelieving her? *Please,* but begging wasn't my way.

Once inside, we were taken to a dressing room, where we wordlessly changed into our costumes. I glimpsed Helen's scar, and my entire body ached for her.

Someone knocked on the door.

"Come in," I called, using my lilting professional voice.

Ed Sullivan entered and closed the door behind him. For someone who was so powerful through his writing he didn't seem to have much personality. He scanned us up and down, nodding approvingly at our satin shoes, our fuchsia-colored costumes that showed plenty of thigh, and our hair and makeup that made us look simultaneously American healthy and accessible and Chinese exquisite and alluring.

"Do this right, young ladies," he said, his voice toneless, "and I'll have you back plenty of times."

We may have been hurt and disheartened, but when a man like that presents you with *the world,* you get swept up in the possibilities. Grace put a hand on the small of my back, where it met Helen's hand.

"Would you consider returning next month to do an Indian number?" Ed asked. "I'm imagining something to Artie Shaw's rendition of 'Indian Love Call.' Viewers will get a bang out of seeing three girls come out dressed as squaws and then turn into little Chinese dancers with pretty American voices. Hilarious!"

"Anything for you, Ed, darling," I cooed. But could I work with Helen again? And what about Grace? *Ha!* What was I thinking? Maybe *they* wouldn't want to work with *me.*

"No question about it," he went on in his monotone, "I'm going to make the Swing Sisters a household name."

After he left, the hands that had been holding the three of us together behind my back loosened and dropped as Grace and Helen twisted away. How many times over the years had we been in a dressing room together? Too many to count. How many times had an opportunity like this come along? Never. Adrenaline pulsed through me. I was sure that a similar buzz surged through Helen and Grace too. I motioned for them to come close, then solemnly pinned white gardenias over each of our left ears. Something flickered in the air around us as ambition and hope tried to push away blame and self-reproach.

"We truly are going to be famous now," I declared. "All across the country, like Ed said."

"What about Joe?" Grace asked.

"If he can keep flying for pleasure, won't he want you to keep performing?" I replied. "If he can do what he loves, won't he want you to do what you love too? Do you think he really wants his very own China doll at home with a new vacuum cleaner, washing machine, and dryer—"

"Five minutes! Five minutes!"

We hurriedly made last checks in the mirror. Then we left the dressing room, went stage right as we'd been instructed, and waited as a man spinning plates finished his routine. I peered around the curtain to the audience and spotted Joe. Man, talk about looking like something the cat dragged in. The expression on his face, however, painted a very different picture. He seemed excited and proud. *That's my future wife and the mother of my children up there.* Joe, what a boob, but he'd probably make a great husband and father. Tommy sat next to him, dressed in a seersucker suit. It was hard to imagine what was going to happen to him in the future. But this wasn't the time for me to start getting maudlin! I needed the Swing Sisters to be fantastic, which meant putting last night—and many more months and years before that—behind me, behind us all.

"We owe it to ourselves and those who sacrificed for us not to have regrets," I whispered to the others. "That's what I feel in my heart. This is what we always wanted."

"What we all wanted," Grace murmured in a vague, distracted manner.

I took Helen's hand. I could forgive her all she'd done if she repaid me by going out there and dancing and singing her drawers off. Helen nodded. Together, we each clasped Grace's hands.

"Friends?" I asked, because I was the only one who could speak the word and have it be meaningful.

"Forever," Helen and Grace answered together. What passed between us—as we stood there with our hands linked—wasn't just a matter of the-show-must-go-on or personal ambition. After everything that had happened, we needed to make this moment perfect—perhaps even make it the beginning of Heaven and Earth, epoch-making, as Helen hoped.

Ed Sullivan began to speak. "I have three little gals I'd love for you to meet. Ruby, Helen, Grace, come on out here and say hello to the folks."

I went first. My smile was warm and enveloped everyone in the studio. I extended my fingers like the undulating tentacles of a sea anemone, luring Helen to come to me. More applause. Wouldn't you know it, but Ed gave Grace special preference. "I bring you the toast of New York for *Toast of the Town.* Miss Grace Lee."

The three of us chatted with our host, following our script perfectly. Then he stiffly raised his arm, awkwardly lurched back, and announced, "Ladies and gentlemen, please give a hand for the Swing Sisters . . ."

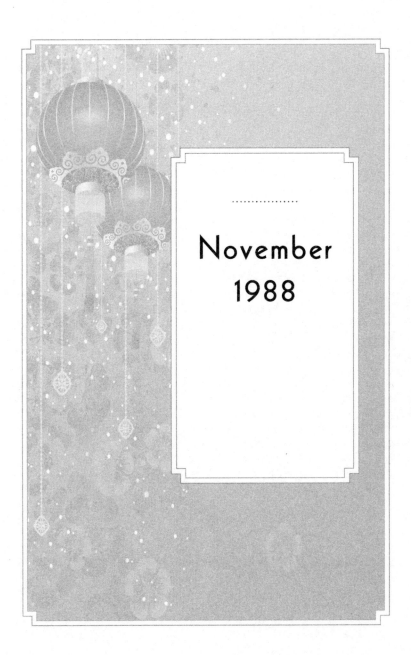

November 1988

GRACE

Once a Chorus Girl

I take a look in the mirror. Makeup: perfect and modest. Hair: cut in what the women at the beauty parlor call an auntie bob and dyed exactly the right color for a Chinese woman of my age and station. Pantsuit: red, never wrinkles, and shows off my still-slim figure. Jewelry: three bracelets and a fun necklace I picked up last year on a trip to Bali. I give myself an encouraging nod and go out to the living room. Joe sits at the computer, a slight frown crinkling his brow. I put a hand on his shoulder. He gazes up at me.

"You don't have to go," he says for what feels like the hundredth time this week. He's worried, but I know him very well. He'll be disappointed in me if I chicken out now.

"It will be strange if I don't make an appearance. It's for Eddie, after all. Everyone wants to help out."

"Try to have fun then."

"Yes, of course. It's bound to be fun . . ."

Joe covers my hand with his own, pressing it into his shoulder.

"Won't you come with me?" I ask. "You knew everyone too . . ."

"I'll come to the actual show," he promises.

"I told you I don't want to do that part of it. I'll sell tickets or whatever."

"Now, Grace, stop with that—"

I pull my fingers out from under his hand and give him a kiss on the top of his head. He turns back to his keyboard, and I head for the garage. I pull out the car and make my way down the tree-lined streets of the Berkeley Hills. When I reach the freeway, I steer toward the Bay Bridge. *They'll see me, and they'll know my life is perfect.* And it's true. My life does look perfect: the nice house, the practical blue Volvo, two professional sons, their perfectly adequate wives, the adorable grandchildren, and the pleasant retirement days of tending my rose garden, teaching Jazzercise to seniors at the local sports club, taking walks with the wives of other retired partners from Joe's firm, and reading books and listening to music at night with him in the den. My mother's recitation comes into my mind like a dark vapor: *When fortune comes, do not enjoy all of it; when advantage comes, do not take all of it.* Except I had wanted *all* of it, and I got *most* of it.

For ten years, Helen, Ruby, and I had shared our dreams, successes, and failures—as women, friends, daughters, and performers. As long as I live, I'll never forget that night in the dressing room at the China Doll or our performance on *Toast of the Town* the very next day. Two weeks later, Joe and I got married. I didn't invite Ruby and Helen to my wedding. My emotions were still too raw. I'm sure that hurt them, but I wasn't ready yet, and I doubt they were either. Our act had gone over big, nonetheless, and lots of fabulous offers came our way. We didn't take them. No one in the world knew me like Ruby and Helen did and we would be forever invisibly linked, but we all still needed a break from each other to mend and to heal.

Mr. Sullivan made good on his promise, though, to invite us back on the show. Ruby wanted to parlay the Swing Sisters into "Occidental stardom"; Helen still wanted to make up for what she'd done to both of us; I was the holdout. I just couldn't do it. After that, we had no contact, although messages were passed through our agent and our circus of mutual friends. The thought that I might never see Ruby or Helen again felt devastating, inevitable, and insurmountable.

Two years passed in a flash, and we were still standing. The three of us had always shown resilience and the courage it took to keep moving forward. And now we did it again. *Toast of the Town* became popularly known as *The Ed Sullivan Show.* He was a persistent so-and-so. Eventually, I caved. The Swing Sisters ended up performing on the show five times. We also did three appearances on *Texaco Star Theater,* which was hosted by Milton Berle, followed by one-shots on *Your Show of Shows, The Lawrence Welk Show, Broadway Open House,* and some other variety programs. While colleagues we knew got parts in *Flower Drum Song* (the Broadway show and later the movie), and Goro Suzuki, Ruby's friend, got rich as Jack Soo, playing Detective Nick Yemana on *Barney Miller,* Ruby, Helen, and I picked up occasional guest spots—together and separately—doing character roles on shows with tropical locations like *I Spy, Hawaii Five-O,* and *Magnum, P.I.* Joe had been fine with it. He always said, "As long as there's a beach and golf and someone else is paying, I'll come with you, baby. We'll bring the kids too!" Occidentals may not remember us today, but we were—and still are—big in the Chinese-American community. I mean, *big.* We made everyone proud. They even love Ruby, who, by now, is accepted as being more "Chinese" than most Chinese.

That doesn't mean we were all buddy-buddy. No touring for us ever again, but we got together to rehearse our television appearances as the Swing Sisters, ran into each other on sets, and gabbed like old friends on special occasions. Helen came and stayed with me when I had my babies. I also saw her when she visited San Francisco for what she called compound business—funerals, weddings, and one-month birthdays for that extended family of hers. She became a real estate tycoon, just as I predicted, first selling houses to veterans, then building tracts, then developing condo complexes. She's a seriously wealthy woman. Together we went to all five of Ruby's weddings. (So much for Ruby not being the marrying kind! Her most recent hubby is twenty years her junior. I'll bet any and all takers a hundred bucks he won't be able to keep up with her.) Ruby is the only one of us who never retired from show business. She's followed every wave: she had her Dancing Chopstix drop their pasties when the topless fad came in, she put them in white go-go boots in the sixties, and taught them to gyrate to a disco beat in the seventies. Journalists still like to interview her, and she's as vivacious and naughty as she was when that reporter from the Associated Press interviewed us in our beds. She's had staying power, our Ruby.

I exit the freeway and maneuver up Nob Hill to the Mark Hopkins Hotel. After leaving the car with the valet, I take a deep breath to steel myself, construct a pleasant expression on my face, and enter the lobby. Eddie spots me right away. Even though he's considerably older than I am, he's as handsome as ever—tall, graceful, nattily dressed, still and forever the Chinese Fred Astaire—but the gauntness around his eyes, the sores on his neck, and the hollowness to his cheeks let me know just how sick he is with this new disease that's taken so many men in the city the last few years.

"You look exactly the same," he whispers softly in my ear as he wraps his arms around me.

"How many others have you said that to already today?" I tease him.

"Oh, plenty. You know me." He chuckles. "Come on. Everyone's asking for you." He loops his arm through mine and sweeps me down a hallway and into the Room of the Dons, with its murals of early California painted in sumptuous earth tones against a background of gold leaf. Almost as one—and before I have a chance to search for Ruby or Helen—my old cohorts glance in my direction to see who's come through the door. It looks to be about fifty people so far. Some sit at tables. Others mill around a buffet, where coffee and some treats have been laid out. Those closest to me hurry over. Well, they hurry as fast as anyone who is fit and in his or her sixties, seventies, or eighties can. *Once a chorus girl, always a chorus girl!* (I'm not sure of the male equivalent. *Once a show boy, always a show boy*?) And they all talk at once.

"You look great."

"Where have you been hiding?"

"Are you going to join us for our follies?"

"You look great too. I'd know you anywhere," I answer Chanchan. "I've been where I've always been, just over the bridge," I inform Bernice Chow, who was once billed as the Chinese Ethel Merman. "I don't think so. I'm pretty busy at home. I have grandchildren now," I say, offering my regrets to Irene. I take in the disappointed faces and add a small salve. "But I'm sure there'll be other ways I can help."

The Lim Sisters elbow their way through the little crowd.

"Hi, Grace. What's cooking?" Bessie, the eldest, has to be something like eighty-five, but to my eyes she hasn't changed one bit. Ella and Dolores stand on either side of her, and one foot back as always. They wear matching kelly-green polyester jumpers over cream-colored turtlenecks. I bump into the sisters occasionally—in the Chinese markets in Oakland, at funerals, or at the Chinese Historical Society's annual banquet. Sometimes I see only two of the sisters, which makes me wonder if one of them is on the outs or dead. Then I'll see a different pair, or just one Lim sister out on her own, and it's all so confusing. But all three are still alive, still connected, and still living just one mile apart from one another.

A man—middle-aged, with a bit of a paunch, and a young woman in tow—approaches. It's Tommy. I remember how comfortable Helen had been holding him as a newborn, and the ways she'd both smothered him and let him have his way—out of love and fear. I never thought he had much of a future, but he grew up to be a doctor, just like Eddie's father, and married a woman not unlike Helen. Go figure.

"Auntie Grace," Tommy says, "I'd like you to meet my daughter, Annie. She's a graduate student at Cal. She's living in the compound with Dad, my aunts and uncles, and the rest of the family while she's in school."

Annie is pretty—long, silky black hair, and high cheekbones.

"You look a lot like your grandmother," I say.

"I've heard that before," Annie answers in a voice that mysteriously combines petulance, challenge, and pride. She reaches into her bag, pulls out a pen and a notebook, and rattles off a string of questions. "When did you first know you wanted to dance? What was your first break? When did you meet my grandmother? How did you feel being billed as an *Oriental* performer, dancing in an *Oriental* club?"

I've heard this accusation—or is it criticism?—from my sons and my grandchildren too, and I answer Annie the same way I answer them. "Oriental, that's what we were called back then. And whites were called Occidentals." I leave out that in my head I still say Oriental and Occidental. I'm stubborn and set in my ways, and I think, *What's the big deal? Why do these young people make such a fuss about this? It's not like saying Jap—like Helen and Joe always said—or colored or something even worse. Or is it?*

Annie peppers me with more questions. "Did you know you were perpetuating Asian stereotypes? How could you dance at a place called the China Doll or even tolerate being *called* a China doll?"

That smarts, and I glance at Tommy. I want to ask, "Have you not taught this girl any manners?" In response to my unspoken question, he says, "Annie's doing research on the Forbidden City and the different clubs where you all performed." He gestures to the others in the room. "She wants to capture this history before it's lost."

My eyes drift back to Annie. "We aren't *that* old."

"Things happen. People die," Annie replies, and it seems pretty callous, given that the reason for today's reunion is to help raise money for her ailing grandfather. "What you did was extraordinary for your time. Don't you want there to be a record? Will you let me interview you? Wouldn't you like to share your stories?"

Hell, no! Instead, I ask, "Is your grandmother here?"

"Not yet. She's flying in from Miami."

I'm saved from having to continue the conversation by Charlie Low, who claps his hands to get everyone's attention. After I sit down, I notice a small dance floor and a piano, which give my heart a little hiccup. I shift my focus to Charlie—shrunken and frail now—to calm myself. If only he'd used his noodle, he would have been a rich man at the end of his life. Instead, he spent it all on wine, women, and song. Women, especially, were his downfall. Too many wives. (Fortunately, he still owns the Low Apartments, which continue to stand as a gleaming gem on the edge of Chinatown.) I peer around the room and spy Walton Biggerstaff, who taught me so much and choreographed our shows. Jack Mak and George Louie are gone, though. So many men have passed already, and that knowledge feels like a heavy weight.

"You all know why we're here," Charlie begins. "We're going to raise money for our old friend, but no bake sales for us! I've come up with a better idea. The Forbidden City opened on December 22, 1938. Here we are in 1988. We're going to put on a revue for the fiftieth anniversary. We're going to re-create the Forbidden City and all our best acts. We're going to put on a show!"

"Put on a show?" Bessie Lim drawls languidly. "Take a look around. We aren't young Mickey Rooneys and Judy Garlands anymore."

"Don't tell me you've forgotten how to sing," Charlie responds. "I know you girls. No one can keep the Lim Sisters from making harmonies as sweet as honey."

"I wasn't there the night the Forbidden City opened," someone else calls out. "I didn't work there until close to the end."

"That's all right," Charlie says so quickly that I realize he's come fully prepared to deal with all complaints and whiners. "We're taking a broad approach. We're going to use everyone we can, whether from the Forbidden City, the China Doll, or any of the other clubs some of you played in for one- and two-night stands out there on the road."

"I haven't performed in front of an audience in years," Irene says, speaking for all of us. "I can't do it."

"Performed in front of an audience?" Charlie snorts. "What do you call all the magic shows you and Jack did at our kids' and grandkids' parties?" He then addresses the whole room. "Don't be such a bunch of old ladies . . . and men. I know what Irene and the rest of you have been up to. You've been taking ukulele lessons, traditional Chinese dance, tai chi, yoga, maybe even learning how to moonwalk. So don't tell me you can't perform. We're going to put on a show. We're going to invite our friends and the press. We're going to get even more people—old customers and total strangers—to come. And we're going to raise money for our dear friend, like I said."

"But what's the show? Who's going to write it? Who's going to choreograph it?" a former chorus girl asks, and the ponies she sits with nod in agreement.

"We don't need new material," he answers. "We're going to do the routines you were famous for—"

"I'm not going to work with any kittens!" a woman's voice sirens through the air.

Everyone laughs. Charlie goes on: "Can't you see it? Nostalgia! We're going for an era that's disappeared, see?"

I hear this with a good deal of anxiety. I want to help Eddie, and I'm perfectly willing to make a donation to his health fund, but dance? (And honestly, why do we have to do this at all? Helen and Eddie stayed married. He's on her insurance policy, and she's as rich as Croesus to boot. All right, I know the answer. We're show kids. We want Eddie to know we're with him 100 percent, even if we don't understand this new disease.)

"There's Ruby Tom!" Charlie suddenly exclaims.

So she came. I process that information before glancing over to where Charlie points. Ruby sits at a table on the far side of the room. She still has her figure, and her skin looks great. She wears a sequined gown . . . in the middle of the day . . . with sparkling clips in her hair . . . and diamond and ruby bracelets climbing her arm. What a spectacle. Even at—what?—seventy?—Ruby has to show off. But damn, she looks good—still seeking the spotlight, still addicted to glitter, and still sly as ever. I notice that my old pal is peeking at me out of the corners of her eyes. I keep my face bland.

I've had other friends—mothers to be when I was pregnant with Ben and Stephen, moms of the other boys in my sons' schools, and the gals I played tennis with over the years—but none of those women knew me as a girl. None of them could ever really *know* me, not like Ruby and Helen know me. I'm convinced this is so, because I'm staring at Ruby and seeing not the sexed-up old woman who is just this side of grotesque, if I'm honest, but the girl who loved to laugh with her two best friends.

"And, of course, our beloved Grace Lee," Charlie barrels along. "Still famous. Still a lady."

I nod politely at the acknowledgment, but inside I'm gloating like I'm seventeen, because I received more applause than Ruby. If Helen were here, I think, she might be smiling too.

Right then I see Helen, standing in the doorway, wearing a Chanel suit, with matching purse and shoes. She somehow manages to appear bemused, critical, and bitter. With another of those hiccups in my heart, I remember when Helen and I were the very best of friends, sure that no one could come between us, and then later when the deepest friendship was between Ruby and Helen, and how much that hurt me. I loved those two, but together and separately, they caused me some of the worst pain of my life.

Charlie, in the astute way he handled a room in the old days, has noticed Helen too. "Ruby Tom, Grace Lee, and Helen Fong! Come up here! Let's see if you three still have it."

Ruby is first on the dance floor, naturally. More applause as Helen comes to stand next to Ruby. Now everyone stares at me. I don't want to get up, but how can I not? It would be rude not to participate. So I find myself joining Ruby and Helen. Goose bumps rise on my arms from the pleasure of having so many pairs of eyes on the three of us.

"Shall I do my Princess Tai act?" Ruby asks. Yes, she still plays clubs way off the Strip and senior centers, where, as I've heard her say, "I put a little bump in those old geezers." But the idea that she might take off all her clothes is horrifying.

"I don't want to be seen in a show with a stringy and naked old bird," Helen states, half in jest, half on the square. She's probably thinking of her political ambitions. She's put together an exploratory committee to look at the feasibility of running for an open congressional seat in Florida. She won't win, but I'm proud to say I was the first person to write a check.

"I have a different idea," Charlie says diplomatically. "Will my glamour girls do me the honor of performing 'Let Me Play with It'?"

It would have to be that. If I first became famous for the dance I did in *Aloha, Boys!*, then the Swing Sisters became even more renowned for the routine we did for Ed Sullivan. *Best known for singing and dancing to "Let Me Play with It"* will be in each of our obituaries and probably end up on our tombstones as well.

Someone starts to pluck the piano keys. At the sound of the opening bars of "Let Me Play with It," something we've danced to maybe ten thousand times, the three of us arrange ourselves in the proper order. How can my feet know what to do? How can my hips sway and my shoulders shimmy? I can feel that I'm clumsy and stiff, but I don't seem any worse than the two women who dance beside me. Like I've always said, friends are better than sisters and three are stronger than one.

Beyond Ruby and Helen, I see the faces of people I've admired, envied, and maybe even hated on occasion in a fractured kaleidoscope of images. They're smiling at me, and I decide against everything that tells me this is a terrible mistake that I'll be a part of this revue or follies or whatever they want to call this reunion show we're going to mount. I wonder if Joe will still be awake when I get home. Will he run his hand through his hair, throw his head back, and laugh when I tell him how I stumbled through the old routine? When I announce that I've decided to be in this performance thing for Eddie after all, will he say "I told you so"? Of course, because Joe loves me, I am his China doll, and he knows that Helen and Ruby will be the sisters of my heart for all eternity. In my mind, I count. *One, two, three, four.* As I make the slow turn that initiates the break, I glimpse Ruby and Helen making their turns as well. After all this time—despite the secrets revealed and the hearts broken—we are still in sync on the dance floor. Love envelops us, and we dance and dance and dance.

ACKNOWLEDGMENTS

The characters in *China Dolls*—apart from Charlie Low, Walton Biggerstaff, David Butler, Ming and Ling, Dorothy Toy, Lee Mortimer, Tom Ball, and Ed Sullivan—are wholly fictional. That said, I have incorporated many anecdotes from people who lived through the Chinese-American nightclub era to create my fictional characters. I'd like to start by thanking Jodi Long, daughter of Larry and Trudi Long (nightclub performers); Michael Ching, son of Larry Ching (the Chinese Frank Sinatra, who in real life was much nicer than the one portrayed in this novel); and Nellie Lew (a Forbidden City chorus girl); and Joyce Narlock, whose mother, Betty Wong, danced at the China Doll and moved on to the Forbidden City, where she married Charlie Low. Their behind-the-scenes stories and Jodi's documentary *Long Story Short* gave me a kid's-eye view of these two clubs and what it was like to travel on the Chop-Suey Circuit.

In 2011–2012, I also met performers: Trudi Long, eighty-eight, shared stories of being interned, Lee Mortimer sponsoring her to go to New York, and life on the road; Mai Tai Sing, eighty-eight, recounted her childhood love of glitter and dancing in a gown made from monkey fur; Mary Ong Tom, ninety-three, spoke about her journey from Arizona to California, where she became one of the eight original Forbidden City chorus girls; and Dorothy Toy, ninety-two, the first and forever best Chinese Ginger Rogers, had me laughing at her exploits. I feel extraordinarily fortunate—and honored—to have met these inspiring, audacious, humorous, and energetic women.

I wouldn't have met Dorothy or Mai Tai if not for a great group of women, some of whom danced at the Forbidden City and the China Doll, and traveled the circuit themselves, who are keeping the flame alive with their troupe, the Grant Avenue Follies: Pat Chin (I loved our extra e-mail exchange), Lillian Poon (with a special thank-you for making the initial introductions), Ivy Tam (one of Charlie Low's ex-wives), and Cynthia Yee (who grew up in the apartment building where Dorothy Toy and so many performers lived). We met at San Francisco's Hotel Whitcomb, where there is a continuing exhibit on the Forbidden City, and where the hotel's manager, Ralph Lee, graciously treated us to tea and desserts. That afternoon was further highlighted by Chuck Gee's hilarious stories of costume malfunctions and such.

I wish to acknowledge several others who consented to be interviewed: Phil Choy, for his historical perspective on San Francisco Chinatown; Susan Lee Colby, who grew up in a traditional family compound in San Francisco Chinatown; Florence Helzel, for her memories of Treasure Island and San Francisco during World War II; Deborah Kirshman, who took me on a tour of San Francisco architecture and introduced me to her mom; Mei Ling Moore, for her photographs and encouragement; and Karen and Bernie Vance of the Plain City Historical Society, who shared memories and details of their town. (Please forgive me for the unpleasant characters I made up for my version of Plain City.)

I wouldn't have been able to capture the details of the Chinese-American nightclub scene if others hadn't interviewed performers and collected materials in years past. (All locations are real except Pieces O'Eight in Norfolk.) Arthur Dong paved the way with his 1989 documentary *Forbidden City, U.S.A.* He found clips from long-forgotten movies, and he filmed Noel Toy, the Chinese Sally Rand, as she recited her classic line about "eating corn on the cob." He has been astute and insightful, always seeming to e-mail me drink menus, photographs, or an anecdote at just the right moment. Ben Fong-Torres, the music journalist, shared with me the time he spent with Larry Ching as they recorded the singer's first and only CD, *Till the End of Time.* I'm deeply indebted to Eddie Wong for giving me transcripts of his 1981–82 interviews with Forbidden City performers. Trina Robbins interviewed two dozen people and gathered nightclub ephemera for her oral-history volume, *Forbidden City.* I also found online interviews with Mary Tom, Noel Toy, and Dorothy Toy. For those who'd like to *see* some of the performers in their heyday, allow me to recommend David Wells's postings on YouTube and his website: softfilm .blogspot.com.

The Museum of Chinese in America proved to be an invaluable resource. Alice Mong, then executive director, and Yue Ma, archive librarian, opened *all* the museum's research materials that had been brought together for a 2002 exhibition entitled *Gotta Sing, Gotta Dance: Chinese America in the Nightclub Era,* which included Lee Mortimer's collected columns, costumes and headdresses, videos, programs, articles, photographs, Jadin Wong's scrapbooks (great for piecing together daily life on the Chop-Suey Circuit), contemporaneous interviews with stars, Walter Winchell's musings, and the coverage of the murder of dancer Midi Takaoka, which served as the inspiration for Ida's death. The museum also provided me with transcripts of the oral histories it conducted with fourteen Chinese-American performers and New York Chinatown locals who were familiar with the China Doll. Sue Lee, executive director of the Chinese Historical Society of America, opened those archives, allowing me to pore over the Kubla Khan nightclub collection, Forbidden City waitress costumes, and old issues of the *Chinese Digest,* as well as other materials on Charlie Low and the Forbidden City.

I also relied on the works (and numerous personal kindnesses) of others. Ben Shahn's 1938 photographs of Plain City taken for the Farm Security Administration put me on Grace's hometown streets. For information on Treasure Island, I'm obliged to the writings of Patricia F. Carpenter and Paul Totah (*The San Francisco Fair*), Jack

James and Earle Vonard Weller (*Treasure Island: "The Magic City," 1939–1940*), Jason Pipe (*Images of San Francisco's Treasure Island*), and Richard Reinhardt (*Treasure Island—1939–1940*). Treasure Island's website and the exhibition in the old Administration Building / Air Terminal were also helpful. For details on clothes and theatrical costumes, I looked to works by Joan Nunn, Jonathan Walford, and Doreen Yarwood. For general information on nightclubs, dance, dancers, and San Francisco Chinatown, thank-yous to Raymond Chung (who sent me an early draft of his article on the Kubla Khan), Gloria Heyung Chun (*Of Orphans & Warriors*), Lorraine Dong ("The Forbidden City Legacy"), Amy Gorman (*Aging Artfully*), San-San Kwan ("Performing a Geography of Asian America"), Him Mark Lai (*Him Mark Lai: Autobiography of a Chinese American Historian*), Anthony W. Lee (*Picturing Chinatown*), Dugal O'Liam ("Playboy of the Eastern World"), Harley Spiller ("Late Night in the Lion's Den"), Rusty E. Frank (*Tap!*), Susan Waggoner (*Nightclub Nights*), Leong Gor Yun (*Chinatown Inside Out*), and Judy Yung (*Unbound Feet* and *Images of America: San Francisco's Chinatown*).

Much has been written about the Sino-Japanese War and World War II. I relied on the following works for historical accuracy: Honda Katsuichi's *The Nanjing Massacre,* Iris Chang's *The Rape of Nanking,* Marjorie Lee's *Duty & Honor,* the essays in *The Home-Front War* (edited by Kenneth Paul O'Brien and Lynn Hudson Parsons), and the remarkable (if bigoted) coverage in *Time* and *Life.* The Virtual Museum of the City of San Francisco was invaluable for its time line and details of events that happened in the Bay Area during the war. Patsy Sumie Saiki's *Ganbare!* and Yasutaro Soga's *Life Behind Barbed Wire* gave me a vivid sense of what life was like for *Issei* and *Nisei* in Hawaii in the hours and days immediately following the bombing of Pearl Harbor, as well as the experience of those who were sent to internment camps.

I grew up hearing stories of internment from friends and family, but I'd also like to acknowledge the wonderful oral histories of Janet Daijogo, Fumi Hayashi, Chizu Iiyama, and Masaru Kawaguichi about their experiences at Topaz, which can be found on the Telling Stories website. I have long been a fan of Kyoko Mori's memoir, *Polite Lies,* in which she writes about the differences between American and Japanese culture. Writer Naomi Hirahara gave me some eleventh-hour advice on Japanese words and phrases. *You Don't Know Jack,* a documentary about Jack Soo, né Goro Suzuki, illustrated how yet another performer was able to navigate difficult times. Regarding the concept of "they all look alike," I recommend the following website to see how good you are at telling the differences: http://alllooksame.com/exam_room.php.

A few special words about Bob Loomis, my longtime editor, now retired. Bob spent a lot of time in Plain City as a little boy, and he filled my head with many colorful stories. Bob was also an airman, who visited Los Angeles (and its myriad nightclubs) during the war. I studied his *The Story of the U.S. Air Force,* and asked him dozens of questions about training and planes. Beyond all that, I'm grateful for his friendship, generosity, and encouragement to me over the years. I would not be the writer I am if not for him.

All this leads me to the people without whom my words would be as vapor. My agent, Sandra Dijkstra, and the industrious women in her office are unfailingly loyal, caring, and compassionate. My editors, Susan Kamil and Kara Cesare, were forthright, thoughtful, and meticulous. Gina Centrello and everyone else at Random House—Benjamin Dreyer, Vincent La Scala, Barbara Fillon, Maria Braeckel, Sally Marvin, Laura Goldin, and so many more—believe in me, support me, and help me in innumerable ways. Closer to home, I wish to thank Nicole Bruno and Mari Lemus for their hard work and thoughtfulness. My mother-in-law, Elaine Kendall, told me wonderful details about clothes during World War II. My mother, Carolyn See, and my sister, Clara Sturak, read the manuscript and gave me loving advice. Last, none of this would matter if not for my husband, Richard Kendall; my sons, Alexander and Christopher; and my daughter-in-law, Elizabeth.

Thank you, everyone.

About the Author

Lisa See is the author of seven previous novels, including the critically acclaimed *New York Times* bestsellers *Dreams of Joy*, *Shanghai Girls*, *Peony in Love* and *Snow Flower and the Secret Fan*, a Richard & Judy pick which sold 2 million copies worldwide. She is also the author of the widely acclaimed memoir *On Gold Mountain*. She lives in Los Angeles.

www.lisasee.com
www.facebook.com/lisaseebooks
@Lisa_See

About the Type

This book was set in Sabon, a typeface designed by the well-known German typographer Jan Tschichold (1902–74). Sabon's design is based upon the original letterforms of sixteenth-century French type designer Claude Garamond and was created specifically to be used for three sources: foundry type for hand composition, Linotype, and Monotype. Tschichold named his typeface for the famous Frankfurt typefounder Jacques Sabon (c. 1520–80).